Bruce Ai
has lived and worked for most of his
life in a small village in the Exmoor
National Park, Devon, England.

Hope Island

Bruce Aiken

For my grandchildren and
generations to come

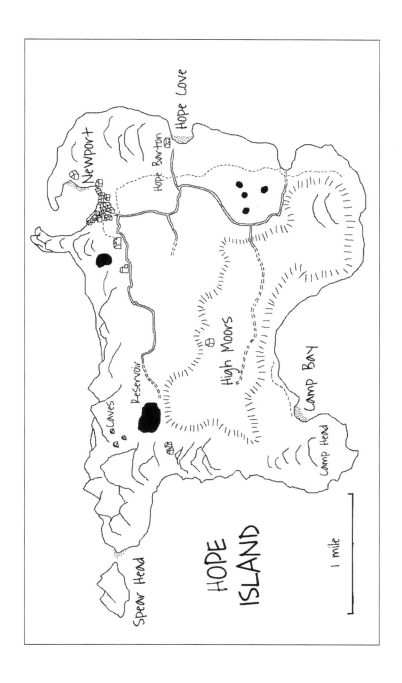

Chapter 1

Hannah dived, leaving only a ring of ripples on the mirrored surface of the sea as it closed behind her. A trail of bubbles marked her progress. She knifed deeper, hands pulling confidently against the cool water. Easing between the roof timbers of a submerged house she hung in a space lit by flashes of shattered sunlight on the swaying weed-covered walls. Swimming down the line of the stairs she searched for the kitchen where she knew any valuable items would most likely be found.

That day a soft mist had stretched along the horizon. Hope Island appeared to be afloat in an endless ocean. Even though it was not yet noon, the sun-baked rocks had burned against her bare feet, the sea shimmering with ice-cold clarity. It appeared to be no more than a few feet deep, but the rafters of the roof were clearly visible, stark beneath the surface, a skeleton, carrion picked clean by time. A shoal of small silver fish had flashed against the bare ribs of the abandoned house.

Most buildings covered by the rising seas had been stripped in the decades before she was born, but Hannah enjoyed the silence when exploring old drowned houses. She would sometimes imagine a family there, clustered around a television set, each with their own personal phone, chatting to friends and to each other – technology that was not available to her generation. Occasional discoveries of aluminium pots and pans, copper bowls, even iron tools could all be weighed and exchanged for small luxuries when the packet steamer called each month. Most of the credits she earned from salvage would be saved towards a gift for Ethan.

After drifting out through the open back door, still empty-handed, she glanced to one side and saw two large bunkers. They must have been overlooked when the house was abandoned to the waves. The timber covers were rotten and between missing planks they looked to be full of coal – worth investigating with fresh air in her lungs. Hannah pushed off from what had been the doorstep, a slab of dressed slate that might also be worth retrieving. She let her natural buoyancy pull her upwards. In no great hurry, Hannah watched the ever-changing patterns of sunlight and blue sky flash and dance on the surface above her. With only a few feet to go a shadow cut across the water. The hull of a small boat sliced through the sea above her, the keel missing her shoulder by inches.

Hannah broke the surface and gasped for air as she looked along the line of white water left by the dinghy. Wood ground against shingle when the boat rode onto the beach. The sudden contact unbalanced the woman holding the tiller. The sail slapped like sheets drying in a gusting wind. The boom swung, it struck the woman on the side of her head and pitched her into the water. Hannah took a deep breath. Her cupped hands dug hard as she swam towards the beach and the body, now face down in the shallows.

When Hannah reached the shore she gripped firmly under the woman's armpits and rolled her over, on top of her own body, lifting her clear of the water. Hannah's feet slid on the pebbles as she heaved against the waves dragging at the woman's clothes. Only when she had her clear of the water, her arms still round her, did Hannah realise that she was young, in fact no older than herself. The girl rolled onto her side, coughed and retched salt water.

"Are you okay?" Hannah asked, still with a hand on her

shoulder. "Where have you come from?"

The breeze that brought the boat to the Island was blowing from the south. There was no land in that direction for hundreds of miles. Coughing again, the girl spat salt and saliva from her mouth.

"Do you speak English?" Hannah asked.

She wondered if that small dinghy could have made it to Hope Island from the continent. The girl wiped her mouth with the back of a hand and took a deep breath, letting it escape slowly before replying.

"Yes, I speak English" she said, glancing at Hannah. She turned away again. "I have money in my bag. I can pay you. I need to hide. I can't be found here."

She looked towards her boat and struggled to her feet. The long, white, linen dress she wore was wet and heavy and the girl half stumbled, half threw herself, at the prow of the boat. She grabbed a rope and leaned her weight against the hull to pull it further up the beach, but she was slender under her heavy dress and the boat wouldn't yield to her.

Hannah moved behind the girl and took the loose end of the rope in her hands. The girl glanced back, eyes wide and frightened. Hannah tightened her grip on the rope and their combined bodies worked against the dead weight. They both groaned with the effort of each concerted pull and the hull inched further up the beach until Hannah let go her end of the rope – the boat was above the high water mark.

"It's safe now," Hannah said.

The girl looked at the line of dried seaweed wriggling along the top of the shingle bank. Still holding the rope taut, her feet slid forward until she was sitting on the beach.

"My name's Bethany," she said without turning to look at Hannah. "But everyone calls me Beth – almost everyone."

"I'm Hannah."

They were both facing out to sea. Hannah wasn't used to

3

finding strangers washed up on the Island and certainly not strangers who were still alive. Beth had long, black hair, tangled by salt and wind. Two thin, plaited braids were tied at the back of Beth's head with a white silk ribbon. The ends of the ribbon hung loose, any decorative bow long undone. A small yellow flower remained caught under one braid.

"I can't lose my boat," Beth whispered.

It was small, clinker built, with no cabin and looked almost new, not like the Island boats that had been repaired so many times that it was difficult to identify which parts were original.

"You can't tell anyone I'm here. I can pay you."

"We don't use money," Hannah said, proud of the principles of her island community.

"I forgot. I suppose I didn't really believe it was true."

Hannah shrugged, but Beth could not see her. The subject of money occurred only occasionally, usually when someone moved to the Island, but even then it was rarely more than a handful of silver coins. They used to welcome new people to the Island years ago, but not many came now, in fact not a single person had arrived for over eight years.

"You know about our island? About our community?" Hannah asked.

"My father..." Beth stopped before she finished the sentence. She turned to Hannah.

Beth's eyes were almost as dark as her hair, fierce, wild, searching Hannah's face with an intensity that Hannah had only previously seen in a frightened animal.

"There are lots of stories about the community here."

Hannah never thought of her island as being a subject of speculation on the mainland, but maybe it was the fact that they hadn't had an outbreak of the fever for the last nine years that made them interesting. The Recorder always implied that they were safer away from the regular epidemics that swept the mainland.

"Can I stay here?" Beth turned back to look out to sea.

"We don't turn anyone away."

"But you can't..." Beth hesitated. "You can't tell the Recorder I'm here."

"Have you run away from someone, stolen something?"

"I haven't stolen anything. The boat, the money, they're mine. If I can't stay here, can I buy some food? I've had nothing to eat since yesterday morning."

"Where would you sail to? Your boat's not suitable for the open ocean."

"I know," Beth said. Her head dropped and she reduced her voice to a whisper. "You're not wearing any clothes."

"They're just over on the rocks, I was diving. Are you okay here if I leave you for a moment?"

Hannah wore as little as possible when she was diving. Loose clothes dragged against the water and could also snag on rusted nails or other sharp objects. It was rare to see anyone on this part of the Island so she had stripped down to her pants. She would have kept a t-shirt on if anyone had been around, but today her clothes would be dry for the walk home.

Beth nodded and Hannah went to retrieve her skirt and t-shirt. When she reached the rocks she glanced back and Beth was watching her. Hannah dropped into a gulley, out of Beth's sight. She carried her shoes with her as she returned, walking where the wash of the sea cooled the sand and shingle. Beth was leaning into her boat and turned when she heard the crunch of the shingle and shells when Hannah climbed the tidal ridge.

Hannah didn't know what to suggest to Beth. Until she came of age her uncle was acting as a Bailiff on the Island. It was a position he had taken on when Hannah's parents died almost nine years ago. She wasn't sure he was going to

5

be happy to relinquish the power and status it gave him. If he knew of her arrival he would be bound to report Beth to the Recorder when the steamship next visited.

"I'll take you to Ethan's farm," Hannah said, the words spilling from her mouth before she could change her mind. "Nobody needs to know you're here if that's what you want."

"Who is Ethan?"

"My boyfriend. You can trust him."

"Thank you."

Beth pulled a large leather holdall out of the boat and a canvas satchel, slung the satchel over her head and held the bag in one hand. She was stronger than she looked or determined to appear so. Hannah admired her spirit, but closed the gap between them and took one handle of the bag.

"We can share the weight." Hannah looked down at Beth's feet. They were pale, the skin smooth and her toenails painted a deep red. "Do you have any shoes?"

"I lost them last night."

"You can take mine. I'm used to walking these tracks barefoot."

"I'll be okay."

"No, you won't. Put them on."

Hannah dropped her shoes in front of Beth. They were canvas, sewn onto leather soles. Beth let go her grip on the holdall and sat down to lace the shoes tight. She looked up at Hannah.

"Thank you, but I would have been all right."

"It's three miles. We'll take the coast path to avoid meeting anyone. It's a rough track in parts."

"What about my boat?"

"I'll ask Ethan to come back for it. He can sail it round to Hope Cove for you. It will be safe there."

Beth looked back at the boat and bit her lip.

"It's above the tide line," Hannah said. "The weather's set fair, there's no need to worry."

"Why can't I stay with you rather than Ethan?"

Hannah grabbed both leather handles on the holdall and set off. Beth, a few paces behind her, had to run to catch up and took one handle back when they reached the top of the beach. Large stones, sea kale and poppies marked the margin between the land and sea. They walked in silence for a while, side by side, along a grass track close to the shore. Hannah wanted to ask who she was, what she knew of her island and what she was running away from.

"My uncle is the acting Bailiff here," Hannah said.

Beth pursed her lips and nodded. "You're Hannah Cotton then?"

"Yes. That's why you can't stay with me? I live in Newport, It's a small village, you would be noticed and my uncle would report you to The Recorder"

Beth stopped walking. The holdall dragged Hannah to a halt too.

"The Recorder is my father," Beth said.

Chapter 2

The path along the south coast of the Island was little used, barely more than a trodden strip of grass worn thin by children who went to Camp Bay to play in the sea or fish from the rocks. The beach was protected from westerly winds and was a favourite spot for catching mackerel and bass. Hugging the shoreline there was a wide grassy margin grazed by rabbits, sheep and even goats, when they ventured off the hills.

A fresh breeze was blowing in from the south, the same one that had rescued Beth. Hannah's hair, already dry, blew across her face and she kept lifting a hand to push it back.

"I could braid your hair for you," Beth offered.

"Thanks, but I usually just tie it back, it's easier."

"It doesn't take long. I could do it when we get to Ethan's place. Honestly, it would be no problem."

"Thanks, but let's just get there first."

Hannah didn't want her hair braided. There was a small group of girls in Newport who were always trying to copy pictures from old magazines that turned up on the Island – Hannah had never been interested. When she was young she had always had her hair cropped as short as the boys. It was Ethan who had asked her to grow it longer.

"What's Ethan like?"

"He's tall," Hannah said. "He has dark hair and hazel eyes. You'll like him, everyone does."

She could have described him in the finest detail. She had been looking at him all her life. The five moles in a crescent on his neck, the way his mouth sometimes set a little to one side, a tiny birthmark under his left eye and his dark brown, curly hair – which he hated and she loved.

"Is that it?" Beth asked.

"You'll see him soon enough."

The path veered to their left, away from the sea and climbed to a low moorland plateau. Hannah told Beth to wait when they neared the top. She ran ahead, stones biting into her feet, but she ignored them.

Hannah crouched, half hidden behind a gorse bush, searching across the pasture for any sign of movement, even a dog that might alert someone. A few sheep looked up, lost interest and returned to their grazing. She beckoned for Beth to come forward.

"We can follow the old roads from here. If anyone comes you must hide in the heather. I can distract them and turn them away from you while you move on. Then I'll catch you up."

They walked on for another fifteen minutes. The road dropped down a gentle hill. The land to both sides of them was now cultivated. Crops grew in regimented rows, marching over the undulations of the landscape, separated by banks and low hedges.

"We strip farm here. All this to the right was a golf course many years ago," Hannah said. "My great-great grandfather built it on part of his farm."

"Is that how you came to own the Island?"

"I don't own it. I'm a caretaker. We farm collectively here. Nobody owns anything, everything belongs to all."

She was repeating the mantra her grandfather had coined around the time of the first outbreak of the fever. He repeated it when the solar storms destroyed all electronic communication. Hannah could have made better time, even without shoes, but Beth was either tired from her ordeal or not used to walking.

"We can cut across here." Hannah pulled Beth off the road and along the edge of a field of maize.

The plants were tall enough to afford them cover, but Hannah still made Beth stop every hundred yards or so to listen and look for any signs of people.

"How did you meet Ethan?"

Hannah smiled. "We've always known each other. There's not that many people on the Island. Each solstice and equinox we have a sort of party. There's a big meal and we dance and sing and tell stories. Ethan and I have always been together at those gatherings."

"And it's your island, you own it?"

"I suppose technically I own it, or I will when I'm eighteen or when I marry. But we all work the land and benefit equally. Like I said…"

Beth finished the sentence for her. "Nobody owns anything, everything belongs to all."

Hannah fell silent for a few minutes while they continued towards Hope Cove.

"We make decisions collectively here," she said eventually. "It works for us."

"Did your parents arrange for you and Ethan to marry?"

"No," Hannah paused. "Anyway, my parents died when I was nine. Ethan and I are not actually engaged, he hasn't asked me to marry him yet, but he will."

"I'm sorry, I didn't know you'd lost your parents. Is that why your uncle is the Bailiff?"

"Guardian Bailiff," Hannah corrected her.

"Did he arrange your marriage then?"

"No," Hannah laughed and raised her eyebrows at the thought of her uncle marrying her off to Ethan. Had it been Isaac's choice she would have had to marry someone from the mainland, someone with money and influence.

"Ethan and I both lost our parents in the last outbreak of

10

the fever."

"You still call it that? The fever?"

"What difference does a fancy name make?"

Hannah pulled Beth down. She put a finger to her lips. There was a soft whistling, not quite a tune and laughter cut it short, a girl's laughter. There were muffled voices, intimate silences. They waited until the couple drifted further away and Hannah pulled Beth onwards, still half crouching.

"Does Ethan live alone?" she whispered

"No. His father is still on the farm with him."

"I thought you said he'd lost both his parents?"

"His father survived, but he's not been the same since."

"I'm sorry," Beth nodded. "My mother survived the fever, but had to be cared for and barely recognised anyone."

"Daniel won't bother you, he won't reveal your presence. If he did say anything, people would take no notice. He remembers how to work the land, but little more than that."

"How old is Ethan? He must have been young to take on a farm by himself?"

"You ask a lot of questions, don't you?"

Hannah led the way along a narrow, sunken path between high hedges. The holdall separated them, distancing any more questions. The path ended at a junction with a wider track. Grass and weeds grew between wheel-worn ruts. They set off downhill again, now side by side, Beth looking down.

"I ran away from my own wedding," she said quietly.

Hannah didn't respond. She wanted to ask why, but she had accused Beth of asking too many questions and was reluctant to display the same level of inquisitiveness.

"My father arranged the marriage. I'm not in love with Simon, I never was."

"He arranged your marriage?"

"I told you, my father is the Recorder. People generally do what he asks."

Hannah knew the Recorder of course. He was always on the Pride, the packet ship that visited the Island. He oversaw exchanges of goods and validated the registers of births, deaths and marriages.

"I ran away yesterday, the day of my wedding. I'd managed to stow what I needed on my boat and escaped when my father was getting the horse and trap. Everyone else had left for the church."

"Where were you planning on going?"

"Here of course, but I knew that I would attract too much attention if I landed at Newport."

"But why here? Your father is bound to look for you."

"The currents took me away from the Island and I lost my bearings at night. It was fate that delivered me to you."

Beth looked directly at her, an intense stare that made Hannah feel somehow responsible for her safety.

"You will help me, won't you?"

"Our life here is very simple. We work the land, we have craftspeople and we care for the sick as best we can."

"I can work. I can be useful. I have money."

Hannah was almost more concerned about Beth's money than she was about hiding a fugitive from the mainland. Hope Island worked by everyone being equal, everyone contributing what skills they had. There was no hierarchy based on wealth, except perhaps for her uncle who made much of his semi-official duties and record keeping.

"Your money has no value here. I can see by your hands that you haven't worked on the land, do you have any skills?"

"I studied medicine."

"You're a medic?"

"No, not a medic. I was a sort of nurse I suppose. I helped

12

set fractures and attended at childbirths. I can dress wounds and I can prepare herbs and natural medicines."

Medical skills were rare on the Island. Although everyone had some basic knowledge, they didn't have a dedicated midwife or anyone with medical training.

"But why here?"

"I have immunity to the virus, so your island doesn't scare me."

"Why would it scare you?"

Hannah never thought much about the fever. They hadn't had an outbreak since the one that took her parents.

"My father says the virus is endemic here."

"But we haven't had anyone sick for nine years, the last outbreak came from the mainland, my parents caught it on their last visit there. Anyway, you have epidemics every few months don't you."

"Are you sure there's no virus here?" Beth asked.

"Of course I am. I live here."

Beth pursed her lips, thinking. She shook her head as though dismissing a thought.

"We haven't had a case for over three years. If you don't have the fever here they must both be lying, my father and your uncle. They must want things to remain as they are."

Beth fell silent, a frown fixed on her forehead. When she did speak she sounded calm and serious.

"Do you know the price your produce fetches in the markets in Freetown?"

"It's all recorded, my uncle keeps the accounts."

A doubt formed in Hannah's mind as she spoke. She didn't really know much about their trade with the mainland. Uncle Isaac always said there would be plenty of time for her to learn when she came of age. She had trusted him in those matters of trade, but now doubts surfaced in her mind and she realised they had been there for some time.

"That's Hope Barton, down there," Hannah pointed and Beth shielded her eyes to look down the valley where a simple building stood at the water's edge, hunkered in under a cliff.

"It's very close to the sea," Beth said.

"There was a village below Hope Barton – flooded now. The cove is sheltered as none of the winter storms blow in on this side of the Island and the seas have stopped rising now."

Beth stared at the farmhouse, her holdall lying on the ground between them.

"There's someone outside, sat on a bench I think."

"That will be Ethan's father." Hannah squinted. Her sight wasn't perfect at that distance. "Ethan must be around, he wouldn't leave Daniel by himself for too long."

They walked on towards the farm. A black and white sheep dog scampered up the road to greet them, but stopped barking as soon as he recognised Hannah. She ruffled the fur around his neck when he leaned against her. Beth had taken a few paces back and when Charlie moved towards her she lifted her hands clear of him, shaking visibly.

"Is he safe?" she asked, her voice rising in pitch.

"He won't bite you."

"I mean fleas, the fever." Beth was looking down at Charlie but not moving. "You know what I mean."

"I told you, we haven't had a case here for nine years and I thought you were immune."

"We don't have any dogs or cats."

"You mean at home?"

"No, I mean in Freetown, nobody has any pets, they're too dangerous to keep that close."

"Charlie's not dangerous."

Beth dropped one hand slowly. Charlie pushed his head

14

against her and Beth gasped as her fingers touched his head.

"He's so soft," she whispered.

"Daft would be a better word. His parents are both working dogs, but Charlie is mostly company for Daniel rather than actually useful on the farm."

"Hannah?" A man's voice echoed up from the farmhouse.

Charlie looked round at the sound of Ethan's voice and bounded down the road to join him on the small patch of lawn in front of the house.

"Let me do the talking," Hannah said. "And don't mention money."

"Okay, but why?"

"Just trust me." Hannah didn't explain.

Ethan waited for them. Charlie had returned to sit on the ground next to Daniel. The afternoon sun was in Ethan's eyes. He shielded them with one hand, his other dropping to rest on the dog's head.

"Hannah, I wasn't expecting you today."

"I found something that might be worth looking at."

Ethan ignored Hannah and turned to Beth.

"Hello, I'm Ethan," he said, offering a hand to Beth. "You're new?"

"She was sailing round Camp Bay and we... sort of bumped into each other."

"We don't get many visitors, any visitors. You're from the mainland?"

Beth and Hannah exchanged glances.

"Can I get her something to eat Ethan? Beth missed breakfast."

Ethan looked at Hannah, glanced back at Beth and sighed.

"Sure, help yourselves. I have to go water the horses. I'll be in directly."

Chapter 3

Hannah had hoped that Ethan would take her hint and not ask any more questions when she evaded his first one. They had known each other for so long that they could sense each other's moods and thoughts. Ethan was inquisitive, but he was always able to hold himself in check and wait for the right time. It was one of the things she liked about him, especially compared to the brasher, pushier boys in Newport who would try to tease and taunt opinions from her.

The farmhouse, Hope Barton, had been built in the 2030s, after sea levels had risen faster than expected. Originally it was going to be two cottages, so there were two entrances, but the world had changed fast and the two dwellings became one, linked by connecting doors on both floors.

"Are you sure it will be all right for me to stay here?" Beth asked.

"Ethan will be fine with it."

"What about his father?"

Daniel was still on the bench, warmed by the sun. He rarely moved once settled, spoke even less frequently and it was difficult to know how aware he was of what was going on around him.

"Daniel won't give your secret away. Come on, let's get you something to eat."

Hannah led Beth inside the house. Light filtered through the small front window to reveal three mismatched armchairs with throws over them and a sofa that sagged so much that the seat touched the floor. Hannah walked to the far wall and drew back the curtains covering a larger window, which looked out onto a now choppy sea. Beth turned around a full circle taking in the room from the large wood-burning stove to a series of family pictures and a mixed assortment of china on a large dresser. A low table in the middle of the room had a piece of carved driftwood on it

"Is that Ethan's?" Beth asked, picking it up. She ran her fingertips over the intricately detailed scales of a serpent that was emerging from the sea-ravaged wood. "It's beautiful."

"No, not Ethan's, that's Daniel's work. We all save pieces of driftwood for him that look promising, but only Daniel can see the creatures that hide inside them."

"I've seen his work before. I never really thought about who the artist was. Daniel looks quite old to be Ethan's father?"

Hannah explained that he looked older than he was, that the fever and losing Mary, his wife, had taken a toll on him physically. But she was surprised that Beth recognised his work and that she referred to him as an artist. She asked where she had seen his carvings.

"They're sought after in town. My father has two pieces – they have to be Daniel's. Father's always kept their origin a bit of a mystery. He said they came from the Island, but wouldn't say anything more than that."

"Why?"

"It adds to the mystique I suppose, the price rises with each new carving that arrives and nobody dares come over here to find the artist in case they catch the fever."

Hannah nodded thoughtfully. Her uncle had always given Ethan something in exchange for them, sugary treats, new tools, but he had never mentioned that they had a significant value. Daniel was content with creating them and, although the new tools took pride of place on Ethan's workbench, they were rarely used. It also explained why the crew of the Pride of the Ocean stayed on the ship when it moored. They were scared of catching the fever too.

"We need a plan if you are to stay here," Hannah said. "We'll have to change your name for a start. You can't hide forever, people in Newport will hear about you eventually and someone will mention you to my uncle, they're bound to."

"I could cut my hair, I've always hated it long like this. Would you do it for me?"

Hannah was surprised, but saw Beth's reasoning. Her black hair was beautiful, but also so distinctive that it made her easy to identify.

"Okay, and we could use honey and vinegar to lighten it a little. Although you never quite know what colour it will end up."

Beth pulled the remains of her braids out of her hair and gathered it in a ponytail behind her head, holding it in both hands. She turned to Hannah, smiling.

"How would I look with short hair?"

"Different, but maybe not different enough to fool anyone looking for you."

"Can you get me some clothes," Beth asked. "I can pay."

"What sort of clothes?" Hannah ignored the renewed offer of money. "Didn't you bring any with you?"

"Could you get me some boy's clothes, I could disguise myself that way."

Hannah wasn't sure if that would work, but she could see some merit in the idea. If Beth's father searched for her, reports of a boy turning up on the Island wouldn't trigger so much suspicion.

"I'll see what I can do," Hannah said. "Now, egg and bacon? We have potatoes and bread too."

"That sounds amazing. Are you sure you can spare it all?"

"It's no problem. The hens are laying like crazy right now and Ethan doesn't like bacon so there's always plenty to spare. Come on."

Hannah disappeared through a door at the side of the room and Beth followed, tying her hair in a knot to keep it back from her shoulders. The room was a mirror version of the lounge, but it was fitted out as a kitchen. There was a large wooden table in the centre and a wood burning range against the far wall. Pale cream cupboards lined two sides with pine plank shelving above. Two deep ceramic sinks were set into the work top-side by side. Everything looked like it had been repaired several times and the cupboard doors didn't match.

"Grab a few rashers of bacon from the fridge will you?"

Beth looked round the kitchen and stopped when she saw a tall fridge with two doors. She stood in front of it, but didn't immediately open either door.

"You have electricity?"

"Of course, we have wind turbines on the Ridge and Ethan's got two small ones here as well, on top of the cliff."

"I didn't expect you would be so... organised," she said under her breath.

"How many eggs do you want?"

Hannah had to repeat the question because Beth was still standing in front of the fridge, not moving or responding. Her answer, when it came, sounded uncertain, as though she was thinking of something else.

"Two please," she replied, adding. "My father said you lived a very basic sort of life here?"

"We do."

Beth opened the fridge and took out a plate with several rashers neatly arranged on it.

"But good bacon is expensive," she said, sniffing it. "Where shall I put it?"

Hannah opened the door of the range, knelt down to poke the embers into life and threw in a couple of dry sticks.

"Just put it on the table for now," she said over her shoulder.

Satisfied that the fire was going, she stood and leaned against the rail along the front of the hob while it came up to heat.

"I think your father and my uncle have been spreading lies. I'm not sure why, but we need to find out."

Hannah filled a kettle from a large jug, cracked two eggs into a cup, scooped fat out of a bowl and rested the laden spoon in an iron skillet. She looked at Beth, wondering how much she could trust her and decided that Beth had more to lose than her. She was about to say something when the front door burst open.

"The land's bone dry," Ethan said. "I'm going to have to run the field gutters this evening."

"I've got your fire going for you – again."

"I was going to let it out for a few days, eat cold, it's too hot to cook in this weather." Ethan turned to Beth. "We don't get many visitors here and the Pride isn't due until next week? Have you been hiding in Newport since it last came? I'm surprised Hannah didn't mention you."

Beth glanced to Hannah, who answered for her.

"Beth sailed here, she happened to beach her dinghy in Camp Bay where I was diving."

"So what did you find this time? More pots and pans?"

"Coal. Two bunkers. Both full."

"How deep?"

"Maybe thirty feet, twenty-five on a low tide."

"Worth salvaging then. Did you grab a sample?"

"I didn't think to." Hannah bit her lip, hesitated and then launched into her appeal. "Ethan, Beth needs to stay here for a few weeks. Would that be okay with you and Daniel?"

"Yes, I guess so, but why here, Newport would be better. Someone could offer her a bed there."

Hannah took a deep breath and glanced at Beth, who was biting a fingernail. Ethan looked at Beth and back to Hannah.

"What's happened Hannah? What should I know?"

"Beth's run away, she needs to hide for a few weeks. Someone will be looking for her. That's why she has to stay here, out of sight."

"Who's looking for her?"

Hannah felt she had revealed as much as she could without Beth's permission, but Beth took over anyway.

She explained about her arranged marriage and who her father was and why she needed to hide until she worked out what to do and where to go.

"People will find out you're here," Ethan said. "Hope Barton is fairly isolated, but word will get round. We're too small a community to hide someone for very long."

"We have a plan," Beth said eagerly. "I'm going to disguise myself as a boy, cut my hair and bleach it. Hannah said I could stay on the Island. I have some knowledge of medicine, herbs and..."

"Whoa, hang on a minute. You're still going to have to explain to everyone how you got here and where you came from."

"I speak some French," she said. "I could say I sailed here from another island."

Ethan shook his head and sighed, obviously not convinced by Beth's plan. Hannah knew Ethan was thinking by the way his eyes dropped to the floor and after a minute he started to slowly nod. She put her fingers to her lips to advise Beth not to say anything for the moment.

"If you've run away it would be too much of a coincidence for someone to turn up here pretty at much the same

21

time – even if it was a boy. You will need to hide for a while. We can work out a story of how you got here and I still have some old clothes of mine in the box room – they might fit you."

Nothing was discarded on the Island. New clothes were costly and hard to come by. Everything was stored or recycled. Ethan looked Beth up and down, assessing her. Weighing up the problem without undue haste. He shook his head again.

"I'm not convinced you'll pass as a boy. Are you sure that's the best plan?"

Hannah turned to the range and tested the cover with the flat of her palm.

"It's our only plan Ethan, unless you have a better idea?"

Ethan shook his head. "I'll go up while you're fixing Beth's breakfast, see what I can find."

Hannah lifted the cover and slid the pan onto the plate. She went back to the fridge and took out a couple boiled potatoes left over from a previous meal and roughly chopped them with a knife. The potatoes sizzled as they hit the fat. She inverted a tea plate over them and left them to heat up.

"What can I do?" Beth asked.

"Maybe practise a deeper voice?"

She turned to look at Beth and both of them burst into a fit of giggles. Hannah inverted the pan so that the potatoes were on the plate and slid the browned, course mash into the oven to keep warm. She put three rashers of bacon in the pan and pushed them around with a fork, flipping them over as they crisped. Beth retrieved a loaf from the bread crock, which Hannah pointed her to, and cut and buttered two slices.

After the eggs were fried Hannah took one piece of bacon for herself and wrapped a slice of bread around it. Beth tucked into her plate of food like someone who hadn't eaten for weeks. Hannah cut another slice of bread, dropped it into the pan to soak up the fat before putting it in the oven.

"Ethan will have that when he comes down." She stood wiping her hands on a cloth and looking at Beth. "So, how short are we going to cut your hair then?"

"I thought Ethan didn't like the taste of bacon?"

"He likes the taste, just doesn't like chewing it. Ethan is a law unto himself. My mother used to say that about my dad."

Ethan returned with an armful of clothes, most of them a variety of browns and buffs and all well worn. He ate his slice of bread and fat while the girls sorted through the clothes, holding them up against Beth and giggling.

"Right," Ethan announced, pushing his plate across the table. "I'm off out to work. I'll take Dad with me to get him out of your hair – literally I suppose. You can take the spare room Beth, but it might need a bit of tidying up first."

They heard Ethan chatting to Daniel about what they needed to do as the two men set off. Charlie barked and Daniel's staff tapped occasionally on the surviving patches of tarmac, slowly fading as they walked up the lane.

"Time for the scissors then," Hannah said. "Are you sure about this?"

Beth pressed her lips together and nodded once. Hannah gathered a handful of hair at the back of Beth's head.

"I ought to warn you that I've never actually cut anyone's hair before. It might not end up quite how you imagine."

"I'll trust you. Go for it."

The scissors took off twelve inches of salt-encrusted black hair and the old Beth began to disappear.

Chapter 4

Hannah became more confident as she attacked Beth's ever-shorter hair. After the first half dozen cuts with the scissors it looked a complete mess, but Beth didn't complain and Hannah noticed how Beth's shoulders relaxed as her hair fell to the floor.

"I think I'm almost done," Hannah said, working her way round Beth's head and snipping off stray strands.

"Is there a mirror somewhere?"

"In the bathroom, upstairs."

Beth started to climb the stairs at the back of the room and Hannah called after her.

"It's the yellow door to your right."

It was a few minutes before she came back down. Hannah wondered if Beth had regretted her decision, but she had wet her hair and brushed it so that it was flat against her head, her small, pink ears stark against her remaining black hair.

"We'll have a go at bleaching it tomorrow. Do you want to try on some of Ethan's old clothes? They should be clean, if not in the best of condition. I can show you your room too, it's on the left at the top of the stairs."

Beth followed Hannah back up and into a large, gloomy room at the end of a corridor. Hannah drew back the curtains and wafted her hand in front of her when dust flew from the rail. The motes twirled as though caught in panic in the light now flooding into the room.

"Might need a bit of a clean-up," Hannah said.

They both looked around them at the sparsely furnished

room. An iron and brass bedstead stood against one wall, blocks of wood were wedged beneath two legs to compensate for uneven floorboards. A tall mahogany dresser was covered in ornaments, candlesticks and old picture frames. Dust, like a recent fall of snow, covered every surface and a threadbare woven rug lay in the centre of the room.

"I can deal with the dust," Beth said. "It will be fine. I can't believe how kind you and Ethan are. I'll have to repay you somehow."

"I hope you're not going to talk about money again, we don't need paying, we help each other here, it's a given."

Beth nodded and smiled. Together they sorted through the pile of clothes they had taken upstairs with them. There wasn't a great deal of choice as he had worn most of them until their only useful function would be as rags in the yard. Beth selected a pair of heavy tweed trousers, but the waist was so loose they had to tie a string through the belt loops to keep them up.

One of his shirts was in better condition, but wide on the shoulders and long in the arms. Beth rolled the sleeves up and tucked the bottom of the shirt into her trousers.

"How do I look?"

Hannah screwed her mouth sideways. She knew Beth was a girl so couldn't really see past that, but maybe it would work, maybe she could pass as a boy if she was a bit less 'clean'.

"You don't look like you've ever done a manual job in your life."

"I haven't I suppose."

"You'll need some boots or shoes. Ethan should have some."

They heard the front door open. Hannah put her fingers to her lips to stop Beth from calling out.

"Are you girls upstairs?"

It was Ethan. Hannah wasn't sure who else it might have been, but she felt her heart beating fast, even after she recognised his voice. She let escape the breath she was holding.

"We need some old shoes of yours for Beth," she called from the top of the stairs.

"I'm not sure I've got any, I gave them all to Martha."

Martha ran what was the closest they had to a shop. Fresh produce was stored there and any items of clothing – in fact almost anything could be left in the communal resource. Martha also kept meticulous records of the Island's population, of donations and withdrawals, but the records were rarely needed nowadays. During the early years they were kept to ensure everyone shared equally, suffered equally and celebrated equally. Those cautious years were, thankfully, long gone and Hannah only knew them from stories that had been handed down.

Hannah came down first and when Ethan saw Beth he swore under his breath. Hannah scolded him playfully, but his mouth remained open for some time.

"Your hair," was all he managed to say.

"Do you like it," Beth asked.

"I preferred it long, but I suppose it wouldn't have worked like that."

A gruff voice interrupted them. "Who's the boy?"

Daniel had entered the house quietly and surprised Hannah when he spoke. It was rare for him to utter more than one or two words at a time. He turned to Ethan.

"Is he here to help with the bees?"

"Yes sir," Beth cut in.

"Mary makes the honey here, but she's not well, don't know what's wrong with her. She's good with the bees."

Daniel turned away and wandered through to the other room.

"Well you passed inspection there," Ethan said. "Although

I'm not sure how much that counts."

"Mary was Ethan's mother," Hannah explained. "She made the best honey on the Island."

"My mother made honey too. I helped her when I was young, then when she..." Beth hesitated for a heartbeat. "I took over afterwards."

Beth walked over to the window, which looked out onto a close-cropped lawn. Rabbits had come out in the late afternoon sun and were scattered across the grass like pale molehills. Every now and then one would lift its head, alerted by a sound or smell, then, satisfied there was no immediate danger, it would return to grazing.

"Where are your hives?" Beth asked.

"Just across the dry steam bed, above the orchard."

None of them had noticed Daniel's return. He was in the doorway between the two ground floor rooms, a small knife held loosely in one hand, his driftwood dragon in the other. A few shavings of wood still clung to his cord trousers.

"Can I see them?" Beth asked. "The bees I mean."

"I'll take him," Daniel said. "What's your name boy?"

"Ben," Beth answered quickly. "My name's Ben."

Daniel grunted and turned away. Beth followed him through into the other room. Hannah watched from the door as Daniel sat down in a chair and turned the dragon over and over in his hands as though looking for the place where he'd stopped working the wood.

"Beth," Hannah whispered. "Leave Daniel alone for now, Ethan will show you the hives later."

Beth sighed and turned back towards them.

"It's like my mother was. We thought she was with us sometimes, but she never really was. She lived in another world."

"Ethan," Hannah said. "Could you sail Beth's dinghy back here from Camp Bay, it will be better protected in

Hope Cove, although we did manage to drag it above the high water line."

Ethan glanced out of the window, ducking slightly to look at the sun.

"Bit late today, the tide will be against me, but I can do it first thing tomorrow."

"It should be safe there overnight," Hannah said.

"I don't want to lose it," Beth interrupted. "My mother gave it to me."

"If Hannah says it's safe, it will be," Ethan assured her. "She probably knows the waters round the Island better than I do. First thing tomorrow I'll fetch it back."

"I can't get here early tomorrow," Hannah said. "I have to spend some time with Uncle Isaac. Beth, can you keep an eye on Daniel while Ethan brings your boat round?"

"Ben," she corrected. "Not Beth, Ben. And yes, I'll be happy to get to know Daniel, I like him actually."

Ethan was scratching his head. "It's going to take me a while to get used to calling you Ben. Will you grow your hair again, once this is all over, when you don't have to hide?"

"I hated my hair. It's much better short like this. And we're going to lighten it too."

"But it was beautiful," Ethan protested.

Beth touched the side of her neck and ran her fingers behind and over her ear.

"Well it's gone now, and good riddance to it."

"I ought to be getting on," Hannah said. "I'll be back as soon as I can tomorrow."

"You'll remember the vinegar, and the lemons?" Beth asked.

"Of course. You've got honey haven't you Ethan?"

"Yes, but what do you want it for?"

"To lighten Beth's hair."

Ethan looked at Beth and raised his eyebrows, his mouth

set, lips pressed firmly together. "Seems a shame," he eventually mumbled. He made an excuse that he had some chores to do and walked out through the kitchen door.

"Not sure what's got into him," Hannah shrugged.

They both watched Ethan through the window as he stood on the weed-studded lawn in front of the house, rabbits scattering to the shrubs and the safety of the longer grass lining the lane. His hands were thrust deep into his pockets and he was staring across the sea to the mainland. Some days it looked so close you would think you could swim there, but the tides and currents were strong and it was, Ethan knew, more than twelve miles.

"He dreams about leaving the Island," Hannah said, as much to herself as to Beth. "He always says we should explore the world, that it must be growing and healing now and that we should be a part of it."

"It's not that special. Just greedy people and the fever to look forward to."

"I thought you said it was quite rare now."

"We get an outbreak every few years, usually in late summer. A traveller will bring it in, rats, stray dogs, mosquitoes, nobody knows when or if it will appear and everyone panics when it does."

"Sounds like we're lucky here."

"Or immune," Beth said. "Maybe your isolation works for you. Maybe that's your uncle's reason for those rumours."

Hannah wondered if exposing Ethan to Beth's experiences might temper his desire to explore.

"Do you have a radio on the Island?"

"What would we want with a radio?"

"To hear the news."

"But radio hasn't worked since my grandfather's days. He told me about it, but even my parents never actually heard one."

"They started some broadcasts a year or so ago. You must have heard about it."

"Nobody told us."

"My father would have told your uncle."

Both girls looked at each other, suspecting what the other was thinking.

"There is an old one at my grandfather's house I think, but I don't know how it works, or even if it works."

"Can you get it? Can you bring it here?"

"I don't know. Isaac might notice if it goes missing. He'll be suspicious."

"Does Isaac live in your grandfather's house?"

"No. It's mine, but I don't live there either."

Hannah knew exactly where the radio was. She had sat in front of it and her grandfather had said how he remembered it when he was little. She had played with it, turning the knobs, and her grandfather had pretended to make voices come from it.

"I'll try to get those lemons from Martha. She's protective of them as we can't grow many here, but the juice will definitely help lighten your hair in the sun."

"I can't wait to see what I look like with fair hair."

"You won't be fair, just a bit lighter and hopefully brown, not red."

"I can live with red. As long as nobody recognises me I'd settle for green."

Both girls laughed and Hannah hugged Beth, saying that she really ought to get going.

"It's only a half hour to Newport, and Isaac will be wondering where I am."

"Thanks for everything Hannah, you've been so helpful. I owe you so much."

Beth hugged her even tighter and Hannah heard her sniffle as though she was holding back tears.

"Ethan will take care of you and don't worry, it will work out okay, I promise."

Hannah wondered why she was promising something she couldn't guarantee, but she now knew that Uncle Isaac was keeping the full truth from her. Just how many lies he was spinning was something she was going to have to find out, and Beth might be able to help in that quest.

Chapter 5

Hannah set off towards Newport, walking slowly, thinking about the things Beth had said and those she had only hinted at. Somewhere in the back of her mind she had always been suspicious of Uncle Isaac. He spoke to her as though she was a child, even though she would be taking over from him soon. She couldn't even remember what Isaac did before her parents succumbed to the fever and he took charge.

A small patch of sweetcorn on her left looked almost ready for harvesting. The long stems were sturdy but the wispy tips caught the breeze and fluttered in unison. Hannah pulled an ear of corn towards her, the silks had just started to turn brown and when she exposed and punctured a kernel with her nail a milky juice oozed out. She would mention it to the pickers.

A voice, in full song, but wandering slightly off key, carried across a crop of broad beans on the other side of the road. Hannah recognised it as Abby and smiled. She cupped her hands around her mouth and called.

"Hey, Abby, is that you?"

"Who else sings so beautifully Hannah?"

"Keep singing, I'll come and find you."

Hannah followed the voice, checking each strip of crops, smiling with the welcome relief of meeting Abby and her particular brand of normality. Abby's mother had helped in the walled garden at the Manor and they had spent many happy hours playing together.

"Have you been diving again?" Abby asked, looking at her hair. "Did you find anything interesting?"

"Nothing special, just some coal."

"Coal's good, we can always use more coal."

"How's the picking coming on?"

"You're beginning to sound like your uncle already. Mind you, we're all looking forward to you taking over on your birthday and you and Ethan getting married."

Hannah frowned, not sure she liked the comparison with her uncle and not quite so sure about Ethan either.

"You know we're not actually engaged."

"Come on Hannah, you've been drawing pictures of the two of you holding hands since you first picked up a crayon."

Hannah broke a pod from the plant beside her, split it open and popped a couple of broad beans into her mouth. She made a point of concentrating on the flavour and texture to buy her time.

"They're ready. We should be picking."

"What do think we're doing?"

Only then did Hannah look further down the row, past Abby, and saw a whole team there, picking beans and filling wooden crates.

"Has something happened between you and Ethan?"

"No, nothing's happened really."

Nothing had happened between Ethan and her, but the way he looked at Beth and admired her hair had cast doubts in Hannah's mind. She didn't think she was jealous, but she was no longer so confident about their relationship. She wanted to tell Abby what had happened, sure that she wouldn't breath a word to Uncle Isaac, but it would betray her loyalty to Beth.

"It was just something he said, nothing really. It doesn't matter."

She had to keep Beth's presence secret, even from Abby, and couldn't explain her concerns without at least hinting that someone else might have caught Ethan's eye. The island was small and gossip was like salt that could easily be sprinkled into any conversation to make it more flavourful. Hannah waved to a woman who had glanced at her from further down the row. The woman waved back, but continued with her work.

"I ought to get back to Newport," Hannah said. "I promised to help Martha with a stock take."

She hadn't, but knew that Martha would be checking all their reserves now they were picking, so it made a plausible excuse.

"You'll be up here tomorrow with us?"

Hannah nodded.

"Maybe we can catch up then. You can always tell me if something's bothering you. You know that don't you?"

Hannah smiled, nodded again and backed off a couple of steps.

"I really ought to be going."

"There is something else I wanted to talk to you about," Abby said.

"What's that?"

"It will keep. We'll have plenty of time tomorrow."

They were close friends, but Abby had always been cautious when it came to Hannah's uncle. Nobody knew why.

Hannah passed more crops on her walk home, but her mind was now a jumble of concerns about her uncle, about Beth and about Ethan. She was also wondering why Abby wanted to talk to her.

Hannah's cottage was half way through the village, not too far from the harbour. She hadn't wanted to live in the Manor after her parents died and chose Canary Cottage because the yellow windows and door made her feel cheerful. They could do with a new coat of paint, but that was an expensive import, not easy to come by and not easy to justify.

Closing the front door behind her she leaned against it and looked around the living room. There was a small kitchen and a toilet at the back of the cottage, but most of her growing up had been in this room. Martha had lived with her to start with, sleeping on the sofa, but for the last few years she had insisted she could take care of herself.

There were some odd items collected from the Manor, framed sketches of her parents, old photographs of long dead relatives, a chessboard of her father's and her mother's sewing basket. The rest of the clutter, by the fireplace and on bookshelves, were objects she had found on her dives or odd items collected from Martha's store that nobody else wanted.

Uncle Isaac only used the Manor when the Recorder stayed the night, so nobody lived there permanently. She had told her uncle quite firmly that she would move back in when she was married. Now she wasn't so certain, either of getting married or her desire to leave Canary Cottage. A sharp knock on the door made her jump.

"Hannah. Are you in there?"

Uncle Isaac's deep voice made her shiver. She looked round the room as though there might be some clue there to Beth's existence, even though she knew that was ridiculous. Hannah wasn't used to having secrets, not important secrets.

"Hannah?"

She turned, shrugged her shoulders to loosen the tension in them and pushed back her hair before opening the door.

"Ah, Hannah, you are here. Someone said they saw you coming through the village barefoot.

"Oh, yes, I lost my shoes."

"Careless. How did that happen?"

35

She had to think quickly and lie – both were unfamiliar territory for her.

"I haven't actually lost them, just forgot to put them on again. They're at Camp Bay where I was diving. I can pick them up tomorrow."

Hannah hadn't moved from the doorway, leaving Isaac standing in the street.

"Aren't you going to invite me in?"

"Of course, sorry. I wasn't thinking."

Hannah still couldn't get over the feeling that there was something that was going to give her secret away. She scanned the room again, let out the breath she had been holding and sat down in an old armchair, which was covered in a ragged tartan throw.

"You were back late," Isaac said before settling his considerable form on a sofa of worn, torn and repaired leather. The sofa squealed in protest.

"It's my day off," she said defensively.

"You don't really have to work Hannah. You won't have time to when you take over the management of the Island."

"Why would I not want to work?"

Isaac shrugged and sighed as though the answer should be obvious.

"And did you find anything of interest today – when you were diving?"

Was he hinting about Beth? Could he possibly have found out already? Hannah told him about the coal, but he didn't show any great enthusiasm for her discovery. She realised that she should have kept it quiet for now because Beth's boat was still there and she didn't want anyone chancing on it, especially Isaac.

"The house was stripped bare. There was nothing else left."

Isaac nodded, his eyes perusing the room. Hannah's discoveries were mainly of interest only to her. The shelves behind her bore testament to an eclectic collection of useless items. Chipped china ornaments, coloured pebbles and plastic toys. Some would be likely to survive millennia. They littered almost every available surface in her room.

"I stopped by Ethan's on my way back," she said to divert Isaac's attention from Camp Bay. "Daniel is carving a sort of serpent, it might be a dragon."

She knew of Isaac's interest in Daniel's carved mythical creatures and that mention of a new one would intrigue him.

"Is he now? I might just ride over and see it before the Pride arrives."

Isaac rarely walked any great distance, his weight made him breathless with very little exertion.

"It's nowhere near finished yet. I would wait a week or two otherwise you might make him nervous. You know how Daniel can get."

"I do, yes, and of course it's not of any great importance, I'm merely curious."

Hannah felt a silence fall between them. She hoped Isaac would take it as a cue to leave, but he made no indication that he was ready to go.

"Are Daniel's carvings very popular on the mainland?"

"Popular?" Isaac looked up to the ceiling and pursed his lips. "There is some curiosity about them, some interest, but I wouldn't say popular exactly. Why do you ask?"

"I just wondered – that's all."

"But you doubt this particular carving will be ready any time soon?"

"It's difficult to tell with Daniel, but no, I don't think so. He's barely half way through it."

That was another lie, Hannah was getting better at them – the carving was almost finished. Isaac nodded, seeming to accept Hannah's judgement, but she was now doubly nervous that he would either hear about the boat or discover Beth at Hope Barton. She decided to warn them that her uncle might drop by. She didn't trust Isaac.

"Will the Recorder visit this time?" Hannah asked.

"I believe so. He rarely fails to be on the Pride."

"I'd like to meet him, not just to say hello. After all I will be dealing with him when I take over."

"That is true," Isaac said cautiously. "Maybe you should join us for supper at the Manor. But you'll find it terribly dull."

"Thank you for the invitation, I think I will join you."

Hannah was affronted that her uncle was in effect inviting her to her own house, but she hoped she hadn't revealed her thoughts in her sarcastic response – she didn't want him to notice her growing mistrust in him.

"There will a few papers to sign. All very boring to be honest and quite routine."

"You'll let me know what time on the day?" Hannah asked as Isaac hauled himself to his feet.

"And you'll keep me updated on Daniel's current carving?"

Hannah nodded and went to open the front door. Isaac didn't leave immediately, he stood, his eyes half closed, studying Hannah.

"Is there something worrying you my Dear? You seem a little on edge."

Hannah shook her head. "No Uncle, nothing, just tired I suppose."

"Maybe you shouldn't dive quite so recklessly and so often. You never know what sort accident could occur when you are alone like that. I've said the same to Martha and she is quite concerned for your safety too."

"But I've done it for years Uncle," Hannah said quietly. She had a horrible feeling in her stomach that he was issuing some kind of veiled threat.

Isaac touched her cheek with the palm of his hand, smiled and left the cottage. He turned back towards her after he taken a couple of steps.

"You will remember to let me know about Daniel's carving?"

Hannah nodded again, not trusting her voice, and Isaac turned and walked away. She leaned her back against the door once it was closed. She needed to warn them at Hope Barton about Isaac visiting them unannounced. Everything felt more complicated now she was in Newport.

She started at another sharp knock on the door behind her. Hannah closed her eyes, counted to ten to calm her breathing and opened the door, fully expecting Isaac to have returned with some more questions.

"Hannah, can I come in? Can we talk?"

It was Abby. The relief was so great that Hannah closed her eyes and muttered a faint "Thank heavens it's you."

Chapter 6

Hannah pulled Abby inside and looked out onto the lane to check it was clear and that Isaac had gone. Satisfied that he wasn't returning, she closed the door and leaned back against it.

"Abby, I have something to tell you and you have to promise that you won't tell anybody else."

Abby frowned. She had seen Isaac waddling down the lane, hands in his pockets and whistling tunelessly.

"Is something wrong, something Isaac's said? I saw him leaving."

"No, nothing to do with Isaac. This has to be really, really secret."

Abby sat on the sofa, which Isaac had vacated only minutes earlier. It didn't protest at her presence. She leaned forward towards Hannah who was barely perched on the edge of the armchair facing her. The tartan throw had slipped off the back and one arm. Hannah hadn't straightened it. She was biting her lip, wondering whether she was making the right decision, but she knew she could trust Abby above everyone else and she couldn't carry this alone.

"You know you can trust me," Abby said.

Hannah told her everything, about Beth, about the boat and the money and about taking her to Hope Barton and about the radio. Once she started, it all poured out, even her fears that Ethan was showing more interest in Beth than he had shown in her for months.

"Well," Abby said, taking a deep breath. "We don't have new people turning up here so it's probably natural that

Ethan's going to be a little bit curious."

It was the kind of sensible explanation that Hannah needed to hear from her best friend and she wondered if she had been imagining it all.

"There's another thing I haven't told you. I think I know why we don't get any visitors here."

Abby frowned when Hannah told her about the rumour that the fever was endemic on the Island and that the frequency of outbreaks on the mainland were also wildly exaggerated.

"That sort of makes sense with what I wanted to talk to you about," Abby said. "It's a bit awkward really because it's about your uncle."

"What about him?"

"A lot of people don't trust him." Abby took a deep breath. "They don't think he's being honest with us."

"How?" Hannah asked, genuinely puzzled.

Abby explained about Isaac's deals with the Recorder. That people who remember her parents' time didn't think they got as much in return on trades as they used to.

"Isaac blames it on fluctuating markets. He says that when we have a good year the mainland does too, but it still doesn't really make sense because they buy everything we can spare."

"You mean he's cheating us?"

Abby said people were asking questions, rather than making accusations, but that they were worried about her taking over.

"They don't trust me either?"

"They do, but they don't believe Isaac will hand over the reins that easily. They think he'll find a way to stay in charge."

"But he can't, he's only the Guardian Bailiff. I take over when I'm eighteen."

Abby reached out and took Hannah's hands in hers. She spoke quietly and slowly, looking Hannah directly in the eyes to convince her of what she was about to say.

"Unless, of course, you catch the fever, or have... some sort of accident."

Hannah listened, not wanting to believe what Abby was saying. In her heart she knew there could be some truth in her words, but couldn't believe that her uncle would harm her deliberately.

"Surely he wouldn't..."

Abby kept hold of Hannah's fingers, her thumbs gently massaging the back of her hands.

"Nobody has actually said he would, but a lot of people are worried for you. Isaac and the Recorder are two of a kind and, from what you've said, even this Beth is not too trusting of her own father."

Hannah looked down and pulled her hands back, burying them in her lap. Her world had turned upside down and she wanted it to be yesterday, before Beth, before Abby had voiced these suspicions.

"Will you come with me tomorrow," Hannah asked her. "I'm going back to Hope Barton first thing in the morning."

"Of course I will. And I can squeeze a lemon or two from Martha, that way it won't look suspicious if Isaac hears."

"What will you tell her you want them for?"

"I don't know yet, but she's usually got some hidden away."

Hannah felt the tension drain from her body now she had shared her secret. Abby had always been there to help her throughout her whole life.

"I wish there was something I could do to thank you."

"Apart from marrying me instead of Ethan," she laughed and Hannah smiled, shaking her head at the same time.

"You never give up do you?"

It was a joke they had shared ever since Abby had come out to her as being gay. With the Island population so small, Abby had often threatened to sail over to the mainland and bring someone back with her – or grow old alone and be miserable to everyone, including Hannah.

"I'll come by in the morning and we'll go and sort Ethan out for you – and this Beth or Ben or whatever she's calling herself."

The next morning Hannah sat by the window in her cottage, waiting for Abby. She was worried that Beth would think she had betrayed her confidence by bringing someone else along with her, but hoped she could persuade her of the benefit of another voice to corroborate whatever story they came up with. Abby arrived a little later than Hannah had hoped, but with a cloth bag hung over her shoulder that bulged in a promising way.

"Martha took some persuading, but I have three lemons. Is that enough?"

"More than enough. How did you prise them off her?"

"Two bottles of last year's elderberry wine and a promise of lots of jam. I told her I needed the lemons to help set my strawberries – you only need the juice don't you?"

"Yes, just the juice. I'd never have thought of that."

The two of them set off for Hope Barton with a hastily fabricated excuse in case they bumped into anyone. Abby had told the picking team that they would return later but were going to check the coal that Hannah had found.

"I thought we could bring a few lumps back with us from those bunkers to cover our story."

When they arrived at Ethan's there was no sign of Beth, Daniel or Charlie. Ethan was sat on the doorstep sharpening knives on a whetstone wheel.

"I wasn't expecting to see you today Abby?"

"She knows," Hannah said.

Ethan kept turning the wheel, but it slowed and he eased the pressure on the blade as it scraped over the stone.

"I told her about Beth, the boat, Beth's father, the wedding, she knows everything."

"Why?"

"We need help. I need help. Isaac dropped in on me yesterday and I was certain I was going to make some mistake, give Beth up by accident."

"And Abby knowing makes it safer for Beth?"

The wheel stopped turning. Ethan tested the edge he'd made, pulling the pad of his thumb across the blade. He put it down on the doorstep, in a line with the others he'd sharpened.

"It's okay for you," Hannah sniped. "You just have to carry on as normal. I have to meet people, pretend nothing's happened and that everything is just how it was – and it isn't, is it?"

Ethan looked up at her – his face neutral, unsympathetic. "They're up with the bees," he said.

"What about the boat? It's not here yet?" Hannah asked.

"I'll fetch it directly."

"I could bring it round here. No problem," Abby offered cautiously, an attempt to thaw the icy reception they had received.

Hannah sensed the usual friction between Abby and Ethan. It was always there, but today you could almost see it like a piece of barbed wire they were both pulling on.

"If you want," Ethan said.

"Come on Hannah. We'll fetch the boat back and you can introduce me to Beth then."

She took Hannah's arm and gently pulled her back in the direction of the coast path to Camp Bay. Hannah kept looking back at Ethan as they walked away. The wheel spun faster now with no blade applied to slow it. Ethan kept his eyes on the two of them until they disappeared round a corner and out of sight of the farm. Abby didn't say anything until they were well out of earshot.

"That was fun," Abby said.

"I don't know what's wrong with him recently."

"His head is off in some imaginary land across the sea. Some place that probably doesn't exist any more."

"You really think he wants to leave?"

"He's always said so, right from when we were kids. He was always the pirate sailing away to some foreign island and coming back rich and powerful."

Hannah knew that Ethan was a dreamer, but she hadn't thought it mattered, hadn't thought it real. They both fell silent. It took almost half an hour to reach Camp Bay. There was a fresh breeze in their face once they had left the valley where Hope Barton sat.

"The wind is perfect," Abby said. "We should make it back in good time."

The boat was where Hannah and Beth had left it, untouched by the tide. Abby walked ahead and ran her fingers along the varnished timbers of the hull, letting out a long, low whistle of approval. Hannah hung back a few yards.

"It's beautiful," Abby said quietly, almost to herself. "Not very practical of course, too small, but it looks almost new."

"Beth said it was a present from her mother."

"Her mother must be wealthy. I suppose she is being married to the Recorder."

"I don't thing she's alive. I got the impression that the fever took her."

Abby nodded, more focussed on the boat than Beth's misfortunes. She put a hand on the mast and checked the stays to make sure they were still taught.

"This is going to be recognised by her father if we ever take it round to the harbour. I can't see how she can keep it without word getting back."

"I thought the same. I haven't solved that problem yet, but we need to get it off this beach before someone else finds it."

Abby was biting her lip, walking round the boat, deep in thought.

"We could scupper it. That's probably the best plan if she doesn't want it to be found."

"Can we just get it back to Hope Cove for now. That can't be our decision to take."

Hannah couldn't imagine Beth agreeing to destroy her dinghy, but maybe it was the only solution. While Abby checked the dinghy over for any damage to the hull, Hannah left her shoes on the beach and went back to the outcrop of rock from where she had dived the previous day. This time she left her t-shirt on, it would dry while they sailed back.

She dived twice. The wind scurried across the sea and broke the surface of the water. The magic of diving through a sheet of glass and into a silent world was lost in the more practical task of recovering a few lumps of coal.

After bringing a couple of fist-sized lumps of coal up each time, Hannah wrapped them in an old piece of cloth she had brought with her. She picked her way over the rocks to the beach. Abby had turned the boat and pulled it into the shallows.

Abby looked up at the few wisps of cloud that were floating lazily past. "You walking back or coming with me?"

"I'll come with you. I want to see if she sails as good as she looks."

Hannah climbed in and Abby pushed the boat out and

slid easily over the gunnels to take the tiller. Hannah balanced her weight against the sail as it took the wind. She leaned forward when she had a chance and examined the coal in her makeshift parcel.

"It looks good quality. Anthracite I think. See how it's keeping a shine even when it's dry."

Abby took a piece, examined it, and tossed it back to Hannah.

"A couple of bunkers you say? That'll keep someone warm for two or three winters."

"The smithy might want it if the quality is as good as it looks."

"Coming about, now," Abby called, her eyes firmly on the sea ahead, and they both changed position – years of experience showing in the ease of their movements.

They sailed Beth's dinghy back to Hope Cove without incident. Hannah's hair blew in the wind and she could taste the salt cracking as it dried on her lips. Hannah closed her eyes, felt the sun warm her eyelids.

When they got to Hope Cove the wind died in the lee of the headland and their progress slowed. They tacked towards the beach where Beth, Daniel and Charlie stood waiting for them on the sand. One of Daniel's hands was resting on Charlie's head, scratching him lazily behind an ear. His other hand lay on Beth's nearest shoulder. One of Beth's arms crossed her body, her hand covering Daniel's. They looked more like father and daughter than newly made friends.

Chapter 7

The dinghy rode onto the beach on a small wave and pitched softly in the fine sand of Hope Cove. Beth waded into the sea and held the craft steady while Abby dropped the sail. Charlie had left his station next to Daniel and jumped with all four paws landing in the water at the same time, eager to be amongst the action. Abby slid over the gunnels and into the water, she and Beth easily pulled the boat onto the beach with Hannah still in it.

"You must be Abby," Beth said across the boat. She instinctively put a hand up to push her hair back from her face, but looked awkward when she remembered that it was no longer necessary. "Ethan told me that you were bringing my boat round. Thank you."

"It's a beautiful dinghy, sails well too. When was it built?"

"It was my sixteenth birthday present, my mother's idea before she died. I don't suppose there's any way I'll be able to keep it now."

Hannah climbed out of the boat, a lump of coal slipped from her bundle, which Charlie pounced on. He ran away with it in his mouth, but stopped and turned half way up the beach to see who was going to play with him. When nobody chased him, Charlie dropped the coal and lay down with it between his paws, panting.

"You could put it on the trailer." Daniel said. He must have been listening more carefully than anyone thought. "You could put it round the back of the house. Nobody would see it there."

They all turned to look at him, surprised at his grasp of the situation.

"Good idea Daniel," said Abby.

Charlie had brought the lump of coal back to Daniel and dropped it at his feet. Daniel's attention wandered, more interested in ruffling Charlie's neck.

"Daniel took me to see the bees," Beth said. "He knows what's going on most of the time, but rarely sees the point in talking."

"Where's Ethan now?" Hannah asked.

"He went to check the sheep, said he wouldn't be long. He's got the dogs with him."

Charlie whimpered, happy to be by Daniel, but eager to play. He shuffled even closer and leaned against his leg. Daniel's fingers found a favourite spot behind Charlie's ear.

"Come on Daniel," Abby said. "You can show me where that trailer is."

With just the two of them left on the beach, Hannah sat and watched Beth as she furled the sail tightly against the boom. She waited until the last knot was tied before saying anything.

"You can trust Abby you know, she won't betray you. And I've had an idea about your boat."

"She seems okay," Beth shrugged.

Beth took the rope attached to the bow and, wrapping a couple of turns around her hand, she pulled it tight and sat next to Hannah.

"So what's your idea?"

"We'll have to do it soon, probably today. In fact if I'd thought about it earlier we needn't have brought the dinghy back here."

Hannah took a deep breath and let it out slowly. She explained her idea that they could beach the boat at Spear Head and pretend to find it by chance the next day.

"Won't that just mean they will come and look for me?"

"Not if they think you went overboard and drowned."

"My father knows I can swim quite well."

Hannah explained that the currents around the Island could be treacherous if you didn't know them. She said that in the dress she was wearing she wouldn't have stood a chance. "If your dinghy is found at Spear Head it would be a miracle for you to have survived."

"We could leave my holdall in it. It's only got clothes that I don't need now."

"Maybe," Hannah hesitated, hoping to dispose of another problem at the same time. "I thought your satchel might be more convincing. With the money still in it."

"But I always wear my satchel over my head. It would have gone overboard with me."

"You weren't wearing it when I found you."

"I'm not giving up my satchel. You can have the holdall. The plan will have to work with that."

A fresh breeze caught the hull and the rope pulled on Beth's arm. The boom swung round as far as its tether would allow and both girls sprung up to hold the boat steady and pull her onto the beach a little further.

"It would be even more convincing if we left some blood on the boom," Hannah said.

Beth looked at the boat, looked back at Hannah, and nodded. "My blood?" she asked.

"It doesn't have to be yours. We could use a chicken, anything really. Everyone will assume it's yours."

Abby was coming down the beach with the trailer, it was rusty and the wheels squeaked on every turn. Daniel had stayed at the house. They could see him on the bench watching them, Charlie at his feet. Beth and Hannah floated the boat back out and Abby guided the trailer under it. The fit wasn't perfect, but good enough. While they secured the boat Hannah explained her idea to Abby.

The three of them sat on the beach, looking at the dinghy. Abby was running sand through her fingers. "If I found it, there wouldn't be a connection back to here."

"But we can't get it there on the trailer," Hannah said. "So someone will have to sail it round."

"Back against the wind?" Abby raised her eyebrows.

"I could do it," Beth offered.

"You don't know the waters," Hannah said. "It's not going to be easy, and look what happened to you last time you tried to navigate round here."

Abby said she was due to check the aqueduct on the western ridge, before the autumn rains set in, and that she could easily spot it at Spear Head from there. She said that if she raised the alarm nobody would find it surprising.

"I wish we'd thought about all this before we brought the dinghy back here," Hannah mumbled. "I'll have to sail all the way back past Camp Bay, we can't take it round past Newport, somebody would be bound to see us."

Because they had all been facing the sea, looking at the dinghy, nobody had heard Ethan return. Hannah spun round when he spoke, her nerves on edge.

"The wind will be more favourable tonight, it'll be coming off the mainland. I could sail it round there if Beth's here to look out for Daniel."

"Ben," Beth mumbled, then lifted her head and turned towards Ethan. "You've got to call me Ben from now on."

"Why do you want to take it round there anyway?" Ethan asked. "It's safe enough here."

Abby explained their idea to Ethan who listened without interrupting, nodding thoughtfully.

"You could take the pin out of the gooseneck," he said. "It would cause a real problem in a strong wind with the boom swinging free, it could easily cause the sort of accident you're talking about."

They agreed that Ethan would sail it round to Spear Head that evening and that Abby would make the discovery early in the morning and raise the alarm.

"How long do I need to stay hidden?" Beth asked.

"A couple of weeks should be long enough," Abby said. "By then nobody will link you with the dinghy."

Ethan suggested waiting until after the steamer had visited before Beth made an appearance and they all agreed.

"My uncle was asking about Daniel's carving. Apparently his work is popular on the mainland."

"More than popular," Beth snorted. "People almost fight over them. There is a sort of unofficial waiting list that my father manages."

Hannah shared her concern that Isaac might turn up at Hope Barton before the steamer arrived to see if Daniel had finished his latest piece.

"We'll have to be ready for that," Ethan said. "He always comes by horse so we should hear him. There will be plenty of time for Ben to hide."

They all knew that the weak point in their plan was Daniel and they also knew that there was very little they could do to prevent him giving away Beth's presence.

"How are we going to explain my being here when the time comes?"

"I haven't quite thought that one through," Hannah sighed. "But we'll come up with something."

In the end they only pulled the boat to the end of the beach, out of sight from the house and the lane. Abby said that they ought to get back before people wondered if there had been an accident and came looking for them. She handed her bag, with the lemons in it, to Beth.

"Keep the skin and pith for me. I need them for jam."

"Jam?" Beth asked.

"Long story," Abby replied, smiling at Beth. "I'll bring you a pot next time I see you."

Abby and Hannah headed off, back up the track towards Newport. Abby set a brisk pace up the hill and, being several inches taller and with correspondingly longer legs, she made it hard work for Hannah to keep up with her.

"Slow down a bit will you?" Hannah joked.

"Sorry Shorty, I forget you've only got little legs."

"They're not little, you're just built like a daddy-long-legs."

"Is that why you always throw me out of your house?"

Hannah never quite knew whether Abby was flirting with her or testing her. She never took it seriously and it never bothered her. Right then there were more important issues to consider.

"What are we going to do about Beth? How are we going to explain her presence on the Island?"

"Well, that depends on whether she's going to insist on being Ben or not. What did she look like with long hair?"

"Pretty. She's still pretty I suppose, but her hair was beautiful, just ask Ethan."

"Shame she cut it off."

"I know, but it makes sense. Even if finding the boat on Spear Head works, people would still make a connection if a new girl suddenly appeared out of nowhere."

"So, how are we going to explain her or him, when the time comes? She can't have swum here."

"Sailing is just as tricky. We'd need another boat for her to have arrived on."

They walked on, both deep in thought. Abby stopped and, when Hannah turned back to see why, a familiar cheeky grin was spreading over her face.

"I've got it. I'll borrow a boat and fetch her from the

mainland. I'll bring her back with me."

"How is that going to work when she's here already?"

"I've always joked that I'd have to go to the mainland to get a partner," Abby laughed. "And everyone knows I'm gay."

"No they don't, I've never told anyone."

"Come on, Hannah, people here aren't dumb. It's an open secret."

"Nobody has ever said anything to me."

"They're being tactful, they know you're my friend and don't want to offend me or you. Why do you think none of the boys here have ever made a pitch at me when I'm such a stunningly attractive woman?"

"Because you're taller than most of them."

Abby laughed. Hannah was not convinced that everyone did know about Abby, but it was true that none of the men on the Island did seem to be interested in Abby in that way.

"But if everyone knows you're gay wouldn't they expect you to bring a girl back with you. And how are you going to bring Beth back when she's here already."

"Oh that bit's easy. I'll take her over with me."

It took Hannah a second to see the simplicity of the plan. If Beth's boat is found on the Island, nobody will link it to a new girl arriving with Abby. She could only see one prominent flaw.

"But Beth's not gay."

"When we get back she can say that she didn't realise what I'd intended or something like that. She'll be free to do whatever she wants."

"And if she's recognised when you get to the mainland?"

"Beth can stay in the cabin. We don't have to be over there for long, just one or two nights should be enough. And I don't want to risk catching the fever, not that it sounds likely now."

"It's a crazy idea, do you think it will work."

"Have you got a better one?"

There was a shout just off to their side. A team of pickers were in the field next to them. Hannah and Abby diverted off the track to show them the coal. There wasn't as much enthusiasm as Hannah expected, but then it wasn't like she'd found something precious, not like the cellar full of bottles she had discovered a few years earlier. Those bottles were useful for all sorts of things, even though the wine in them had been undrinkable. The coal would simply mean they didn't have to buy quite so much for the Smithy this winter.

Chapter 8

The next morning Hannah woke to the sound of rain scurrying in rapid bursts against her window. She pictured the aqueduct, the channel that followed the contours around the western hills, gathering the water as it slid and slithered down the slopes.

Abby would already be there, her hair wet, plastered against her face as she picked her way along the narrow path on the northern side of the Island. She would be clearing any scree that had fallen into the channel and uprooting plants that threatened to block the flow. The path, gently rising, followed the aqueduct to its high point under Button Peak. From there it would flow in the other direction, down the west side of the ridge and through a pass in the southern end of the hills to the main reservoir.

At that high point Abby would have a clear view of Spear Head and the spit of gravel and sand that ran out to the small rocky island. It was normally frequented only by gulls and cormorants, but Beth's dinghy would be there if everything had gone according to plan.

There was nothing she could do until Abby returned with news of her discovery. Hannah would have to act normally and that meant joining the picking crew or liaising with Martha on what the Island needed in trade exchanges. She decided to visit Martha as that way she would be in the centre of the village and among the first to hear Abby's news on her return. The door was open when Hannah got there, but Martha wasn't in the large barn that served as the main store.

"Martha, it's me, Hannah," she called and received a muffled reply.

"In the cellar Dear. Come on down, but be careful on the steps."

Hannah made her way to the end of the barn, picking her path through crates stacked on platforms that were in turn balanced on stone mushrooms. Rats weren't a common problem on the Island, but mice had been known to wreak havoc in the grain bins during the early years of the community.

"Can I help?" Hannah asked, descending the shadowed steps with care.

The stone steps were badly lit. Martha claimed that electric light hurt her eyes and preferred to work with the warm glow and aroma of beeswax candles. She made them herself so nobody tried to argue against her choice.

"Are you stock-taking?"

"Just checking records. If you're offering to help you chose your time well because I've almost finished."

"Sorry, I meant to come by yesterday, but got side-tracked."

"It's fine Dear, there wasn't much to do. Just rearranging before this year's supplies start turning up."

Martha kept all the bottles and jars in the cellar, where the temperature was almost constant throughout the year. Vinegar, cider, fruit juices, pickles, preserves, fruit wines and even mead would fill the shelves by the end of October.

"Can I put the kettle on and make a cup of tea?"

"That would be very nice Dear, I'll be up directly."

Hannah made her way back up the steps, with more confidence than on her descent.

Every household on the Island has its speciality when it came to preserving food for storage. Tasks had been divided for decades and pride was paramount in keeping standards high. Only rarely did this division of labour change, usually through marriage or because of a death.

Martha's own skill was in making soap from rendered fat. The lye she needed was produced in two large barrels. Her arms bore the scars of her work – the lye being caustic and temperamental. She always claimed that the potatoes hated her when she was testing the alkalinity by floating one in the bucket. Her cursing could be heard throughout the village when she dropped one and the lye splashed her skin.

Hannah moved the kettle onto a hot plate and stared aimlessly out of the window at Martha's barrels. A shout came from the street.

"Martha? Is Hannah in there? We're making up a search party."

Abby must have returned with news of the abandoned dinghy already. Their plan was in action.

"Martha," Hannah called down to the cellar. "I have to go, something's happened."

"What's that?" Martha said, climbing the steps slowly.

"I don't know, there's a search being organised."

"You get on Dear, I'm too old for clambering over the hills."

Hannah followed the sound of the commotion coming from the harbour. She hoped Abby would be there, making sure the two of them got the south coast to search. Not that many people had turned out, only a dozen or so, but they didn't need more.

Three parties were formed. Four people elected to go west from Newport, beneath the hills. Abby said she didn't see anyone there, but fresh eyes might find something she missed. The second group, just three of them, would check the east side of the Island. Given that the boat had been found on the west side it was deemed unlikely they would come across anything.

The third party, with Hannah, Abby and two others would cut across the Island to Camp Bay and work their way round the southwest coast to meet the first party at Spear Head and the spit of sand where Abby had found the dinghy. One other volunteered to go inland, past the reservoir, in case someone had taken that path to the village.

Abby said that she found blood on the boom and that the gooseneck had come unattached at the base of the mast. Everyone hoped for a good outcome, but all were resigned to the worst, knowing the fierce currents around the Island would have made survival unlikely.

Abby stuck close to Hannah on the way across and took her arm to hold her back and let the other two push ahead a little.

"We need to warn Ethan and Beth," she whispered.

Hannah nodded in agreement. They hurried and caught up with the others. When they got to the lane that dropped to Hope Barton, Hannah turned off and called out. "I'll warn Ethan and see if he's seen anyone. I'll catch you up at Camp Bay. I can check that bit of the coast on my way round."

Hannah was certain that something would go wrong, but couldn't think what – unless Beth was seen. She didn't linger at the farm and spoke only to Ethan.

"They're searching the whole coast. Keep Beth out of sight. There's a search group coming round to you from Newport."

"No problem. We guessed something like that would happen so Beth's inside."

Hannah didn't wait, she cut along the low, grassy cliffs around the south east coast, running, hoping to catch the others before they got too far ahead of her. She cut across a section of moor, following tracks sheep had made. The others were only a few hundred yards in front when she reached Camp Bay.

"Hey," she called to them. "I'm coming."

Abby was laughing when she caught them up. "Need to get your breath back after making those little legs work so hard?"

"Shut up you," she replied, making a face and punching Abby on the arm.

Neither of the other two would have teased Hannah like that, being aware that Hannah would soon be the bailiff. From Camp Bay the search was simple for the first half mile. A footpath followed the coast to Camp Head, shingle bays and a few outcrops meant there was little chance of missing anything or anyone. When they rounded the head, the shore became rockier, with small undercut inlets making the search slower.

A voice called from under a rock outcrop where he had picked his way.

"I found something."

"What is it? A body?" Abby asked.

"Just a jacket of some sort. Coming up," he shouted.

A bundle of wet, deep red cloth was thrown up and landed a few feet from them. Abby picked it up and it fell open to reveal a short, red jacket, not very practical and not the sort of clothing anyone on the Island would own.

"Any ideas?" she asked.

Nobody recognised it. Abby managed to catch Hannah's eye, but Hannah had no idea what it was. As they pressed on with their search Abby quietly asked her if she had seen it before, but Hannah said that she had never looked in Beth's bag so it might or might not be hers.

They found nothing else by the time they arrived at Spear Head. The dinghy was beached on the spit of sand. The other team had beaten them there by some time.

"We found a jacket," Abby said and handed it round for everyone to see.

Nobody recognised it, but Sophia, always inquisitive, dug into the small decorative pockets and discovered a tiny bone carving of a rabbit with extra long ears, there was a small hole worked through it, which made it look like it should be on a string as a necklace. Nobody had seen anything like it before and had no idea what it was. Abby was busy checking the boat.

"The pin's missing on the gooseneck," Abby said. "But I reckon I can jury rig it good enough to get it back to Newport."

She rejoined the group and took the small carving, turning it over in her fingers and shaking her head.

"Anyone fancy joining me to sail the dinghy back?"

Out of sight of the others she put a hand on Hannah's arm to hold her back from volunteering.

"I'll come," Sophia said. "I'd like to see how she sails. She looks almost new."

Sophia was often out all night fishing off her small rowboat. She was wiry and strong and could handle almost any boat given a chance.

"Maybe we should check the shore again later?" Hannah suggested.

Everyone knew that it probably a waste of time and energy, that the most they would be likely to find was a dead body, but nobody wanted to say that out loud.

"I'm up for it," said Sophia and everyone else mumbled their assent.

"I'll go back round the coast again to Camp Bay," Hannah said. "Just to check we didn't miss anything."

A couple of people offered to join her and when they got to where the jacket had been found they did another thorough search of the area, but there wasn't anything there. Following the coast back to the east they met the other search party and updated them.

The walk back was peppered with speculation as to who it might have been, where they had come from and how slim their chances of survival were. When they passed by the lane to Hope Barton, Hannah made an excuse to check on Daniel and Ethan, waved the group goodbye and said she'd join the second search later on. She loitered making sure nobody had decided to follow her before heading down the lane. The farm looked deserted, not even Daniel was on his bench. Hannah knocked on the door as she entered. Not sure why she felt the need to do that as she never had before.

"Anyone here?"

"In the kitchen," came Beth's reply.

She had a cloth wrapped tightly around her head and was sitting at the table, her chin in her hands.

"I put it on last night, the honey and vinegar I mean. It needs to be on for hours for it to work."

"Have you looked at yourself in the mirror?" Hannah asked, not managing to suppress a smile of amusement.

"Yes I have thank you."

"I mean you still look like a girl. Even in those clothes"

"I know."

"I don't think fairer hair is going to help much either."

"It has to. Unless you've got something I can smear on my face so that I can grow a beard?"

Hannah laughed. It was difficult not to laugh when Beth was being herself.

"You may not need to grow a beard. Abby's had a brilliant idea – although you might not agree."

Hannah explained the plan, which sounded even more fanciful when repeated. She wasn't sure it would work, but disguising Beth as a boy probably wasn't going to either.

"Would she really do that for me?"

"I said you could trust her."

Hannah told her about the boat being discovered and that

all had gone exactly as planned. She explained that Abby and Sophia were sailing it back to the harbour. "When the Recorder arrives, I mean your father, he's bound to see it and recognise it."

Beth turned half away from Hannah, staring into the distance. "He'll think I'm dead," she whispered. Her voice gave away no emotion.

"That red jacket was a stroke of genius," Hannah said, trying to engage Beth again. "I assume it was yours."

"Yes, but it was Ethan's idea to leave it there. The netsuke was my idea."

"Is that the little carved thing we found in a pocket?"

"Yes, it was my father's, he collects them. That one was his prize possession. I don't know why I took it, spite I suppose, but he'll recognise it for definite."

Ethan came in the kitchen door.

"Hello Hannah. All go off all right?"

"Yes, exactly as we planned. I was just telling Beth."

"My father is bound to take my boat back."

"That's a small price to pay to escape him," Ethan said.

"I suppose so."

Ethan put a hand on her shoulder to comfort her.

Hannah looked at them and remembered how strong and confident his fingers felt when he held her. He hadn't even kissed her since Beth's arrival.

"It was a good idea," Hannah repeated. "I mean throwing that jacket on the rocks."

"And Beth was clever thinking of that netsuke," Ethan said, squeezing her shoulder.

"There's going to be another search later this afternoon, so keep a lookout for anyone coming by. Probably best for you to stay inside Beth."

"I wasn't planning on going anywhere, not with this on my head."

"I ought to get back," Hannah said.

Ethan's hand was still on Beth's shoulder when Hannah closed the door. Daniel had reappeared on his bench and Charlie looked up with sad eyes as though trying to commiserate with her.

Hannah trudged up the lane, trying to work out what had gone wrong between her and Ethan. She wondered if they had been growing apart for some time and she hadn't noticed. She sighed, stopped for a moment and looked up into the pale sky to clear her thoughts. A skylark was singing, but she couldn't see it, she hadn't been able to see clearly for several years. Hannah shook her head angrily and walked on at a more determined pace.

Chapter 9

There was a small gathering of people looking at Beth's boat. It was now moored snug against the harbour wall. Hannah joined them to see what was being said and in the centre of the group was Isaac, speculating on the value of another search. Abby and Sophia had just finished furling the sail and were climbing onto the quay.

"I doubt we'll find anyone now, not alive anyway," Isaac said. "But I suppose it would be wrong for us not to make an effort."

The tide had dropped and, looking down onto the dinghy, it seemed far too small to have sailed from the mainland. From close to Hannah, Jacob, one of the Island's fishermen, spoke slowly but with a measured authority.

"From where that jacket was found I reckon they'd have had no chance of survival. The currents will have taken the body way beyond our island – it was just chance that the dinghy grounded where it did."

"It's not large enough to be of any practical use is it Jacob?"

"Too small. The kids might use it to catch bass off the rocks, but I wouldn't advise taking it too far offshore."

Isaac sighed as though rather bored by the whole affair. "I suggest you organise a second search between yourselves. I will let the Recorder know whatever details we manage to gather when the Pride calls next. It's possible he will recognise the dinghy if it's from the mainland."

"I was thinking of sailing over there myself," Abby said to nobody in particular, sounding out reactions.

There were one or two knowing smiles. Many had heard her propose this trip before and were sympathetic to her plan. Isaac, however, turned to her with a fresh frown creasing his forehead.

"We're at full stretch right now Abby, what with the harvest and this boat. Maybe you should wait until after the Recorder's visit and we can get an update on the fever over there."

"I suppose I can wait a week or so," Abby smiled at Isaac, but without warmth in her eyes.

Isaac looked slightly confused and Martha, who had joined them purely out of nosiness, nudged him hard in the ribs.

"Isaac, you know why she wants to go you fool."

His eyebrows lifted and he looked up to the sky remembering the stories he had been told over the years.

"Quite, quite," he cleared his throat. "Well, Abby, Spring might be the best time to sort out that business. We're so busy at this time of year. Or I could have a quiet word with the Recorder if you'd like me to."

"I'm quite capable of sorting out my own life thank you Isaac. I don't need a man to organise it for me," she stared him straight in the eyes, "as you know perfectly well."

Hannah pulled Abby away. More people were joining the group and nobody noticed their withdrawal to the railings along the edge of the harbour wall. "You shouldn't have said anything, you should have just gone. He'll try to stop you now."

Abby said that she would go when she felt like it, not when Isaac said it was okay.

"I'll take the Crabber, it's got a decent cabin and it's solid enough for the journey. It will get me to Freetown without any problem. Anyway, I can't take Beth over there until after the steamer has been and gone – Isaac will have forgotten about it by then."

"You might need money on the mainland. I can ask Beth about that. I think she has some." Hannah made a small laugh of disapproval. "In fact I know she has money."

Abby said she would ask her herself, and that they needed to get to know each other a little better before they pitched into this. She asked Hannah how Beth had reacted to the idea.

"She was grateful, but people are going to take against her afterwards."

"Why do you say that?"

"You may want to pretend that you're independent, but everyone likes you, they won't like Beth, not when you bring her back and she dumps you."

Abby leaned back against the rail alongside Hannah and twisted her mouth to one side as she thought. A seagull screeched past behind them, swooping along the edge of the harbour wall looking for discarded fish heads from the boat that had just arrived.

"Maybe I could dump her," Abby suggested. "Then I'd be the one to blame."

"That would look a bit odd if you'd just brought her over here."

"We didn't think this through did we?"

The group of onlookers were splitting into new search parties. Isaac joined Hannah and Abby, leaned over the railing and looked down at the dinghy.

"It's not really of any practical use is it?"

"I suppose we can keep it Uncle, if nobody claims it. It will useful for something and it's practically new."

"It could be a suitable boat for children to learn how to sail – if it handles well. Maybe you should take it out Hannah, let me know what you think."

Abby looked hard at him. "After the gooseneck has been

properly repaired of course."

"Of course, of course. We wouldn't want you coming to the same fate as whoever sailed it here. I'd take it out myself, but as you know I've never been comfortable on small boats."

Martha pulled on Isaac's arm. "I need to talk to you Isaac and these girls will want to join the search party. We're low on several items and I want to make sure you get them ordered when the Pride comes."

She eased him away from Hannah and Abby. It was some days before the Pride of the Ocean was due to call, plenty of time to get an order together. Hannah was glad that Martha had separated Isaac and Abby. There was always a sense of impending danger when the two of them were in close proximity and Martha had often acted as the peacemaker.

"Why does he want you to sail it?" Abby asked. "Sophia and I have already said how well it handled – even with a makeshift repair to the boom."

"I don't know. You really don't trust him do you?"

"I have my reasons."

"Did something happen between you two? Something you've never mentioned."

"It doesn't matter. Water under the bridge."

Hannah wanted to push her friend, sure that she was concealing something, but she also wanted to respect Abby's privacy – it was an unspoken rule on such a small island.

"Well, we can't do anything until after the Pride's been and that gives us time to work on our plan. But we'll have to make sure nobody sees Beth until I bring her back with me."

"By then her hair should be quite a bit lighter."

"She will still need to change her name, to be on the safe side."

While they were talking, the second search party was being organised. Hannah and Abby offered to take the east side of the Island, from Newport to Hope Cove and beyond, the least likely stretch of the coast to find anyone or anything. Nobody else wanted that section.

One group was designated to check the old caves above the main reservoir in case someone had taken shelter there overnight, but they didn't have a realistic expectation of finding anyone. Excitement of this nature was rare on the Island and everybody wanted to be part of it. Before they set off, at Sophia's suggestion, each group took a shotgun with the express understanding that it should only be fired if a body was found – dead or alive.

Hannah and Abby were able to walk side by side for most of their route round the headland and towards Hope Cove. They didn't need to scour the sea's fringes and the rocky inlets – they knew there was nothing to be found.

"How are we going to work this with Beth and you when you bring her back?"

"I don't know, maybe we could just share my place for a while and gradually drift apart."

"Or what if you don't bring her back as your partner, but as someone who just wanted to come to the Island?"

"Wouldn't that be stretching it a bit? I just happened on someone who wanted to come here when nobody has for years."

"No more of a stretch than you finding a soul mate in two nights on the mainland."

"Thanks for your vote of confidence in my magnetic and attractive personality."

"You know what I mean."

"Okay, so we need to think of another reason for her to return with me."

"And what would be the chance of you finding someone who wants to be with you and move to Hope Island - all in a couple of days?"

Abby said she had no idea, but maybe Beth could come up with a suggestion. "After all, she knows more about life on the mainland than we do."

The walk to Hope Cove was no more than a mile and, as they approached the farmhouse along a narrow stony track, both Ethan's sheep dogs started barking. Even before they could see any buildings Samson, a border collie, bounded towards them, his tail wagging furiously. Hannah squatted down to greet him, ruffled his ears and talked to him. Delilah stood a little way off as usual, friendly but wary, her tail wagging furiously in her excitement.

"Come on you two, take me to your master."

Both dogs appeared to understand Hannah's request and ran ahead, occasionally turning to check the girls were following them. At the house Ethan was sitting on the bench, in the sun, nursing a mug of tea. Beth was half hidden in the doorway, ready to scurry away from anyone she didn't recognise.

"Afternoon." Ethan smiled, shading his eyes from the glare of the sun. "Just out for a stroll?"

"We're all doing a second search round the Island. People are saying this is the most exciting thing that's happened for years."

"My death is exciting?" Beth sounded offended.

"Sorry," Abby said. "But then you're not actually dead are you?"

"I know, it just sounds odd, sort of uncaring."

She came out of the doorway and walked to within a foot or two of Abby. She held out a hand as if she was going to touch Abby's arm, but hesitated and withdrew it.

"I haven't seen you to say thank you for what you've

offered to do. You won't get into trouble will you?"

"No," Abby laughed. "Nothing serious anyway, but Hannah has spotted a small problem with our plan."

"What's that?"

"The unlikelihood of me pitching up on the mainland and finding someone who wants to live me in such a short space of time. And, to be honest, neither of us know what life's like over there."

"It's quite different from here," Beth said. "People are more wary, not so willing to help a stranger and you'll need money too – for food if nothing else."

"I can stow enough provisions for a few days. I'll borrow the Crabber as it's got a decent sized cabin. You might have to hide in it for a couple of nights while we're there."

"Can you do that, just borrow it?"

"Of course."

Ethan had been listening, sipping his tea, and spoke quietly.

"Can you get me something while you're over there?"

"What?" Abby asked.

"I'd like a map, a proper one that shows what the world looks like now. We've only got old books and they're useless."

Beth cocked her head to one side and frowned.

"Are you planning on travelling then?"

"I don't know, maybe. I'd like to see more of the world, not just live and die on this lump of rock."

"Maps are expensive," Beth said. "But I could give Abby the money for one, especially when you're doing all this for me."

Beth and Ethan's eye contact lasted far too long for Hannah's comfort.

"Well we can't do anything until the Pride has been and gone," Hannah said.

"I presume my father will be on it." Beth had finally turned to look at Hannah.

"He usually is. In fact Isaac has asked me to join them for a meal this time, to get to know the ropes."

"Beth will be fine here," Ethan said, putting his arm round her shoulders in a protective gesture.

Beth looked slightly uncomfortable and Hannah suspected she was embarrassed at such an obvious display of affection in front of everyone.

"So," Abby said, breaking the icy stare with which Hannah was trying to freeze her boyfriend. "How would I go about finding a like-minded woman in Freeport - if I was actually looking that is?"

Beth turned to Abby, but dropped her eyes to the ground when she answered.

"I've heard about a pub near Clear Bay. I've never been there of course, just heard about it. It's about three miles down the coast from Freetown. It's only ever mentioned in whispers, but I think it's where you would go."

Beth said she thought it was called The Three Troubadours.

Chapter 10

Over the days before the steamer arrived Hannah visited Hope Barton regularly. It was Abby's suggestion that she didn't draw attention to the farm by changing her pattern of behaviour. Hannah knew there were other girls only too willing to step into her shoes if they thought Ethan was available. Beth was using the lemon juice during the day, in the sunshine, and the honey and vinegar at night, sleeping with her head wrapped in a towel. Her hair had lightened to a dull copper and stood in spikes, refusing to lay flat.

Hannah was resentful at how easily Ethan, Daniel and Beth had settled into a routine with Beth taking over the cooking and household duties. Even Daniel was talking more, although not always making sense. He often referred to Mary as though she were still alive, simply away from the farm for some unexplained reason. He occasionally became confused and thought Beth was Mary. Hannah stayed for supper one evening and wanted to help, but Beth brushed her offer away.

"No, it's fine, I have it all under control."

She produced a large casserole dish from the oven. It contained a knuckle of ham, whole carrots, potatoes and even a cabbage. Hannah had to admit that it smelled wonderful. Beth turned it over with a wooden spoon and put it back in the oven with the lid off.

"I'll need to thicken the stock a little. Do you have any cornflour?"

"Where did you learn to cook?"

"At home. Since my mother..." she took a deep breath

and closed her eyes for a second. "Since my mother died, I helped our cook in the kitchen. She taught me most of what I know."

"Martha taught me."

"The woman the lemons came from?"

"Yes."

Hannah wasn't sure how much of her life she wanted to share with Beth – she appeared to be taking over so much of it already. Ethan made a noisy entrance and Beth called for him to take off his boots.

"I know it's not muddy out there," she told him. "But I've washed the floor and I don't want you messing it up again."

"Always nagging you are," he laughed. "I'll be glad when you find somewhere else to live."

"No you won't," Beth replied. "You'll probably come round there to eat."

Ethan spotted Hannah leaning against the wall when he closed the door. She had been hidden by it until then.

"Hello Hannah," he said. "I didn't know you were here."

"Apparently not."

"Beth's hair is getting lighter isn't it?" His voice dropped to a more measured tone. "I think it really suits her. Mind you she still doesn't look like a boy, good job you gave up on that plan."

Hannah said nothing. She was thinking how happy and bright Ethan had sounded before he had noticed her.

"Beth's been telling me about all the places she's seen," Ethan said with renewed enthusiasm. "She went on the Pride with her father when she was younger. She's seen most of the south coast and the western islands."

Beth was fussing over the casserole, tactfully keeping her back turned to Ethan and Hannah.

"Tell her Beth, tell her about all those places you told me about."

74

"They were nothing special," Beth mumbled. "Just places like everywhere else. You haven't really missed anything."

"But you said about the steel works and the weaving mills and the printers. There's a whole load of stuff happening that we've never heard about."

Hannah wondered what would happen if the Recorder found Beth. Would she be in a lot of trouble? Would Ethan follow her back to the mainland?

"It's really not that exciting," Beth said quietly. "It's much nicer here from what I've seen."

Ethan shook his head even though Beth couldn't see him. She was stirring flour into the stock with her back to him.

"There's not that much here to see," Ethan said. "Just a big old rock sat in the middle of the ocean. Not even the middle, we're more like an afterthought the mainland had."

Beth lifted the spoon to her lips and muttered something. She reached for the salt pig and sprinkled a generous pinch into the pot.

"Simon would like it here too. He doesn't want adventure, just a simple life."

"So why did you run away?" Hannah asked.

Beth turned round and looked straight at her.

"I told you. I didn't love him. I didn't want to marry him. I didn't say he wasn't nice."

Daniel wandered in from the lounge just at that moment.

"Supper smells good Mary."

They all looked at Daniel.

"What did I say? Just said that supper smelled good. Beth's a good cook."

Over supper Daniel was chattier than he'd been for years, he talked about the farm, about crop rotation, when they should bring the sheep in and that they were likely to be short of winter feed again with another dry summer.

Soon after they cleared the dishes Hannah said she ought

to go. Ethan gave her a cursory peck on the cheek when she left. She heard the door open again and Beth calling for her to stop a moment.

"I wanted to talk to you, in private," Beth said and took a deep breath. "I think Ethan has got things wrong. I'm not trying to steal him from you. I don't want him."

"Well, thanks for that," Hannah said. "But it's about what Ethan wants too, and that doesn't seem to be me right now."

Beth shook her head and Hannah could see her eyes liquid in the low sun, but she didn't care about Beth's feelings right at that moment. She just wanted to be away from the farm, away from Ethan, and away from Beth. Hannah turned and walked off without saying another word, just shaking her head at Beth before she left.

Hannah stayed in Newport the following day, helping Martha, not wanting to go out and face anyone. The harvesting team would be close to Hope Barton. She didn't want to bump into Ethan. A part of her half hoped that Beth might be discovered and everything could go back to how it was before she had arrived.

That evening Hannah was sitting on her sofa, distracting herself by unpicking a woollen jumper and winding the wool onto a board ready to be steamed. There was a soft knock on the front door. It wouldn't be Isaac as his approach would be louder and more confident. He would also be unlikely to call round so late and Abby always rapped on the door with a particular rhythm.

Hannah put down her wool and opened the door a few inches. She was never afraid on the Island but a visitor this late was unusual. Ethan was there, standing a couple of paces back from the door as though not sure of his welcome. Hannah was certain this was the end of their relationship and that he was there to finish it. It always took something important for Ethan to come to Newport, even though it was less than an hour's walk.

"What's happened? Has someone seen Beth at the farm?" Hannah asked, hearing the fear in her own words.

"No nothing's wrong, nobody has seen Beth. I just came over to ask you something."

She invited him in, without enthusiasm, like he was an acquaintance, not even a friend, and certainly not a boyfriend. Hannah was convinced that Ethan was going to break up with her.

"You haven't been over here for ages?" she said, her back turned to him.

"No, I suppose I haven't. With the farm work and Daniel…" Ethan shrugged, unable or unwilling to flesh out his answer.

"So, what is it you want to talk about?" she asked, sitting back down in her armchair.

"Lemons."

Hannah looked at him blankly.

"I wondered if you could get any more lemons for Beth. She says she wants to get her hair as light as possible."

"I don't know. I could ask Martha I suppose."

Hannah doubted that Martha had that many lemons left and she might get suspicious as Hannah never made jam.

"She's amazing isn't she? Beth I mean, not Martha."

"Beth is different, but then she's been brought up on the mainland," Hannah conceded. "But I'm not sure about amazing."

"You haven't had the chance to talk to her as much as I have. She's done so much, been so many places."

Hannah thought 'and now she's here', but didn't say it.

"She was so brave, just setting off like that, alone, risking her life. I wish I could just go off somewhere, but there's

Dad and the farm... and you."

"Don't let me stop you."

Hannah didn't mean for Ethan to leave, but she wasn't going to be reduced to begging him to stay.

"You're going to be busy taking over from your uncle soon. There's no great rush for us is there?"

"Rush for what?" Hannah asked, staring at him, her arms folded across her chest.

Ethan had been wearing a hat when he arrived. It was now screwed up in his fingers and he was looking down at it, puzzled by how it had got that crumpled. He mumbled with his chin tucked hard against his neck.

"Getting married I suppose."

"You haven't asked me."

"Sorry. I... just sort of thought we both..."

"I'm not as exciting as Beth am I?" Hannah said.

Ethan took a deep breath and let it escape audibly.

"You're always so bloody certain about everything. Why can't you be easier to be with, and yes, Beth is easy to get on with, she's fun and exciting and doesn't take me for granted."

An uneasy silence ensued. Hannah couldn't bring herself to stand up and move closer to Ethan, to make physical contact. She feared he would shrug her off and their life together would end before it had really begun.

"I'd better be going. Dad will be worried if I'm not back soon."

"Surely Beth will be taking care of him." Hannah regretted her words as soon as they escaped her lips.

"I'll see you tomorrow maybe."

Ethan turned and slid through the still half-opened door without looking at her. His eyes firmly fixed on his hat, which he reshaped and forced onto his head.

Hannah went to the door, her fingers white where she

was gripping the wood. She watched him walk up the street, his shoulders rounded and his head dropped forward. She wanted to run after him, turn him round and kiss him, say sorry, but feared he would have pushed her away.

For the last couple of days before the steamer was due she found excuses not to go to Hope Barton. Hannah busied herself in Martha's storerooms, helping her tidy and check that nothing had spoiled. Ethan didn't return to her cottage, but Abby dropped by early one evening, wondering where she had been, why she hadn't been out on the fields. Hannah told her about Ethan's visit, how badly it went, and what she feared had happened. Abby hugged her and Hannah finally let go her tears and buried her face in Abby's shoulder.

"I've lost him haven't I?" Her words were muffled.

"No, not necessarily. Ethan's just distracted. I'm sure it will all work out okay in the end."

"They're going to go off together, her and Ethan," she sobbed. "They'll sail off to all the places that Ethan's always wanted to see."

"I doubt it Hannah. Beth seems to like it here. I can't see her going through all this just to leave again."

Hannah wished she hadn't saved Beth. Wished that she had washed up somewhere else. Wished that she'd never existed. Abby stroked her hair and held her.

"When we go over to the mainland I'll have time to talk to her and you'll have time to talk to Ethan without her around."

"But what if he doesn't love me? I'm not even sure I love him any more. There's no one else for me is there. He's right, this island is so bloody small."

"Shush Hannah, it's all going to work out somehow. I know it will."

Hannah wanted to believe her best friend, but she couldn't see how life could ever go back to how it was before Beth turned up. Abby poured her a mug of milk and stirred two spoonfuls of honey into it. She stayed with her all evening, making her eat, even though Hannah protested that she wasn't hungry, and settled her in bed before kissing her forehead and quietly closing the front door as she left. Hannah slept restlessly and only woke at the sound that was familiar to everyone on the Island.

Chapter 11

The noise that woke Hannah was the long, piercing steam whistle of the Pride of the Ocean as it approached Newport Bay. The sound was familiar to everyone on the Island and a small crowd of curious volunteers always gathered to help move goods or simply witness the presence of such a large ship.

Hannah had spent a restless night, slipping in and out of sleep, and her eyes were heavy and didn't want to open. She splashed cold water over her face and stared at herself in a small mirror, propped on the shelf above the sink.

"What am I doing with my life?" she mumbled, but her reflection in the mirror didn't answer, it simply returned her stare.

She shrugged on a shirt that fell almost below her shorts, which were fashioned from cut-off jeans that had acquired too many holes and tears to be patched or recycled. After slipping her feet into canvas shoes, Hannah left her cottage and walked down towards the quay. Her neck prickled with the fresh morning breeze at her back. The sun would warm the day soon enough and everyone involved in loading and unloading on the quay would seek rest in the shade whenever they could.

The Pride was moored temporarily in deep water at the entrance to the bay as the tide was still on the rise. Hannah heard someone say that a rowing boat was being lowered from the main deck, but she couldn't see it clearly, let alone who was in it. She stood on the edge of the quay, fingers thrust into the pockets of her shorts. A voice behind

Hannah interrupted her speculation about the nature of life on the mainland.

"It will be a couple of hours yet before it's sensible to start transferring anything." It was Isaac, his voice quiet and relaxed. "No point in rowing cargo that distance when she can be moored nearer the quay in an hour or so."

The Pride never moored right alongside the quay and the cargo was always transferred by rowing boat. As the boat drew nearer Hannah could see there were two passengers. Usually only the Recorder would land to negotiate the exchanges with Isaac.

The onlookers moved back instinctively as the Recorder and a younger man climbed the rusted metal ladder fastened to the quay wall. Fear of the fever being carried from the mainland made everyone apprehensive about visitors. Isaac shook hands with the Recorder.

"Gideon, always a pleasure to see you." He turned towards Hannah. "You know my niece of course."

Hannah nodded to the Recorder. He was someone she was going to have to deal with, but she didn't have to like him. They had met before on several occasions, but only ever exchanged courtesies. Hannah had always excused herself from his company on the pretext of having to help Martha.

"Delighted to see you Isaac and your beautiful niece. Hannah has grown into quite the woman now hasn't she?"

The Recorder's words, or the way he looked at her, made Hannah squirm. He rarely spoke directly to her and often as though she wasn't even there.

"Hannah will be joining us for supper tonight," Isaac said. "To learn the ropes so to speak."

The Recorder nodded slowly and smiled.

"Excellent."

"And who is this young man you have with you?"

Isaac reached out a hand in greeting. Simon hesitated, looked to Gideon, who half smiled and nodded almost imperceptibly. Simon took Isaac's hand, but for the shortest possible time.

"Allow me to introduce you to Simon. My soon to be son-in-law."

"Ah, wonderful," Isaac said. "I have heard so much about Gideon's daughter over the years." He turned to Gideon, a curious puzzled smile creasing his face. "Didn't you bring her with you on one occasion?"

The Recorder said he had, but that she remained on board during their visit for obvious reasons.

"Ah, just so, just so," Isaac said, and handed a sheet of paper to the Recorder. He cleared his throat. "We have a fairly standard list of requirements this visit."

Gideon scanned the list nodding his head and mouthing the occasional items with raised eyebrows.

"Well I can't see any problems here. We should have everything you require on board. Of course some items are subject to market forces and scarcity. You know the sort of problems we face."

"I do, I do," Isaac responded sagely and sympathetically.

"We can tally everything up tonight over supper... with Hannah of course. Your produce has always been of good quality and I'm sure we can balance the books somehow."

"May I ask you something?" Simon interrupted. "There's a small boat in your harbour, just over there."

All four turned to where Simon was pointing. Beth's dinghy gently bobbed in the chop created by a strengthening breeze.

"That's my daughter's boat," Gideon said.

"Exactly what I thought," Simon added.

The Recorder frowned. He kept his eyes on the boat but addressed Isaac in a tone suggesting the boat's presence might solve a puzzle. "How long has Bethany's boat been here?"

"We had no idea it was your daughter's when we found it," Isaac replied, slightly flustered. "Ah, we discovered it beached on the far side of the Island ten, maybe twelve days ago."

"And my daughter?"

"The boat was empty." Isaac looked worried and glanced to Hannah before continuing. "Oh dear. We fear that whoever was sailing it has been lost at sea. I'm sorry Gideon, I had no idea."

"No reason you should have known. But I would like to talk to whoever found it."

"Hannah knows more than I do, she was involved in the search for... clues."

Hannah noticed Isaac's pause, she guessed he was going to say survivors, but decided to be more tactful. Isaac asked her to explain the circumstances of the boat's discovery and the subsequent searches.

The Recorder appeared relatively unshaken by the possible death of his daughter, but when Hannah mentioned the coat they found and the small, carved figure in the pocket he immediately asked to see it.

"Is there any chance Bethany might still be alive?" Simon asked. "That she might have washed up on the shore and be safe, taking shelter somewhere?"

"I'm sorry," Hannah said quietly. "We've searched the whole island. We would have found her if she were here."

Hannah felt awful concealing Beth's survival from Simon, who was more concerned for her than her father appeared to be.

"You said that you have that jacket and carving," the Recorder reminded her.

"Yes, it's in my cottage, the jacket is with Martha. It will only take me a minute or two to fetch them if you want to see them."

Simon reached out and held her arm. "Is there even the slightest chance that she might be alive?"

"I'm sorry," Hannah said and saw the sadness in his eyes, the way his face had dropped, his previous alertness blunted by the news. She wanted to offer him a morsel of hope. "I suppose she could have made it to safety somewhere else, maybe she's still on the mainland."

"I would have been informed." The Recorder's voice sounded hard and certain. "That carving Hannah? You were going to fetch it?"

It was less a question than a command and Simon's hold on her arm slackened enough for her to turn away.

The carving was on her mantelpiece, amidst plastic fig-urines and small models of things she had never identified. Hannah wrapped it in a piece of clean cloth to protect it and put it in a small drawstring bag she often used when diving. Martha had told her the jacket was in the stores, in the clothing room and said to pop in and pick it up to save her the walk. She said she couldn't see it being of use to anyone but a child and not very practical even then. She was happy for it to be returned to the Recorder, especially as it belonged to his daughter.

When Hannah returned to the quay she could see the process of rowing goods out to the Pride had already begun – even though the ship was still moored at the entrance to the bay. A second rowing boat had been lowered from the Pride and the small derrick on the harbour wall was being used to lower crated goods into it while the first made slow progress against the swirling wind. The crew from the Pride never alighted on the quay and nobody from the Island ever went aboard the Pride or its boats. It was a long-standing arrangement, each group hoping to be protected from contracting the fever they believed the other might carry.

Hannah still felt bad that she was allowing Simon to believe Beth was dead, but she was less concerned about the Recorder as he had showed little emotion at the news. If Simon knew about Beth and persuaded her to go back with him, maybe Ethan would be more like his old self. Maybe he would remember he was in love with her. But Simon might not be what he seemed and she knew she couldn't betray Beth by letting anyone know she was still alive. She approached the group at the quay and offered the red jacket to the Recorder.

"Here it is," she said.

Gideon glanced at it briefly and passed it to Simon.

"And the Netsuke?"

Hannah pulled back the drawstrings and handed the small cloth-wrapped parcel to him.

"Ah, yes, that is it," the Recorder said, turning it over carefully in his fingers. "And it appears not to have suffered any damage."

"What did you call it?" Hannah asked.

"It's a katabori-netsuke. One of the commoner kinds, but exquisite none the less."

"Was it your daughter's? You said she was called Bethany?"

"She is. And no, it was not my daughter's, not hers to take."

Simon had been holding the jacket, feeling the cloth with his fingertips. He held it to his nose to smell it.

"And that is Bethany's jacket?" Isaac asked.

"I bought it for her as a wedding gift," Simon said quietly. "She loved the colour and the buttons."

The Recorder wrapped the netsuke in the cloth Hannah had used and slipped it into his pocket.

"She is dead then?" Simon said, a statement, but phrased

more like a hopeful question that might still be denied. "You're sure?"

"We found the jacket on the rocks and there was a bag in her boat. We think she must have fallen overboard when the wishbone came apart."

"The wishbone broke?" the Recorder asked, suddenly more alert.

"Well, the pin had come out, Sophia said it had probably been working loose for some time."

"This Sophia is an expert?"

Hannah shrugged. She didn't want to drag anyone else into this subterfuge as she still felt there might be a flaw in the plan. The Recorder sighed and shook his head.

"Silly girl. She should have known better than to try to take that dinghy onto the open ocean. I'll go back to the Pride on the next boat Isaac and organise your order. We can sort out the finer details tonight."

"About six o'clock then. That will give you time to get back to the Pride after supper and before the light fails."

"And I will look forward to getting to know you better Hannah. We will of course be dealing with each other before too long."

The Recorder's smile was practised. It looked friendly, but Hannah didn't trust him. His demeanour was far too relaxed for someone who had just discovered his daughter had drowned.

"Would it be okay if I stayed here?" Simon asked.

"If you wish, but beware of anyone with early symptoms of the fever, we wouldn't want you going down with something on your first visit here."

Simon turned to Hannah. "I'd like to see where the boat was found and where Bethany's coat was discovered. Can you take me there?"

Hannah turned to Isaac, not to ask his opinion, but to

87

gauge his reaction to Simon's request, but Gideon had put his arm round Isaac's shoulder and they had turned away to discuss something in private.

"I suppose it would be all right. We will have to walk, it's probably three miles to Spear Head."

"I think I can manage that if you lead the way."

Chapter 12

They set off up through the village and Simon asked where Hannah lived. She pointed out her cottage and thought how small it must look to him.

"My parents died some time ago and the Manor, where we lived, was too big for me to live in by myself, so I moved into Canary Cottage."

"Was it the fever that took them?"

Hannah nodded, not sure why she was offering so much personal information so readily. "What about your parents? Are they still alive?"

"Yes, both of them. I've been lucky."

"What do you do on the mainland?"

Simon thought for a second before replying. "I work in imports, keeping the books mainly."

Simon's answer was vague and he didn't expand on it.

They were soon clear of the buildings and the road climbed up to fields where barley and wheat had already been harvested and a sun-warmed breeze blew across the stubble. A dry, dusty aroma of gathered hay swept past them.

"Did you have a good harvest this year?" Simon asked.

"Yes. The summer came early and we cut in late May, but now the land's dry. We are going to have to run water for all the pulses. We need a good crop to store for winter."

Hannah kicked herself for giving him a lecture on farming, he must know all about this stuff, everyone did.

"You don't seem to buy in much from what I gathered from Gideon."

"The Recorder you mean? No, we don't. There are things we can't grow here, sugar, some citrus fruits and, of course, we have a smithy so we need coal and charcoal and then there's timber for repairs to our boats."

"You have no woodland?"

"Not as such. We have enough to cut for fires in the winter, but not enough for timber. And we don't have a sawmill so we'd have to cut by hand anyway."

"And the fever...?"

Hannah thought for a few moments before replying. She didn't want to reveal the knowledge Beth had imparted and thereby disclose her presence.

"We haven't had the fever for nine years. How about you, on the mainland?"

"It seems to have run its course. We get the occasional case, but there hasn't been an epidemic for several years." Simon kicked a pebble. It skittered along the road before leaping sideways into the scrub at the edge of the fields. "Everyone says it's still here on the Island."

Hannah stooped to pick some wild strawberries she had spotted. Simon squatted down to help her. She tried one herself and offered a particularly large, ripe one to Simon. She looked sideways at him.

"Everyone here thinks the fever is still running wild on the mainland."

"That's odd," Simon said, sounding puzzled, savouring the strawberry.

They walked on in silence, past the rows of sweet corn and beans, and followed a path leading up onto the high meadows and moorland. As soon as they crested the rise the wind strengthened bringing a fresh tang of ozone from the ocean. A sudden gust blew Hannah's hair across her face. She retrieved a ribbon from her pocket and tied her hair back in a ponytail.

90

Sheep scattered lazily as they walked across the rough grass and heather, but soon lost interest in the new arrivals and returned to their grazing.

"It's beautiful here," Simon said, shielding his eyes from the sun and scanning the moorland.

The wind sent ripples through the longer grass and a faint smell of coconut drifted from the gorse, which flowered all year round on the higher ground. A dog barked in the distance and a man's voice, much closer to them, called him back.

"Samson, here boy. Samson."

"That will be Ethan," Hannah said. "He farms at Hope Barton with his father. They keep an eye on the sheep up here."

"He's a shepherd?"

"Not really. Everyone does a bit of everything here."

"He works for Isaac I suppose?"

Hannah explained the way the Island worked, their collective ownership and responsibilities.

"I always got the impression from Gideon that Isaac ran Hope Island?"

"No, Isaac's just acting as my Guardian Bailiff."

"So who does own it?"

Hannah didn't really want to answer. Legally she knew that she owned it, but she never felt proprietorial about the Island. She simply believed that she would have to make decisions when she was Bailiff, and only when necessary, that would be in everybody's best interest.

"Me I suppose." She shrugged, dismissing the importance of the fact.

"You're Hannah Cotton? Sorry I didn't make the connection."

"You know me?"

"From Gideon. He's mentioned you. I should have

guessed when we met on the quay."

Hannah didn't like the idea that she was not only known on the mainland, but that Isaac was spoken of as the owner of Hope Island. Being Bailiff had always been such a distant obligation that it hadn't weighed heavily on her shoulders, not until recently. Ethan's voice saved her from further explanation.

"Hannah. Over here."

Ethan was stood on the crest of a small hillock waving to them. Samson bounded across the moor, weaving artfully between the larger, thornier bushes and jumping over the smaller ones.

"You have dogs here?"

"They're safe, they don't bite and you don't have to worry about fleas."

"Are you sure?"

Hannah laughed, remembering the same reaction from Beth. Samson sat in front of her and pushed his nose into her tummy, his tail wagged furiously.

"Hello," Ethan said as he caught up with Samson. He had Delilah held on a short rope. "Not seen you before," he said to Simon. "Did you come on the Pride? I heard it arrive."

"I did."

"I'm Ethan Webber, Hope Barton."

Ethan was in a particularly good mood, maybe because he could learn more about the mainland from a man who lived there.

"I'm Simon, Simon Delancey."

"Nothing to do with the sugar I suppose?" Ethan laughed at the idea that this dark skinned stranger was connected to one of the richest families and most valuable commodities.

Simon took a deep breath and let it out slowly. "Yes, as it happens that is my family's business."

Everyone on the Island would know the name emblazoned on the sugar bags that were brought there on the Pride.

"Wow, sorry, I didn't realise you…" Ethan turned red with embarrassment. "Er, what are you doing here then? Not that you shouldn't be here."

"It's okay. People are often surprised when they meet me for the first time." Simon smiled, brushing off Ethan's awkwardness. "The girl whose boat was found here was my fiancée, we were going to be married the day she disappeared."

Ethan looked flustered and Hannah was worried that he would use Beth's name without having any reason to know it.

"Her name was Bethany," Hannah said quickly. "She was the Recorder's daughter."

"Sorry, bad business," Ethan mumbled and glanced in the direction of Hope Barton.

"Do you need to get back," Hannah prompted. "Daniel will be on his own."

"Yes, good point, I do. It was good to meet you mister… Simon."

"And you too." Simon offered a hand that Ethan shook rather too enthusiastically. "Maybe we'll bump into each other again. Hannah says it's a small island."

Ethan gave another mumbled goodbye and hurried off in the direction of the farm. Samson hung around Hannah, reluctant to leave her until Ethan called him. Simon watched Ethan disappear as the path he had taken dropped off the higher ground.

"I'm used to some unusual reactions to my family's name, but he seemed to be almost scared."

"Ethan spends a lot of time alone, don't worry about him, he's not used to meeting strangers. Actually we haven't had any visitors here for years."

They followed a track forged by goats and sheep, which narrowed and zigzagged across the moor. They had to walk in single file to avoid the thorns of gorse bushes. Hannah led the way and, without having to look Simon in the eye, she found it easier to ask him about Beth.

"You said you were going to marry Bethany?"

Simon didn't answer immediately and when he did his voice was subdued.

"She ran away the morning of our wedding."

"I'm sorry, I didn't mean to pry, all this must be terrible for you."

He didn't answer for a while and Hannah was about to apologise for being nosey.

"It may sound odd," he said. "But we didn't know each other that well."

"But you were getting married?"

"It was an arranged marriage, between my family and hers."

"But you must have known her?"

"We'd met, at parties specifically arranged for us to get to know each other."

"Did you like her?"

"I did actually. And she was very pretty."

Hannah bit her lip to stop herself from correcting Simon and telling him that Beth was still alive, that he didn't have to mourn her.

"I don't think she loved me, she didn't even really know me, but it wasn't that. I don't think she wanted to get married to anyone."

"Was it something she said?"

Simon explained that it was something he sensed, not an animosity towards him, but an aversion to the whole idea of marriage. "And she did run away that morning. Maybe she

94

preferred risking death to living with me."

Hannah asked whether there were a lot of arranged marriages on the mainland. It was a totally alien concept to her as, on the Island, people only married for love – although they did occasionally make mistakes.

"It's not common," Simon said. "But my father said it was my duty. It was a union of business and politics and the strongest way forward for our family to continue to prosper. He made quite a speech about it and my mother reluctantly agreed."

"But what about love?"

"I didn't have anyone else in my life."

They arrived at Camp Bay and, not thinking, Hannah almost let slip that she had found Beth's boat there. They stood side by side on the grass above the bay and Hannah pointed out where the submerged house was that she had been diving on recently and the reserve of coal she had found there. Simon was interested in the way the Island was almost self sufficient and impressed by Hannah's story, admitting that he had never dived down very deep.

"I could teach you if we had more time."

"I'd like that, maybe next time."

"You're planning on coming here again?"

"Yes I think I might."

It was a short and not definitive answer. But Hannah was getting used to, and rather liked, Simon's sometimes simple, direct way of answering her questions. She pointed off to their right where there was a dip in the hills that ran down the west side of the Island.

"We can cut through South Col to where we found Bethany's coat, then follow the coast to Spear Head where her boat was beached. It's not far now."

She turned away from Camp Bay and soon they picked up an old road that wound past a dilapidated farm and through the hills to the rocky west coast. Nobody had wanted to take over those particular buildings as the westerly gales funnelled through the valley and kept the house locked into winter far longer than the rest of the Island. The sea was, as often, rougher on the west side of the hills. Waves broke on the rocks and the spray carried to them, making both of them laugh as they jumped from rock to rock to avoid getting soaked.

"We found her coat just over there, beneath that overhang. The sea cuts under the land in places and there are lots of small inlets and snags. But we searched them all for any sign of her."

The strong wind tore Hannah's words from her mouth, forcing her to almost shout to Simon. He nodded, looking at the rocks to each side of them. Their jagged edges would make climbing from the sea difficult, especially with a strong swell.

"Where did you say you found her boat?"

"A bit further up the coast. There's a spit of sand and shingle that runs out to Spear Head, we found it beached there."

"Can we go there please?"

They had to pick their way over the jagged rocks. There was no clear path along the shore. Conversation was difficult so not much more was said until they arrived at Spear Head. The sea was slightly calmer as the offshore island offered some protection and the water was shallower.

"Just over there, on that spit of sand." Hannah pointed to a spot where the sea had almost covered the sand, separating Hope Island and Spear Head for an hour or two at high tide. "The wishbone had lost its pin. It would have been near impossible to repair and we think that Bethany must have been struck by the boom or knocked overboard."

"Such a lonely end. She should have spoken to me. I

wouldn't have pushed the marriage. She could have gone her own way."

Hannah wanted desperately to tell him that Beth was still alive, still safe. Simon didn't deserve to feel guilty about what had happened, or what he thought had happened. She determined to talk to Beth, to ask her if Simon could be told. It wasn't a decision she could make by herself.

"I suppose we'd better get back," Simon said. "Thank you for bringing me here and for what you did to try to find her."

"It was the least we could do. I'm sorry it wasn't better news."

Simon wiped the back of his hand across his nose and sniffed loudly. He turned, facing back the way they had come, but not before Hannah had seen his eyes welling up.

Chapter 13

"I was wondering," Simon said, turning to face Hannah. "What do you do for a water supply here, you said you have very dry summers?"

Hannah was thrown for a moment, but assumed he wanted to think or talk about anything other than Beth.

"I can show you. We can take the path back past the main reservoir, it's actually a bit quicker than going via Camp Bay again."

The sun was high by that time. Once the path had wound back between the hills they were sheltered from the wind. A herd of some twenty goats had gathered in front of them and Simon hung back as they approached them.

"The goats are nothing to worry about Simon. They can get a bit twitchy in the spring when they've got kids, but at this time of year they couldn't care less about us."

"I'm just not used to animals, especially goats."

"I know..." Hannah almost let on that Beth had told her about the lack of animals in Freetown, but checked herself just in time. "I know some people can be a bit scared, but our goats aren't really wild, we keep them for milking and for cheese."

"Cheese from goats?"

"It's nice."

"I'll take your word for it," Simon replied, laughing.

Hannah held his elbow and led him along the path. The goats glanced up at them and wandered out of their way. She liked being his guide and protector and let go of him reluctantly once they had passed the last nanny.

"What do you do on the mainland, in your family's business?"

"Get bored mostly."

"It can't be that dull."

"I'd much prefer to be outdoors, like this, not stuck in some office tallying columns of figures like I am most of the time."

Hannah and Simon walked on in silence until the reservoir came into view a few minutes later.

"Well, that's it," she said. "We have another smaller one, closer to the village."

"It looks so blue."

"It's lined with white clay. It was my great grandfather's idea. He had it built before we became an island. Apparently lots of people thought he was mad, thought he'd been affected by the fever."

Simon was looking at the hills that rose behind the reservoir. There were two separate peaks, the highest points on the Island. The lower slopes were covered with pine trees, but higher up the rock was exposed and only a scant smattering of shrubs clung to the barren facade.

"It is so beautiful here, so quiet," Simon said in a hushed voice.

They both stood in silence for a few minutes. Hannah was seeing it through Simon's eyes, as if for the first time.

"We ought to get back," she said reluctantly.

"What are those caves up there?"

"Old mines we think. Nobody really knows what was mined there, but everyone likes to believe it was silver, or maybe even gold. We used to climb up there as kids, but Isaac was worried they were dangerous. The entrances are sealed now and the doors padlocked."

"Bethany couldn't be hiding up there could she?"

"I'm sorry Simon. We did check them. And the boards are

untouched, you can't go in more than a few yards."

They followed a leat through the valley and past the mill. Hannah told him how she used to help there with her parents when she was a little girl and still does when the grain is harvested.

She always thought the village looked like a model when approached from the reservoir. From their elevated view they were looking down at a jumble of different roof styles and colours, all appeared to be angled and aligned randomly, but followed the contours of the land. Simon stopped and Hannah turned to face him.

"What is it?"

"I'd like to live here."

"You don't really know it. You'd get bored pretty quickly."

She liked the idea of Simon living on the Island, but felt guilty as if even thinking of that possibility was being disloyal to Ethan.

"I wouldn't be much use here though. I don't know how to farm, I'm hopeless with my hands and you wouldn't have much need of a bookkeeper from what I hear."

"And your family wouldn't be too keen on you moving here either."

"I don't know. Dad's hardly ever home."

Hannah realised that if he moved to the Island he would be bound to recognise Beth, even if her hair was short and blonde. She also suspected that Simon was only dreaming out loud. Once he got back to the mainland he would forget about the Island and about her.

They strolled back into the village, Hannah nodding and saying hello to everyone they passed, too many to introduce each one to Simon. The Pride was moored closer to the quay. The tide was now almost full. Acrid smoke from the Pride's stacks wafted across the harbour, stinging Hannah's nostrils. It smelled of power and adventure, the sort of aroma Ethan was always drawn towards. The last few crates were being lowered into the two rowboats. Martha was organising people to pile everything from the quay onto handcarts and wheel them to her store.

"I'm sorry I wasn't here to help you Martha."

"Don't worry Dear, there's plenty of hands available as it is."

"You mustn't blame Hannah," Simon said. "I dragged her away to show me where Bethany's boat was found."

"That was just as important. You have to put these things to bed in your mind before you can move on. Anyway Hannah's going to be taking over as Bailiff soon and won't have time to go stacking things on shelves when she does."

Martha shouted to a young boy to be careful. He was in danger of spilling bags from an overloaded cart. She bustled over to help him.

"When do you become Bailiff and mistress of all you survey?" Simon asked, cocking his head to one side and smiling.

"Soon enough," Hannah answered obliquely, not wanting to mention the now slightly doubtful plan for her to marry Ethan in the near future."

Martha returned, having taken half the load off the cart to the boys disgruntlement.

"The Recorder went back to the ship on the last boat," Martha told Simon. "He said he'd like to have a word with you on your return."

"I'd better get back on board then. They will be wondering what kept me all this time."

"Simon," Hannah touched his arm just as he was about to turn away. "Would you like to come for supper tonight? The Recorder and my uncle have asked me to join them. I'd like you to be there too, you might be on my side."

"What do you mean by being on your side?"

"It's difficult to explain. In fact I'm not sure I can explain. It's more a feeling than anything specific. I don't think either of them have been quite truthful with me."

"Will it be okay with your uncle?"

"It's okay with me. That should be enough. Uncle Isaac is only acting for me as Bailiff so it's time he was reminded of that fact."

It was the first time Hannah had ever exercised the authority inherent in her position and she stood slightly taller as she spoke.

"I'll look forward to seeing you later then," he said.

His smile was so wide that it revealed perfect teeth and a warmth and sparkle in his eyes.

Simon held onto the rope dangling free from the arm of the derrick. He casually pushed off from the quay, hanging in mid air by one arm and waving with the other. The winch man was smiling too as he lowered Simon down below the edge of the quay and out of sight.

Moments later the boat emerged from the lee of the harbour wall, two oarsmen rowed it back towards the Pride and Simon was in the stern. He turned towards Hannah and waved again.

She waited until she couldn't make out his face, but waved until the boat was alongside the Pride because she assumed his sight was sharper than hers. She walked, smiling to herself, back up the lane towards Martha's store-rooms. When she opened the door she could hear Martha and Isaac talking and she hung back, listening to them.

"I hadn't met Simon before today," Isaac said. "I had heard of him of course. Gideon had spoken of him."

"Terrible business, losing your daughter like that."

"So it is Martha."

"It didn't strike me that the Recorder was all that upset."

"I'm sure he is, but he has a position to maintain. His feelings come second to his duties."

"Family should always come first."

"I suppose so Martha."

There was the sound of boxes being moved and Hannah was about to make her presence known when Isaac spoke again.

"Simon would make a good match for the right girl."

"He would. He seems a nice lad. More concerned about that Bethany than her father was."

"I got the impression that he and Hannah were getting on well. Did you think so?"

"Hannah's spoken for already. Her and Ethan are practically wed."

"My understanding is that Ethan hasn't actually proposed. I presume he would want my blessing before any formal arrangement was announced?"

"That's as maybe, but Ethan and Hannah have always been together."

Hannah didn't like her uncle interfering in her life, but at the same time he was right about Ethan, he hadn't proposed to her. Until a few days ago she wouldn't have hesitated, her answer would have been yes. Now she was less certain of Ethan and of her own feelings. Hannah coughed and made a point of closing the door quite noisily. She didn't need to hear any more.

"Hello, do you need any help here?"

"Just about done Dear," Martha replied cheerfully.

"Ah, Hannah, just the person I wanted to talk to."

"About the stores?"

"No, no, I think Martha and I have that sorted. It was about Daniel and that new carving."

Hannah regretted having mentioned it. Now she knew how valuable they were to him she realised that he would keep chasing until he had his hands on another one.

"Daniel's not finished it yet, at least not the last time I saw it."

Hannah was trying to think how much Isaac might know about her visits to Hope Barton.

"Maybe I should ride over and check for myself."

It wasn't really a question and Hannah didn't know what to say. Isaac was difficult to judge. If she tried to discourage him it would probably have the opposite effect.

"I don't know Uncle. I could ask Ethan when I see him."

"I'd need to have it before the Pride leaves. Maybe I will go over there. I could do with a distraction after all this work."

"Do you need me to do anything here Martha?" Hannah asked.

"No Dear, you go off and enjoy yourself, I can cope."

"I'll see you later tonight then Hannah, for supper, you haven't forgotten?"

"No Uncle, I'll be there."

"Maybe I could send a message out to the Pride to invite Simon. Would that be all right with you Hannah?"

"He seems a nice lad," Martha added. "You two were getting on well today I thought."

"We were and he is," Hannah said. "And there's no need to send a message, because I've already invited him."

Isaac smiled and nodded his head just once, as though he was almost bowing to Hannah.

"Not that there's anything between us. I thought I ought to make some contacts for the future – for when I take over."

She tried to out-stare Isaac, but he didn't take on her challenge. He turned to Martha and said he would see her tonight and for her to let him know then if there was anything they had forgotten. He smiled at Hannah.

"I will see you later too."

He left the stores quietly and without a backward glance.

"That Simon is a nice lad," Martha said, looking directly at Hannah. "But you need to sort out what you really want young lady, don't go making any rash decisions that you'll regret later."

"I won't, I promise Martha, but I have to dash now. There's something I have to do and I don't have much time."

"Go on then my dear, run along and leave me in peace."

Martha watched Hannah as she hurried to the door, checked the street in both directions and set off almost running towards Hope Barton.

Chapter 14

Hannah walked briskly up the road out of Newport. At the top of the village she turned left down a narrow lane and, as soon as she was out of sight of the last house, she broke into a run. She had to get to the farm before Isaac and didn't know how much of a head start she had.

Her uncle would have to fetch Autumn and saddle her, so she should have fifteen minutes' grace with any luck. Hannah cut across the lower side of the cornfields, a short cut to Hope Barton that was rarely used. Brambles had grown over the path, they caught at her clothes and scratched her legs and arms, but she increased her pace, ignoring the pain.

The path eventually linked to the farm track. At the junction she stopped and looked to the right to listen for a horse clattering on the patches of concrete and tarmac on the main road. There was only birdsong and the occasional bleating of ewes. Hannah slowed to a walk on her way down the track to Hope Barton to steady her breathing before she arrived. She couldn't help but keep glancing back over her shoulder, fearing that Isaac would catch up with her.

Daniel was on the bench in front of the house as usual, a rag in his hand and a small pot by his side, carefully polishing his latest driftwood carving with small circular motions. Hannah knew it must be almost finished, but this was the stage that Daniel could fuss over for days. Gently bringing the colour out in every detail and making minor alterations with a small knife.

"Hello Daniel," Hannah said quietly, suspecting he hadn't noticed her arrival.

"Hello Lass," he replied without looking up.

He dipped the rag back into the pot and continued with his work.

"Is Ethan around, or...?"

Hannah hesitated for a moment. "The boy who's staying with you."

"Oh, the young lad? Yes, he's in the kitchen."

As Hannah turned Beth opened the door. "I saw you arrive. Is something wrong? We weren't expecting you for supper."

"I'm not here for supper, I'm eating with Isaac and your father tonight – and Simon."

Beth looked down at the ground. "Ethan told me that he'd met Simon earlier. You know who he is now I suppose?"

"Yes I do, but I actually came over to warn you that Isaac is on his way here. Where is Ethan?"

"Do you know why Simon is here?"

"Looking for you, what else? I've been with him most of the day. I even had to take him to where you supposedly died."

"Is he okay?"

"I didn't think you cared for him."

"I don't love him, I didn't want to get married, but that doesn't mean I don't care for him."

Hannah realised she was being harsh on Beth and softened her approach.

"He's all right I think, upset – but he's okay."

"You won't tell him about me will you, please?"

"No, of course I won't. But is it fair on Simon and your father to let them keep thinking you're dead, that you drowned?"

"There's no alternative is there? If my father thinks I'm

107

alive he'll look for me everywhere. And he doesn't care about me really, just who he can marry me off to."

"Simon cares about you though."

"I never gave him any encouragement. The marriage was all my father's idea."

Hannah looked back over her shoulder, expecting her uncle to appear there at any time.

"We haven't got long. Isaac will be here soon. Where's Ethan?"

"Can't you deal with your uncle? I can hide. He's not looking for me is he?"

Hannah shrugged her shoulders to dispel a shiver at the thought that Isaac might have guessed they were hiding Beth.

"He's coming to see Daniel's carving. He wants to sell it to your father tonight." Hannah bit her lip and held Beth's shoulders firmly.

"We don't have much time and I don't want to risk Isaac questioning Daniel, so do you know where Ethan is?"

"He said he was putting the horses out to grass."

"He'll be in the bottom meadow, I'll go and get him. Don't go outside. If Isaac comes, hide upstairs."

"Why can't you deal with him?"

"It would look odd if I was here. I didn't say anything about coming over when we were talking. I'll explain later."

Hannah looked outside and listened for any sound of horse's hooves. There was enough tarmac and stone on the track that the approach of Isaac's Suffolk Punch would be clearly audible. She ran across the grass and Charlie whimpered, half wanting to go with her.

Ethan was draping a loop of rope over the gatepost to the meadow to hold it shut. A bridle lay over the top bar of the gate. She explained that Isaac was on his way over and that he couldn't see her or he'd be suspicious. As they approached the house they heard Isaac riding down the lane, the slow steady walk of a heavy horse and a heavy rider.

Hannah ducked behind a water barrel at the side of the barn. Ethan looked at her and she put a finger to her lips to silence him. He walked across the yard and stood on the grass in front of Daniel, shielding him from Isaac.

"Ah Ethan. I'm glad I caught you. I was afraid you might still be out on the fields or with the sheep."

"What can we do for you Isaac?"

"Just a social call," Isaac said, dismounting and rubbing Autumn's nose, who shook her head vigorously in response.

"I'd offer you a drink, but I've let the stove go out in this weather, so can't brew tea, but I have some fresh cold water if you want a glass?"

"No, no, nothing for me thank you. Is that Daniel's latest piece he's working on?"

Autumn found an interest in the grass in front of the house when Isaac let go of her reins. He moved past Ethan and watched Daniel, still polishing, giving no acknowledgement of Isaac's arrival.

"May I see it Daniel? It's a dragon isn't it?"

Daniel stopped polishing and tucked the rag carefully back in the pot, still not looking up.

"The boy likes the scales," he said quietly. "He said they look realistic."

He held the piece up to Isaac in both hands and only then raised his head to look at him.

"It's not for sale. I'm going to give it to the boy."

Hannah considered breaking her cover and causing a disturbance to distract her uncle.

"Which boy is that Daniel?" Isaac asked absentmindedly while examining the detail of the carving.

"The boy that helps with the bees. He looks after the

109

hives for me. He's a good lad."

"Do I know him?"

"He's inside. I can fetch him for you if you want to talk to him."

Daniel got up and noticed Autumn for the first time. He walked over to her and ran his hand down her neck. Autumn looked up and rubbed her nose into Daniel's shirt.

"I haven't seen you for a while girl."

"Dad always liked Autumn," Ethan said. "He foaled her."

"Yes I do remember that. She's a fine horse."

Daniel patted her neck again and shuffled indoors.

"Don't take any notice of Dad. He sometimes imagines people, bit like his carvings, they mostly live in his head."

Hannah settled back behind the water barrel, feeling the tension leave her body when Ethan invited Isaac to sit on the bench with him while they waited for Daniel to return. Isaac kept the driftwood dragon and rested it on his lap when he sat down. He turned it over, examining it from every angle.

"He doesn't like to let them go until he's satisfied they're finished," Ethan said. "It can take a while, even when they look done to you and me."

Hannah thought about trying to sneak round to the back of the house. Hoping she could get in through an open window and keep Daniel indoors. She saw Beth inside the kitchen doorway, to one side of Isaac. She put a finger to her lips to tell Hannah to keep quiet.

"They always look finished when he starts to polish them," Ethan added. "But Dad will probably take his knife to it again. Give him a couple of weeks and he'll have forgotten about it. I'll bring it over to you then. It wouldn't be right to take it from him now."

"Who is this lad he says he's promised it to?"

110

"Oh Dad's got some idea in his head that there's a boy here helping him. It's best just to let him be. He gets upset if you try to argue with him."

Even from where Hannah was hiding she could hear Isaac's exaggerated sigh as he handed the carving back to Ethan. He kept looking at the dragon even though he'd relinquished possession of it, picked up the pot next to him on the bench and sniffed at it.

"What is it Daniel uses for polish? I've never asked him. It smells like beeswax"

"It is, but it's thinned out with turps."

Hannah saw Daniel coming back out the kitchen door. He was nodding to himself and stood in front of Isaac.

"It takes time," Daniel said.

Isaac frowned and looked at Daniel, not understanding him.

"It takes beeswax and a lot of time," Daniel said. He was standing directly in front of Isaac.

"Ah," Isaac said. "I understand."

"I put lots of layers on. It takes time."

Isaac stood, realising that Daniel was waiting for his seat back so that he could continue with his work.

"Did you find the boy?" Isaac asked.

"What boy?"

Daniel was looking for telltale patches where Isaac's fingers had touched his carving and dulled the finish.

"And I'll have my jar back if you've done sniffing it."

Hannah suppressed a giggle at Isaac's obvious discomfort. He held out the jar, which Daniel looked at for a few moments before Isaac placed it carefully on the bench next to him.

"I had better be making my way I suppose," Isaac said. "Things to do. You ought to be careful with that turpentine Daniel, it's extremely flammable I believe."

111

He collected Autumn's reins and tried to remount, but unsuccessfully. Ethan offered his cupped hands and Isaac managed to get his leg over the saddle although he was half sat, half lying across it at an awkward angle. Autumn stood patiently while Isaac shuffled himself into a sitting position, the weight and lack of agility in her rider was quite familiar to Autumn.

She set off up the lane, knowing where she was going and seemingly eager to make a start. Isaac had to turn in his saddle to say goodbye to Ethan and Daniel. Hannah only came out of her hiding place when Isaac vanished round a bend near the top of the track.

"That was close," she said.

She turned to Ethan, not sure whether to kiss him or simply slip her arm through his. She wasn't sure how welcome any physical contact from her would be. Beth came out through the kitchen door, pre-empting either action and Ethan turned to her.

"How did you get Dad to change his story about a boy being here, helping him with the bees?"

"I told him I was only here to cook, not to do his work for him. I'm not sure if he'll forgive me in a hurry. He got quite grumpy."

"Brilliant," Ethan laughed. "He'll forgive and forget soon enough."

Hannah felt like she was intruding in a cosy domestic situation. Ethan and Beth had such an easy way of getting on.

"I ought to be getting back in case Isaac calls in on me."

"Will we see you tomorrow?" Beth asked.

Ethan didn't say anything. He sat next to Daniel and tilted his head back to catch the warmth of the late afternoon sun.

"I don't know. I should be working really."

"It's not a problem if you can't, but I'd like to see you."

Ethan had his eyes closed. Beth looked at Hannah, raised her eyebrows and shrugged. Hannah didn't know what to say. She looked at Ethan, who still wasn't moving and Daniel, who was occupied with his polishing, both oblivious to all around them.

Hannah gave Beth a tight-lipped smile and turned away from the scene she'd once fitted into so easily. Walking back up the track, away from the farm, she was tempted to turn and see if Ethan would at least acknowledge her departure. But she didn't. She cut off on the track, the same way she had come, breaking first into a jog and then running, pushing the ground behind her to put distance between herself and Ethan. She ran as fast as she could to vent her anger and stave off her tears – not even aware of the brambles tearing at her legs.

Chapter 15

When Hannah arrived at the outskirts of Newport she slowed to a walk. There was no sign of Isaac on the main road, so she continued down to her cottage, listening all the time for the telltale clatter of Autumn's hooves on the paved track.

Once in her cottage Hannah leaned back against the door and thought about how close Beth had been to being discovered and the lasting image of her and Ethan together, easy with each other.

The scratches on her shins started to sting and Hannah examined the long abrasions she had also picked up on her arms – red, jagged lines of drying, caked blood.

"Oh shit," she muttered and walked through to her small kitchen.

As she left the door she heard the click-clack of Autumn's return echoing off the walls of the houses in the street. Hannah waited for a knock on the door, expecting a cross examination from an inquisitive Isaac, but the sound of hooves receded slowly down through the village.

Hannah took two cloves of garlic and crushed them on a piece of marble that she had rescued from a submerged house. The smell caught at her nose. She made the garlic into a paste and wrapped it in a small piece of muslin, making a pad that oozed sticky juice.

Back on her sofa Hannah started to dab the garlic paste on her cuts, on both arms and legs, wincing as she did so but knowing that it would clean them. The pad grew redder as she worked her way over the worst scratches.

"You're an idiot Hannah," she mumbled to herself. "If he wants her, he can have her. I don't care any more."

But she did care and the tears from her eyes were not just from the sting of the garlic. She lay back on the sofa, knowing she had only an hour or so before she was due at the Manor and wondering what she really felt about Simon. He was like nobody she had ever met before, certainly wealthy, definitely good looking and his life had nothing in common with hers at all. She drifted off to sleep and was relieved that not much more than twenty minutes had passed when she woke. She had half an hour before she was expected at the Manor.

The stinging in her wounds had eased. She climbed the stairs to her bedroom to sort through the sparse collection of clothes in her wardrobe. She had working clothes, course skirts and shirts and trousers, but only the one dress. She had worn it to the last quarterly gathering and she held it against her. It had short sleeves and would show all the scratches she had picked up on her wild run back from Hope Barton. They would prompt too many questions. She hung it back up and took down some light, baggy cotton trousers and a cotton shirt that was free from tears and major stains.

Before she dressed, Hannah washed the garlic from her cuts and smeared the worst ones with a little honey to staunch any further flow of blood and to protect against infection.

The Manor was only a short walk through the village and then a hundred yards along the road towards the main reservoir. As Hannah approached the house her parents' laughter rang in her memory, the same laughter she remembered from when she had been helping them weed the garden or playing games on the lawns in front of the house.

Simon had just come out of the front door, strolling towards the walled garden. He saw her walking up the path and waited. He held her shoulders lightly as he kissed her cheek. Hannah was familiar with the gesture, but unsure how she should reciprocate. In the end she did nothing but smile awkwardly.

"This is your place then?" Simon asked, looking back towards the house.

"I live in the village."

"I know, you said, so who lives here?"

"Nobody does. I said it was empty."

"That's a shame, it's such a fabulous setting and it's your family home?"

"It is, or it was, but I don't have a family now."

"I know, sorry." Simon bit his lip. "I didn't mean to…"

"It's okay. You're right. It is a shame that it's empty."

Hannah looked out over the lawns and fields of winter vegetables. The low sun glinted off rich green leaves. The house was high enough that it had clear views over the fields to the moors, beyond which a thin strip of sparkling blue sea glittered beneath the sky.

Very soon the sun would drop below the western ridge. The heat of the day had already softened. A warm breeze blew across the land bringing the sweet, nutty scent of heather to them in gentle waves.

"I was just going to have a look in the walled garden. Do you want to give me a guided tour?"

Hannah led the way through an arched opening in the west wall of the garden. The formal layout was still evident, but weeds had taken over empty spaces between overgrown plants. Grass poked through on the gravel paths, turning them into a patchwork of green and grey.

"I remember how well my parents cared for this garden. It was their pride and joy – and useful too."

"Did they grow fruit here?"

"Some, but mainly it was for medicinal plants and culinary herbs." She squatted down as she spoke and picked the weeds out from around some marigolds that had survived, but were being suffocated.

"Most of them are probably still here, they just need some care and attention. I really should come up and sort it out."

"Do you know about herbal medicines then?"

Hannah thought about replying, saying that she didn't but she might know someone who did. Could she give Simon just the tiniest clue about Beth and see how much he knew her and whether he was still thinking about her?

She persisted at the weeding, freeing the marigolds and leaving what she'd pulled out in a small pile on the bare earth.

"Damn, I need to wash my hands now."

"We probably ought to go in anyway. I only popped out while we were waiting for you. I met Martha again. She's quite a force isn't she?"

"She's helping with the food tonight?"

"Her and someone called Sarah."

"So you've met silent Sarah. She had the fever when she was a young girl and recovered, but she doesn't talk much."

"Do you often come to these dinners?"

"No, Isaac's never asked me before. I don't quite know why he did this time. I don't even see why these dinners are necessary."

"A waste of your precious supplies?"

"No, not that. The Recorder always brings food over in the boat with him. Martha says we end up with more than we started with most times and often something we would never buy."

"What sort of things?"

"Tropical and citrus fruits. We can grow lemons in the big

glass house, and grapes of course, but we have never been successful with oranges."

"So why don't you come to these suppers?"

"It's like Isaac is playing some sort of role as Lord of the Manor. My parents never did that. It goes against the whole ethos of the Island."

"I understand what you're saying, but doesn't someone have to be in charge?"

"I suppose so, but they don't have to enjoy it quite so much as he does."

Simon laughed and said he knew what she meant and that it's just the same on the mainland – his father always described it as a natural order of things.

"That's what the people at the top always used to say."

Hannah's unwitting jibe at Simon's family made the walk back to the house uncomfortable and quiet. Hannah hadn't intended to insult him, but she felt strongly about the old structures and had a sense of loyalty to what her own family had done to replace them. Simon might be one of the 'ones at the top', but it wasn't entirely his own fault he was there.

"Sorry," Hannah said as they stopped at the front door.

Simon wrapped his fingers around the door handle. His thumb was on the latch but not pressing it down.

"You don't have to apologise to me. I wish I wasn't part of that structure, but I don't know anything else I could do."

"You could learn a skill," Hannah said quietly, wanting to encourage him if she could.

Simon nodded and then smiled. "You're right of course. I could. Any suggestions?"

Simon held the door open for her, and Hannah hesitated, a bit uncomfortable at being treated so politely after what she'd said. She edged, slightly sideways, through the door to avoid obvious body contact with him. Martha was there, carrying a jug of water through to the dining room.

"We were just about to send out a search party for you two," she laughed.

The dinner was uneventful with the exception of the wine. The Recorder had brought two bottles with him from the Pride and Hannah tried a small glass, but found it sour and it made her screw her mouth up. She drank a glass of water to take away the taste.

"I think I might have spotted a bottle of cider in the kitchen," Isaac said. "Would you prefer that?"

Hannah nodded, not trusting her throat to work properly and feeling embarrassed at her naivety in front of Simon.

"I'll go and fetch it myself. I know just where I saw it. Easier than trying to tell Martha and have her hunting high and low."

Isaac opened the bottle for Hannah when he returned. It made no welcoming fizz, but their island cider was unpredictable. Slightly flat was better than those lively bottles that sprayed half the contents over the table when opened.

The three men drank the wine and Hannah stuck to her cider and water for the rest of the evening. Contracts were produced from a briefcase and signed by both the Recorder and her uncle, a mere formality as far as Hannah could tell. She wondered why she was even there as all the deals and trading had been concluded earlier. After dinner they walked down through the village towards the quay, Hannah and Simon hung back behind the two men.

"I might come over on the next trip too," Simon said. "That is if it would be all right with you?"

Hannah was not sure it would be a good idea as Beth would be back with Abby by then and it would be hard to keep it a secret from Simon. Her arrival as Abby's partner would be the talk of the Island for several weeks. But she would like to see Simon again.

"It would be okay by me. Not that it's up to me."

They walked on a little way and Hannah had a thought.

"How easy is it to get maps on the mainland?"

"Why would you want one?"

"Ethan would like a map of the world – as it is now."

"Simple. My family have lots of maps. We need them on our ships so we keep them updated every year. The old ones are still pretty accurate and just sit around in drawers."

"They're not expensive?"

"I'll bring you a set, it's no trouble."

They said goodbye on the quay and Simon leaned in to kiss Hannah on the cheek again. This time she was prepared and didn't feel so awkward – not until she saw her uncle smiling at her.

Early the next morning Hannah rose, intending to get to Hope Barton and return before anyone noticed she'd gone. She wanted to tell Ethan her news in person. He was outside in the yard when she arrived, checking the shoes on one of his horses. Samson was the first to spot her, barking and wagging his tail and setting off both Delilah and Charlie.

"Morning Hannah, what brings you over here so early?"

"I thought I'd tell you I have a present coming for you."

"It's not my birthday, not for months yet."

"I was talking to Simon at supper last night and he's promised to bring some maps over for you next time he comes."

Ethan didn't look excited at the news. Beth appeared in the doorway.

"They will have the best maps. They sail all over the world."

"And Abby won't have to risk looking for one when she goes over with Beth," Hannah added, but clasped her hands to her tummy as a pain struck her.

She had suffered a couple of stomach cramps during the night and thought that the rich food from the previous night was to be blamed.

"Are you all right," Beth asked, coming across and taking her arm.

"Just a tummy ache, something I ate I think. Nothing to worry about."

"You look so pale, do you want to come in and sit down for a while? I'll get you a glass of water."

Hannah protested that it was okay. The pain had subsided. She straightened up and said she had to get back – she had missed too many days in the fields recently.

"You ought to take it easy if you have food poisoning. Drink plenty of water, keep hydrated."

Beth ran indoors and came back with a glass of water, which Hannah drank while protesting that she really did feel much better. She said she only came over to give Ethan the news about the maps.

"Yes, thanks Hannah," Ethan said without much enthusiasm. He was still holding onto his horse, while she stood patiently, waiting to get her leg back.

During the morning the pains in Hannah's stomach increased and became more frequent. Abby was working alongside her and decided that she had to go home and rest no matter how often she claimed to be fine.

By the time the two girls got back to Canary Cottage, Hannah was almost doubled in pain and running a fever. Abby ran to get Martha and both of them were concerned that Hannah had caught the virus, that Simon or Gideon might be unwitting carriers, but Martha said it doesn't usually come with stomach pains. Abby told her she knew someone who might be able to help.

"No don't," Hannah protested. "Don't tell her."

"What's she talking about?" Martha asked.

"Oh God," Abby said. "I'm going to have to tell you something, but you must promise not to breathe a word to anyone, not anyone."

Martha had no idea what Abby was talking about, but she sounded so desperate that she agreed. Hannah was still mumbling not to tell Martha, almost crying in pain as she did so.

"Keep her comfortable Martha, I'll be back as quick as I can."

Abby left in such a hurry that the door slammed back on its hinges before crashing closed. Even in her befuddled state Hannah could hear Abby set off at a run up the street and protested once more that she mustn't bring Beth into the village. Suddenly she gripped both hands to her stomach and threw up over both Martha and the floor.

Chapter 16

Hannah was unaware of time passing and couldn't judge whether minutes or maybe hours had passed when the door opened again and Beth knelt next to her. A cool hand rested gently on her forehead and Hannah felt any remaining energy drain from her body as she relinquished her struggle and submitted to Beth's care. Martha watched from the end of the sofa where Hannah lay, not commenting on the stranger who had arrived from nowhere.

"Don't tell anyone... please Martha." Hannah panted between shallow breaths.

"You worry about yourself right now Hannah, I'm not about to go gossiping about stuff I don't know, or people I've never met before."

Hannah turned her head towards Beth and touched her arm. "You shouldn't have come."

"Nonsense," Beth said. "You were there for me when I needed you."

"So, who exactly are you?" Martha asked.

Abby put a finger to her lips to silence Martha. "Shush, I'll explain later, it's complicated."

Beth dug into her satchel and produced a watch on a short chain. She took Hannah's wrist between her fingers and waited until the second hand was at twelve. They watched as Beth counted silently, her lips moving almost imperceptibly.

"She's running a temperature, but her pulse is normal. It doesn't look like the fever to me – more like a stomach upset."

"It doesn't look like the fever to me either," Martha said. "I never knew anyone throw up with it like that."

"It could be food poisoning. Do you know what Hannah's eaten recently that might have caused this?"

"I cooked them all supper last night," Martha said defensively. "And I ate the same myself. I know it wasn't supposed to be for me, but why should the Recorder be treated so special. And I'm not ill and nor is Isaac, I saw him not that long ago."

Beth checked Hannah's neck for any swelling and got her to poke out her tongue.

"Am I going to live doctor?" Hannah managed a smile.

"You're that Recorder's daughter aren't you?" Martha said quietly. "The one that's supposed to be drowned."

"I am," Beth replied, concentrating on Hannah.

"So I suppose you have a good reason for all this subterfuge?"

"Yes, I do. I'll explain later."

Abby was mouthing remonstrations at Martha and shaking her head, trying to stop her asking questions for the moment.

"You don't look like her though. She's supposed to have long black hair according to the Recorder." Martha half closed her eyes. "Those lemons. They were for you weren't they?"

"What did you have for breakfast?" Beth asked, ignoring Martha's speculations.

Hannah shook her head, too weary to say anything.

"I'll go and have a look," Martha said and went into the small kitchen at the rear of the cottage. "Not much, just a mug of tea by the look of it," she said.

"Cider," Hannah murmured.

"You had cider for breakfast?" Beth repeated, surprise showing in her voice.

124

"She did have a cider at supper last night. Said she didn't like the wine, can't blame her, that foul foreign stuff."

Abby snorted. "And what makes you an expert Martha?"

"I've tasted what's left in the bottles after their fancy meals," Martha replied.

"It was bitter," Hannah said frowning at the memory.

"What was?" Beth asked.

"The cider." Hannah closed her eyes and breathed out heavily before opening them again.

"You need to keep hydrated," Beth told her. "Keep sipping water as often as you can, but don't try to force it down." She turned to Abby. "Can you stay with her today?"

"Of course I can."

"You need to keep her cool and comfortable. Use a cold cloth on her forehead and arms, but don't make her too cold."

"Is there anything else we can do?" Martha asked.

Beth dug into her satchel and produced a tiny wrap of brown paper, which she unfolded, careful not to spill any of the powder held inside.

"This is powdered white willow bark. You need to dissolve a little in boiling water and let it cool before giving it to her. It should ease her pains and reduce her temperature."

She delved into her bag again mumbling, "I'm sure I had one." She brought out a metal rod that had been flattened on both ends. One end was a small circle, the other a longer more oval shape.

"Use the small end to measure the powder – only one spoonful to each cup of water and no more than two cups a day. The concentration is not easy to judge accurately."

Abby took the spoon and examined it. "Where did you get this?" she asked.

125

"I'll need it back afterwards. It's the only one I have."

"Our blacksmith could make these easily enough if you want another one."

"You said the cider was bitter?" Martha asked again.

Hannah nodded, sipping at the glass of water Abby had fetched for her and wincing as her stomach cramped again.

"I'm going to pop back up to the Manor," Martha said. "I just want to check something."

Beth looked up at her, still kneeling on the floor next to Hannah. "You won't tell anyone I'm here will you?"

"I think we've got other things to worry about right now, but I am curious why you'd let that nice Simon think you were dead."

Hannah was only half aware of what was happening around her, time had ceased to have any meaning and she was sure Martha had not long left when she heard her return.

"I found the bottle," Martha said as she closed the door behind her. "It's not been washed out yet so I brought it back. See what you think."

She handed the bottle to Beth who sniffed at it cautiously.

"It smells sort of bitter, but I don't drink cider so it might just be stale. Does it smell strange to you?" she asked, handing the bottle to Abby, who took sniffed at it too.

"It doesn't smell right to me."

"Mistletoe," Martha said knowingly. "We were clearing some from the orchards last October, same time as we were harvesting the apples. It stunts the growth of the trees if you let it take over."

Abby sniffed at the bottle again and frowned. "You're saying it got into the cider by accident?"

"Not by accident," Martha said. "Isaac brought that cider up to the Manor himself. And we haven't had this happen to anyone else."

"Why would he want to poison Hannah?" Beth asked.

"I think we know the answer to that one don't we Abby," Martha shook her head slowly. "But we don't need to go into it right now?"

Martha put her hand into one of the voluminous pockets of her skirt and pulled out some long, pale, leaves. "I found these hidden in the scullery. I reckon he was planning to go back later today and get rid of the evidence."

Abby took the leaves and examined them, rubbing one between her fingers and sniffing at it gingerly. "Definitely mistletoe."

Martha nodded. A knock at the door stifled any further speculation and Beth looked up, startled. "Who is that?" she whispered.

"We won't know until we open the door," Martha replied and waved her hands at Beth to usher her into the kitchen and out of sight.

Beth didn't need a second prompting. She scrambled up from the floor and ducked into the kitchen, half closing the curtain that screened it from the rest of the cottage. Martha made sure she was out of sight before opening the front door.

"Isaac," she said louder than necessary. "What brings you here?"

"Someone told me there was a crisis, that they had heard Hannah wasn't very well. I did hear the word fever used and thought I ought to check."

He had a hanky in his hand and when he saw Hannah on the couch, pale and quite obviously unwell, he raised the hanky to cover his mouth.

"She's been poisoned," Abby stated. "It's not the fever. You're quite safe... for now."

"Poisoned? Who would want to do that?"

"I didn't say somebody did it on purpose, it was probably

127

an accident. Unless you know better?"

"But everyone loves Hannah. It must have been accidental." Isaac withdrew the hanky from his face. "You're certain it's not the fever. She spent a lot of time with Simon yesterday. Who's to say he's not a carrier?"

"I'm okay," Hannah said, pulling herself up into a sitting position. "It's just something I ate. Nothing for everyone to panic over."

Isaac spotted Beth's satchel on the floor by Hannah's feet. They all saw him look at it and Hannah shuffled sideways to try to hide it.

"Whose is this?" he asked, bending down to pick it up. "I've not seen that satchel before."

Nobody moved to stop him and Isaac opened flap to see what was inside. He pulled out some strips of dried bark.

"It's mine," Abby said suddenly. "They're medicine."

"Really? I didn't know you had any leaning in that direction Abby?"

"I'm trying to learn about natural remedies,"

Abby claimed that she hadn't told anyone yet. She said she had been experimenting on herself to make sure her remedies were safe.

"A rather dangerous pursuit if I might say so."

"I have some books," Hannah said, wishing she sounded more positive. "I've been lending them to Abby."

"Very commendable. We could do with someone with more knowledge about these sorts of things."

Isaac walked over to the where Hannah had glanced when she mentioned the books and put his index finger on one, tilting it back off the shelf. The front cover remained where it was.

"Please be careful Uncle, some of them are a bit fragile."

"Where did you get these from?"

Martha piped up at that point saying that she had found a

whole load of books in the back of one of the storerooms and that they must have been there for decades.

"The stores used to be part of the old hotel," Martha continued. "They probably had some sort of library way back."

"And you're applying your new knowledge with Hannah's current sickness?"

"It's only willow bark. I collected it in the spring."

"Well I do hope you know what you're doing, we wouldn't want you making Hannah any worse with your experiments."

"I know what I'm doing," Abby replied, staring out Isaac and sounding confident.

"Then I'll leave you to it." He turned to Hannah. "I do hope you feel better soon. Excuse me if I don't come too close, I'm afraid I'm not entirely convinced that it's a simple case of food poisoning, but I do hope it's nothing more serious."

Isaac opened the door, nodded to the three women, smiled and left. He closed the door softly behind him. Abby rushed to the window, trying to hide behind Hannah's thin curtains. She watched Isaac and told everyone that he was strolling leisurely back towards the quay. Abby stayed there until he was out of sight.

"He's gone," she said, turning back to see Beth standing in the doorway to the kitchen.

"Did he believe you?" she asked.

"I think so," Abby replied.

"And it's time someone filled me in on what's going on here," Martha said, settling herself on the sofa next to Hannah. "Would anyone care to start?"

It didn't take long to fill Martha in with the basic details of Beth's arrival and her subsequent sheltering at Hope Barton.

"So, this father of yours, are you afraid of him?"

Martha always had a way of getting straight to the point and asking what nobody else dared.

"Not afraid, not physically, but it's difficult to say no to him. He doesn't listen. I used to talk to mother about… stuff, but I can't talk to him in the same way. He wouldn't understand."

"Hmm," Martha said. "And Simon?"

"He's nice, but I'm not in love with him, I didn't want to marry him, but my father wouldn't listen."

"So you ran away, or rather sailed away?"

Beth head dropped and she didn't say anything else.

"Well," Martha said. "It seems to me that you need to get back to Hope Barton. Abby can stay here and take care of Hannah and I need to go and find all those books I'm supposed to have."

Martha stood up shook her head at the three of them and opened the door. "You two girls have always been trouble, but I'll take your side against Isaac any day."

With that, she shook her head again and left. Abby asked Hannah if she'd be okay for ten minutes, just while she set Beth back on a safe route to Hope Barton.

"I feel a lot better already. I'll be fine. Go, quick, before my uncle decides return."

Hannah did feel better, but she still felt weak and lay back on the sofa, sipping water and wondering whether it was going to be easier now Martha was in on their secret.

Chapter 17

Abby stayed with Hannah all night. She slept on the floor by her side and every time Hannah woke from a disturbing dream, Abby was there to sooth her back to sleep.

The next morning Hannah was feeling better but still weak from the poison and couldn't face any breakfast. Abby made her a mug of chamomile tea and gave her another glass of Beth's willow bark water.

"What else is in Beth's bag?" Hannah asked between sips of her tea.

Abby was sitting on the floor, leaning back against the sofa. She pulled the satchel towards her and Hannah leaned over her shoulder to see what it contained. The bag was made of soft, waxed leather and it smelled of the sea and some sort of oil. Hannah wrinkled her nose slightly as a medley of aromas wafted up when Abby opened the flap. Some were sweet, some musky, none of them particularly unpleasant.

"Anything familiar?" Hannah asked as Abby bent her head to examine the contents.

Abby pulled out a bottle with a vivid green oily liquid in it. "Do you think she might be a witch?" she asked and opened the bottle to sniff it.

Hannah laughed and her stomach muscles cramped. "I doubt it," she groaned.

"I have no idea what any of this is."

"Isaac's going to expect you to know now you've told him you've been studying herbal medicines."

"I'd better do some reading up then, or get Beth to teach

me, at least enough to fool Isaac." Abby got up and looked at the small row of books on Hannah's shelves, picking out the one Isaac had looked at the night before.

"I didn't know you were interested in herbal remedies and medicine?" Abby murmured, flipping through a few pages.

"I brought a couple of books back from the Manor. You know my mum and yours grew all sorts of things in the walled garden. I've kept promising myself I'd read up on it, but I never seem to have the time."

"I know what you mean, but I'll have to now. Can I borrow this?"

Abby turned the pages to the index at the back and ran her finger ran down the page.

"It's got something in here about willow bark, wasn't that the powder Beth left for you?"

"I wasn't really paying that much attention, if you remember I wasn't feeling all that well."

"I'm not sure we have many willow trees. Would Isaac know about trees?"

Considering she had known him all her life, as had Abby, they both realised that they didn't know that much about Isaac. He had always lived in the same house in the village, never married, never worked on the land and he wasn't a fisherman. Before her parents died he made cider and pressed fruits and she knew he worked with Martha in the stores, but beyond that she had no real idea of what Isaac might or might not know.

Abby put the book on the arm of the sofa and slid out another one.

"Poetry? Have you actually read any of this?"

"Some," Hannah replied looking at Abby's back, hunched over, head dropped forward while she read. "Did something happen between you and Isaac once? It's not exactly a secret that the two of you don't get on."

Abby ignored her and pushed the book back into its slot.

"There are willows up by the village reservoir I think, but I've never taken that much notice of them. When I go to the mainland I could always try to bring some plants back. Can you buy trees?"

"I have no idea. We'd have to ask Beth?"

"Are you feeling okay now? I ought to get to work, everyone will be wondering where I've got to."

"I think Martha might have told them by now."

Abby laughed, knowing that Martha doubled up as village notice board.

"I think I'm going to go up to the Manor," Hannah said. "If anyone asks after me tell them I'm still ill. I'll have a look for some more books for you and see if I can find some to help Martha with the 'secret hoard' she's supposed to have."

"Does this mean I'm going back to school and will have to become the Island medic? It's not a role I cherish."

"Let's worry about that when you've brought Beth back from the mainland, she can probably take over from you. I doubt you'll kill anyone in the meantime"

"Thanks for your confidence, but you'll be the first one I try all my potions on."

"Beth will need a new name too. She seemed dead set on Ben, but that's not going to work now."

"Yes, well, I'll get on. Let me know if you need any more of my services as your doctor."

"I'm feeling remarkably well now," Hannah smiled and giggled.

"So ungrateful," Abby retorted as she opened the door, blew a kiss goodbye to Hannah, and left.

Hannah was so much better than the previous evening, but she still didn't feel like eating anything. She folded up the blankets that Abby had tucked round both of them the previous night and hid Beth's satchel, out of sight, in the kitchen. Hannah looked round the room to check there was no other trace of Beth and set off for the Manor on her hunt for books.

From the lane, Hannah looked up over sloping lawns to the Manor. It appeared to be basking in the morning sun. The sandstone walls, that had at one time been painted, were almost back to their original colour. Decades of neglect had returned the house to something resembling its original design – at least it looked like that from a distance.

When Hannah got closer she could see where the slate roof needed attention and that some of the windows were sorely in need of repair. She hadn't taken the care she should have over the Manor and wondered whether it wasn't time to move back in.

The main door was unlocked and the latch slipped easily on its pivot. Someone must have kept it oiled – probably Isaac. She wondered whether he was hoping to move in if anything happened to her. The taste of the cider revisited her tongue and she shuddered.

The stairs didn't creak as she climbed them, unlike Canary Cottage. Hannah hadn't been upstairs in the Manor for several years, but nothing had changed. She ran a finger along the bannister rail and was surprised to find that there wasn't a layer of dust settled on the wood. She looked at an old trunk that lived on the landing – that was dust free too. Someone had been cleaning the house.

The door to her parents' bedroom moaned when she pushed it open. Hannah was concerned that everything would still be the same as on the day her mother died with sheets tumbling to the floor and a still-wet flannel laying on the pillow to sooth her mother's fevered brow.

The bed was made and the room tidy and clean. It looked

as though it was waiting for a guest to arrive with two fresh towels lying over the end rail of the bedstead. Hannah ran a finger across one of the towels – it was soft, newly laundered.

Most of her parents' books were downstairs in the study, but Hannah remembered her mother as always having a few beside her bed, to dip into on a whim. There was still a pile of four books there, waiting to be read.

Hannah turned them round with her index finger to examine the titles. One book was on herbal medicines, the others titles were unfamiliar – a slim volume on psychiatry, another about social structures and the last was 'Pride and Prejudice'. Hannah had only read the last one and found it strange to read about a world so different from the one she knew and so long in the past, yet strangely familiar in some ways. All the books were very old and suffered from many years of love.

The top one was titled 'The Natural Doctor' and Hannah picked it up to give to Abby. The cover was loose and some pages were trying free themselves from the binding. She went back downstairs with the book in her hands. Her parent's bedroom was not somewhere she wanted to linger by herself.

Hannah propped herself on the window seat in the lounge. The light was good and the warmth from the early morning sun was welcome in the old house. Turning the cover, Hannah started to read. It was full of notes in her mother's hand and it was like being close to her again, hearing her soft voice and the laughter of her father teasing them.

Hannah lost track of time. When the front door clicked open, she jumped. Someone was moving through the house and not caring if they were heard because there shouldn't be anyone there to question their presence.

"Right, where the hell did they hide it?"

Hannah knew Isaac's voice instantly, even though he was only muttering to himself. She put the book down and crept to the door to the hall, hid behind it and spied on Isaac through the narrow slit below one of the hinges. If he came into the lounge he would be bound to see her, but instead he went into the study on the opposite side. She tiptoed carefully across the hall, flattened herself against the wall next to the grandfather clock and listened to Isaac rummaging around, opening and closing drawers and cupboards.

"Okay," he muttered to himself angrily. "I know it's not in the bloody desk and I've searched the cupboards before, so where did they put it?"

She couldn't make out what he was doing, couldn't risk peeking round the door in case he saw her, so Hannah went back to hide in the lounge. From behind the door she could see into part of the study, but not what Isaac was doing in there.

When the study door opened fully and Isaac stood there with his hands on his hips she knew he hadn't found whatever he was looking for. He looked straight at the door she was behind and shook his head, his lips tight in a thin straight line and his eyes half closed. He shook his head and left the house, the door slamming angrily behind him.

She went to the window and watched him stride down the path with more energy than he usually displayed. He slammed the gates with the same force he'd exerted on the front door. The gate bounced back off its latch but Isaac ignored it and walked away down the lane.

The study was a mess. Books had been taken from every shelf and left in cascading piles on the floor. She knew that whatever Isaac was looking for must be important and therefore her parents would have put it in the safe.

If you didn't know where the safe was you would never

find it. Her great grandfather had installed it and her grand-father had let her play with the spinning dial, trying to guess the correct numbers. He gave her clues but she never guessed the combination and it amused both of them that it was so difficult. Hannah crossed to the main bookshelves, now empty of their burden. She counted five shelves up from the floor in the central rack and pushed firmly on the backboard of the shelf at one end. It didn't move. She counted again and struck it hard with the heel of her hand. There was a creak and the panel moved a fraction of an inch. Pressing again it pivoted just enough for her to get her fingers behind the end and pull on it. The panel hinged out and revealed, just as she remembered, a dull, horizontal, grey metal panel with a large silver and black dial in the centre.

Hannah needed a clue. She knew she would never be able to guess the correct three numbers in the combination. At least her grandfather had told her the principle by which it worked. She just needed to find those numbers. An image from the book she had been flicking through, with all her mother's annotations, flashed into her head. The one that hadn't made sense was a series of three digits scribbled hastily at the foot of the title page. Maybe they hadn't been written in such haste, but simply in a different handwriting – her grandfather's handwriting.

Chapter 18

After retrieving the book and turning to the right page, Hannah looked at the dial on the front of the safe. "Be right," she said trying to convince the lock to open.

Her fingers rested lightly on the dial and tried to turn it clockwise to the first number. It wouldn't move. She took a deep breath and let it out slowly, gripped the dial harder and tried again. It started with a jerk and then moved more fluidly. She entered the digits, turning the dial in alternate directions. On the last number it resisted for a moment and gave a sharp click. She knew that if the numbers weren't correct, she had no second guess. Hannah gripped the handle and pulled. The door swung open with only a hint of resistance.

Inside the safe was a pile of documents and, on top of them, a small book with a thin strap round it. Sorting through them Hannah found that the documents were her family's history, everything her parents and generations before had deemed worthy of preserving.

Hannah's grandfather, Benjamin Cotton, had shown her the old deeds to the farm, which included most of the land on the Island. Those parcels of land he didn't inherit from his father had been annexed during his lifetime. After years of the fever, many farms and cottages had been abandoned. The families who once lived there left buildings and land empty and unattended. The previous owners having either died or scattered to places unknown.

Sorting through the bundle of documents one by one, a smell of dust and age infused Hannah's nostrils. It reminded

her of Martha's office when she had tried to tidy it once –
until Martha shouted for her to stop messing about with her
filing system. The deeds were familiar from her childhood,
including the small collection of documents pertaining to
land and buildings.

She didn't spend too much on them because there were
two items she had never seen before. They were on hand-
made paper, folded into three and tied with ribbons. Hannah
ran her fingers over the visible fibres on the surface of the
cream paper, feeling how it had been pressed hard to
produce a smoother finish.

In shiny black ink the name of her father, Jacob Cotton,
was written in a flowing script. Just above, in a smaller
hand, it said 'The Last Will and Testament of'. Her mother's
will was the same, written in the same hand. The 'y' of her
first name, Sally Cotton, looped at its lowest point into a
series of decorative swirls.

She didn't want to open them. Inheriting the Island and
being the legal owner of her whole world was not something
she dreamed about or really wanted. With a sigh she pulled
the ribbons off her father's will and read it slowly.

As far as she could understand, if she didn't marry, or
have children, Abby would succeed her as bailiff, and
Abby's children after her. The language was strange, but
Hannah couldn't see why Abby inherited, rather than it
passing to her mother's side of the family. She shook her
head slowly and slid the ribbon back over the re-folded
document. Her mother's will was almost identical, naming
Abby as the beneficiary if anything happened to Hannah,
both were witnessed by Martha and Peter, their miller.

Hannah put the wills and the various land deeds back in
the safe where Isaac had been unable to find them so far.
Only the notebook with a soft black cover remained to be
examined. She opened it to the first page and written in a

wavering script it read 'For Hannah – We will always love you'.

The house suddenly felt huge, empty, cold, even in the middle of summer. Hannah shivered, the sound of her father's voice was in her head and she shut the book without turning a page. She needed to be back in Canary Cottage before she could read it.

The documents were safe. She would take that book of her mother's still laying beside her, the journal and maybe she should take some books for Martha as promised to help with her imagined hoard she had told Isaac about.

Back in her parents' bedroom, Hannah dug around in the wardrobes until she found two large canvas bags that had belonged to her mother. One had a headscarf in it that her mother had worn for gardening and Hannah decided to take it with her for luck. She put the journal and a book entitled 'Garden Apothecary' in the bottom of one bag, looked at the other books by the side of the bed and decided to leave them in case Isaac noticed them gone. She had no idea if he ever went upstairs but would be surprised if he hadn't snooped everywhere looking for those wills. Returning to the study she scooped books up randomly and filled both bags. Fortunately Isaac wouldn't notice anything missing as he had left the room in such a mess.

She tried to heave one bag onto her shoulder, the other had handles so short that she could only grasp them in clenched fingers. Realising how heavy they were, Hannah took a couple of books out of each. Martha would have to make do with what she could carry.

Walking back towards the centre of the village she stopped and listened every so often for anyone else who might be on the path, this gave her a rest from carrying what were still very heavy bags. The path was clear, even the lane back into the village was quiet, everyone was out working on the fields or involved in some task indoors. It was still an hour or so to go before people broke for lunch.

Without pausing at her cottage, Hannah headed straight for Martha's store, praying that Isaac wouldn't be there. She rehearsed excuses for having two large bags of books with her – none of which sounded plausible. The door was ajar and Hannah leaned her shoulder against it, trying to hear if there was any conversation, any clue as to whether Martha was alone. The welcome sound that reached her was Martha's tuneless singing, something she would never do if she had company.

"Hi Martha, where are you?"

The main barn was so cavernous that she could be hiding almost anywhere.

"Over here my dear, just airing the potato sacks."

The old, used sacks needed to be turned once a week to stop heat building up in the stack. Many years ago, when Hannah was a small child, there had been a minor fire when the sacks started to spontaneously smoulder. Fortunately it had been caught in time, but used sacks were never left for more than a week now without turning.

"What are you doing here my dear, you should still be resting in bed?"

"I'm okay. Whatever it was has passed pretty much. I brought you some books."

"What for?"

"So you had that hidden stash you're supposed to have found. In case my nosey uncle comes asking about them."

"Oh, he won't bother me, but thanks all the same. Did these come from the Manor?"

Hannah nodded, unloading the books from the two bags and stacking them on the end of a table.

"What were you doing up there?"

"I went up to get these." She couldn't look directly at

Martha. "Isaac was there, looking for something. He left the study in a complete mess. Books were scattered everywhere."

"Do you know what he was looking for? Did he see you?"

"He didn't see me, I hid behind a door. But I'm sure he was looking for the safe, and for my parents' wills. He might have wanted this too"

Hannah reached into one of the bags and brought out her father's journal.

"I know what their wills say," Martha said quietly.

"You've seen them before. Do you know what they mean, why my parents included Abby in them?"

"Did you find anything else in that safe?" Martha avoided her question.

"Deeds and titles to land," Hannah looked up. "And this journal, written by my father."

"You've not read it yet have you?"

"How do you know?"

"I witnessed those wills, along with Peter. We had to read them first, your parents insisted. When we'd signed them he, your father I mean, told us what his journal contained, why Abby was to inherit if anything happened to you. He said the journal was for you, that we should give it to you when you came of age, but we needed to know who Abby was and why she was named in both their wills."

"Why is she in their wills?"

"You need to read that journal yourself. Peter and I... we've never spoken about it since that day, not specifically. Your father gave me the combination of the safe and told Peter how to find it. We were only to make their wills public if something happened to you. And after last night I was worried. I almost went round to get Peter this morning, but I saw Abby and she said you were much better."

"I'll read it tonight."

Martha came round the table and hugged Hannah. She whispered in her ear. "Don't act hastily on anything you read. That journal was written nine years ago."

"Okay." Hannah frowned, even more apprehensive at what it may contain.

"And remember, you can come and talk to me about anything, anything at all."

Hannah eased herself out of Martha's arms, bit her lip and played with a stray thread on the bottom of her shirt.

"There was something else I wanted to ask you about."

"What was that my dear."

"Do you have a radio here? One that works?"

Martha pouted and looked carefully at Hannah.

"Now why would you want one of them. None of them work. Nobody's heard anything on a radio my whole lifetime. Now, your grandfather was a one for them. He used to go on about radio all the time, convinced it would all come back."

"I was hoping you might still have one. There's a radio up at the Manor, but I didn't want to take that one in case Isaac notices it's missing."

"Well, I probably have got one somewhere, tucked away in one of the lofts, but I don't know that it will be of any use. They used to try turning one on every so often when I was a girl, years ago that was." Martha laughed. "What makes you think it's worth trying now?"

"It was something Beth said."

"Hmm, Well, I'll pop it up to you when I find it, but I doubt it will work."

Martha started to pick up the books from the table, reading the titles and making grunts of approval or dismissal.

"Your father was a good person Hannah and your mother

too. He never had a harsh word to say about anyone, always did his duty. Just remember that when you read his book."

Hannah thanked her, promising she would keep an open mind and that she would come back to talk to Martha after she had read the journal. She took a couple of potatoes, a few carrots and a chicken breast – all at Martha's insistence and put them carefully on top of the journal in her bag. If Isaac stopped her now she would have an excuse for visiting Martha and for carrying a bag.

Back in her cottage Hannah set the journal on a high shelf in the kitchen and started preparing the vegetables and chicken for a casserole, which she would put on the stove later. The simple, familiar task gave her space to think and settled her nerves. She had no idea what the journal would reveal, but she had a feeling that it was going to change her world forever.

Once the casserole was ready and she'd washed her hands, Hannah reached up, took her father's journal off the shelf and went back into the lounge. She stopped for a moment, looking at the front door, went over and slid the bolt across, something she never did. Hannah settled on the sofa and turned to the first page, to that inscription and read it again, running her fingers over the slightly raised surface where the ink lay black and shiny.

Chapter 19

Before turning to the next page, Hannah arranged a cushion behind her back, closed her eyes, took two deep breaths and let each out slowly. She was ready for her father to talk to her.

'For Hannah – We will always love you'
August 19th 2112

Dear Hannah, If you are reading this then it is almost certain that your mother and I are no longer here to take care of you, but you are eighteen now and must make your own decisions as to how to go forward. My last trip to the mainland was selfish and I should never have risked bringing the virus back with me. I hope you will forgive my foolishness when you read this journal.

Your mother is seriously ill as I write this. She loves you very much and cares not so much for her own well being, but that she will not see you grow, marry and have children of your own. I fear that neither of us will have that pleasure.

If you have already read them, you may be wondering why Abby Gliddon features so prominently in both our wills and to explain I must start at a time before I was married to your mother. Grandpa Benjamin may be able to help you understand all this if he is still alive.

Hannah let her head drop back against the sofa and stared at the ceiling. She could remember her grandpa well, even though he had died only a year after her parents. She looked up at her shelves where she still had the picture she had drawn of him a few months before he left her. Aunty Rebekah succumbed to the fever soon after he did. The picture was small, drawn in pencil, and was typical for an eleven-year-old, but he had insisted that it was of high artistic merit and Hannah had kept it ever since in the old silver frame in which he had mounted it.

The fever had taken them all and left Hannah in the care of Martha. Abby was deemed old enough to claim her independence and lived during the summer months in a shepherds' hut near the main reservoir, only returning to spend her winters in the village after the end of October. Hannah dipped her head back to the journal and turned another page. The writing was dense, packed onto the page as though her father feared he might run out of space or time.

The walled garden at the Manor is our island's apothecary – it has grown as such over a period of years and with much research and expertise by several people, inspired by your grandmother. Abby's mother, Rebekah, also worked in the garden as a girl. When I was young, Rebekah was bright and cheerful, only a couple years younger than me and we got on well. I had thought about asking her to marry me, but she left suddenly for the mainland. Nobody knew why.

I missed her, but there was a lot of work to do in those years. The island was thriving both in its produce and its population. We were the success that my grandfather had hoped we would be.

Your mother took over Rebekah's work in the garden. We knew each other of course and had been friends, but nothing more than that. Maybe it was our proximity in work or maybe it was always meant to be, but we fell in love and were married within the year. We lived in the Manor with my parents.

You were born in the February of the next year. We always hoped to give you a brother or sister, or both, but it never happened. Despite that, our life was near perfect, the Island had settled into its own pattern and, barring occasional disagreements or minor tragedies, everyone was happy.

Rebekah returned to the Island, just after your second birthday, with her own child, a girl she had named Abigail. She joked that she would work her way through the alphabet and said if she had a boy, Benjamin would be her first choice of name, in honour of my father. She refused to talk about Abby's father, only saying that their relationship hadn't worked out the way she had hoped. She accepted our offer for her to return to her old work in the garden. Rebekah also took to maintaining the channels that feed the reservoirs and took on many other solitary tasks. She kept Abby with her wherever she went.

It was delightful to see you and Abby growing up together even though she was a year or two older than you. Rebekah claimed that she wasn't even sure of Abby's precise birthday, as their life had been in so much turmoil at that time. We took to celebrating it on the same day as yours.

When I came back from my trip to the mainland, with a high temperature, Rebekah insisted that she care for me, that your mother not risk catching whatever I had in case it was the fever. Unfortunately her precautions were to no avail. Your mother came down with the fever only a few days after I returned.

We both suspected that something bad had happened to Rebekah when she was on the mainland, maybe her partner had died. We pressed her repeatedly to tell her story and finally she relented.

Her first words were 'Abby's father lives on the Island'. I confess I knew what she meant almost immediately and couldn't believe I had been so blind not to suspect. I asked her

147

directly if I were the father and she said I was.

Your mother told her she should have said something earlier, not kept it to herself. She also asked why she had left, why didn't she just tell someone she was pregnant.

Rebekah was reluctant to reveal all, but we persuaded her and, I think because we were both ill, she felt compelled to tell us the whole story.

Your Uncle Isaac, in whom she had confided, told Rebekah that everyone would think she had tricked me, that she had become pregnant by someone else and just wanted to secure her place on the Island as the future Bailiff's wife. He had dated Rebekah when she was a teenager and held a grudge against her after she rejected him. She apologised to your mother for speaking out so harshly, but said that Isaac wanted to be Bailiff of Hope Island, and he wanted his sister to marry me to provide him with a substantive claim some time in the future.

Your mother understood. She assured Rebekah that she knew her brother well and that we would make sure his plans would not come to fruition. We never told Rebekah what solution we agreed upon, but you and Abby are half-sisters and we felt that if the fever or anything else prevented you from carrying on our family's heritage, then Abby should be the rightful successor.

Hannah let the journal fall onto her lap, digesting everything her father had written. It made sense that Abby was her half-sister. They had always felt so close. It also explained the friction between Abby and Isaac. There were several more pages to read, but Hannah decided she needed a break and wanted to talk to Martha to confirm how many people knew the full story. She looked for somewhere to hide the journal, but it didn't feel safe to leave it anywhere other than at the Manor so she put it back in one of the canvas bags and kept it with her. After she had finished reading it she would put it back in the safe, but until then it wouldn't leave her sight.

It was late afternoon and Martha was still at the store. Hannah called from the door and she answered her immediately.

"In the kitchen," she called and came out drying her hands on a towel. From the other side of the barn she guessed from something in Hannah's voice or her expression. "You've read it haven't you?"

"Some of it. Enough."

"Come on into the kitchen. I'll make us a cup of tea. You're bound to have some questions."

Hannah followed her into the kitchen, a huge room with a long pine table running down the centre. The bare wood had been scrubbed and scraped so often the surface was now uneven, dipping in areas where the grain was softer. She sat on the bench on one side, put her bag in front off her and kept hold of the handles – in fear that it might be snatched away from her.

"You know about Abby? About her being your half-sister?"

"Yes," Hannah answered quietly. "But does she know?"

"Her mother told her before she died and that both Peter and I knew the truth. Rebekah left it up to Abby whether she told you or not."

"She never did tell me."

"I know. She thought it would complicate your relationship. She didn't want to lose your friendship."

"She would never have lost my friendship. I would have loved her even more if I'd known – as a friend and a sister."

Martha set two mugs of tea on the table. Hannah's tilted sideways and spilled. Martha rubbed the spilt tea into the wood with her fingers, not bothering to mop it up. She sighed, the air blowing from her mouth as though it had been trapped in there for years.

"She was worried about Isaac."

"But Isaac has no claim before myself and Abby. My parents' wills are quite clear about that."

Martha sighed again, more quietly, and shook her head slowly.

"Isaac is a powerful man. He's built connections on the mainland over the time he's been Bailiff."

"Guardian Bailiff," Hannah corrected her.

"A name is but a name. He has been in charge of all trading, all dealing with the Recorder and he's well connected with Joseph Delancey too."

"Is that Simon's father?"

Martha nodded. "A very wealthy family, you must have guessed that, and with wealth comes power."

Hannah thought for a moment about all the time she had spent with Abby, how she had always been there for her.

"Why does Abby hate Isaac? She does hate him doesn't she?"

"Hate is a strong word Hannah. Isaac threatened her when she was just a young girl. He scared her then, but she's grown since, and not just in height."

"What did he do?"

"I wasn't there to hear it myself, but I believe what Abby told me. She overheard him talking to her mother when Rebekah was ill, near the end. He told her that he would see her daughter dead rather than let her get her hands on the Island."

Hannah fell silent. She had always thought their island was a haven, a place of safety. Now she knew an undercurrent of hatred and power was the background to her life – and all because of her uncle's greed.

"I want to tell Abby I know," Hannah whispered and

nodded her head slowly, "I want her to know that having her as a sister is the best thing that could have happened to me."

"A half-sister to be accurate."

Hannah looked at Martha, her eyes narrowed. She vowed to herself that she would stand up to Isaac. He wouldn't win.

"Who else knows about this, about Abby being my sister?"

"Ah, that's not so easy to say. I know, Peter knows, Isaac knows of course, Abby knows and now you. But I reckon half of Hope Island has guessed something close to the truth. But nobody else knows about the wills and, if Isaac found and destroyed them, it would only be our word against his."

"But people trust you and Peter, they would believe you."

"And that's where money and power start to work their evil Hannah. People believe things, but they're not always ready to stand up against someone they fear."

"I want everybody to know the truth. Nobody should have to fear Isaac, not even if he was the real Bailiff and not just a stand-in."

"But it's not only up to you. You'll have to ask Abby how she feels about it. And I take it you haven't quite finished your father's journal?"

"No. Why?"

"You might have some more questions for me when you have."

Martha finished the dregs of her tea and reached across the table to take hold of Hannah's hands.

"Sleep on it tonight my dear. Come back and see me in the morning. We can talk again then."

Chapter 20

When Hannah left the barn it was still only mid afternoon, most people were working and the village had a curious deserted feel. In an hour or two it would be buzzing with people, but it suited Hannah not to be seen. She stopped off at Canary Cottage and moved her casserole to the warmer side of the hob for it to start cooking.

Out on the street she was lucky again, not bumping into anyone on her way up through the village. The lane that led up to the Manor and continued to the reservoir was rarely used and she was confident of remaining unseen. At last she relaxed a little and thought about Abby and how that close feeling she had for her now made sense.

Hannah opened the door to the Manor quietly, just in case Isaac was searching once again for her parents' wills. She had no doubt that was what he was after, most probably in order to destroy them. She waited, but there was no sound.

The study was in the same turmoil as when she had left. The safe remained concealed by the false panel.

Clasping the canvas bag firmly in front of her, Hannah climbed the stairs to the first floor. When one of them creaked she stopped, waiting for someone to appear and ask her what she was doing, but she was alone. The door to her parents' room was ajar. She couldn't remember whether she had closed it. She pushed it open cautiously, her heart beating fast, but the room was empty. Isaac hadn't ransacked it as he'd done in the study, but he had probably searched it at some time in the past.

Leaving the journal on the bed, Hannah stowed the canvas bags back in the wardrobe. It would be one less thing to explain if Isaac asked her where it had come from. There was a small sofa in the room and an upright wooden chair. Both still had her parent's clothes draped over them. Her fingers caressed the hem of her mother's favourite gardening dress, a light cotton print with so many small repairs that they appeared to almost be part of the floral pattern. She lifted it to her nose, hoping that a remembered scent would still cling to the material, but the dress smelled old, slightly musty, with no trace of her mother. She let it fall back onto the sofa.

Sitting on the bed she tested its springiness, remembering the times she had bounced on it to wake her parents in the morning. She lifted her feet up, kicking off her canvas shoes, which fell to floor with soft thuds, and she lay down, head resting on the pillow, trying to picture her parents.

With a sigh Hannah propped herself up and reached for her father's journal, turning to the page she had read last. The handwriting on the next page was more spidery. Hannah assumed he was quite fatigued by the fever and maybe his hand, as well as his mind, was wandering. She wiped a tear from her cheek.

You have to be ready Hannah. When the virus has run its course, as it eventually will, the Island will need to adapt to the world again.

There was an undecipherable doodle filling the rest of the page. Hannah assumed that her father's mind was going even as he wrote. She turned the page. There was a single word at the top, 'MONEY', in capital letters, followed by lines of minute writing, like bullet points, but only a few were decipherable.

Find the gold
Don't tell Isaac
Martha will know where to hide it
The two of you must be strong
Trust your sister and believe
Everything will return, it must

Those lines Hannah could read made little sense to her. Maybe that's what Martha had meant when she said to talk to her again tomorrow. From that page onwards Hannah couldn't read anything other than the occasional word. Her father's pen wandered across the pages with words and lines crossed out vigorously and drawings that made no sense. Ink blots became frequent to the point where it looked like he had been attacking the page with his pen, rather than attempting to write. On the last page he had written one line, remarkably clearly.

You must find the mine.

Hannah wasn't sure whether her father had become delusional. She remembered that he kept drifting in and out of consciousness and eventually he found her visits to his bedside more distressing than comforting. Her mother's end had been kinder, simply slipping away into unconsciousness.

But Hannah's memory of that time was confused by the trauma of losing both her parents within days of each other. It was real then, but now more like a dream and she hardly trusted her memories. She never knew he was writing a journal and none of the pages were dated. It would be simple for her uncle to dismiss it all as the unfortunate ramblings of an ill man. And maybe her father was confused, about the mines, about the need for money, about everything in those last days.

Hannah lay back on the pillows and stared at the ceiling, a cobweb trailed from the light fitting, moving gently in the air. The journal, open on that last page, rested on her tummy. She hoped she could keep Hope Island the way her parents had known it when she took over. Their system worked fine without money. Everyone was happy. Hannah closed her eyes, to rest for a while and work out what to do, but she drifted off to sleep, exhausted. She woke to the sound of the front door closing, the sharp click of the latch falling back into its keep. Footsteps on the stairs made her sit up. She needed to hide the journal, but could do no better than tuck it under the pillows behind her.

The footsteps stopped outside her door. She was holding her breath, convinced that Isaac somehow knew that she had found the wills, the journal and the truth about his plans. He must have followed her.

The knob turned and the door swung open slowly. A head appeared round the edge of it to check if the room was occupied. It was Abby.

"Hello Hannah. Martha said I might find you up here if you weren't at home. She said you had read your father's journal."

"If you mean our father's journal, then the answer's yes." Hannah frowned. "Why didn't you tell me?"

Abby edged into the room and leaned back against the door.

"I didn't know what your reaction might be. I didn't want to lose you as a friend."

Hannah swung her legs off the bed, and walked to within a few inches of Abby. Hannah saw her stiffen, her eyes fixed on Hannah.

"You're pretty dumb," Hannah said. "You do know that

don't you?"

Hannah slid her arms round her, pinning Abby's own arms to her sides. She hugged her tightly.

"You're my sister and you kept it a secret from me. I don't know if I can ever forgive you."

Hannah felt the tension leave Abby's body when she started to tickle her like she had when they were young. Abby had no resistance and fell back against the door, trying to escape Hannah's fingers and failing. Her strength gone, her body turned to jelly and she sank to the floor.

"Stop, stop, I'm sorry," she gasped for breath. "Oh please stop. It hurts." Abby fumbled to grab Hannah's hands without success.

Hannah relented. She was sitting on the floor in front of a crumpled Abby. She kept hold of one of her hands while Abby got her breath back.

"Seriously though, why didn't you say something, what happened wasn't your fault and I could have had a sister all these years."

"You did have one."

"But I didn't know."

"I didn't know either, until my mother was taken ill. It was less than a year since you'd lost your parents, it just seemed wrong to bring all that up again." She paused looking into Hannah's eyes. "The longer I left it the harder it got to say anything."

"I remember your mum so well. She was really kind to me when my parents died, but she must have been grieving too. She must have been in love with Dad. And when she died you were left with nobody."

"Well you only had your uncle," Abby whispered. "And I'm sure you know what I think of him."

"Have your read our father's journal?"

"No, but Martha's told me about it, she knows what's in

156

it. That's why she told me that you were reading it."

"It doesn't all make sense, not the stuff towards the end. I've got it here. Do you want to see it?"

Abby nodded. "If that's okay with you. I mean he wrote it for you really."

Hannah pulled Abby up and they sat side by side on the bed. She slid the journal out from under the pillow and handed it to her. While Abby read, Hannah watched her, wondering how she hadn't guessed that she was her half sister. Everything about their relationship made sense through this new perspective. Abby's lips started to move as she reached the erratic writing that was so difficult to decipher.

"It's hard to make out the words," she said. "Your father must have been quite ill when he wrote this."

"Our father you mean."

"I never thought of him as my father. He was always Uncle Jacob to me."

"But he was your father."

"I know, but I always struggle to think of him like that. I loved him, but of course it wasn't until a year after he died that I learned the truth and by then I was probably too old to change the way I saw him."

Abby flicked back a couple of pages to the strange spidery drawing that Hannah had assumed was no more than a doodle.

"If you turn this sideways what does it look like to you?"

Hannah looked, trying to make some sense out of it. "I think he must have been drawing something he could see in his head, the same way Daniel sees all those monsters in pieces of driftwood.

"It's the reservoir," Abby said. "And the mines. Look, there they are, on the hill above it."

Hannah looked again. It made sense now Abby had

157

pointed it out. "Do you think that's what Dad was trying to draw – a map?"

"They were gold mines at one time."

"That's just a story. Nobody really knows what was mined there. And anyway, whatever it was, they were abandoned hundreds of years ago."

"So why did your uncle have them boarded up?"

"For safety," Hannah replied. "He was worried that someone might get trapped in there, that the roof might come down."

Abby looked at her and raised her eyebrows.

"Okay, you're right," Hannah conceded. "He boarded them up because there's something hidden there."

"It doesn't totally make sense," Abby said, looking at the drawing again. "If Isaac had found something why would he board it up, why not move whatever he'd found to somewhere safer?"

"Too big?"

"Or he hasn't found it yet." Abby pointed at a mark on the map. "Is that another cave?"

"There is another one. I'd forgotten, it's beneath the water level in the reservoir."

"You mean it's completely underwater?"

"I found it when I was diving there years ago, when the sea was too rough to for swimming. It's not far under the surface. You can almost see it when the water level drops at the end of summer."

"So it would be visible now?" Abby asked.

"Yes, probably, but you wouldn't notice it if you didn't know it was there. You can be standing right above it and you wouldn't see it."

"And you've been in it?"

"Not very far. There wasn't any reason and it's very dark in there."

"Do you think your father might have meant that one?"

"Our father," Hannah corrected her again. "I don't know, maybe."

They both sat in silence looking at the map. Both had heard stories about the mines, about gold and hidden treasure. The stories were handed down and exaggerated every year at the solstice meetings. Nobody took them seriously.

"They're just stories aren't they?" Abby asked, as much to herself as Hannah. "There can't really be a hoard of treasure?"

"I wonder what Martha would make of the map. She would know about it if anyone does."

"She knew your grandfather of course? But I remember him, he used to tell lots of stories at the solstice and everyone said he hid truths in them."

Hannah nudged her. "He's your grandfather too, don't forget that."

"Maybe," Abby said. "But Isaac doesn't know about the other mine that you've discovered."

Abby nudged her back so hard that Hannah fell against the pillows.

"Big brute," Hannah said, laughing.

"You shouldn't be so short and easy to push around."

"Remember I have a power over you," Hannah said, wriggling her fingers threatening to tickle Abby again.

The front door clicked as the latch was lifted. They both froze, looking at the bedroom door as though it was about to open. Hannah buried the journal under the pillows again. The latch fell back into place and footsteps crossed the tiled hall floor.

Chapter 21

From Abby's frozen expression, Hannah assumed that she too expected it to be Isaac. She checked the journal couldn't be seen and smoothed the cotton cover as best she could.

"What do we do?" Hannah whispered.

"We don't have to do anything," Abby said. "You've got as much right to be here as he has, more right in fact."

"But what do we say we are doing here?"

"Looking for some of your mother's books."

"That will worry him if he thinks we might go into the study."

A voice, not Isaac's but Martha's, called up from the hallway.

"Girls? Are you here?"

Relieved, they went out onto the landing. "Up here," Abby shouted.

"Well, you can both come down. I'm too old for climbing staircases when I don't have to."

Hannah dodged back in the bedroom to collect the journal. Abby waited for her and they went down together.

"So, I presume you two have had a chat about things?"

"Why didn't you tell me Martha?" Hannah demanded. "You've known all this time and not said anything."

"It wasn't my place, not my secret to tell."

Hannah stared at Martha and decided she was probably right. She sighed in resignation. "Okay, I forgive you, but if I have any more brothers and sisters hidden away I'd appreciate it if you told me now."

"No, no more Hannah, isn't one enough?"

"Well, I couldn't have picked a better sister if it had been my choice." Hannah hugged Abby's arm.

"Have you got to the entries about the money?" Martha asked.

"We have," Abby said. "Do you have any idea what Jacob meant?"

Martha made a puffing sound followed by a little grunt. "I saw those pages back when he was writing his journal, but Jacob never explained it to me and I couldn't make anything of them." She paused and shook her head slowly. "He was quite ill by that time, he wasn't always making sense."

"We think we have an idea what it means," Abby said.

"Well don't tell me unless you have to, I've had enough of secrets to last me a lifetime."

Hannah and Abby exchanged glances and Hannah closed the journal, sparing Martha their thoughts.

"I take it you two are okay." She looked at Hannah. "With you finding out you have a half-sister?"

"I'm fine," Hannah replied. "Although you are sure aren't you? I mean she's so tall."

Abby nudged her hard. "Oh sorry, didn't see you there. Could you stand on a box so I don't trip over you?"

Both girls descended into a fit of the giggles and Martha said she was going to head back, that she had just wanted to check that they were all right.

"We'll put the journal in the safe with everything else and follow you. I can't see Isaac finding it and he doesn't have the combination even if he did stumble across it."

"Well, I don't want to know where it is - but one thing has been puzzling me. How did you know the numbers?"

"They were written in one of my mother's books, it's been beside her bed all this time. I'm not sure who wrote them though, I don't think it's her handwriting."

"That's strange," Martha frowned. "It was lucky Isaac

didn't notice it."

"He would have had to find the safe first, the numbers wouldn't make any sense if you didn't know what they were for."

"That's probably true," Martha said, but not sounding sure. "Anyway, I'd better be getting back to my supper. I just wanted to check on you girls. I'm glad you're okay."

Once Martha left, Hannah led the way into the study, but Abby stopped at the door, seeing books piled all over the floor for the first time and the empty shelves lining the walls.

"What happened here?"

"Isaac happened. Come on, I'll show you the safe."

"Do I need to know?"

"If anything did happen to me, you're going to have to get these documents and make everything public. You'll have to stop Isaac and take over as Bailiff."

"What if I don't want to take over? I'm not the administrator type."

"It's what my father wanted, our father I mean."

Abby reluctantly agreed although she kept her hands firmly in the pockets of her shorts.

"Isaac left a hell of a mess in here didn't he?"

"It looks worse than it is. Nothing's been damaged as far as I can tell. He's not that stupid."

"Shouldn't we clear it up, re-stack the shelves. Do you know what went where?"

"If we do that he'll know we've been here."

"Good point, it may be best to let him think he still has plenty of time. That nobody knows he's looking for those wills."

"Do you think..." Hannah paused. "That maybe we ought to just remain friends for the time being, as far as everyone else is concerned, rather than tell everyone we're sisters?"

"I wasn't planning on dancing through the street with a banner, but I'm glad you know – and that you're okay with it."

"I suppose I've had my big sister looking out for me all along, just without me knowing."

"Are you being sarcastic again?" Abby said, punching Hannah on the shoulder.

"Come on big sister," Hannah said, feigning pain. "I'll show you where the safe's hidden."

"If you have to," Abby moaned.

Hannah showed her the panel on the bookshelf, and how to release the catch by pressing on the end of it. The panel swung open more easily the second time. She showed her how to spin the dial four times before stopping it on the first number, back twice to the second number and forward once to the third. The she turned it back again there was a slight resistance and a satisfying click as the lock mechanism released.

"It's that simple?" Abby asked. "Sixteen, nine, twenty-two?"

"My grandfather told me about how many turns and changing direction, but not the numbers."

"And you never guessed what they were?"

"How could I have guessed, there must be millions of combinations."

"But your great grandfather only had the one birthday. The sixteenth September 2022."

Hannah couldn't believe she'd never thought of that when she was a child and hadn't even recognised it when she saw the numbers in her mother's book. But she had only been so young when her great grandfather died that she didn't remember him too well.

"How come you know his birthday off by heart?" Hannah asked.

"It must have just stuck in my head for some reason."

"Of course he's your great grandfather too."

Abby shrugged off the connection. "I didn't think of him as family, and of course he never knew that Uncle Jacob was my father."

"It must have been horrible for you."

"Not really. And when my mother died at least I knew I still had family, a sister, even though you didn't know and I wasn't sure how, or when, to tell you."

Hannah put her arms round Abby and hugged her. They stayed like that until Abby said they should stow the journal in the safe and leave, before Isaac decided to return. Abby closed the door, spun the lock dial and pushed the panel back into place until it lay flat against the back of the bookshelf.

"I reckon he'll come back and tidy up soon," Abby said, looking around at the books in untidy piles. "He won't want anyone else to find it like this and start asking questions."

Hannah picked up a single book and placed it on the shelf to prevent Isaac from finding the safe by accident. Then took it down again as it might make him suspicious.

They left the house, walking back down the lane towards the village. It was late enough in the day that the heat was beginning to ease and birds were active in the hedgerows, darting across the path in front of them and singing warnings to their families. Around a bend, where the path was obscured, they heard the sound of someone plodding towards them.

"It can't be Martha," Hannah whispered, grabbing Abby's hand.

Before she could answer they saw the bulky form of Isaac lumbering towards them. He stopped in the middle the path, effectively blocking their way unless they pushed past him.

"Where have you two been then?" he asked.

"Oh, just up to the reservoir," Abby responded without hesitation.

"And what would you be doing up there?"

"Hannah was showing me where there's some willow trees. I want to harvest some more bark in spring, from new shoots."

"Planning well ahead?"

"If I stripped the bark now I would damage the trees, possibly kill them."

They could both see Isaac mulling this over, determining whether he could accept it as plausible.

"Where are you off to Uncle?"

Isaac looked flustered by the question, as though he hadn't been expecting to have to justify his presence on the path.

"Oh, just up to the Manor. I think I must have left some papers there after that evening with Gideon and Simon. Quite careless of me."

Hannah could see Abby smirking, enjoying Isaac's discomfort.

"Well I hope you find them Isaac."

"Oh I will, I will, I'm sure they won't have strayed far. Anyway, I must press on, I can't stand here chatting to you girls all day."

They moved to one side to allow Isaac to pass without getting caught in the brambles that strayed across the way. Abby was by then smiling broadly, which appeared to unnerve Isaac even more. Hannah kept nudging her and mouthing for her to keep quiet. When they were round the bend and out of sight of Isaac, Abby collapsed into laughter, leaning back against a large beech tree and holding her stomach.

"You're terrible," Hannah said, trying not to laugh too.

"Why did you say that? You could have given everything away."

"But didn't you see him squirm. Can you imagine how much it annoys him that we're friends and he can't find those wills and destroy them."

"But it's dangerous to provoke him. Remember he's already tried to poison me."

Abby stopped laughing. "You're right I suppose. It's just so much fun that he doesn't know what we know."

"Do you want some supper? I went a bit mad earlier and cooked enough for four I think?"

"That would be delightful. I was going to eat leftovers."

On the walk back to Canary Cottage there were a few people around, loitering on doorsteps in the late afternoon sun, happy to say hello and willing to engage in idle chat. But many were still out on the fields, taking advantage of the light evenings.

In her kitchen Hannah took a jug of cold water out of her small fridge, gathered some mint leaves from a large pot, shredded them and put them in the jug. Her casserole needed bringing up to full heat again so she poured each of them a glass of the mint water.

"So, have you thought about when you are going to sail off to the mainland and bring Beth back with you?"

"Soon," Abby sipped her water. "No point in delaying now."

"Makes sense to me too. The sooner you go the sooner the gossip will die down about the two of you after your return. Hopefully it will be old news by the time the steamer calls again."

"There is going to be gossip isn't there?" Abby said.

"Of course there will be. But you can't just turn up at Hope Cove one morning and bundle Beth into a boat without warning."

"I could actually sail round there tonight. I'd have to wait until later, pretend I was going out fishing. That way we could leave at first light tomorrow."

"In that case I'll walk over after supper and let them know you're coming."

The two of them agreed on a plan of action. Abby would take the Crabber on the pretext of fishing and afterwards claim that the wind took her to the mainland. She would return with Beth a couple of days later.

"Beth will still need a new name," Abby said.

"She can't call herself Ben can she?"

"What about Rebekah? She could shorten it to Becky then"

"Your mother's name?"

"Why not? You could suggest it to her tonight. At least it would be easy to remember."

Chapter 22

Hannah was in no hurry when she walked over to Hope Barton. After supper she and Abby had gone separate ways. Abby had said she would try to sail round to Hope Cove in the Crabber as soon as she could get away. Hannah needed time to think. Her relationship with Ethan had always been a given, they would get married, everyone knew it, but they had never really discussed it. The thought of Simon returning on the next visit of the Pride was confusing.

If he remembered, Simon would bring that map for Ethan. She had never thought Ethan would ever take off on one of his fantasy voyages, but now she wasn't so sure. When she neared Hope Barton a dog barked from the top of a rise to her left, it was Samson greeting her arrival. He bounded down towards her and circled her twice while she talked to him, calming him down. They strolled down the lane together to the farm.

Daniel was sitting in his usual place with Charlie by his side, his hands cradling a new piece of driftwood. It could have been in Ethan's workshop for a day or a year, Hannah didn't recognise it, they all looked similar to her, and she couldn't see the hidden beasts inside them that Daniel found.

"Hello Daniel. Is that a new piece you're about to start?"

"Maybe."

"Is the last one's finished now? That dragon?"

"What dragon? I don't recollect any dragons around here. They'd take the sheep wouldn't they?"

Beth emerged from the kitchen door, a tea towel in one

hand, the other shielding her eyes from the setting sun. "We haven't seen you for a day or two, is everything all right?"

Beth's hair was another couple of shades lighter and she looked nothing like the girl Hannah had rescued on the beach. Anyone describing her now would mention her short, spiky reddish hair before anything else.

"What have you done with your hair, the colour's changed again."

"Carrot juice," Beth answered.

"Waste of good carrots," Daniel mumbled.

"Did you want some supper? We've already eaten, but I could throw something on the stove easily enough."

"No I'm fine. I ate earlier. Is Ethan around?"

"Up with the sheep. He'll be back soon. Did you want to see him about something in particular? He gave me a whistle in case someone turns up unexpectedly. He'll come straight down if I blow it."

"No, it's okay, it was you I wanted to see really."

Hannah took her into the kitchen, out of Daniel's earshot, and explained that Abby was sailing the Crabber round to Hope Cove and was planning to set off for the mainland in the morning. Beth nodded, taking it all in.

"Good. It's time we sorted this out. I can't stay here forever. Hidden on the farm I mean."

"You can stay with Abby when you return. We'll work something out longer term. Won't you miss living here, with Daniel and... Ethan?"

"Abby is fine, I like her. And no, I won't miss this place that much, although I love Daniel, and the dogs of course."

"And Ethan?"

"He will probably miss having a servant around to cook and clean for him. Why don't I brew us some tea? I never realised you grew it here."

Hannah wondered whether she had misread Beth's

interest in Ethan. She wasn't even sure that it mattered to her any longer. Hannah bit her lip, thinking how to phrase a question that would clarify the situation without directly accusing Beth of trying to steal her boyfriend, or ex boyfriend.

"Is Ethan treating you like a servant then?"

"Oh no, not really, but I've taken on a lot of the work in the house, and the bees, and looking after Daniel. Ethan hasn't exactly objected."

"Sounds like you've almost become a farmer's wife."

"Oh my god, no, nothing like that. I'm not interested in Ethan in that way. You didn't think I was did you? I'm so sorry if you got that impression, especially after all you've done for me."

Beth walked over to Hannah and gave her a hug.

"I would never try to take Ethan away from you," she whispered into Hannah's ear. "Not even if he suggested it – and he hasn't in case you're thinking that."

"I'm sorry too," Hannah said, hugging Beth back. "I should never have thought anything like that of you. It's just that Ethan has been so distant lately."

"I noticed."

Hannah frowned. Wondering how obvious the break-down in their relationship had been.

"Maybe when I'm gone, Ethan will settle his mind back on the farm, but he's obsessed with leaving this island, exploring the world. Heaven knows why. I've told him he's better off here than anywhere else, but he doesn't seem to take it on board."

"I know, he's always been a little like that. I used to think it made him interesting, now it's more like he can't wait to leave me."

The kettle started to whistle and Beth broke away to make the tea. She had her back to Hannah.

"Are you going to stay until Abby gets here?"

"I don't know, I'm not sure when she'll arrive, but it will probably be late."

"Can I ask you about her? I don't really know Abby that well and I'm going to be sharing a house with her after we get back. In fact I don't even know where she lives."

Hannah explained that Abby still spent much of the summer in a small hut near the reservoir, but said she also had a cottage in the village.

"She's something of a free spirit," Hannah said, sipping her tea. "She spends a lot of time alone."

She wanted to tell Beth about how they were sisters, but that would mean explaining far too much. Hannah recounted the story of Abby's mother and her return to the Island with a baby and how Abby and her had grown up together.

"We were almost like sisters," Hannah said and was aware that Beth had caught something in her tone by the way she was looking at her.

"Ethan told me some things about Abby, rumours mostly. He said it was best I knew."

"What's he been saying?"

"That she's gay?"

Hannah nodded, not sure whether to confirm it or not. Abby had said that everyone knew, but Hannah hadn't totally believed her.

"He also said..." Beth hesitated and took a slow breath in, releasing it before she continued. "He said there's always been a rumour that your father may be Abby's father too."

Hannah didn't respond. She was surprised and confused.

"He did say it's only gossip. I mean you're so different, the two of you. You'd know if something like that was true wouldn't you? Surely it would be obvious to both of you?"

Hannah spoke quietly, choosing her words carefully, not

wanting to deny or confirm the relationship – not yet.

"I've always loved Abby. We did grow up like sisters and I'd be more than happy if she were my real sister."

Any further discussion was interrupted by the return of Ethan.

"What are you two nattering about? Is that tea for me?"

"Um, no, I poured one for Daniel but forgot to take it out to him. There's plenty in the pot though."

Ethan took Daniel's tea out to him and came back to pour one for himself.

"So, what are the two of you plotting?"

"I told Hannah what you said about Abby, and that maybe they were half-sisters."

Ethan finished pouring his tea and put the pot down carefully, still with his back to the two girls.

"I told you that was just a rumour. This island likes nothing better than inventing stories about people." He turned around to face them, his mug held firmly in front of him. "I'm sorry, you should have heard that from me if you had to hear it from anyone."

"Sorry," Beth said quietly.

"I'm glad someone did tell me. Does Abby know about these rumours?"

Ethan shrugged and Beth was looking down into her mug of tea.

"She's sailing round here this evening," Hannah said.

"What for?" Ethan asked.

"To whisk me away to a new life, away from all this drudgery of being a farmer's maid."

Ethan didn't respond. Beth's humour was lost on him.

"You've got used to Beth being here I suppose?" Hannah said.

"We coped before," Ethan said curtly. "And we will again when she's gone."

"Why are you so grumpy?" Beth asked. "You should be happy for me."

"It's been easier I suppose with you here. I don't like leaving Dad alone for too long and while you've been here I've been able to catch up with a lot of work."

"You could have asked me," Hannah said. "I could have come over and sat with Daniel."

"I know. I didn't want to put upon you. Now I've got used to Beth being here. If she was staying I was thinking I'd be free to..." Ethan stopped mid sentence.

"Go off and explore the world?" Hannah suggested.

"Something like that," Ethan nodded.

Daniel shuffled into the kitchen with his mug in his hand. "Any chance of a refill boy?"

Beth rose, taking Daniel's mug from him and lifted the pot only to find it empty. She refilled the kettle and put it back on the stove.

"It will take a while to come to the boil Daniel," she said.

Daniel nodded, turned and went back outside.

"Why don't you have an electric stove if you've got wind turbines?" Beth asked as though it had only just occurred to her.

"Takes too much power," Ethan replied. "We don't have battery storage that would cope. In fact I need to check them."

He turned away and headed out the door. Beth called after him, asking if he wanted more tea, but Ethan only grunted that he'd be back directly.

"I'll take that as a yes then," Beth said, but too quietly for Ethan to hear. She looked to Hannah. "I'm really not after him you know."

"But what if he wants you?"

"He'll be out of luck"

"Are you planning on staying single forever then?"

"Not forever. If the right person comes along..."

Beth didn't finish her sentence and the kettle started to spit on the stove where water had run down the side of it.

"We have hydro electric power on the mainland. Not that I understand all that stuff, but even there not everyone has access to it."

"What is it like over there?"

Beth stared up at the ceiling, her shoulders dropped and she puffed.

"I suppose it's all right if you have money."

Hannah was going to ask her how much difference money made when Ethan called from outside.

"There's a boat just rounded the headland."

The girls went out to join Ethan. Even Daniel had stood up to see what was happening. Hannah shielded her eyes against the low sun, but light glinted off the water and she couldn't make out if it was Abby or not.

"It's the Crabber," Ethan said. "Did you say that was what Abby was coming in?"

"Yes, that should be her." She turned to Beth. "Hadn't you better go back inside just in case something's gone wrong and Abby's not alone."

Beth retreated until she was hidden in the doorway.

"I wish I hadn't left all my clothes in that holdall now?"

"That's not a problem," Hannah said without looking at her. "Once you're back here you can get most of your clothes back from Martha. I'll have a word with her while you're gone."

The boat tacked slowly towards the beach and Ethan said he could only see Abby on board. They all walked down to the water's edge to welcome her. Abby brought the boat in close and Ethan held it steady while Abby furled the sail, pulled up the drop keel and disappeared into the cabin. Beth took Hannah's hand.

"Now that Simon's getting that map for Ethan is there anything I can bring you back from the mainland?"

"I don't know what you have over there that I'd want."

"Pretty much anything is available if you have money."

"And you have money of course."

Beth didn't say anything.

"Actually there is something I would like if you can get it."

"What's that?"

"A book, one that I can write in. I'd like to keep a journal."

"That should be easy enough," Beth said gripping Hannah's hand a little firmer.

Chapter 23

"I brought you some clothes," Abby said, holding out a canvas bag. "You can't arrive back on the Island looking like you do now."

Beth was dressed in a baggy shirt and a pair of Ethan's old corderoy trousers, held up with an over-long belt that hung loose over her hip. She was barefoot and looked nothing like the girl who had been washed ashore a few weeks earlier.

Ethan and Abby pulled the boat onto the sand and buried its anchor on the beach. The four of them walked back towards the farm. The sun was just about to set and their shadows stretched across the lawn and angled onto the wall of the barn. Ethan muttered something about having to check on the cows. He kept two house cows, but one was in calf and he would have milked the other earlier in the evening, so it was probably an excuse to get away from three women.

"I'll put these clothes upstairs, and thanks again – for everything."

Daniel had gone indoors so Abby and Hannah sat on the bench and leaned back, looking at the darkening deep blue sky. The sun cast a glow of brilliant red along the line of the horizon, brighter and orange-yellow in the centre where it had sunk below the sea. The colour slowly faded into a rich blue and stars began to appear above them, each switching on in turn.

"When I slept in the shepherds' hut those first summers after my mother died, I used to imagine those shimmering

176

blue-green lights in the sky was her waving to me."

"I thought they were the spirits of my parents and grand-parents dancing with each other."

"They were so bright then, every night the sky was filled with them."

Both girls fell silent. The sky was turning ever darker, stars flickering like pinpricked holes in a deep blue sheet. The front door creaked on its hinges as Beth came out to join them.

"Do you remember the night lights Beth?" Hannah asked.

"Of course I do," she replied, slipping between Abby and Hannah as they shuffled aside to make room for her. "They were pretty, but that's why the radios wouldn't work – and televisions and computers and everything else."

"I miss the colours," Abby said quietly.

"But the radio works again now, or does sometimes. It's on for an hour in the evening, mostly news and informa-tion." Beth didn't sound like she thought it very important. "But not many people have radios. And anyway, it's not that interesting."

Beth leaned forward and stared down into her lap as though not wanting to look at either of them. Abby and Hannah exchanged glances behind her back.

"Do you think Isaac knows about this radio stuff?" Abby asked.

"I would be surprised if he doesn't," Beth said.

"And he's kept it secret," Hannah said. "He wants the Island isolated. I think my uncle and your father have kept a lot of things quiet and a lot of rumours alive – all for their own benefit."

"I know," Beth said, almost whispering and still staring down at the ground. "That's how my father has made so much money."

Hannah wanted to ask her more, but Ethan was walking

towards them across the grass, hands thrust into his pockets, head dropped into his shoulders. He scuffed a molehill flat with his boot as he passed it, stopping several feet short of the three girls. He lifted his head just enough to look at them from under his eyebrows and sniffed.

"What are you lot talking about then?"

It was Hannah who answered. "Just about the night lights in the sky. And how we used to imagine that they were the spirits of our parents."

All three girls were now looking at him and he ran a foot over the molehill he had previously flattened, as though to make sure it was completely levelled. He walked off towards the kitchen door, dismissing their ideas as he went. "They're just lights caused by solar storms, we all know that." The door didn't slam behind him, but closed firmly and the sound of the latch dropping echoed in the still of the evening.

"I suppose I ought to be heading home before Isaac decides to send out a search party for me."

"Would he do that?" Beth asked.

"No," Hannah laughed. "He'd probably just hope that I'd disappeared forever."

"She's joking," Abby said. "Or at least exaggerating a little."

Hannah stood up. Abby stood too and hugged her

"Take care of yourself while we're gone," Abby whispered.

"And don't you capsize or do anything stupid. I can't lose you now I've only just found you."

Beth had risen too. She remained slightly to one side as though not sure of her place. Hannah turned to Beth, gave her a brief hug and wished her good luck before she broke with them both and walked away. She looked back once, from the bottom of the farm lane, gave a final wave of goodbye and blew a kiss to both of them.

On her walk back to Newport the night was quiet save for the gentle whisper of a breeze through the longer grass and the occasional call of a barn owl. A flash of white feathers hovered above the corn stubble and was gone. Hannah walked slowly, she hoped that her uncle's hold on the Island was loosening and a new age was ready to start. But she wasn't sure.

The village was quiet as she wandered through it, passing her cottage and continuing on to the quay. Most people had gone to bed, but a few would be out fishing. She should be able to see which boats were missing because a gibbous moon had risen above the mainland. Sophia's boat would almost certainly be among those out on the water.

Leaning on the rails along the edge of the harbour she scoured the boats, silhouetted against reflections of the fractured moonlight on the calm, sheltered waters of Newport Bay. Beth's boat was moored hard against the harbour wall, small, pretty and entirely unsuited to the open sea. Three of the dories were out, two gaff-rigged boats and Sophia's which, although it was equipped with a fore and aft sail, she insisted on rowing on most occasions. The empty buoy, at which the Crabber was usually moored, appeared to Hannah to leave a huge empty space in the harbour.

Through the mouth of the bay a few lights showed on the coast of the mainland, but Hannah couldn't make out any details. Abby had told her that when the sun was low in the sky and the air was clear you could sometimes see individual houses over there. For Hannah the distant coast had long been no more than a slightly blurred line on the horizon, making it even more mysterious and dangerous in her heart. She was startled when Isaac's voice broke the peace of the night.

"What are you doing down here so late my dear?"

"Just thinking Uncle," she replied, not daring to turn

around lest he saw something in her face and questioned her about the missing Crabber. "I was thinking how far away the mainland is and that I've never even been there."

"There's nothing special to see over there, I wouldn't worry about it if I were you."

"But you're not me are you Uncle?"

Isaac didn't say anything for a minute or two and, if she couldn't have heard his breathing, she might have thought he had left her alone.

"Someone told me Abby had joined the fishing team tonight – in the Crabber. Did you know she was planning to go out?"

"No. I've been over at Hope Barton this afternoon."

"Really? Were you looking for more willow trees?" he chuckled.

Hannah had almost forgotten the excuse Abby had come up with when they met Isaac earlier, but needed something to divert his attention from Abby and the Crabber. She turned to face him.

"Daniel has finished that carving, the one of the dragon."

"So I could pick it up now? He wouldn't raise any objections?"

Hannah nodded. The air felt cooler. A breeze had scurried across the harbour, small waves slapped against hulls and the stays on masts sang ominously.

"I might ride over in the morning then."

Abby was planning on leaving early, soon after first light, but if there wasn't sufficient wind she could be delayed. Hannah wished she hadn't mentioned the dragon as Isaac would have had no reason to go over to Hope Barton.

"I do hope Abby is safe out there by herself. The Crabber is quite a large boat for one person to handle isn't it? Quite dangerous."

Hannah's mind was fixed on the following morning and

she thought for a moment that Isaac had somehow learned of their plan. She remembered with relief that Abby was supposed to be out fishing.

"It's easy enough to handle with one person Uncle – if you know what you're doing. The Crabber's not that big and it's stable."

"Good, good," Isaac said quietly. "We wouldn't want any misfortune to overtake her would we?"

"Maybe I could walk over with you tomorrow?"

"I'll be riding Autumn."

Isaac sounded indifferent to her company, but if she rode with him she might find a way to slow him down.

"I haven't been on a horse for ages. I'd like to go with you. It's never been something I like to do alone. Maybe we could ride over the moor and give Autumn a decent hack, she doesn't get as much exercise as she should."

Autumn was known to be Isaac's preferred mount and, although in theory anyone could ride any horse, most people avoided Autumn for fear of Isaac's disapproval.

"You could take Pepper I suppose."

Pepper was Autumn's stable mate, a gentle mare that Hannah had ridden before.

"What time were you thinking of setting off?"

"Ah, not too early, I have a few things I have to take care of first. Maybe we could meet at the stables at about ten. Would that suit you?"

Hannah cursed inwardly. If she had known Isaac wouldn't be leaving until that late she could have avoided riding to Hope Barton with him – and she had extended the time they would spend together by suggesting a circuitous route. It would sound odd if she pulled out now.

She thought about giving him a kiss on the cheek before she made her excuses and got away, but that would have been out of character and may only have roused his suspicions rather than placate them.

"I'll see you at ten Uncle. I need to get home to bed now."

"At ten then. And don't be late."

Hannah walked away, infuriated by his parting comment. She was never late for anything. It was he who would turn up for meetings when he felt like it, making everybody wait for the great and all-knowing Isaac to arrive.

Back in her cottage Hannah was too jittery to go to bed. She made a cup of camomile tea and sat on her sofa sipping at the steaming liquid. Everything was going to plan, but there were so many uncontrollable factors. Ethan was the most volatile, most worrying, or rather her relationship with Ethan and his attachment to Beth. Her stomach turned over when she thought of Simon. They had only met for one day and she already thought she knew him better than Ethan, had more of a connection and would maybe even leave the Island if he asked her to.

Hannah needed to sleep. Abby wouldn't be back for a couple of nights, maybe three. Simon wouldn't return for a few weeks and he might not even be on the Pride when it next visited Hope Island. That night Hannah kept waking from dreams where she was being pursued, but she never remembered from what or whom she was running away. Eventually she settled into a deep sleep and woke much later than planned.

Chapter 24

The sun was no longer on her bedroom window when Hannah woke, which meant she might already be late for her meeting with Isaac. She cursed as she rolled out of bed, rubbed the sleep from her eyes and tried to get them to focus on the wall clock that would strike so loud and persistently that it usually woke her by seven. It was the most reliable timepiece she had, even though it was over two centuries old. Fortunately it was not too late to catch up with Isaac. But she didn't have time to wash if she was going to make it to the stables on time.

Hannah fought her way into a fresh t-shirt and wriggled into a long, full skirt, in such a hurry that she popped a button and had to thread a belt through the waist loops. She grabbed socks and donned some old walking boots. Not the most attractive of outfits, but suitable for riding. It would have to do. She rushed out of the cottage, grabbing a hat from the hook on the back of the door to protect her from the sun and flies.

Hannah tried to calm her nerves by controlling her breathing as she slowed to a walk when approaching the quay. Martha was outside her stores, sitting on the step and drinking tea.

"You looked rushed my dear. Where are you off to?"

"I'm going over to Hope Barton with Isaac. You haven't seen him have you?"

"Last time I saw him was two hours ago, walking up out of the village. I haven't noticed him come back, but that doesn't mean he hasn't."

"Thanks Martha." If she hadn't seen Isaac return then he probably hadn't returned yet, not much escaped Martha's eyes or ears.

"What business has Isaac got with Ethan and Daniel? I suppose it's another piece of Daniel's work he's after?"

"Yes it is actually. How much do you know about them? Daniel's carvings I mean."

"I suspect they're more sought after than Isaac lets on. He wouldn't be so eager to take them away otherwise, but I don't know that for certain."

"I think you're probably right from what Beth has said. But I'd better get going, I don't want to miss him."

"Abby's gone fishing has she?" Martha winked at her and smiled. "I hope she catches something that she likes. Now, get on, and go find Isaac, we can talk later."

Hannah walked down to the quay and took the steeply rising lane at the end of it. The stables were in an old barn, barely a hundred yards up the hill. She walked in through the open doors and called out to the girl who worked there.

"Leah, are you here somewhere?"

"Over here." A head popped up over one of the stalls, Leah's tousled blonde hair almost looking like it was made from the straw she was spreading. "Isaac told me you were riding with him this morning – he said you wanted to take Pepper out."

"Yes, but has Isaac left already? Have I missed him?"

"No, not yet. I bumped into him at the top of the village earlier. He was charging off in the direction of the Manor."

Hannah saw Pepper in the stall opposite where Leah was working and walked over to her. She nuzzled at Hannah, looking for a gift, and when none was forthcoming she threw her head in the air and turned away.

"I should have brought her something."

"There are some carrots by the door. Martha dropped

them in when she cleared out the store."

Hannah walked back to the door and found a carrot that still looked fairly crisp and palatable. She took it back to Pepper who munched on it happily and forgave Hannah by rubbing her nose against her shirt.

"I heard Abby went out fishing last night in the Crabber." Leah said while kicking over the straw she had spread. "Not like her to go out at night – and alone."

"She's been out by herself before," Hannah said, although not entirely certain she had.

"I spoke to Sophia this morning when she returned and she didn't see her anywhere. She was quite concerned when I asked her."

"Maybe Abby was trying out some new spot."

Neither of them heard Isaac come into the barn and when he spoke Hannah started at the sound of his voice.

"I also heard she was still out there. Maybe we should organise a search if she doesn't reappear soon. It would be a tragedy if we lost her – and so soon after the Recorder's daughter met her fate."

"She might have sailed to the mainland," Hannah said, not sure if she should be pre-empting Abby and Beth's story. "She did mention it when we were all at the quay the other day."

Isaac frowned and shook his head. "I told her to wait until spring. She's too headstrong that girl." He looked thoughtful for a moment or two and spoke very quietly. "I do hope she doesn't meet with some misfortune over there."

Leah led Autumn out of her stall, already saddled and ready for Isaac. She walked her over to a wooden mounting block and held the reins out to him. He managed to get astride Autumn with surprising ease for such a large man. Autumn stood patiently while he adjusted his stirrups.

Hannah mounted Pepper and the two of them walked

their horses out onto the lane, not even having to duck as they moved through the huge barn doors. Hannah was about to take the track up past the village reservoir, but Isaac turned Autumn in the other direction, back towards the village.

"I thought we were going to go over the moor Uncle?"

"Maybe on the way back. I'm eager to see Daniel's carving."

They walked up through the village and onto the road between cultivated fields. Hannah wondered why she didn't take Pepper out more often as the view from her elevated position gave her a better idea of how far their harvest had advanced and what was left to pick, or ready to plough. When they were half way to Hope Barton, Hannah plucked up the courage to question Isaac.

"I wanted to ask you uncle, Simon said something about radios working again. Have you heard anything about it from the Recorder."

He didn't answer immediately and Hannah was about to rephrase the question when he finally spoke. "Gideon did say something about it. I wasn't paying that much attention to be honest."

"Simon said it's on every evening with news and information." Hannah's knowledge had actually come from Beth, but Isaac wasn't to know that.

"I can't see that it would be of any use to us on the Island, probably just reinforce the fear everyone has regarding the virus."

She thought of confronting him about that too, but his suspicions would only be raised and Hannah wanted stay at least one step ahead of him. They walked on with Hannah chatting about the crops and what changes they had planned for autumn plantings. Isaac had to stifle a yawn at one point and Hannah was reassured that he appeared relaxed, not ruminating about her earlier questions.

When they neared Hope Barton, Hannah could see Daniel in his usual place on the bench and was relieved that the Crabber was nowhere in sight. She slid easily off her horse and held Autumn's reins for Isaac while he dismounted, rather less elegantly without the aid of the block.

"The boy's gone," Daniel said as soon as they walked up to him.

The horses were happy to remain on the grass, grazing quietly in the gentle morning sunshine. Ethan appeared at the kitchen door with a towel in his hands.

"Don't worry about Dad, he's been imagining more than dragons recently."

Daniel turned his attention back to a clumpy piece of driftwood on his lap. He turned it over a couple of times and grunted.

"You've come for his latest piece I suppose?"

"As long as Daniel's happy for me to take it away," Isaac said.

"He won't mind. Do they sell easily on the mainland?"

"Easily?" Isaac mused. "Well there is some interest in them, largely as curios I think."

"Only I was wondering what sort of money we could get for them? It's not like they're part of the Island produce is it, and I might want to go over there some day myself. A little real money might be of use."

Isaac nodded as though he understood and sympathised with Ethan's request. "I'll talk to the Recorder next time he visits. I'm sure something could be arranged if that's what you want, but I don't expect the sums involved would be substantial."

Ethan saw Hannah looking at him as though she suspected him of something. He started to fold the towel on which he had been drying his hands.

"Anyway, I ought to see about the sheep. Are you two going to be here for a while, Dad's been a bit funny recently?" He glanced at Hannah, hoping she understood that she might need to prevent Isaac from questioning him.

"I'll make us some tea," Hannah said. "Would you like a mug Daniel?"

Daniel nodded without looking up from his wood and Ethan told Isaac that the dragon was in the kitchen, on a shelf above the sink. Hannah followed Isaac indoors, taking the towel from Ethan and mouthing a question as to whether the girls had got off okay. Ethan nodded curtly and walked away without saying anything else.

Hannah didn't need to worry about Isaac questioning Daniel – he was too engrossed in the carving he had found. It was one of the most intriguing pieces that had come from Daniel's imagination so far. The dragon had originally been wrapped around a rock, but Daniel had carved the rock into a child, now nestling in the protection of the dragon.

On their return trip, Hannah didn't mention going for a hack over the moorland, she had no desire to remain in Isaac's company any longer than was necessary. When they were approaching the village she told him that she might go up to the Manor. He made no objection and said he had other matters to attend to.

They parted company without Isaac trying to dissuade her and Hannah wondered if that was where he'd been earlier in the morning – tidying up the mess he had left in the study. Once out of sight she urged Pepper into a trot, eager to see if she was right.

When she arrived her suspicions were confirmed. All the books were back neatly on the shelves, as though nothing had been disturbed, but they weren't on the right shelves. Hannah had spent many hours there with her father and, although she hadn't read all of the books, she knew their positions in the same way she knew the paths on the Island – a detailed knowledge born from familiarity.

Hannah looked out of the window to make sure Isaac hadn't followed her and took the books off the special shelf to check the safe was still closed. There were horizontal scratches on the opening end of the panel and Hannah ran her nails down over them before pressing firmly on the other end. The panel swung out to reveal that a sharp object must have been used to pry it open, a knife probably.

She spun the dial a few times then carefully followed the sequence she had entered before. There was a satisfying click as the tumblers fell into place and the dial locked in position. Turning it firmly she held her breath as the door opened. With some relief she checked to make sure nothing was missing, but all was still there. Isaac had obviously found the safe, but not the combination.

After closing it and spinning the dial again, Hannah pushed the panel gently back into position and replaced the books, being careful not to change the order that Isaac had chosen, just in case he'd made a mental note of them.

She didn't know to what extreme Isaac would go to protect his chances of remaining Bailiff. Would he burn down the Manor to destroy those wills, especially now he knew they were almost certainly in the safe? Should she take the documents and hide them somewhere else, perhaps with Martha? Hannah was overwhelmed by everything that was happening and wanted to ask Abby's advise, but she wouldn't be back for at least a couple of days.

Hannah walked slowly upstairs, still trying to make up her mind on a course of action, but determined to take the radio back to her cottage. She wanted to see if she could get it to work. But the radio was no longer there. Isaac had beaten her to it.

189

Chapter 25

When Hannah came out of the Manor, Pepper was missing. She heard a whinny from the walled garden and found her there, happily munching on a variety of wild herbs.

"What are you doing in here you naughty girl?"

Pepper looked up and shook her head. Hannah walked her back out through the garden and into the lane before mounting and riding back to the village. She was wondering whether to mention to Isaac about the radio or let him think she hadn't noticed its removal.

Leah wasn't at the stables so Hannah loosened the girth strap on Pepper and brought over a bucket of water before removing her tack. Although she hadn't had to work too hard, Hannah still checked her hooves and hosed down her legs before letting her out in the paddock.

Walking back through the village, on her way to Martha's store, she decided not to confront Isaac. The more he thought he was still in control, the safer she and Abby would be.

"Hello. Anyone home?" Hannah called from the door.

"In the kitchen," Martha replied. "Now, what can I do for you? I'm guessing you don't need any more lemons now Abby's gone fishing." Martha's smile was just short of turning into a laugh and her eyes sparkled with glee.

"No, I just popped in to see if you'd found that radio you said you had hidden away somewhere. The one in the Manor seems to have disappeared."

"Disappeared you say? I think I can guess who made it vanish."

"So did you find it?"

She invited Hannah to follow her and set off up a narrow wooden staircase into one of the two lofts located at either end of the barn. For a woman who professed to be too old to go on a search party, she could be surprisingly nimble when she wanted to be. The lofts were where everything ended up that was of no immediate use. The storage system had grown organically over the years. Old wardrobes had been shelved out and spare doors and planks were supported by a seemingly random structure of scaffolding poles and timber frames. The density of the layer of dust, which lay over most items, was a clue to how long they had been there.

"Here it is," Martha said, pulling a cardboard box towards her and blowing a cloud of dust off the top.

She put it on a table and unfolded the lid of the box. It had once been sealed with a plastic tape, but the adhesive had dried over the years and fell from the cardboard like crinkled gray ribbons. Martha reached in and removed a radio that was not dissimilar to the one at the Manor, a solid maroon, plastic case with an inset cloth panel the colour of old straw. It looked almost new.

"Don't suppose anyone's taken it out of its box for the best part of ninety years – and it wouldn't have been new then I don't suppose. Are you sure they're broadcasting again?"

"That's the word Beth used," Hannah remembered. "Broadcasting."

"Well you'll need a plug," she said, holding up a lead with bared wires on the end. "It doesn't look like it was ever used. I've got some somewhere. Here, you carry the radio, my balance isn't so good going down these stairs."

Martha found a plug and put it in the box with the radio before tying it up with a length of string, reminding Hannah that she'd have the string, the box and the radio back once she didn't need them any more.

Returning home, Hannah looked around her living room, searching for a hiding place. There was nowhere that Isaac would not notice it. Her bedroom also proved inadequate to the task. She wouldn't it put past Isaac to let himself in and root around the whole cottage. Hannah didn't own a lot of clothes, so a rail and a few open shelves held most of her everyday possessions. Hope Barton was the best bet. With barns and a cluttered house, the radio could easily remain hidden and Isaac would never think of ransacking Daniel's farm.

Hannah wrapped an old sheet around the box, which still displayed the maker's name and a picture of the radio. She checked outside her door for anyone passing by, before setting off up the lane and out of the village. Once again she took the narrow coast path to avoid bumping into anyone working on the fields – feeling guilty that she wasn't there with them.

Daniel was sat outside on his bench when she arrived. Only Samson greeted her and even he walked more slowly because of the heat. The sun was almost at its zenith, but the temperature would be even higher by mid afternoon.

"Is Ethan around anywhere?"

"In his workshop, trying to mend the plough. He should have done it months ago in spring. He'll probably have to take it to the smithy."

She didn't want to argue with Daniel, he was probably right. She had known for some time that Ethan's heart had left the farm, but she had tried to ignore it, or pretend it was simply a phase.

"I'll go and find him."

Ethan's workshop was a ramshackle affair, timber framed and clad in a variety of salvaged materials. The roof was corrugated iron that had been patched wherever rust had eaten holes in it. Makeshift repairs had been made with whatever material came to hand. She had been in there when it rained on more than one occasion, positioning buckets and bowls to catch the drips that Ethan ignored.

He turned to her as soon as she slid through the partly opened door. He was sitting on the floor beside a plough, the furrow wheel was by his side and a spanner hung limp from his hand.

"I didn't know you were coming over," he said.

"Is it fixable?"

"Yes, but I'll need to take it to the forge. What's that you've brought with you?"

"A radio. I need to put a plug on the lead."

"Hand it over, I'll do that for you."

"I can wire a plug by myself thanks. It's just that I'd like to leave it here, I'm worried Isaac will find it if I keep it at my cottage."

"You think he'll snoop around?"

Hannah shrugged and Ethan raised his eyebrows in acknowledgement that they both thought the same, but neither wanted to speak ill of Isaac quite so directly.

"That's for what Beth was talking about," he said. "Those broadcasts. When are they on?"

"Evenings I think. I'm not sure what time."

"There's tools over there," he said, nodding towards his bench.

Hannah took the radio out of its box, examined the plug and selected a screwdriver. Ethan came over and leaned against the bench watching her.

"You've always been so bloody independent haven't you?"

"I've had to be," she said, focussing on the plug.

She bared the wires and fixed them into the plug, blew the dust out and reassembled it. Ethan put the radio back in its box and picked it up. Hannah wound up the lead into a coil and followed him to the house, the only place they could plug it in.

Even Daniel sensed something unusual was happening and followed the two of them into the kitchen. Hannah plugged the radio into one of only two wall sockets, but paused before she switched in on, half expecting an explosion of some sort. There was silence. Ethan reached across her and turned a knob marked 'VOL'. There was a small click and a scratching sound grew in the speaker panel.

Hannah turned the only other knob and the scratching changed pitch, disappeared completely and then returned several times. A thin red marker moved behind a screen inscribed with meaningless numbers.

"We must be too early. Beth said they broadcast in the evenings." Hannah looked at Ethan. "What time is it?"

"Don't know exactly," Ethan replied. "You know we don't use clocks round here."

"But you've got one in the other room."

"I only wind it up because Dad likes the chimes."

Hannah turned the dial back in the opposite direction, much slower this time, listening for anything between the noises.

"If we want to know what's happening on the mainland why don't we just go over there?" Ethan asked.

There was an obvious logic to his suggestion. Now they knew that the virus wasn't a significant problem there was nothing to stop them.

"We'd probably need money from what Beth said."

"I've got some of Dad's earlier carvings in the shed. We could take them over and sell them ourselves, not just leave it up to Isaac."

"Abby will tell us what it's like when she gets back. Maybe we could go over for a couple of nights."

"I don't want to go for a couple of nights, I want to travel, to explore, to see the world. We could take the Crabber, she can get us pretty much anywhere, maybe not across the oceans, but we could see so much."

"I can't just leave the Island to Isaac, I have a duty."

"Yeah, I keep forgetting – you're the Princess of Hope Island aren't you. You'll end up like Isaac – bitter and selfish. I don't want to stay here and watch you change into a version of that fat bastard."

"Is that really how you see me?"

"I don't know you Hannah, never have," Ethan said quietly. "I never asked to marry you, it was just assumed by everyone, including you. I always wanted to get away from this bloody island. But that's not going to happen with Dad here is it? I'm trapped forever."

She had never seen this side of him before, this resentment seething beneath the surface. She turned away before she said something she might regret, only pausing at the door to look back at him.

"I'll take care of Daniel if that's what you want. Just go if you have to."

Hannah walked across the yard and took a rough, narrow path that zigzagged up the cliff behind the farm, up to the wind turbines. Her heart was beating fast, not from the climb, but from anger and frustration. The regular, eerie noise of the turning blades gradually calmed her while she sat on the grass on the edge of the cliff.

From there she could see right across the Island, across the fields and moorland to the high ridge in the northwest. The warm breeze whipped her hair and blew it over her eyes. She turned into the wind to clear her hair from her face and in the other direction she could see the mainland, slightly blurred, indistinct, the place where Abby was right now. She missed her. She missed her sister, her friend. Abby would have explained what was happening, would have comforted her and made everything okay.

Below her, Daniel and Charlie were walking through the orchard, towards the beehives. She vowed she would take care of Daniel if Ethan ran away. Her father had liked Daniel, she remembered them talking about the land, the animals and the love they both shared for the Island. That was what mattered, not the mainland, not change, not progress back to the kind of world that had created this mess in the first place.

Hannah walked down the easier path, which looped back towards the orchard without passing the farm. She found Daniel sitting under an apple tree with Charlie at his side. She sat down beside them and scratched Charlie behind his ear.

"Something happened between you and Ethan?" Daniel asked without looking at her.

"Not really," Hannah sighed. "I think everything's as it always has been."

"He's always had dreams that boy, just like his mother did."

Charlie snuggled against her.

"You maybe need to let him run away, get it done with. He might return a different man."

"How much do you understand Daniel?"

"More some days than others Lass." Daniel laughed to himself.

"I always thought I loved Ethan. Maybe I only loved the idea of being in love."

"He lost his parents too, just like you did. I think that's what threw you two together."

"But you're still here."

Daniel sniffed. "Sometimes," he said quietly.

"We ought to get back to the farm, the sun's low now, it must be near supper time."

"The boy will be taking care of that."

"He's not here now, he's gone away."

"She wasn't a boy anyway was she? I'm not that daft."

They walked back to the farmhouse in silence, birds flashed through the orchard and the constant hum of bees at work followed them. Ethan was still playing with the dial on the radio, turning it so slowly that it looked like his fingers were frozen onto it. A scratchy, distant, voice came and went, then came back again slightly clearer.

"Who's that talking?" Daniel asked. "Where are they hiding?"

"It's a broadcast from the mainland," Ethan said without looking around. "I found it."

Daniel grumbled that he didn't want any part of it, claiming he was too old and that no good would come from someone speaking out of a box like that. "That was the madness that my grandfather used to tell me about. They had pictures too."

"The fever is gone. They called it the FBE7 virus," Ethan told Hannah. "They reckon the solar flares have almost finished too. They said this is the start of the rebirth of civilisation. We have to go Hannah. We have to be part of it."

"I think you might have to Ethan, but I think my place is here, on the Island."

"Well I'm going to find out for real, just as soon as I can get away from all this."

Chapter 26

After her argument with Ethan, Hannah avoided Hope Barton. She spent her days making a start on renovating the walled gardens at the Manor. Hannah enjoyed the physical labour and fell asleep each night fatigued and with a sense of having achieved something that she had wanted to do for some time.

On the third day she took a break from the Manor garden and joined the crews working in the fields. Hannah was aware of Isaac's reputation for remaining aloof and, after Ethan's accusations, she wanted to show everyone she was still willing to do her share of the work.

At lunchtime one of the younger girls ran back to the village to help Martha with lunch. It was only minutes later she reappeared, the girl pushing a handcart and Martha trailing behind, slightly out of breath, fanning herself with a large floppy hat. Martha must have already been on her way.

Their meal consisted of bread, cheese, pickles, cider and apple juice. They all stopped work and sat in the shade of an oak tree – one of whose branches stretched out so far that it had, by necessity, been propped up by a timber support.

There was the usual chatter and laughter about small things that were happening in the community, but Abby's unexplained departure had been the centre of gossip since the day she had left. Speculation was rife, with fears for her about the fever, and the promise she had always made to go and find a partner on the mainland.

Hannah was now included in the references to Abby's

sexuality, a change apparently made acceptable by the fact that Abby had left so abruptly – thus making the subject matter both unavoidable and public.

The same girl pushed the cart back to the village when they had finished, even though Martha could have managed the mostly downhill journey with the lighter load. The girl's return was quicker than anyone expected as she would often stay for a glass of lemonade with Martha and a slice of cake, but she was shouting to them only minutes later from the far edge of the fields.

"She's back, she's come back, Abby's back."

The girl was bombarded with questions, the whole crew crowding round her to catch the news, but she was out of breath and doubled up, panting.

"The Crabber's been spotted outside the harbour," she managed eventually.

"Is it coming in?" someone asked.

"Yes, but," the girl took another couple of deep breaths. "The wind's light and against her. She's having to tack really slowly."

"Hannah, you need to be there," a voice behind her urged.

"You can't leave her to Isaac," someone else added.

"You have to be with her. Go now, quickly."

Hannah didn't hesitate. She dropped the hoe she had been using and started running, pushing the ground back beneath her feet as hard and fast as she could. Tall weeds whipped at her ankles and a bramble snatched at her shirt. She ran over the fields and onto the lane that led through the village, she didn't slow down until she could see the harbour and Abby's boat approaching its mooring buoy.

"I see you heard." Isaac's distaste for Abby was evident to Hannah, even in those few words.

Hannah was now out of breath and leaned with straight

arms on the railings a few feet along from Isaac.

"I wonder what excuse she has this time," he said through half clenched teeth, as though ready to act as judge and jury on her disappearance for four days.

Hannah turned to look at him. Isaac was standing with his hands on his hips, feet apart, showing anger in every taught neck muscle.

"Abby's never done this before."

"Hmm, maybe not this, but she has often proved a problem in her obstinacy."

The rowboat, tied to the buoy after Abby left, had been retrieved by Sophia and she was now rowing out to pick Abby up. Even with Hannah's eyesight she could see that there were two people on the boat, but chose not to say anything until Isaac commented on it. This was one of the few occasions where being known for having poor distance vision proved an advantage.

"Who in heavens name does she have on there with her." Isaac muttered, not expecting an answer. "Do you know what's going on Hannah?"

"I have no more idea than you Uncle, but maybe she's made a friend on the mainland. She always said she would one day."

Isaac turned his head away from the boat to look at her for the first time since she'd arrived. He frowned, as though trying to determine whether Hannah was telling the truth or playing with him. She held his eyes and shrugged. The rowboat was gliding smoothly over the calm water, already nearing the quay. Isaac cupped his hands around his mouth and shouted.

"Have either of you been in contact with the fever?"

"There is no fever Uncle," Hannah said quietly. "Simon told me the truth."

Isaac didn't look at her. "You shouldn't believe everything

you hear from the Delanceys. They have their own agenda."

Sophia pulled the boat in close to the quay. It was high tide so the boat was almost level with Hannah, Isaac and the small crowd that had gathered to get the news first hand. Sophia passed a rope to Hannah, which she threaded through a metal ring set into the stone. Beth was avoiding Hannah's eyes and there was an awkward silence until Abby stepped off the boat and offered a hand to Beth to join her.

"Isaac, Hannah, this is Becky."

Isaac remained still, if anything he had managed to lean back, away from the new arrival – as if afraid of contact.

"And might I ask the purpose of your visit?" He turned to Abby without waiting for an answer. "And I'd also like an explanation for your unofficial borrowing of one our most valuable boats."

"It's not one of the most valuable boats Uncle," Hannah corrected.

"All of our boats are valuable."

"Yes, and they belong to everyone, so Abby didn't have to ask to use it."

"It was just a spur of the moment thing," Abby said. "I wanted to go to the mainland and find... well, it turns out I wanted to find Becky. I just didn't know who she was or what her name was at that time."

"Ridiculous," Isaac muttered. "What on earth do you mean?"

"I'm with Abby," Becky said.

"I can see that much," Isaac said impatiently.

Abby put an arm round Becky's shoulders and Becky slipped her arm round Abby's waist.

"She means she's with me Isaac. Just like I threatened I'd do so many times, I went to the mainland and found

201

someone who wants to be with me."

Hannah said it was nice to meet her and Becky freed her arm from Abby and shook hands with Hannah.

"Abby's told me all about you, about Hope Island too, it sounds amazing."

Isaac didn't make a move to take Becky's hand when offered and she withdrew it.

"So if you're from the mainland, might I ask who your parents are, what your surname is and what made you want to come here?"

"Hmm," Becky said, furrowed brows showing her serious contemplation of Isaac's questions. "I don't know. I don't really have one. Abby. In that order."

"How do not know who your parents are?" Isaac was turning an unattractive shade of red, his fists clenched and knuckles turning white in frustration.

"I'm an orphan. I was abandoned just after I was born."

Sophia had climbed up onto the quay behind them, she coughed to make her presence known and asked if they were engaged.

The two of them looked at each other and Abby responded. "Sort of, I suppose."

"We're in love," Becky said more positively.

"So you're going to live with each other?" Sophia asked, trying to determine how these things worked. Sophia hadn't had a boyfriend yet and Hannah realised they needed to have 'the chat' that her parents had obviously skipped.

"That's the plan," Abby said looking down at Becky and smiling.

"But your place only has one bedroom."

Sophia's sailing skills were legendary, but her grasp of relationships still had a way to go.

"Who is this then Abby?" Martha asked, having only just arrived at the quay.

"I'm Becky and you must be Martha, Abby told me about you too. She said you don't have anyone who knows about medicines here. I know something about herbs and tinctures and some basic first aid." Becky bit her lower lip. "Just stuff I've picked up helping here and there," she added quickly.

"Well, that's something you have in common with Abby," Isaac sneered.

"Not just that though. We love each other."

Hannah was not sure if this was all an act or if it was real. If it was an act they were very good at making it convincing and Hannah wondered for a moment if they actually were together. Abby's arm was round Becky's shoulder and she gave her a reassuring hug. It had to look like convincing for Isaac's benefit.

Martha leaned close to Hannah and whispered that it looked like everything had turned out rather well. Isaac muttered that he had better things to do.

"Martha, would you like to record this Becky whatever she's called in our logs." He turned back to Becky. "You must have a full name that you use on the mainland?"

"Rebekah Martini."

"Martha will record you as resident here... with Abby. We'll sort out everything else later."

As Isaac walked away and the crowd dispersed, Hannah asked Becky where that name came from.

"It was the name on an old bottle my mother had. It was the first thing that came to mind."

"And using Abby's mother's name?" Martha asked.

"That was my idea," Abby said. "I suggested it, I think my mum would have liked Becky."

"Well, welcome to the Island Becky," Martha smiled and gave her a hug.

"I didn't put the Crabber to bed," Abby said. "I ought to row back out and furl the sails properly and we have a few

203

things that need bringing ashore."

Sophia offered to give her hand.

"We'll wait for you at Martha's," Hannah said. "Maybe you could have a chat with Sophia while you're out there." She winked at Abby, who raised her eyebrows and mouthed 'why me'.

Hannah took Becky's arm and followed Martha up towards her storerooms. Martha offered to put the kettle on and find something to eat.

"You must be starving after your trip."

"Not at all, we brought some food back with us that you might like, different cheeses, spices, all sorts of stuff."

Once Martha was busy in her kitchen Hannah confronted Becky.

"What's going on? Aren't you two over-acting a bit, specially if you're going to break up in a few weeks time?"

"Why do you think I didn't want to marry Simon?"

"Because you didn't love him."

"I was never going to fall in love with a man."

Hannah was about to say something else but she stopped with her mouth half open.

"Oh my god, I'm such an idiot. Why didn't you say something? And are you and Abby really together then, like properly together, as a couple?"

"We do like each other – a lot."

Martha came back with three mugs, one without a handle.

"Isaac is going be suspicious," she said. "You and Abby are going to have to be very careful what you say."

Martha opened a drawer under her table and slid out a large book. She flicked through it until she came to a page with lists of names and notes next to them.

"Now, Becky, how do you spell Martini?"

Martha carefully inscribed Becky's name in the left hand

column and wrote 'herbalist' next to it.

"Well that's it. You know how we organise things here?"

"Sort of. I'd like to see Daniel again. I feel bad about the way I muddled him up with the whole boy and girl thing."

"He'd like to see you again," Hannah said. "He's was more talkative when you were there. I think you had a really positive influence on him."

"I saw that Daniel and Ethan didn't talk much, other than what was absolutely necessary, farm stuff, nothing else. And I have to sort things out with Ethan too. I think he hoped there was more to us than there was."

"Let's leave that until tomorrow," Martha said. "You two have been on a bit of journey in more ways than one. It's your first time in Newport of course, you must be a little curious about the village. And you should take time to settle into Abby's cottage."

"Someone mention my name?" Abby said, smiling broadly.

Chapter 27

Abby said she'd unloaded the Crabber, but couldn't carry everything so she had left it all on the quay. She wondered if they could borrow Martha's handcart to move it. "I don't know how we brought quite so much back with us in just one trip," she said.

"I'm not taking the blame for that," Becky laughed. "You wanted to buy everything you hadn't seen or tasted before. It was only my sense of restraint that stopped you buying enough to capsize the boat."

"But there is so much we never get here. There's some runny cheese that is amazing Hannah, you have got to try it, it smells like wet wool but tastes beautiful."

"Hmm, I might pass on that for the time being."

"We were going to leave all the food with Martha," Becky said. "So everyone can taste it if they want to."

"Take the cart," Martha said. "But I'm not sure I like the sound of that cheese smelling out my store room."

Abby and Becky wheeled the cart out into the lane and set off back to the quay to load it.

"They really seem like a couple don't they," Hannah said after they'd left.

"Maybe they are. Stranger things have happened. And I would be glad to see Abby settled, she's always had something missing in her life and maybe Becky will fill that gap."

Hannah flipped back through the record book, while it was still out on the table. Martha tidied up the mugs and fussed about in the kitchen. Most of the book was a diary of island events, but the pages nearer the back, where Martha had noted Becky's arrival, showed information on each of the Island's inhabitants. Their birth dates, skills, marriages and of course their deaths, were all recorded for the last ninety years.

"What does this say opposite Abby's name?" she called to Martha. "It doesn't make sense."

"Ah, Pater eius fuit ballivus – if I remember correctly."

"What does that mean?"

Martha walked back from the kitchen, stood close to Hannah and put an arm across her shoulders.

"It's Latin, a language I learned when I was young and your father used for his plants. It was another of his ideas to record Abby's entry like that."

"Why did he use a foreign language?"

"A dead language to be accurate. Plant names are better described in Latin, it's more precise."

"So, what does it mean?" Hannah asked, running her finger along the line of writing and repeating it.

"It says 'Her father was the Bailiff'. Jacob wanted it on record."

The handcart rattled on the stones outside the store and they heard Abby laughing with Becky and warning her that something would fall off if she didn't grab it quickly. They unloaded the food items for Martha, who couldn't stop herself from trying the smelly cheese.

"My heavens," Martha spluttered, spitting the small piece of cheese back into her hand. "What is wrong with you Abby, nobody wants to eat something that tastes like that."

Martha rushed back to the kitchen and they heard her washing her mouth out with water and spitting it into the sink. When she returned she was surprised to see Hannah tasting the cheese and agreeing with Abby.

"You're mad, the lot of you," Martha said. "It tastes like unwashed socks."

"Well, we can be sure you won't eat it all yourself then," Abby teased.

Martha shooed them out of the door, telling them she had better things to do than poison herself with their foreign food.

"Let me have the cart back when you're done, I'll need it tomorrow."

Becky said she wanted to see as much of the Island as she could and as soon as possible.

"I'd really like to see where that girl's boat washed up, the one who drowned so horribly."

"Very funny," Hannah replied. "But don't go joking about things like that in public, you never know who might be listening."

Becky pulled her finger and thumb across her lips and the other two stared at her, puzzled by the gesture.

"I won't utter another word," she said.

It was still only mid afternoon with several hours of daylight left, so they were in no hurry. They took the handcart to Abby's tiny cottage. Even Canary Cottage looked sumptuous in comparison. Several slates had slipped on the roof, the windows were covered in dust, inside and out, and a spider had spun a near perfect web across the door.

"Yes, well," Abby sounded awkward and embarrassed. "I'm still living in the hut at the moment, more convenient for looking after the stock and checking the water channels."

"It doesn't look like it's been lived in for years," Becky said, trying to peer through a window.

Hannah knew what a mess there would be inside. Abby was a beautiful person and would help anyone, but was a total shambles when it came to tidying up or cleaning her cottage. In complete contrast, her hut on the moorland was immaculate. Her work tools would be kept spotlessly clean and hanging in their rightful place in a small lean-to, her bed would be made every morning and fresh herbs hung from hooks outside to dry in the summer sun. Abby didn't bother with many possessions up there so there wasn't that much to keep tidy. The cottage in the village was where she left all her rubbish, only to be sorted out in autumn.

"Needs a bit of a spring clean," Abby mumbled. "As I said, I've not spent any time here recently."

"Good job," Becky said and turned smiling at Abby. "If you had been you'd probably have come down with some new and untreatable disease."

"Very funny," Abby sneered and then broke into laughter with Becky.

"Of course you know a lot about herbs I suppose?" Hannah asked to distract Becky from the cottage and give Abby a chance to at least clear some floor space before they went in.

"I know a little."

"Maybe you could help me up at the Manor. I want to restore the old physic garden. I don't even know what half the plants are, or what they're for."

"I'm not an expert, but I'd be happy to help if I can."

"My parents' books are still there, in their study, there are loads on herbs and medicines. I've skimmed through them, but not read many of them properly."

Abby stuck her head out of the door and said they could come in now if they wanted. Hannah stood aside for Becky to go first.

"Sorry, it's not very big, but at least it's warm in the winter."

The stove was in a corner of the room, not much more than a firebox with a single cooking plate on top of it. A sofa was the only seating, facing the fire, a small table next to it.

Unworn patches on the underside of the sofa's arms hinted at a once bright geometric patterned material, but most was now threadbare, half covered by a dark green woollen blanket. One wall was decorated with a floral paper that must have predated Martha. The other three walls had at one time been cream, or maybe even white.

"It's cosy," Becky said cautiously.

"It will look better when I've had a chance to tidy up." Abby surreptitiously used her toe to nudge an old pullover out of sight behind the sofa.

"It's not very nice in here," she admitted. "I don't use it during the summer and haven't got round to... well, anything really."

"Living out on the moorland sounds really romantic," Becky said. "Watching the sun go down every night, nothing but birds to wake you in the morning."

"Well, there's no toilet and no running water, so I'm not sure it's quite as 'romantic' as I may have made it sound."

Hannah intervened. She didn't want their great romance, if it was that, to falter on the hurdle of Abby's cottage. She thought it better to get them out of there and distract Becky while they made alternative plans for accommodation.

"I was asking Becky about the walled garden at the Manor, whether she could give me some advice on the plants."

"I'd love to see it. It's where your mother worked wasn't it Abby?"

"Both our mothers," Abby said.

"And our father," Hannah added, smiling at Abby.

They left the cart outside Abby's cottage and walked up to the Manor. The heat of the afternoon had eased a little and the breeze had veered and freshened. The wind must have stirred the sea, causing breakers to scatter spray on the rocks because the air carried a faint hint of ozone as it swept across the fields. The path to the Manor took them higher and they could see white horses on the crests of waves blowing in from the south. Hannah was glad they arrived before the weather had changed.

"There are a few other empty houses," Hannah said. "But to be honest, they're not in much better condition than Abby's. I'm sure we can get a party together to patch it up before winter, once the harvest is in and the autumn ploughing's done."

They walked on in silence knowing that it would be some months before the autumn tasks were done and people had more free time.

"Well, that's the Manor," Hannah said as it came into view round the last bend in the lane.

Becky ran ahead, bursting through the gate, which clattered shut behind her. She stood on the overgrown lawn staring out across the fields to the sea beyond.

"Why don't you live here if it's empty? The views are amazing."

"It's too big for one person, and there are too many memories, that's why I moved out after my parents died." She stood next to Becky sharing the view while Abby lingered at the gate watching them. "And I couldn't stand living with the echoes my previous life."

"It needs children doesn't it? A family, lots of noise."

"It used to be like that when I was young. My parents, Abby, her mother Rebecca, we all spent so much time right here, on this lawn – and in the walled garden."

Abby caught up with them as they entered the physic garden through a stone arch in the wall. Becky identified plants that Hannah would have missed – her knowledge greater than she claimed. Some of the names were familiar to Hannah, but some were new. Becky rattled them off as they walked around the outer path. Chamomile, feverfew, goldenseal, milk thistle, she kept enthusing over the diversity of the planting and wondered how they had come to collect so many species.

"My great-grandfather started it," Hannah said. "The rest of the family simply kept it going."

Inside the Manor Becky stood in the hall and spun around slowly, looking up at the carved, dark, panelled ceiling that imposed its quiet, cool presence, even on a bright day.

"My father said it was a beautiful house."

"Do you mean Mister Martini?" Abby joked.

"It was the first name that came to me," Becky replied grumpily. "Your uncle would have found it strange if I'd spent ages trying to think what my name was."

She realised that Abby was teasing her and pulled a face. Hannah suddenly realised the solution to their housing crisis.

"Why don't you two move in with me for now. I can sleep on the sofa and you can have my room. It would be fun living together."

"We couldn't," Becky said, but looked at Abby for approval.

"Well you can't live in Abby's place, it's a tip."

"Thank you," Abby said sarcastically.

"You know what I mean."

"Or I suppose I could move back in here, I've got to sometime. That way I could keep an eye on the place, guard it against Isaac. You two can have Canary Cottage. I won't need it."

"You'll have to move your stuff up here first," Abby said. "You can't just camp out tonight."

"We could do that tomorrow," Hannah said enthusiastically, warming to the idea. "Tonight we can share – unless I'll be in the way?"

"It's a wonderful offer," Becky said. "And of course you won't be in the way, but why did you say you need to keep an eye on the Manor?"

Hannah told her about the wills and safe. She showed her how to find it, how the secret panel worked and the marks that Isaac must have left in the wood.

"My father has a safe like that."

Becky turned her attention to the books lining the walls and away from the safe and its contents, she found several on herbs and medicines. Opening one of them, she pointed out some of the plants in the garden.

"People on the mainland die of infections because antibiotics are so expensive and not everyone can afford them. My father controls the imports and taxes them, although the free hospital do make their own. Simon probably knows where they come from and the real cost. My father wants to make a profit out of everything – including me."

Becky found a section in one book on how to make penicillin. She showed it to Hannah, but said they would need a microscope to identify the right bacilli and lots of equipment and even a sterile room.

"How do you know all this?" Hannah asked.

"From the hospital. I helped, but really I just followed instructions."

"Could you make it here if you had the right equipment?"

"I don't know, maybe, but if you get it wrong it can do as much harm as good."

"Are all those things you would need available on the mainland? The equipment, the microscope?"

"Sure, if you have money," Becky said. "And I do have money. Abby didn't spend it all on cheese."

Chapter 28

After Hannah had given Becky a tour of the house the three girls walked further up the lane towards the small village reservoir. The only other building they passed was the mill. Nobody slept there permanently, only when there was grain to be ground, but Peter was there that day. He was repairing the millrace several feet above the path and called down to them.

"Hello." All three looked up to see him balancing astride the race. "You must be Becky, welcome to Hope Island."

"How did you hear about Becky?" Hannah called. "She's only been here an hour or two."

"It's a small island. You know how it is. Anyway, it's nice to see a new face, I hope you'll stay."

"Oh I will." She cuddled into Abby, holding her arm and looked up at her. "I know I will."

"Do you need any help Peter?" Abby asked.

"No, I'm okay, I've got it all under control. But when we start milling I could do with a spare pair of hands or maybe two pairs if you're offering."

"We can help," Becky said.

"Me too," Hannah added. "I'm moving back into the Manor tomorrow so I'll be close by. Call for me when you're passing."

Peter said he would, but not for a few days yet.

It was only a short walk up to the village reservoir and when they arrived the three girls sat on the grass on the high side of the water. They had a view out over the fields of vegetables in one direction and towards the mainland in the other. Abby promised to take Becky on a complete tour of the Island the next day.

"Are you okay with heights?" Abby asked.

"Yes, no problem. Why?"

"The path on the seaward side of the ridge is pretty narrow and there are some sheer drops, but you will get great views from there and it leads round to Spear Head and the Spit where we 'found' your dinghy."

"What's going to happen to it?"

"Your father didn't claim it, so I don't know. I guess it belongs to the Island now."

Hannah said they ought to go and sort out everything they had left with Martha. They made their way back down to the village, picked up the handcart and unloaded it at Hannah's cottage. They had left the food at the store, so it was mainly the clothes Becky had insisted on buying. She said it would look odd to only have what she had travelled in. She had also persuaded Abby to buy new trousers, tops and even a dress. Abby was still embarrassed at having such luxury items, and said they were all far too new for her to work in.

To get away from the teasing she offered to pop down to see Martha and prise some cider off her for a celebratory first night party for Becky being on Hope Island – officially.

"None for me," Hannah said quickly. "I've lost the taste for it ever since that night at the Manor. I'll stick to water."

By the time Abby returned there was cheese, pickles, jam and bread scavenged from Hannah's cupboards, all laid out on a small table. Becky had even found some serviettes that Hannah had rescued from the Manor but never used. Hannah had taken them because they had been embroidered in each corner by her grandmother with leaves and flowers of medicinal herbs.

They ate and chatted late into the evening, filling Becky

in on as much of the Island history as they could. Hannah told Becky how her great-grandfather owned most of the farmland and a small golf course. And that it was he who had rented out the original farm and bought the Manor. As the waters rose and created an island, Hope Barton and all the land surrounding it became Hope Island.

Becky was fascinated and told them legends about the Island that circulated on the mainland. She said that there was supposed to be buried treasure here, but that anyone who came to look for it would succumb to the fever – the Islanders being immune. That the Island was also armed and fortified and those who survived the fever were kept to work as slaves or put to death with ancient weapons. She said that nobody really believed the stories, but everyone feared there might be some truth in them.

Abby yawned and announced that it had been a long day and she needed to get some sleep. Hannah was still turning ideas over in her head and wondering which rumours and myths might have some truth behind them. She needed to face up to her responsibilities and if that didn't suit Ethan, then maybe they weren't destined to be together after all.

Either Abby or Becky was soon snoring upstairs. Hannah was dozing, still dressed, when she woke to the smell of something burning.

"Abby?" she mumbled.

The smell was sharp, acrid, not at all like something cooking, burnt or not. She knew Abby and Becky had taken a candle upstairs with them as Hannah didn't have any electricity in her bedroom, but it couldn't be that, Abby knew to be careful.

Hannah struggled off the sofa, disorientated and confused. The smoke was coming from the kitchen. She pulled the curtain back, that screened it from the rest of the cottage and a great cloud of dark smoke swept towards her, stinging her eyes and making her grasp the newel post on the end of the stairs. She coughed and called out.

"Abby. Becky. Wake up. There's a fire."

Hannah staggered up the first two steps, covering her face, her eyes squinted.

"Quick," she shouted. "We need to get out."

"What's happening?" Becky replied, the first to respond.

By the time Becky had stumbled out onto the landing, competing clouds of smoke were tumbling over each other, climbing the stairs and threatening to engulf them.

"The bathroom." Hannah coughed and opened the door, dragging Becky in by her hand.

Abby followed them, now fully awake, and with an armful of clothes. She pushed a towel against the gap where the door didn't quite meet the floor.

"Open the window," she said. "Get Becky out."

Hannah pushed Becky onto the windowsill. "The shed roof is just below us, only a few feet. You can slide down it and drop to the ground."

Hannah was next, pushed ahead by Abby because she was coughing from the smoke she'd already inhaled. Hannah didn't argue. She landed in the garden, half caught by Becky. Abby slid off the roof moments later, clothes scattering around them.

"What happened?" Abby asked, struggling into a pair of jeans.

"I don't know," Hannah said. "I woke up and smelled smoke coming from the kitchen."

"But we didn't cook anything and there were no candles in there when we went to bed," Becky said. "I took the only one upstairs."

Smoke was now seeping out through the gaps between the roof slates and a large dark cloud billowed through an open bedroom window. All three of them backed towards the fence between the garden and a narrow communal path behind the row of cottages.

"We need to raise the alarm," Abby said. "You go down, we'll go up."

The only way to get to the front of the cottage was either by taking the path around the end of an old warehouse and out onto the top of the lane or following it down to the quay. Both routes were about the same distance.

Hannah set off at a run, still coughing, but not slowing down. Stones bit into her bare feet but she ignored them. She was shouting, trying to raise help to tackle the fire. People tumbled out of cottage doors in the lane to see what the commotion was about. By the time Hannah made it to the front of Canary Cottage there were already a group trying to form a bucket chain – even though Hannah couldn't see any flames. Peter came out of her front door, a wet cloth draped over his head. Billows of dark swirling smoke followed him.

"It's okay Peter, don't go back in," she heard Abby shout. "We're out, we're safe. All three of us."

"I can't see anything in there," he said. "The smoke's too thick. I couldn't breathe."

He bent over, coughed and retched, then straightened up.

"Where's Hannah," he asked, seeing only Abby and Becky.

"I'm here. I'm fine."

Someone threw a bucket of water as far as they could through the front door, but it made little difference.

"Don't take any risks. Drench the adjoining roofs," came a loud authoritative voice. It was Isaac, standing next to the line of people with an assortment of buckets and bowls. "We don't want to allow the fire to spread."

"We're safe Isaac," Abby shouted at him. "We're all safe, all three of us."

The smoke was reducing in volume and the immediate danger of the fire taking hold and spreading to neighbouring properties seemed to be over.

Abby moved behind Isaac, who had approached Hannah. She was unscathed and safe next to Peter.

"Good job Hannah was sleeping downstairs and woke us all. I can't imagine what might have happened if she hadn't been there."

Becky was next to her, looking down at one of Isaac's hands and frowning.

"Have you hurt yourself?" she asked, seeing a piece of cloth wrapped around his fingers.

"Oh that, nothing to worry about," Isaac said hurriedly and thrust his hand into his pocket to hide it. "Just a bit of a burn I must have got it while helping out here."

"Would you like me to look at it for you. If it's serious you should run cold water over it for a while to prevent further skin damage. I did have some aloe vera but I think it might have been lost in the fire."

"Don't worry about me my dear, I'll be fine."

Isaac moved away from them and turned to address the crowd.

"We'll assess the extent of the damage in the morning. Thank you for turning out and especially whoever it was who raised the alarm so promptly. You probably saved three lives tonight."

"That was odd," Hannah said. "It's not like Isaac to offer his thanks so readily."

"He has a burn on his fingers," said Becky quietly. "I noticed it before he hid his hand in his pocket."

"He probably picked that up here," Peter offered.

"I haven't seen anyone else with burns," Abby said. "Not even you Peter, and you were inside the cottage."

"It was mostly smoke by the look of it," Peter said,

frowning. "I don't know what it was that was burning but you could hardly breathe as soon as it hit your face."

A new voice cut in from behind Peter.

"That was rubber burning," Ethan said.

"What are you doing here?" Hannah asked, surprised that he'd arrived all the way from Hope Barton so quickly.

"Just happened to be out walking, couldn't sleep. And it's rubber that you can smell, I recognise it from when we burned some old rubbish on the farm. Makes you choke something rotten if you breathe it in."

"I don't think I had anything made of rubber in my kitchen."

"Then someone put it there," Ethan said, his voice flat and unemotional.

"But why?"

"I don't know the answer to that, but I doubt it was by accident."

A silence fell over the group. Nobody wanted to voice the thought that the fire might have been started on purpose. If it had been, Hannah knew there could only be one reason and Ethan obviously thought the same.

"You three need somewhere safe to stay tonight Hannah. Might be best if you come back with me to the farm. Our dogs will see off anyone who comes sneaking around. And it's a long way to walk for some people."

They all knew who he was referring to and nobody contradicted him.

"Sounds like a good idea," Peter said. "I'll stay and make sure the cottage is safe, although I can't see you moving back in anytime soon."

Hannah thanked Peter and, in a subdued mood, the four of them started the walk back to Hope Barton. Nobody felt like chatting and Hannah was suddenly so tired that every step became an effort and her mind spun with a myriad of thoughts. None of them had managed to rescue shoes and when they got to the farm all three girls washed feet and faces and huddled together in the big iron bed in the end bedroom, safe and secure in each other's company.

Chapter 29

The next morning Hannah woke wondering if it had all been a bad dream, but she could feel a warm back against hers in the bed. She didn't turn round to find out if it was Abby or Becky, but slid her legs out from under the covers, lifting them carefully so as not to disturb either of them. She picked up her clothes and tiptoed across the floor, only releasing the breath she had been holding when she closed the bedroom door quietly behind her. The clothes she had been wearing the night before reeked of smoke and brought the fear of the fire back to her.

In the bathroom Hannah stared at her reflection, smudges of grey still on one cheek and on her forehead. She had washed the worst off when they got back to Hope Barton, but there had only been candle light to see by and the morning sun brought back the reality of how close they all been to dying.

Hannah scrubbed her face and hands hard, trying to cleanse herself not only of soot and smoke, but the desire to scream. She had no other clothes with her so she pulled on the shorts and shirt she had been wearing, realising that she wouldn't even have any fresh clothes at the cottage as everything would have been caught by that smoke. Ethan was in the kitchen when she went down.

"Morning, do you want tea, I've just boiled the kettle?"

Hannah nodded. She didn't know where her and Ethan stood any longer, but he was completely at ease, as if nothing had changed between them. Abby appeared before the kettle had come to the boil so any discussion over her and

Ethan's future had to be suspended. She had a pinch of her t-shirt between finger and thumb and was sniffing at it.

"I've left Becky sleeping, but we ought to get back and see what state your place is in."

"You're together then," Ethan stared at Abby. "You and her. It's true what people are saying?"

"Yes, we're together, for now. Is that okay with you?"

"Doesn't make any difference to me," Ethan sniffed. "You're welcome to stay here, the two of you. Can't see Becky, it is Becky now isn't it, wanting to live in your hut up on the moor."

"Thanks. We'll see what Becky says, but I know she likes this place, and Daniel. After last night I think she could do with staying somewhere she feels safe. Actually, I think we all could. So thank you, and yes."

"Well we've only got that one spare room, I'm not bunking up with Dad."

Hannah said she was going to go back and stay at the Manor.

"I'm not sure you'll be safe there alone," Abby said.

"Why not," Ethan looked puzzled. "Nobody's going to burn down the Manor."

Becky came into the room, dressed but still rubbing her eyes and yawning. She walked over to where Abby was sitting and put her arms round her neck from behind, kissing her head.

"Why didn't you wake me?"

"I only just got up. We've not had breakfast yet."

"I'll make it," Becky said and opened Ethan's fridge to see what was in there.

"I'm away for four days and look at the state of this kitchen," she said. She turned at the sound of the door opening and saw Daniel framed against the light of a new day.

"I see the girl's back," Daniel said, without taking his eye's off Becky. "What are you called now?"

"Becky," she said and walked over to give Daniel a hug.

"You stink of smoke girl. You all do. Ethan told me what happened last night. Thought you would have been more careful with candles lass."

He was looking at Hannah who insisted they had all been careful.

"From what I hear you need to take care. Bad luck comes in threes they used to say."

Ethan made an excuse that he had to check the cows and Hannah got up to help Becky with the food. They talked about how the fire might have started, but it made no sense to any of them. Hannah said she would walk back to the village after breakfast to see what state the cottage was in. Abby apologised that she would have gone with her but had to check the filters up at the main reservoir today. Becky offered to stay with Daniel and said that she would sort out the kitchen.

"Don't stay at the Manor by yourself Hannah, you could sleep at Martha's until this is all sorted," Abby suggested.

She sounded so serious that Hannah agreed and found she was relieved to follow Abby's advice, the prospect of being alone at night filled her with trepidation.

"Some people are ruthless," Daniel muttered. "That Isaac's one of them. I've never trusted that fat scoundrel, he terrorised us as kids."

Daniel wandered outside with a mug of tea in his hand before anyone could ask him why he had mentioned Isaac, not that the name had been far from Abby's lips. Before anyone could comment, Daniel's voice came back through the open door.

"Now you're back maid, you going to help me with the bees?"

They all agreed to meet back at the farm after lunch. Hannah said she would try to find some spare clothes and shoes for them all at Martha's and Abby said she'd got a change up at the hut, so she was okay.

The walk back to Newport cleared Hannah's head. The wind had turned and freshened, signalling that the fierce heat of summer had passed its peak.

The island had been Hannah's whole life, her playground and her place of work. Now it had changed. The stability she had taken for granted had now been disrupted by Isaac, by Ethan, and even by Simon. She didn't know whether Simon would return as promised or had he simply forgotten her and Hope Island as soon as the Pride pulled out of Newport harbour.

When she arrived at her cottage the door was open, a cart was in the lane with two chairs and her table already loaded on it. She could hear the sound of people inside. Were they emptying her cottage in the belief that she wouldn't want to move back in? She stepped over the threshold and called out.

"Hello, who's here?"

Peter came out from her kitchen, his hands and face smudged with soot.

"I thought I'd get a couple of people to start clearing up the mess, I didn't know when you would surface again."

"Has the fire done a lot of damage?"

"Only smoke damage. It looks like something caught alight just inside the back door, on the floor, it looks like rubber of some sort? Did you leave some old boots there?"

"No, nothing like that. Are you sure it was rubber?"

"Come and look for yourself."

Peter showed her a black, melted pool of something no longer identifiable. He pointed out a larger patch, nearer the door, where the floor was scorched.

"It's like a liquid caught fire and then burned whatever was just inside the door."

"I didn't have anything like that in the kitchen, just some cooking oil."

Hannah turned round to check a bottle on the work surface. It was still there, still half full, but it too was now covered in a layer of soot. She picked it up by the neck with finger and thumb and showed it to Peter.

"Did you have any paraffin, for a lamp maybe, left it burning by mistake?"

"I used to have a lamp, but I used it so rarely I let Abby have it for her hut. I don't have any paraffin anywhere."

"Well, it doesn't look like an accident to me. It looks almost like someone did it on purpose, but who would want to burn your cottage down?" Peter frowned and added slowly, as though exploring the idea as he said it. "Unless it wasn't you but Abby or Becky they were after?"

Hannah wanted to mention Isaac, to see how much he knew or had guessed, but held herself in check for the moment. She needed to talk to Martha first.

"You'll need somewhere to stay for the next few nights, or probably weeks. It's going to take time to clean this place up, but as it is mainly smoke damage, there doesn't appear to be anything actually burnt."

"I was going to ask Martha if I could stay with her."

"You come of age soon don't you? Then you'll take over from Isaac?"

"Yes. I suppose so." Hannah wasn't sure about anything anymore.

'Well, take care, you can always stay with me if you want to, but I imagine you'll be moving back into the Manor sometime?"

Hannah didn't want to confirm or deny Peter's guess. She went over to the sofa, a bitter aroma wafting from the blankets as she lifted them. Underneath the pillow was the brown paper parcel Becky had brought her back from the mainland. She hoped that the wrapping had protected the precious contents.

Taking it outside she set it down on the end of the cart and untied the string. The paper was dusted gray around one end and smelled of smoke, but inside her new journal and four pencils were all untouched. She flipped through the pages. They were still clean and unsullied, although the smell of burning lingered even on them. Hannah decided it would remind her to be cautious in the future. Peter had come out to join her.

"What's that?"

"Something Becky gave me."

"A book?"

"A blank journal."

"I'll organise someone to drop your clothes and curtains down to Martha's. I'm sure they just need a good wash."

"Thanks Peter. I wish we knew how the fire started."

"I've been thinking about that too and I don't think it was an accident."

"Really?"

"But I doubt we will ever know for certain. It's bad that something like this could happen, that it could be one of us."

"I think I know who it might have been."

"We're probably thinking of the same person, but how would we ever prove it?"

Hannah sighed and said she had no idea, but that she planned to get everything out in the open, which might make it less likely to happen again. Peter asked what she was going to do. She said he'd hear at the same time as everyone else, but if he thought about it he might guess. Peter laughed and said he could wait, but for her to take care in the meantime and to come to him if she needed any help. She promised she would and said she was going to see Martha and warn her that she was acquiring a lodger.

Martha was pottering about in her kitchen when Hannah arrived a few minutes later. The first thing she did after hugging Hannah and asking if she was all right was to push the kettle onto the hot side of the stove.

"Now," she said firmly. "You're going to be staying here for the next few weeks where I can keep an eye on you. There's already a rumour going round about how that fire started. I don't think Isaac will dare do anything else, but best be careful."

"I'm going to restore the cottage."

"Well, there's plenty that will lend you a hand, but it will take a bit of effort. I reckon a good clean, a fresh coat of lime wash and it will be back to normal from what I hear."

"My birthday is only a few weeks away. I'm thinking about announcing that Abby and I will be joint Bailiffs from that day. Isaac will know he's lost then."

"That will certainly annoy him, but I'm not so sure it will stop him."

"I'm going to write it all down, like my father did, so there's a record of everything."

Hannah showed her the present Becky had brought back from the mainland. Martha examined the book, smelled it and wrinkled her nose.

"That lingering smell might not be a bad thing - it will remind you to be careful."

"It will, but I hate the idea of having to lock doors all the time." Hannah sighed, closed the journal and turned to look at Martha, to see if her eyes betrayed any secret thoughts she had. "My father's journal has a map drawn in it, at least that's what we think it is. There's a cave submerged in the reservoir and we believe there might be something hidden there."

"There were always rumours my dear, but I don't remember anything about a cave under the reservoir. Isaac would have drained it if he'd known. He had those others sealed up and only he has the keys to get in."

"I might dive there again, take another look. If I do it late in the afternoon the sun should be shining on that side, I might be able to see into the cave more easily."

"Take someone you trust, Peter or Abby, or both of them. I don't like the idea of you being alone anywhere right now."

"I will, I promise. Now what about that tea, the kettle's singing."

Chapter 30

Hannah walked back to Hope Barton later that day to see how Abby and Becky were getting on. She took the coast path, not wanting to bump into anyone on the fields and have to discuss the fire and its possible cause. A sharp breeze was blowing in from the east, carrying a fine spray from the larger waves when they broke and fragmented on the rocks.

The end of summer was a welcome time for Hannah and almost everyone on Hope Island. With the autumn solstice, apple harvest and Mabon it was a satisfying time of the year. The fields would be almost cleared, the storerooms full and they would honour the changing season when night once again outwitted day.

Daniel was in his customary place in front of the farmhouse with Charlie at his side. He wasn't working on a carving, simply sitting there, with a mug in his hand, enjoying the afternoon sun.

"Hi Hannah," Becky said from the kitchen door. "Perfect timing, can I pour you a tea, I just made a brew?"

"I could probably drink the whole pot, I think it must be the after effect of the smoke."

They stood in the kitchen, the sun was low enough to flood through the window and cast the room into sharp contrasts of light and shade. Decades of scratches on the kitchen table were thrown into relief and dust motes floated aimlessly in shafts of light.

"Where's Abby?"

"She went back up to the reservoir. There's a lot of

blanket weed to be cleared, she said she'd be back in an hour or two."

"How is it working out here?"

"It's okay, it sort of feels like home to me, and I don't think Abby really wants to live in the village. The only problem is she and Ethan are a bit edgy together."

"They always were, even when we were kids. I don't think there's anything in particular between them, just differences in personality."

"Ethan asked her if he could use her hut while we were staying on the farm. He said it was convenient for the sheep and I offered to milk the cows. Daniel helped me today."

"You're a good influence on Daniel, he seems to be more aware when you're around."

"How old is he? I didn't like to ask Ethan."

Hannah had to think. She knew he was around the same age as her own parents had been, but Daniel and Mary had married young.

"He's in his early forties I think. The effects of the fever and losing Mary aged him."

"I think Ethan hopes we'll stay here and take care of Daniel. He probably sees us as a way to gain his own freedom, he's so desperate to leave the Island."

"I know, he's said the same to me, about travelling. You've seen a lot haven't you?"

"Not that much. I only accompanied my father on a few trips when I was younger. It was pretty boring most of the time, you only saw harbours and were never there long enough to really explore."

"Is your father very rich? You don't mind me asking do you?"

"I suppose he's wealthy. Not like the Delanceys though, Simon's family."

"Are they very rich?"

"Mega rich." Becky shook her head slowly as though nobody would be able to believe the truth of their wealth. "Like you can't imagine."

"Aren't you going to miss the mainland, there must be so much more going on over there? We lead such a simple life here."

"I hated it after my mother died, she was my only friend, the only person I could talk to. Anyway, it's all about showing off and power. Nobody cares who you actually are on the inside."

"You do know that if you and Abby stay together you will sort of be in power yourself? Not quite in the same way of course."

"How do you mean?"

"Abby and I are going to be joint Bailiffs of Hope Island, share responsibilities."

"So you'll both own the Island."

"Nobody owns Hope Island, we all own it. I explained that when we first met."

"I know, but technically someone has to own it. What about Isaac, what happens to him when you take over?"

"To be honest I don't know. I've got a feeling that Isaac has got money stashed away somehow, although I don't know how or where."

"Gold," Becky said simply, nodding her head.

"You mean like gold jewellery, gold rings, that sort of thing?"

"Real wealth is kept in bullion coins. They're still around from the time before."

"Have you seen any then? What are they like?"

Becky explained that her father uses them and that he keeps them in a safe. She told Hannah that they were made of pure gold and incredibly valuable.

"Some countries used to have special coins, just bought

for their gold value."

"I've never heard of them before, but I suppose I wouldn't have." Hannah frowned, trying to imagine them. "What do you use them for?"

"People hoard them, buy things, do deals - I never really got involved in all that."

There was a clatter of something outside and the sound of Abby cursing in irritation. She appeared in the kitchen door, looking hot and tired.

"Well, I'm glad I've finished that bloody job for another year. You wouldn't believe what hard work clearing that weed can be. Oh, hello Hannah, didn't know you were back. How's the cottage looking?"

"Sorry," Becky said, clasping her hand to her mouth. "I never asked."

"It's okay, just smoke damage. But everything's going to have to be washed – at least twice I would think – even your new clothes."

"I've still got stuff here I can wear for now."

"I'm going to be sharing a bed with a boy am I?" Abby laughed.

"I'm the same inside whatever I'm wearing. Don't be so judgemental."

Becky was obviously joking and Abby came over and gave her a hug.

"Yuk, you're wet and sweaty, get off me."

"I'll make you help me next time. In fact you can help when we load the weed onto a cart. It will make a proper man of you," Abby laughed.

Hannah let Abby get herself a mug of tea. Becky offered to make a fresh pot, but Abby said that tea didn't grow on trees and as long as it's wet it would be fine. Becky grimaced as Abby drank half the mug in one swallow.

"So," Abby put her serious face on. "We weren't in any

233

danger of being burnt alive, just choked to death by that smoke?"

"Peter thinks it was lit on purpose."

Becky looked to Abby for reassurance and back to Hannah

"You mean someone tried to kill us?"

"Isaac," Abby spat the name out. "I wouldn't put anything past him."

"But why would he try to kill us all, he hardly knows me?"

"When Hannah comes of age he's out of a job and it will be an end to the schemes he's been running for years."

"And out of power," Becky added. "I know his type."

"Exactly," Abby said. "He's come to the end of the road unless he manages to get rid of both Hannah and me."

"No wonder he and my father get on well, they're the same type, ruthless, they only care about money and power."

"We'll have to be careful," Hannah said quietly. "And I need you to help me with something Abby."

"Sure, what do you want me to do?"

"I need you to stand guard while I dive."

"The seas picking up, it's not the best time to dive right now."

"Not in the sea, in the reservoir."

"Of course," Abby slapped a hand on her forehead. "With everything else that's been going on I'd completely forgotten."

"What's in the reservoir?" Becky asked.

Hannah explained about the map in her father's journal and that they thought there might be something in the underwater cave.

"But what do you expect to find."

"We've no idea," Abby shrugged.

"From what my father wrote, or rather our father wrote," Hannah corrected herself, "there could be something valuable, maybe even gold coins like you described. But it's just as likely that he was delirious by then, so there could be nothing there at all."

"When do you want to do it?" Abby asked.

"It will need to be late in the afternoon, so that the sun's low and shining on that bank of the reservoir. I'll let you know which day, I've got some other things to catch up with first."

"I wish I could be there when you dive, but I'll have to stay here with Daniel. You will take care won't you?"

"Maybe Sunday would be a good day," Hannah said. "Isaac usually drinks at lunchtime and sleeps it off in the afternoon. There would be no danger of him stumbling on us."

"I don't think Isaac's been up to the reservoir for years, but it's a good idea to be careful."

"I might ask Peter too, just for added protection."

"Sounds good to me," Abby said. "Now, I have to get out of these clothes, I brought my stuff back from the hut as Ethan's going to use it."

Becky started preparing supper and asked Hannah if she wanted to stay, assuring her there was plenty to go round even though it was only going to be cold cuts until she got the place organised again.

"Thanks, but I'd better get back to Newport before dusk."

Hannah shouted goodbye to Abby, who was in the bathroom.

"Do I need to bring anything on Sunday?" she called back, her voice muffled.

"Maybe a length of rope, and something heavy we can use as an anchor."

"Wouldn't a rock do? There's plenty of them up there already."

"Of course it would, I'm not thinking straight. I'll see you before then but I don't think we need anything else unless you've got a light that would work underwater."

"Ask Martha. You never know what she's got hidden away."

Hannah laughed at the suggestion and hugged Becky before leaving. Daniel was still on his bench enjoying the last of the sun. Becky stood next to him and rested a hand on his shoulder. Hannah saw the hint of a contented smile spread across Daniel's face.

"We'll see you soon I hope Hannah. Take care."

"I'll be fine. I'm with Martha."

Abby had emerged with nothing but a towel wrapped round her shoulders and a pair of shorts. Hannah cupped her hands round her mouth and called back.

"Better put more than that on before Ethan comes back for supper."

Abby held the towel up in defiance before Becky grabbed it and covered her up. Daniel had taken no notice of the performance. She waved a final goodbye before the lane turned a bend and took the farm out of sight.

Over the next few days Hannah stayed indoors, fuelled by tea and sandwiches, which Martha, with a second sense, brought her just as she thought about them. She recorded everything in her new journal, from her earliest memories after her parents had died, through to the fire in Canary Cottage. Hannah had never written quite so much in her life. She had to think carefully before she started each passage – she didn't want to be continually crossing bits out. Every now and then she took a break, helping Martha with whatever she was doing, her fingers cramped and ached from the unaccustomed business of gripping a pencil. After a while she learned to hold it looser and her writing style improved at the same time.

Isaac only visited once. Martha made a show of not leaving him alone with her even when he made it clear that he wanted to speak in private with Hannah.

"All right, you may stay Martha," Isaac said begrudgingly. "But I hope you will appreciate that some things need to be kept confidential."

"My tongue only wags when it needs to Isaac. You know that."

Isaac sat opposite Hannah so that his back was to Martha.

"I wanted to talk to you about Simon," he said.

"What about him?" Hannah sounded surprised.

"I simply wondered how much you liked him, you appeared to get on rather well."

"We only spent the one day together, and a meal of course. You were there."

Hannah wasn't going to tell him that her stomach felt like it was full of butterflies every time she thought about Simon.

"I suppose if we were to meet a few more times..." Hannah teased. "He is quite nice and really wealthy too."

"Just so," Isaac cleared his throat. "And if something were to come of it I presume you would want to move to the mainland with him?"

"Of course, we'd want to be together, and his families business is on the mainland."

Isaac nodded sagely as though he understood entirely.

"But I have to stay here I suppose when I come of age. There's no real alternative is there?"

Isaac's face revealed his thoughts. A simple solution was opening up for him. Martha was practically giggling behind his back, stifling any sound coming from her mouth with both hands clasped tight over it.

"Well, I could carry on for a while I suppose – as a favour to you. I was looking forward to some peace and quiet, but your needs are more important than mine."

"Maybe we could talk after I meet Simon again, assuming he does return on the next boat."

"Quite, quite, no need to rush these arrangements. I'm glad we had this chat Hannah. I'm sure it will all work out in the end."

"How is your hand now Uncle?"

"Oh that, nothing, nothing at all."

Isaac hid his hand under the table and made an excuse that he really ought to be going.

"Things to do, always things to do," he said and made a hasty retreat from the store and from Martha, who shrieked with laughter as soon as the door closed behind him.

Chapter 31

Sunday arrived without further incident. After a lunch of bread and jam, Hannah walked down to the harbour. She checked that nobody was watching and pressed her ear against Isaac's front door. There was silence. She bit her lip, wondering if he had gone out for a walk. It would be uncharacteristic of him and she wanted to be sure where he was while they were at the reservoir. A loud snort from inside the house startled Hannah, but it was followed by Isaac's familiar rhythmic snoring. She knew they would be safe – from him at least.

Hannah had a couple of hours before she was due to meet Abby and went back to the store to think. She wrote in her journal that she was about to go to the reservoir and explore the submerged mine that was shown on her father's map. She sat with her pencil poised above the page, but didn't want to write down her fears in case it made them come true. She wasn't entirely sure if she wanted to find some mythical hidden treasure because she knew it would change her island forever, but it was time to go. Hannah sighed put down her pencil and slid her journal back into the drawer under Martha's huge table.

"I'll be back later Martha," she called and scurried out before she could be questioned. Hannah wasn't sure that Martha would approve of her plan. For the same reason she hadn't included Peter, also believing that the fewer people who knew about anything they found, the easier it might be to conceal it.

The sky had the crispness that only early autumn brings

when the air is free from the dust and heat of summer. Trees were turning shades gold and yellow, each in their own turn, and the rocks high on the ridge were so sharply picked out by the sun that they looked ready to tumble from their lofty perches.

Abby was sitting on a boulder, quite high above the reservoir, a perfect position to see anyone approaching. She waved to Hannah when she saw her but didn't call out. They both knew not to draw the attention of anyone who might be out for a walk.

"I brought the rope like you asked," Abby said, indicating a coil of brown platted twine at her feet. "This should be strong enough I hope."

"That will work fine, I only need it as a guide line."

Hannah led the way to a large, flat outcrop of rock above the water. She looked around and selected a substantial stone that was irregular in shape and easy to tie the rope around securely. Abby took over that task, saying she was probably better with knots. Hannah didn't argue, she was preoccupied with diving into water that looked black and more forbidding than she remembered. Abby lowered the line and its weight where Hannah indicated, just to one side of the ledge.

"What now?" Abby asked, knowing the answer, but wanting to break the silence.

"I go in and explore I suppose."

Hannah stripped down to her t-shirt and pants and stood on the edge of the rock, hesitating for only a moment before jumping into the water. She surfaced again, almost immediately, and wrapped a hand loosely round the line.

"Let it out slowly when I pull on it. I'll lodge the stone as far inside the cave as I can."

"Don't take any risks."

Hannah nodded to Abby, but didn't smile. Most of her

dives were fun, never knowing what she might find, never looking for anything specific. But she was used to diving in the open ocean where the sunlight penetrated further than on the reservoir.

The light from the watery autumn sun didn't show everything as clearly as she had hoped and it took her the first dive simply to find the opening to the cave. It wasn't as far down as she had expected because the water level was lower at the end of a dry summer. Her first dive was too deep and she only found the cave on her way back to the surface, where Abby was watching intently.

"Got it," she said, spitting a few drops of water from her mouth. "It not far below the surface, but it's difficult to see down there."

"I wish there was something I could do to help."

"Knowing you're at the end of that rope is good enough."

Hannah was more confident on her second dive. She carried the stone several feet into the mouth of the cave and lodged it as securely as she could manage. It was darker than she had hoped, the sun hardly penetrating the cave, except for occasional flashes illuminating protruding rocks. By remaining still, the topography slowly revealed itself like a picture being uncovered one section at a time.

The line guided her back to the entrance where could see the light of day above her. She broke surface again.

"It's going to take several dives to explore it all. I can't see much down there."

"I wish we'd brought Peter with us, at least he can swim if you get into trouble."

"Don't worry, I'm okay down here. I've done this all my life."

Hannah dived repeatedly. Each time she took the line and its anchor weight deeper into the cave, but the light diminished the further in she ventured. After half an hour she hauled herself onto the rock for a rest.

"Is it worth it?" Abby asked. "There might not be anything there anyway."

"You're probably right, but I can't not know. That drawing and the message in Dad's journal were important to him."

"I know what you mean."

"Four more dives. I'll stop if I don't find anything after four more dives."

"What if you do find something valuable? What do we do then?"

"I don't know," Hannah said quietly. "Use it to deal with Isaac I guess."

Hannah lay back on the rock, which was warm from the sun, and stared at the wispy clouds hanging over the top of the ridge.

"If there is gold in there of some sort, if it's a lot," Hannah said as though thinking out loud, "the island will never be the same again will it?"

"Not if we tell everyone."

"Could we keep it a secret? Would we have a right to leave it hidden?"

"Your father kept it hidden. He had a reason."

"But he told me. He must have thought it would be needed some day."

"Let's see if it's there before worrying too much."

Hannah stood and pushed her hair back from her face.

"I'm going straight in," she said and dived at an angle to the bank.

The line was trailing into the cave, but Hannah ignored it. The sun had dropped lower in the sky and was now illuminating the cave somewhat better, although the flashing and waving shafts of lights were as much confusing as helpful. She held the line and stayed in the mouth of the cave trying to see details as the refracted sunlight danced over the floor and walls.

She could now see that the cave was some thirty feet deep and near the far end, on the floor, she thought she could see something like a box. It was too rectangular to be a stone, but she didn't have enough breath left on that dive.

Hannah turned, pushing off from the bed of the reservoir and surfaced, spluttering, trying to talk before her face was completely clear of the water.

"I've found it, a chest or box of some sort, it's at the far end of the cave."

"Oh my God, there's actually something there?"

"I'm going back down. I'll try to tie the rope to it. Can you take the rock off the end?"

"Is it safe?"

"The caves not that deep, there's no obstructions. I'll be fine."

Abby hauled up the rope and untied the weight. Hannah had heaved herself onto the ledge again, took the end of the rope and wrapped three or four winds around her hand and wrist.

"Pay it all out as I dive," she told Abby. "I wish we'd brought a crowbar or something like that."

"I've got a knife," Abby said, holding out a long, sturdy blade with a wooden handle.

Hannah took it, holding it backwards like a dagger so that it wouldn't snatch against the water when she dived. She took a few deep breaths and exhaled as far as she could each time, then one more breath, nodded to Abby and she was gone. A small splash and a few bubbles was all there was to be seen while Abby waited.

Hannah swam straight to the back of the cave, lodged the knife into an iron ring on top of the wooden chest and tied the rope through a handle on one end. Hannah tried to lift it, but the chest was either fixed to the cave floor or very heavy. She tried to open it, but gave up after pushing the blade into a small gap under the lid, which had no effect. She returned to the surface for more air.

"Okay," she said to Abby once she had regained her breath. "Can you tie your end of the rope to something safe?"

She took a few more deep breaths and tuck-dived back underwater. Confident now that she knew the layout of the cave. Hannah found a stray rock and gripped it between her knees so that she could kneel by the box. She found the catch, it was a simple hasp over a loop, there was a small metal bar pushed through the loop to keep it closed, but no lock.

The bar came out with minimum effort, just a couple of taps with the butt of the knife. Hannah prised the hasp open with the dull edge of the blade. The lid resisted for a moment but, with the knife to lever it open, the rusty hinges gave up their resistance. The lid opened just enough for Hannah to slide a hand inside.

There were smooth cloth bags in the chest, bags containing coins. One bag had rotted over the years and a few coins slipped easily into Hannah's palm. Her fingers closed over them and she only just remembered to pick up Abby's knife before it floated away.

Hannah swam awkwardly to the ledge with coins in one hand and the knife in the other. Before she hauled herself out of the water she reached up and dropped her finds in front of a kneeling Abby.

"Look."

The coins shone in the daylight. There was no doubt they were gold. Abby did look, but she didn't touch them.

"How many are there?" she whispered.

"I don't know, but lots. The chest is full of them, there

could be hundreds."

"This is what Isaac's been looking for. He knew they existed. That's why he closed up the other caves."

"What do we do?" Hannah asked, still in the water, her elbows resting on the rock ledge and the coins only inches from her face.

"Check them with Becky, she might know what they are. We need to make sure what we're dealing with and how much they're worth."

Hannah heaved herself out of the water, shivering with excitement or fear, or maybe because the heat of the day was waning with the sun lower in the sky. She picked a few stray pieces of weed off her feet. Abby wound the rope into a coil, pulling it taut against the sunken chest. She laid it at the side of the reservoir, covering it with stones to hide it.

Hannah pulled her canvas shoes over wet feet and wriggled her shorts up her legs. She bent to pick up the coins and saw Abby still kneeling where she had hidden the rope.

"Are you okay Abby?"

"This is going to change everything isn't it? The island can never be the same again."

"We don't have to tell anyone. You and I are going to share the running of the Island, we could just keep this between us."

"I can't keep secrets from Becky."

"You two are the real thing aren't you?"

"I think so. At least I hope so."

Chapter 32

Hannah and Abby were in no great hurry on the way back to Hope Barton with their three coins. Walking partly in the shade of trees, Hannah's clothes were slow to dry. Her feet were cool in her wet shoes and she wished she had brought something to wrap around her shoulders to warm her.

"I suppose we don't have to tell anyone do we?" Abby asked.

"Not unless we need to. And we don't know exactly what's in that chest yet, it might not all be gold coins."

"But we could buy all the coal we need and new tools."

"Do we really need that much, everything works as it is now."

"It works for Isaac." Abby snorted a dry laugh. "And he does have a few people on his side."

"I didn't know that. Who?"

"Mark and his wife, and their son. There are a few others too who I think might be with him."

"But they can't do anything when we take over from Isaac can they?"

"I don't know. Most people just want a simple life, not a civil war."

"What if we told everyone, held an island meeting, told them what we'd found and that it belonged to everyone?"

"Isaac and his friends would want their share at the very least."

"Money is going to change everything," Hannah said quietly. "Maybe Isaac was actually right to keep the Island isolated."

"No he wasn't," Abby said, sounding sure. "We can't ignore the way the world is changing. I saw a lot over there that we didn't know about. They have tractors, even some lorries are running, and there were so many ships in Freeport's harbour. I don't know why Isaac's kept it all so secret."

"Could we get our own steamer if we had enough money?"

"I have no idea, but that's something else Becky might know."

"Do we tell her how much we might have found?"

"We don't really know how much is in that chest do we?"

"It's heavy, but whoever put it there may have weighed it down with some rocks in the bottom. I only scooped those few coins off the top."

"We need to find out what we've got before we do anything."

They were at the top of the lane leading down to Hope Barton. Charlie came bounding up to greet them, barking and wagging his tail. Abby bent down to ruffle his neck and he backed away, wanting to play.

"Not right now Charlie," Abby said and he scampered back down the lane towards the farm.

Becky was in the kitchen when they got there, Charlie in front of the range and Daniel was staring at a virgin piece of driftwood on the table in front of him.

"How was the treasure hunt?" Becky asked, continuing to scrape potatoes with a small knife.

Hannah and Abby exchanged glances, neither knowing quite how to respond.

"It was sort of successful," Abby said.

"So you found something? Your sunken treasure trove?"

"Yes," Hannah said. "But we don't quite know what it is yet."

Becky had turned round to face them, a potato still in one hand and the knife in the other. A piece of peel fell to the floor, but she ignored it.

"Come on then, what did you find?"

Abby nodded her head sideways in Daniel's direction and put a finger to her lips. Becky understood and put the potato and knife back in the bowl.

"These will have to wait," she said for Daniel's benefit. "I need to milk the cows."

"I'll give you a hand," Hannah said, picking up the metal bucket that stood by the sink.

"Do you want a drink Daniel," Abby asked and flicked her head to suggest they left her with Daniel.

"Cup of water would be good Lass."

Hannah followed Becky across the yard and into the barn.

"So, what's the great mystery?" Becky asked.

The cows found their voices as soon as they saw Becky and she grabbed the milking stool, sat down, put the bucket in place and leaned her head against Mollie's flank.

Hannah unfolded her fingers to show Becky the three coins she had salvaged from the chest. Becky looked at them and asked her to turn each one over so she could see the other side.

"I recognise two of them. Is that all you found, just those three?"

"There are more."

"They're gold. Each one should weigh one ounce. You can ignore what it says on it, they're worth more because they're pure gold."

"How do you know this?"

"My father has lots, everyone who trades uses them. That one is a fifty dollar American Gold Eagle."

"What about the other two?" Hannah asked, reading out

the raised lettering on the coins. "Canada, fifty something, does that sign mean dollars?"

"Yes and the third one is a Britannia one hundred pound coin. They are all pure gold. That's why they're still shiny even though I assume they've been underwater for years."

"Why are they so valuable?"

"My great-grandfather told me that when he was a boy, when the banks collapsed, when all that electronic stuff got zapped by the sun, gold was the only safe thing to have. Lots of people who thought they were wealthy and clever lost everything."

"Didn't your great-grandfather lose everything too?"

"No, he never trusted banks, he kept most of his money in jewellery, gold and precious stones. It made him smile when he talked about it in those days."

"It must have been a horrible thing to live through. My great-grandfather died before I was old enough for him to tell me much and my grandfather didn't like to talk about it. I think a lot of people he knew died in the first pandemic."

"I doubt it was any fun to live through that time. But it's history now, things have changed even if people haven't."

"So what are these coins worth, say in terms of produce?"

"My guess is that those three would buy enough food for your whole island for a year. I never got too involved with trade, my father is quite secretive about his wealth."

"A year?" Hannah whispered almost in disbelief. "Just three coins?"

"You could buy other things too if you wanted them. Like a decent pair of glasses to correct your eyesight."

"I have glasses, although they don't work that well."

"They could make them specially for you. I imagine the ones you have are relics from generations ago?"

"Maybe," Hannah said defensively. "But I can get by

without glasses."

"Proper medicines are appearing too, doctors, newspapers, radio like I told you. Since the sun flares reduced and the virus is under control, it's all going back to how it was."

"Is that a good thing? Wasn't it that way of life that caused half the problems in the first place?"

"I suppose there are problems, but there always have been, and there are people who are poor, I mean really poor, you're not really poor here."

"So why do you want to live here? Why did you run away?"

Becky turned her head the other way, so that Hannah couldn't see her face

"Some people want everything. My father, he's one of them."

"And Isaac I think."

"They don't care about anyone else, they're just greedy. I wanted to get away from all that. My father had let slip some stuff about this island. He thought it was funny, he said that everyone here was backward, but I thought it sounded better than what was happening around me."

"I think I understand, even though I've not been there." Hannah leaned back against the wall, closing her fingers round the coins.

"I'm going to milk Gertie and then I'm done for the day. Why don't I see you back indoors. Get yourself a mug of tea, you look cold, you're shivering."

The milking parlour and the heat emanating from Mollie and Gertie had taken some of the chill from Hannah's skin, but she was still damp and the thought of a hot drink was too tempting to resist.

Back in the kitchen Abby was looking enquiringly at her. Hannah shrugged and raised her eyebrows. "Complicated," she said and tested the warmth of the kettle with a quick touch of the palm of her hand.

"I'll make you one," Abby said. "Go out and get the last of the sun to dry yourself off."

Abby threw her a towel and Hannah went out and sat on the bench, prising her feet out of still damp shoes and rubbing her toes with the towel to bring them back to life. Abby joined her a few minutes later and put a mug of tea on the bench to the side of her.

"So, what's the verdict from our girl from the mainland?"

"They're valuable, really valuable, especially if we have as many as I think we have."

"What do we do then? Do we tell anyone else?"

"I'd like to ask Martha's advise."

Abby nodded in agreement. "She's okay, but nobody else for now?"

"I don't think so, not until we know just what we have."

Becky came out of the cowshed carrying a bucket that hung heavy in her hand. Abby met her half way across the yard and took it from her.

"Do you want to stay to supper?" Becky asked.

"I'd better get back. I need to get into some dry clothes."

"You could borrow something of mine if you want."

"No, it's okay, but thanks anyway."

"You know Abby's cooking tonight?" Becky giggled.

Hannah turned to look at Abby, smiling broadly for what felt like the first time for hours if not days.

"I didn't know you were extending your skill set Abby?"

"I'm learning," she grimaced. "Slowly."

A whistle coming down the lane announced the arrival of Ethan.

"Could you smell dinner?" Abby asked. "I suppose we have enough for you to join us – now Hannah's not staying."

"Don't mind if I do, and I'm glad you're here Hannah. There's something I wanted to ask you."

"What's that?"

"Isaac sent me a message to meet him in the village tomorrow to discuss something. I wondered if you might have an idea what it's about?"

Hannah said she couldn't think of anything, but suggested it might be to do with the steamer visiting next week. She didn't want to talk to Ethan at the moment, there was too much on her mind, and she was glad she had refused the offer of supper.

"I ought to be going, the sun's almost down already and Martha will be wondering where I am."

She hugged Becky and Abby, whispering to Abby that they should meet soon to discuss everything, but only raised a hand to say goodbye to Ethan.

Hannah took the lane through the fields on the way home. It was late enough that everyone would have stopped work for the day. She was confident that she wouldn't see anyone and have to talk.

"I was beginning to wonder where you'd got to," Martha said as Hannah closed the door behind her. "Did you have an interesting day?"

"We found it," Hannah said. "We found my father's treasure, or my grandfather's, I don't actually know who hid it there in the first place."

Hannah opened her hand and spilled the three coins onto the table. Martha looked at them and sighed.

"They're gold aren't they?" Martha said. "I've heard about them, but never seen any."

"What do we do Martha? There are more of them, lots more I think."

Martha didn't offer a solution, but changed the subject, or so Hannah thought at first.

"Isaac dropped in today, a waste of space that man. He

seemed to think you might be marrying Simon?"

"I've only spent one day with Simon. I don't even know if he likes me in that way."

"Oh he does Hannah, I saw the way he looked at you. Isaac is also under the impression that you may be moving to the mainland if you marry."

"I did say something like that didn't I – just to see his reaction."

"Well, let's keep him thinking that way, it might also be safer for you. And if he knows you've found these he'll be a real problem."

"They're not mine anyway, they belong to the Island, to the community."

"Nonsense, they belong to you. They were your family's – probably your great grandfather's. He didn't steal them from anyone here, not like whatever Isaac has hidden away."

"Can I leave them in the store somewhere?"

Martha looked nervous. She said that she didn't like gold, it always caused trouble and jealousy, but of course she would hide them for Hannah.

"Isaac could spend a month searching this place and not even find his own feet. They'll be safe here. Now, supper, I have a nice vegetable stew on the stove and you look like you need to change into some dry clothes before we eat."

Chapter 33

Over the next few nights Hannah had recurrent night-mares. She was drowning in a pool of liquid gold, not hot, not burning, but it was dragging her under, filling her nostrils and ears and mouth. She woke in a cold sweat, fighting a tangled sheet from her arms and legs. Isaac was there, watching her drown, laughing and pointing at her as she sunk.

She knew that her and Abby needed to rescue the contents of the chest, bring it to the stores and keep it safely hidden. The papers from the safe needed to be taken there too, in case Isaac stumbled on the correct numbers. She knew he would be trying every combination he could think of to open it. It would only be a matter of time. Hannah was in the kitchen, drinking a mug of water, when Martha appeared.

"Up already? Trouble sleeping?"

"Martha, can we borrow that small handcart of yours to bring the rest of the gold back here? I think it might be too heavy to carry."

"What are you going to say to anyone who sees you?"

"We could say that we are moving stuff from Abby's cottage to Hope Barton."

"And what about when you come back into the village with it still loaded?"

"If anyone asks I could say that I've brought stuff back here from the Manor, for my cottage when it's done."

Martha looked long and hard at Hannah and eventually nodded her approval.

"That should past muster, but you'll need something to put it all in, you can't have a mystery chest on full view. I'll sort you out a solid box."

"I'll have to arrange a good time to do it with Abby, when nobody is likely to wander past. Maybe next Sunday would be okay."

"Or when everyone's working, that way you'll be sure to be on your own."

Hannah sipped a glass of water. Martha pushed the kettle onto the hot plate and stoked the firebox, throwing in a couple of sticks and a few lumps of coal to get it flaming.

"I'll put on some coffee, you look like you need perking up."

"That would be great. Do you have enough?"

Martha smiled. "If I don't have any, then there's none on the whole island. How are those two getting on, Abby and Becky? I hear Ethan's moved out."

"They're good. I think it's real, not just for show."

"That hut is going to be cold in the winter. I can't see Ethan sticking it out there for long."

"Maybe he'll take over Abby's cottage now it's free."

"Or maybe he'll finally leave the Island, like he's talked about doing for years."

"You know about Ethan's plans?"

"Everyone knows my dear. We've listened to him going on about escaping the Island since he was a tot. He read a book about pirates roaming the high seas and I think he recognised the wanderer in himself. Can't blame him after his mother died and Daniel was affected so badly."

"Daniel's better when Becky is there. He's quite different now, more aware, more connected."

"She's a nice girl from what I've seen of her."

The kettle started to whistle gently and they scraped together a breakfast of toast and eggs. Martha said how she had seen Hannah drawn to Ethan when they were both small and thought it was the faraway look in his eyes that had intrigued her.

"We all had a soft spot for him as a child. But he changed when he had to take over the farm so young. It hardened him. It was sad to see him close in on himself and not be able to do anything about it. He wouldn't accept help and we had to leave him to it."

There was a loud knock on the main door and the hinges moaned as it swung open.

"Anyone in here? Hello." It was Ethan's gravelly voice.

"I think he might want to chat with you alone. I'll make myself scarce," Martha whispered. "Morning Ethan, did you want me for anything? I'm just popping down to the cellar, but Hannah's here, she can keep you company for a few minutes."

"Thanks Martha, it was Hannah I wanted to see."

Ethan came over and sat on the opposite side of the table to her.

"You want tea?"

"No, I can't stay long. It was just that I wanted to clear some things up with you. We kind of left it a bit bad. I thought we should talk."

Hannah assumed he wanted something. Maybe he was going to try to apologise and repair their relationship. She knew now that she didn't want to do that, it had run its course.

"We can talk here," she said.

"Are we done, I mean us, as a couple?"

"From what you said the other day it sounded like we never were a couple."

"Yes. I'm sorry, it didn't come out the way I meant it to."

"How did you mean it to come out?"

"I saw the way you were with Simon. You were never

like that with me."

"I wasn't 'like that' with Simon, we'd only met that day, I was being polite, showing a guest round our island."

"You probably weren't aware of it, but I could see it. Everyone saw it, and he likes you too."

Hannah dropped her head and studied the grain in the tabletop.

"It's a mess isn't it?" she said.

"It might have been more of a mess if we'd got married."

"Are you angry?"

"No. You?"

"No."

She looked up and it was the old Ethan she saw, the boy with a dream in his eyes. She knew Martha was right. It was the dream she had fallen for.

"Can we still be friends?" she asked.

"Can't see why not. I need friends now I only have a hut to live in."

He smiled and Hannah did too.

"What was it Isaac wanted with you?"

"I'm not sure. It was a bit of an odd meeting. He kept talking about my plans to get away from here and I told him I didn't really have any plans as such."

"That doesn't sound like Isaac."

"It got stranger. He said that Abby had got away, that the Crabber appeared to be a sturdy little boat, that it was perfect for one person to sail wherever they wanted. It was almost like he was giving me permission to take it."

Hannah realised what Isaac's plan was. If Ethan were out of the running, there would be no obstacle between her and Simon. Isaac was hoping she would leave too and he could stay in charge as bailiff.

"I told him I couldn't leave Dad. But he said he'd heard that Abby and Becky were taking very good care of him."

257

"Simon promised to bring you a map. I wouldn't do anything until you get that – assuming you do want to go."

"Now it all seems possible I'm not so sure. I could take the boat, but I don't have any money and I'll need some on the mainland."

"Daniel's carvings. They sell on the mainland and you have some in your workshop."

"You think that would work?"

"Becky could tell you where to sell them and Daniel's forgotten all about them. I can't see the harm in you taking some to give you a start."

"But what about Dad and the farm?"

"Abby and Becky will take care of them. It will still be there if you decide to come back."

"You want me to go?"

"I want you to do what you want to do. Let's face it, you've always wanted to go and I can't imagine a better opportunity is going to crop up."

Ethan reached across the table and took Hannah's hands in his. "Thanks," he croaked, his voice catching in his throat.

"The Pride is due here next week," Hannah said, squeezing his fingers. "You've still got a few days to think about it."

Martha chose that moment to reappear. Whether she had been listening or whether it was coincidental, Hannah couldn't tell, but Martha did like to know what was going on.

After Ethan left, kissing Hannah on both cheeks as he'd seen Simon do, she asked Martha where would be the best place to hide the chest or maybe just its contents if the chest itself was fastened to the rocks.

"Abby and I don't want anyone to know about it yet, not until we decide what needs to be done with it. It's about this big." Hannah used her hands to show something the size of a blanket box.

"Hmm, too big to just squirrel it away. There is a special place where it won't be found and it's about time you knew about it. Come on."

Martha led the way down the stone steps into the cellar. She lit two candles, one for each of them, and wound her way between the stacks to the back wall. The cellar had wooden pillars, old tree trunks with the bark stripped off. They held up the barn floor and behind them, lining the walls, were rough-sawn planks, laid horizontally.

She stopped in front of one of the many large wardrobes that had been shelved out for storage. It held jars of pickled vegetables and Hannah wasn't sure what Martha had in mind.

"Help me move all these onto that table."

They stripped the shelves and Martha pulled on the side of the wardrobe.

"We need to get this out of the way," Martha said through gritted teeth.

Hannah was amused, wondering what she was trying to do, but gripped the wardrobe with Martha. They wriggled and shoved it to one side.

"I used to be able to do that by myself when I was younger," Martha puffed.

All that was revealed was more of the planking that lined the cellar. Hannah was expecting a secret door or something similarly exciting.

"Reach up to that top plank my dear. See that knothole? Put your finger in it and slide the plank to one side."

Hannah did as instructed and the plank moved easily, freeing the other end from behind a pillar. Under Martha's guidance she pulled it free, revealing a set of soldier bricks in the stones behind it. As more planks were removed, a narrow arched opening was gradually revealed. It led into a dark cavernous space. Hannah couldn't see into it, but any noise they made echoed eerily from the secret chamber.

"Come on, nothing to be afraid of." Martha tugged at Hannah's sleeve to follow her.

Their candles flickered, but lit the room well enough for Hannah to make out a vaulted brick ceiling and dressed-stone walls.

"Your father knew about this of course. He said it would be better lost forever than found by the wrong person, but I reckon it's time for you to make decisions like that."

Now they were inside, Martha's voice bounced back from the far recesses where the candlelight couldn't reach. She was only speaking quietly but the empty space emphasised every word.

What Hannah could see were boxes upon boxes stacked against the part-rendered walls. They were a variety of sizes, but ordered into neat groups.

"I loosened the lid on that one some years ago," Martha said, pointing at one close to them.

Hannah slid the wooden lid across the box, having no idea what she might find inside. She lifted a strange imple-ment out of the straw packing, quickly recognising it as something she had only previously seen in a book.

"It's a crossbow," she whispered, turning it over in her hands. "What's in the other boxes? Do they all contain these?"

"There are crossbows, longbows, bolts, arrows, but I haven't looked in all of them – enough to know that I didn't want to see them fall into the wrong hands."

"But why, what are they for? Why keep them hidden like this?"

"Your great-grandfather was a peaceful man by all accounts, but a pragmatist. Your father admired him. He quoted him as saying that the only reliable weapon in the future might be a bow and arrow."

"Who else knows about them?"

"Only me, and now you."

"Isaac doesn't know they're here?"

"He would probably be the last person I'd tell."

"Why would we ever need them?"

"I don't know, I don't like to think about it, but Jacob, your father, made me promise to protect them and tell you when the time was right. And I think the time is right, at least for you to know this room exists. And it's a good place to hide your gold."

Hannah backed away from the boxes, wishing she still didn't know about them.

"They have to remain hidden," Hannah said in a hushed, but confident voice.

"I agree."

"But Abby is going to have to know where the coins are."

They both looked back at the boxes.

"She's probably the only other person I would trust," Martha said. "And she'll know when and how to use them – if that time ever comes, but I hope it doesn't."

Chapter 34

Hannah tried not to think about the gold or the weapons in Martha's hidden room. Together they had put the boards, and the old wardrobe, back into position and replaced the jars and bottles. Hannah felt like she was in a strange kind of limbo, waiting for the Pride's next visit.

She thought about her damaged cottage and wanted to see it. Having been so preoccupied with other matters, she had left Peter to organise the removal of all her furniture and start the renovation work. Although she had passed it on several occasions, she hadn't ventured in. She walked up from the store and poked her head through the door. Even at a glance the rooms looked bare and sad. Smoke had left dirty grey and black smudges on the walls and ceilings, with pale, dull-cream shapes almost untouched where her sofa and cupboards had protected the plaster. It smelled damp and sooty, a clawing odour that stayed in her nose even when she pulled back into the open air.

"We've left all the windows and doors open to let it air for the last few days," Peter said, coming up the lane and stopping next to her. "It does actually smell better now."

"It will never be like it was though."

"No it won't, it will be better once we've finished. Joanna has already stripped your sofa and chair and got some old curtains from the store. She says the material will be perfect for recovering them. Sophia's out the back in the garden, she's cleaning your collection of salvaged bits and bobs. I think she's rather enjoying it."

"I haven't been in the house yet. I ought to go and see her

and say thank you"

"Well we're going to start scrubbing the walls today. Give us a hand if you have time. It will feel more like your old cottage soon enough."

Gabriel and Leah turned up at that moment with a bucket of hot water each with scrubbing brushes floating in them, and rags slung over their shoulders.

"Have you got the stove going Peter? We're going to get through a lot of hot water today."

"There are pots coming up to heat," Peter replied. "And Sophia's cleaning stuff out the back, so leave some for her."

Hannah moved aside so that Gabriel and Leah could get through the door with their buckets. Gabriel said they were going to start upstairs where there was least damage.

"I guess I ought to help too," Hannah said when they had gone. "I'll just go and see Sophia first."

"I make a start down here. You can help me if you like."

In the garden Sophia was sitting on an upturned wooden crate, humming contentedly to herself and cleaning Hannah's finds in a bowl of soapy water. She had just finished a small plastic figurine, dunked it in a bucket of clean water and put it on a plank in front of her, alongside several others drying in the sun.

"Thanks for doing this," Hannah said, making Sophia jump. "Sorry, I didn't mean to startle you."

"I didn't hear you. I was miles away."

"What were you thinking about?"

"I was wondering who owned this originally." She held up the little dog she'd been washing. "I used to think you were a bit odd collecting all these things, but I kind of get it now. I like this one."

The little resin dog was no more than an inch or so high, mostly cream, but his ears and tail were brown and he had a black nose.

"I mean it's quite cute, but what was it for? Who owned it? Why did they keep it?"

"Same reason I rescued it I suppose. I liked it."

Hannah sat next to her and picked up a pebble from the bowl. It was black with silver flecks sparkling all over the surface and didn't need any further cleaning. She put it on the plank.

"I think that's all it is, just stuff that catches my eye when I'm diving in those old houses. Thanks for doing this. I ought to go help Peter, I haven't done anything here at all – and it is my cottage. I'm feeling a bit guilty."

"No need to feel guilty. Everyone's enjoying helping, it's sort of like sticking two fingers up to whoever started the fire."

Hannah didn't want to get into a conversation about whether the fire was set on purpose and who might have done it. She went back indoors where Peter was washing the ceiling and getting very wet.

"You'd better keep away from me," he said. "I put old clothes on specially for this and that white shirt of yours would never clean up."

"There was something else I was going to do, but I should be helping here."

"We've got plenty of people offering to help. There's not enough room for everyone, so don't worry. We're all eager to see you back in here and settled after that awful night."

"Okay, but only if you're sure."

"I am sure. Go on, buzz off and annoy someone else."

Peter laughed and Hannah promised herself that she would make it up to everyone who had helped her, but she didn't know how.

She thought that now Isaac had discovered the safe she ought to move the contents somewhere more secure. They wouldn't take up much space and she was sure Martha could hide them until they opened up the secret room again and put the gold in there.

There was a light, fresh breeze blowing from the south when she walked up towards the Manor. Soon the wind would veer eastwards for months and the temperature would drop. The autumn equinox was only a few weeks away, but Hannah knew that as long as it stayed dry for their festivities nobody would mind a chill in the air.

Just as she was approaching the Manor she heard the heavy front door slam shut. She ducked behind a tree and waited, her back pressed to the trunk and hands held tight against her sides. The gate clicked shut and footsteps came in her direction, scuffing against the dirt and pebbles in the lane. Hannah held her breath as she recognised the tuneless, sibilant whistling of Isaac as he approached her hiding place. She edged round the tree when he walked past, only daring to peek at his retreating figure when he was almost at the bend in the lane and soon to be out of sight.

She ran up to the Manor, bursting through the front door, scared of what she might find. In the study the safe was exposed, but still locked. The books from that section had been stacked in a neat pile and a couple of pieces of paper lay on top of them. At first she thought Isaac might have already opened the safe and these were the remnants of its contents, but they were just lists of numbers, some with names by their sides, others simply regular sequences. The first page all had ticks against them, as had a few on the second page.

Scanning down the list she realised that Isaac had put down everyone's birthday and the date of their marriages and deaths. Along with the sequences there were lots of groups of numbers that fell into neither category. One set of numbers on the list caught her eye – it was the combination for the safe's lock. Counting quickly she realised that Isaac only has seven more numbers to try before he reached the one that would open it.

Hannah turned to the safe, but fumbled the dial and had to take a few deep breaths and start again. The lock clicked, the dial met resistance and the safe door opened. Everything was still there. She bundled it into her arms, closed the door and spun the dials.

Bounding up the stairs two at a time she shouldered open the door to her parents' bedroom, dumped the papers on the bed and pulled the canvas shoulder bag out of the bottom of the wardrobe. Hannah sat on the bed to think. She couldn't afford to bump into Isaac and she had no idea where he had gone or when he might return. Just when she decided to risk leaving the house, she heard the front door open again.

From the landing she could hear Isaac in the study, whistling and grunting every now and then – she assumed when a combination failed to work. It wouldn't be long before he gained access to the safe.

Hannah crept up a narrow set of bare wooden stairs to the top floor. She and Abby used to play hide and seek up there. She remembered a bathroom with a huge cupboard with just enough room to squeeze in under the bottom shelf and shut the door.

It would be a much tighter fit now, but she thought she could still get in there if she needed to hide. A small, high window overlooked the front garden. Hannah hid the bag on the very top shelf of the cupboard where it couldn't be seen and sat quietly on the floor, listening for any sound from Isaac.

She knew that he must be close to finding the right sequence and she heard a loud bang. It wasn't the front door, but it could have been the safe slamming shut after Isaac found it empty. It was soon followed by the sound of something breaking.

Only a few seconds later the front door slammed shut so hard that a glass rattled on a shelf above the sink where she was. She stood on tiptoe, not able to see much of the garden, but she could see the gate to the lane.

Isaac came into view and wrenched the gate open, kicking it and cursing loud enough for Hannah to hear as it swung back at him. He walked, shoulders hunched, down the lane towards the village.

Hannah descended the stairs cautiously, even though she had seen Isaac leave. A vase was in hundreds of pieces on the hall floor, fragments scattered in a fan shape.

She looked through the door to the study. The pile of books had been knocked over and the safe door was hanging wide open, revealing Isaac's displeasure at finding it empty.

Hannah was clutching her bag to her chest. She looked out of the window beside the front door and, confident that Isaac had left, ran along the front of the house, round the top of the walled garden and onto a unused path that she and Abby had considered their secret route.

Emerging onto the lane in the village, Hannah casually slung her bag over her shoulder so as not to draw attention to it. When she saw Isaac outside the stores she hesitated, almost stopped and turned around, but knew that would look odd if he had seen her.

"Hannah," he said tersely, as though she was late for an appointment and had to be reprimanded.

"Uncle," Hannah replied. "Are you okay, you look worried?"

She used her best sympathetic voice, but couldn't believe he hadn't spotted the bag over her shoulder.

"I'm a bit tired, that's all," he said, recovering his composure. He forced a rictus smile onto his red sweating face. "Are you looking forward to seeing Simon again, it's only a few days now?"

"I am Uncle, but please don't say anything to him, it would be so embarrassing."

She wondered if she was overdoing the little girl act, but Isaac appeared to be getting back into control and was probably happy to hear her sounding so innocent.

"I'm sure it will be all right. You two are made for each other."

Hannah looked down, wondering how to get out of the conversation. The bag on her shoulder was getting heavier and practically screaming that it held secrets. The door opened and Martha feigned surprise to see them both there.

"Oh Isaac, you're still here. I thought I heard Hannah's voice."

She nudged Hannah as though conspiratorially.

"I've altered that dress, the one you want for when..." she glanced at Isaac and spoke even more quietly, "for when the Pride next arrives."

Hannah looked at Martha blankly, and didn't understand for a second or two. Isaac chuckled.

"A new dress eh? Someone you're planning to look nice for?"

"Don't embarrass the girl Isaac, get on with you and leave us women alone with our plans."

Isaac laughed comfortably, turned and walked away.

Chapter 35

As soon as she and Martha were alone Hannah confronted her, having been puzzled by Martha's interruption. "What was all that about a dress?" she asked.

"I wanted to get rid of him. He's in a foul mood about something."

"He managed to open the safe."

"Oh no, did he get everything?"

"It's okay, it's all here," Hannah said, patting the bag on her shoulder. "But it was close."

"We need to hide that somewhere. I wouldn't put it past that devious devil to figure out your father's gold does exist."

"The dress was a brilliant idea, it will keep Isaac focussed on the idea that I might marry Simon and leave the Island."

"It wasn't exactly made up on the spur of the moment. I do have a dress that might be just right for you."

Hannah smiled but shook her head at Martha.

"You are devious aren't you."

"Well you do like Simon."

"We only spent one day together."

"One day can be all it takes."

Hannah said she needed to hide the wills and her father's journal, emptying her bag onto Martha's table.

"I don't fancy opening up that room again until we have to. But I know where to put them for a while. Mind you, I doubt even Isaac would try to search my stores."

"Where's that?" Hannah asked.

"My barrels, the one I make lye in."

"Won't it damage the paper?"

"No, I've just cleaned them out thoroughly and there's fresh straw in them. They'll be quite safe there for a few days. But when are you planning to recover the rest of the coins, or whatever is in that chest?"

"As soon as we can, in the next couple of days I hope, I need to arrange it with Abby."

"It is safe isn't it, diving there?"

"It's really only a few feet down, just well hidden from view."

"Nothing I can do to help?"

"No, I was going to ask Peter to stand guard for us originally, but the fewer people who know the easier it will be to keep secret."

"I'm sure Peter's okay, but I agree, for now at least. You may need help in the future though."

"I'll take the cart up to the Manor tomorrow and bring a couple of things back here, make sure I'm seen, then nobody will think anything of it if they see me with it another day."

"Good idea, you could bring back a chair and some material if there's any spare up there. We left the Manor intact out of respect for your parents, hoping you and Ethan would move in some day, but you'll need new curtains in your cottage"

"Ethan and I are done now, it's officially over."

"Maybe you and Simon then – that house needs a family in it."

"You are awful Martha," Hannah laughed. "You've got me pregnant and I haven't even got a boyfriend yet, never mind a husband."

Martha took all the documents and went out to squirrel them away in one of her barrels. Hannah called out to her from the kitchen as to whether it was okay to grab some old clothes to wear while painting the cottage. Martha told her to help herself from the racks by the door.

"They're all on their last legs, they're really not much use for anything but cleaning rags."

When Martha came back in, Hannah had donned a pair of knee length shorts and an old, torn, oversized man's shirt.

"If you meet Simon dressed like that I think we'll be able to rule out marriage."

"Go and find me that dress then and maybe a bridesmaid dress for you too," Hannah countered and ducked out the door before Martha could answer her.

"Stupid girl," she heard Martha mutter.

Hannah walked up the lane and wandered into her cottage. The walls were looking better but the smoke damage still showed through the first layer of lime wash. Peter was mixing another tub for the second coat.

"It's not very white is it? I can still see the grey smoke stains," Hannah said, quickly adding, "sorry, I'm not complaining."

"Don't worry, it will dry much whiter and it will cover eventually. We'll probably have to give it three or four coats in total."

Gabriel and Leah had already started on the stairs and Hannah squeezed past them to see the bedroom. It looked better than it had before the fire. In the middle of the room was the box Sophia had been using as a seat and in it were Hannah's scavenged collection, packed with straw to keep them safe.

"Sophia put your stuff up there to keep it out of the way," Leah said from the top of the stairs. "We're going to give the walls another coat, but upstairs is almost done."

Hannah pitched in with Peter and helped thin the lime putty with water until it resembled the consistency of milk.

"Why not make it thicker?" she asked. "Won't it cover more?"

"Because it bonds better like this. We have to damp the walls too. You can start doing that with some rags. Actually we're lucky that the heat of the summer has passed because it might have been too hot to do this a week ago."

"I'm not so sure I'd use the word lucky about any of this."

"Okay, you're right, I didn't mean it like that."

"When do we start painting?"

"Now," Peter said handing her a brush. "You've not used lime wash before?"

"No, but how hard can it be?"

Peter laughed. "It's not hard, but I warn you, it's tedious and tiring."

Gabriel was painting the ceiling above the stairs while Leah steadied the ladder. He had a towel over his head and some ancient swimming goggles on to keep splashes out of his eyes.

Peter and Hannah worked round the walls. Peter had showed her how to keep a wet edge to the wash so that it didn't dry too quickly.

"It's going to take forever if it needs four coats," Hannah said, wiping a splash from her cheek.

Peter laughed and said she could leave it to them if she wanted, but Hannah said she needed to help and that she should have been there from the start. At the end of the day her right arm ached from such an unaccustomed task and her neck had stiffened on one side.

She ate supper with Martha and said she was going to walk over to Hope Barton and arrange to meet Abby at the reservoir later the next day.

"Peter said it would be easier to finish the lime wash without me as all three of them would be trying to work in a small space. I can't say I mind, painting is really tiring work."

She didn't linger at Hope Barton as she wanted to get to

bed and rest her neck, which was stiffening more as they evening drew on. That night she kept waking from a nightmare that Isaac had somehow found the cave and sealed it off underwater.

The next morning Hannah got up early and set off to the Manor with the smallest handcart Martha had - not much more than a wooden platform between two solid bicycle wheels and shafts whose hand grips had been worn smooth by use.

Martha put a box on the platform, tying it in place with a length of thick string. She suggested Hannah brought back some books and maybe a kitchen chair, telling her that there were a couple stored in the scullery, which were never used. People were surfacing for the day and the two of them lingered outside the store, giving all who passed a chance to see Hannah with the cart. They both said hello to everyone and a few stopped to chat before starting their daily work.

Hannah told three or four people that she was off to bring a few things back from the Manor for her cottage. After the fourth repetition she thought that she sounded almost too eager to explain her plans and from then on waited until someone asked.

Her intention was to bring one or two small loads back and then leave the handcart at the Manor, out of sight, in the walled garden. All went well and Hannah worried that it was too easy to create this pretence and that someone would see through it and mention her trips to Isaac, but he was nowhere to be seen all day.

She was back helping in the cottage by late morning. Leah had taken her leave to deal with one of her children who had fallen out of a tree picking the last of the plums – fortunately he wasn't badly hurt. The repetitive work took her mind off the reservoir, Isaac and the imminent arrival of the Pride and Simon. By mid afternoon the walls were almost finished, which allowed her to make an excuse to haul some more things back from the Manor.

After retrieving the handcart from the walled garden, Hannah trundled it up to the reservoir, relieved to meet no one on the way. It wasn't a path that was used that often and most people would still be working in the orchards or stacking wood in the dry for winter. Abby was there waiting for her with a couple of small canvas sacks to transport the coins from the cave to land.

"Hi, this is it then?" Abby said.

"I guess so."

Abby got up and retrieved the line that was still hidden under a pile of stones. She gave it a gentle tug to make sure the other end was firmly attached.

"What do you need me to do?"

"Fasten the end of that to something. I'll use it as a guide-line."

They spoke very little. Abby secured the rope and Hannah stripped down to pants and a t-shirt. She folded her clothes neatly on the rock, along with fresh t-shirt, pants and a towel, which she'd put in the crate on the handcart.

"I can't return to the village wet. It would be difficult to explain."

Abby nodded in agreement and Hannah slid into the water off the rock ledge. Before she went down for the first dive Abby reached out and covered Hannah's hand where it was resting on the rocks.

"Be careful won't you," she said and handed her one of the two bags.

Hannah smiled, took a few deep breaths and sank under the water. The sun was higher in the sky, the cave darker than before. She felt her way with her hand loosely closed around the rope until she reached the chest. Clamping her knees around the same stone she had used before, Hannah forced the lid of the chest fully open.

Working almost entirely by touch she carefully transferred loose coins and a couple of intact bags into her own larger sack. She didn't want anything to burst and to lose coins onto the cave floor or especially when she was surfacing. She clasped the bag to her chest and pulled herself out of the cave with the guide rope.

It took several dives. She filled her bag each time, handed it to Abby and went down again with the other empty bag. Abby, as arranged, was transferring everything to the crate as soon as Hannah brought it up. That way if anyone stumbled on them there would be nothing immediately visible. They would be able to claim that Hannah was trying to find a spanner that Abby had dropped into the reservoir by accident. As Abby couldn't swim it would sound plausible. As it was, nobody chanced by them before Hannah brought the last half-filled bag to the surface.

"The chest is bolted to the rocks from inside," she gasped. "The head of the bolt isn't corroded and I think the chest will break if I try to lever it off."

"It would be conspicuous anyway," Abby said. "People would want to know where we found it."

Hannah said she'd like to retrieve it sometime but they would need a wrench to free the bolt. She climbed onto the rock ledge with Abby's help and they threw the end of the rope, tied to a stone, into the reservoir. It would be relatively easy to find again as it was still secured to the chest.

Once Hannah had changed and dried her hair, they wriggled the crate centrally on the cart and started to trundle it back to the Manor. Abby pulled while Hannah steadied the load as it bumped over the stones on the path.

At the Manor they add a couple of small rugs and some

curtains to the cart, covering most of the crate. In the village they didn't hurry, but stopped to chat to people about Hope Barton and Becky. Nobody paid any attention to the cart or its load. Even Isaac wandered by them, distracted by something, giving them a curt nod and a mumbled greeting. Had he known what was hidden from his sight he would have taken more interest.

Chapter 36

When they arrived at the stores Martha had the door open and was waiting just inside to welcome them. She poked her head out and looked up and down the lane to see if anyone was watching. It was all clear, so she opened the door wide and beckoned them to wheel the handcart inside. She closed the door behind them and stood with her back against it, arms spread as though to prevent anyone following them in.

"I'm glad you were waiting for us," Hannah said. "This box is far too heavy to lift, even with two of us."

Martha locked the door before coming closer to the cart.

"Is that it? Is it all there?" she asked.

Abby lifted the top off the crate to reveal a stack of bags and a scatter of loose coins.

"How many are there?" Martha gasped.

"We haven't counted," Hannah said, looking to Abby for confirmation.

"We didn't have time."

"We need to get them safe," Martha said urgently. "I've emptied the shelves but couldn't move the wardrobe by myself."

She couldn't take her eyes off the coins but made no move to touch them. "You'll need some bags for the loose ones. I'll get a couple while you take Abby down to the cellar and open up the vault. Better wheel this over to the top of the steps before someone comes in and sees it."

Even though Hannah had described the hidden room to Abby, she was still surprised by the skilful way the entrance was concealed and the size of the vault.

"Let's get the gold down here first," Hannah said. "I'll show you the weapons I told you about afterwards."

Abby and Hannah ran up and down the stone stairs, transporting the bags to the vault. Hannah found them surprisingly heavy, having only really handled them underwater. She only managed to carry four at a time while Abby took five or six.

Martha kept a watch upstairs and put the loose coins in the spare bags she had found. Once the last coins had been removed from the cart Martha unlocked the door and followed them, taking the crate down there with her.

"Can you get the small table Abby," Martha said. "I left it just through the arch on the right." Martha looked at the bags piled on the floor. "I'll be back in a minute."

The girls started to put the bags onto the table while Martha disappeared back upstairs. Both were in a state of wonder, not having seen them all revealed until then. There were more than either had realised. Martha returned a few minutes later with a set of ancient balance scales and large circular weights.

"You count the coins in one bag," she said. "Then we can weigh it."

The first bag had exactly 80 coins in it, so did the second. Abby put one on the scales and Martha balanced it with a several of the weights.

"Five pounds," Martha said. "Put the next one on."

Martha was staring at her fingers, wiggling each one in turn, in an attempt to count. Her face was screwed up in concentration.

"Each coin must weigh one ounce," she said almost to herself. "That makes sense."

"What's an ounce?" Abby asked.

"The old way of weighing things before everyone changed to grams and kilos."

They weighed the next bag without counting the coins, merely untying the string around the top to check that the contents were similar. Martha weighed each bag and kept a tally on a piece of scrap paper. Abby packed them in the box after putting it in the corner of the room.

Once the intact bags were weighed, noted and stowed, Hannah started to count the loose coins that had spilled in the top of the chest. She looked at the coins as she piled them in stacks of ten. There were four main types but a few other odd versions, all a similar size and all gold. The counted coins filled the new bags that Martha had found except for the last one.

"We're three short of a hundred. I wonder if I dropped some on the cave floor."

"I don't think three will make much difference," Abby laughed.

"Don't be silly," Martha said. "The other three are upstairs, you brought them here before. I forgot to bring them down."

Hannah counted the tallies on Martha's records.

"How many?" Abby asked.

"It makes sixty bags when that last one is added in."

"And eighty coins in each bag. That's..."

Martha was just walking down the steps again when they all heard the front door open and Isaac's muffled voice calling hello.

"I thought you locked the door?" Abby hissed.

"I unlocked it as soon as you moved all the coins out of sight - it would have been odd if someone had turned up and found the place closed and locked – I never lock it in case there's an emergency."

Isaac was calling from the top of the stairs. "Are you down there Martha?"

Martha put a finger to her lips to tell them to keep quiet.

She thrust the last three coins into Hannah's hands and turned to go back up.

"On my way Isaac, I was looking for something."

Hannah and Abby crept to the bottom of the steps to listen.

"Is Hannah here somewhere? I wanted a quick word with her."

Martha hesitated. "Have you checked in her cottage, she was working in there earlier."

"No, I thought I'd stop here first and save myself a walk if I could."

"Can you wait a moment Isaac, there's something I wanted to check with you too, but I left a candle burning in the cellar and after the fire at the cottage I've got so nervous about such things."

Martha wobbled back down the steps, calling to Isaac not to go anywhere for a minute. Abby handed her a candle.

"Will this take long?" Isaac called down.

"Back in a jiffy." She bent towards Hannah and whispered urgently. "I'll distract him. You sneak out the back door and get to your cottage as fast as you can."

Martha went back up with the snubbed out candle and took Isaac's arm, carefully turning him away from the cellar.

"We're you talking to someone down there?"

"Just nattering to myself Isaac. I forget things if I don't keep repeating them nowadays."

"What is it that's so urgent then?"

Hannah crept up the stone steps until she could peek through the rails to see Martha and Isaac.

"I need you come and look at the potato stocks," Martha said, managing to sound very concerned.

She turned Isaac away from Hannah and led him down one the aisles between stacked crates and a haphazard shelving unit, while waving a hand behind her to indicate Hannah should escape.

"Now, how many potatoes do you think the main crop will yield, because as you can see we're quite low on seed potatoes. You have no idea how much I worry Isaac, what with prices always going up on the mainland."

Hannah kept low behind some boxes and made her way quietly towards the back door. As she left she could hear Isaac getting frustrated with Martha.

"How on earth would I know that Martha? It's not my department, you'd do better asking Abby or Leah, or any number of people rather than me."

Hannah lingered just outside the back door unable to resist listening to Martha leading him on.

"Well you did ask about the potatoes didn't you? Was there anything else you wanted to check?"

"I asked if you'd seen Hannah. I'm sorry Martha, I have to go."

Isaac opened the front door, grumbling rather too loudly that she must have lost her marbles.

"Was it marbles you wanted Isaac? I think I've got some upstairs, just let me fetch them."

The door rattled as Isaac shut it harder than necessary. Hannah took the path that led to the back of her cottage. She ran as fast as she could while trying not to laugh, grabbed the gate post and wheeled into her garden, bumping into Peter as he came out the back door.

"Steady on," he said, catching her shoulders. "What's got into you? And what's so funny?"

"I'll tell you later," Hannah said, slightly breathless. "But when Isaac gets here, could you pretend I've been here all day. Please."

"Okay, no problem, but what have you been up to?"

"Me? Nothing at all, it's just that... well, you know what

Isaac's like. He always wants to know everything."

"Okay, you put the kettle on and I'll deal with him when he arrives. You need to get your breath back."

No sooner had they gone back in than Isaac turned up at the front door.

"Hello. Anyone here? Hannah?"

"Isaac, what can I do for you?"

"I was looking for Hannah, is she here?"

"She's just making tea. We thought we'd have a break. Shall I get her for you? Do you want a mug?"

"No, no drink for me, I only wanted to catch up with Hannah, check what she's doing. I'm concerned for her, wanted to see she was okay."

Hannah came out of kitchen having recovered her repose.

"Hello Uncle, do you want a mug of tea?"

"No, no thank you dear girl, I simply wanted to see how you were getting on here."

Hannah said she was cleaning the kitchen one last time and that everything was almost back to normal except for the scorch marks on the flagstones. Isaac looked uncomfortable when she mentioned the kitchen floor, but he recovered quickly.

"It looks almost better than before. Nice fresh new paint, very spacious."

"That's because there's no furniture in here yet."

"It will take a few days to dry properly," Peter said. "Then we'll get Hannah's stuff back in here. But is there anything we can help you with?"

No, nothing I need as such. I'm just going up to the Manor, wanted to see that it's all ship-shape up there. The Pride's due to arrive soon and I... just wanted to look around you know, a quick check."

"Why wouldn't it be okay Uncle?"

"No reason at all, I was just going for my own peace of mind and so on."

"I picked up some rugs and a chair from there, but I didn't look in the dining room or study. I don't expect anything will be out of place."

"I suppose your little fire has made me nervous," Isaac explained. "Always best to be on the safe side."

Isaac made a hasty retreat, muttering that everything seemed to be working out okay and that Peter had been a great help to everyone. When Isaac was out of earshot, walking hurriedly in the direction of the Manor, Peter looked at Hannah, a hint of a smile about his mouth.

"I presume you know what that was all about."

"I think so."

"And I also presume you're not going to tell me."

"I will, I promise, but not right now, it's too long a story and I have to get back to the store."

Peter laughed and told her to get going, calling out after her that he thought she'd given up playing pirates and princesses years ago. Abby and Martha were coming up from the cellar when Hannah burst through the front door.

"What did he want?" Abby asked.

"Just checking where I was. I think he's going up to the Manor to tidy up the study."

"Well, we're all done here, we've put everything back in place."

Martha still had a piece of paper in her hand, on which she had kept track of the counting.

"I could do with a hot drink," Abby said, rubbing her bare arms. "It's surprisingly chilly down there."

"It's not that cold," Martha replied. "Never too hot, never damp, that's why it's such a good storage room."

"For all sorts of things," Abby raised an eyebrow. "As I have now discovered."

"You saw what was in those other boxes - those weapons."

"I did," she said. "And I hope we never need them, but it's good to know they're there – just in case."

"Does anyone want to know the final tally?" asked Martha.

"I worked it out," Hannah said, her voice dropping to almost a whisper. "Four thousand eight hundred coins."

"How much do you think they are worth?" Abby asked.

"Becky said just three of those coins would feed the whole island for a year."

Martha sat down on one of the chairs that Hannah had brought back from the Manor.

I think I need something stronger than tea my dear. There's a bottle of damson brandy in my kitchen. Would you fetch it please Abby? I think the occasion might justify a little celebration.

Chapter 37

One end of Martha's store was kept as a makeshift lounge. In summer she was too busy to sit down, but in winter she often took it easy, whiling away the day by a huge wood burner with a book by her side and, on her lap, whichever stray cat had adopted her that autumn. Transitioning furniture found a home there and Martha sank into an old leather armchair, so soft that it looked as if it was trying to swallow her whole. Abby joined them with a half-full bottle and three mismatched glasses.

"I'd better take the larger one," Martha said, taking the bottle and one glass. "I've had more practise with this stuff."

Martha poured a generous measure into her own glass and slightly less for Abby and Hannah.

"To the future," Martha said, holding up her glass.

"And to the past and those who planned for us so well," added Abby.

Their mood was not so much sombre as tired. Not from physical labour, although Hannah's shoulder still ached from painting her cottage, but brought about by the relief that everything important was now safely concealed.

"What do we do now?" Abby asked.

"Nothing, not until I've spoken to Simon and found out what is really happening on the mainland. You must have seen a lot while you were over there Abby?"

"Not that much really. Becky went into Freetown."

Martha sipped her damson brandy and closed her eyes.

"That was a bit risky wasn't it?" she asked.

"You don't know what she's like. You can argue with her

all you want, but you're unlikely to win."

"You didn't see any tractors working on the fields did you?" Hannah asked.

"There was a lot of noise, they were factories, Becky said, but I wasn't that interested to be honest. I didn't want to leave the boat unguarded as Becky said things were not quite so civilised over there and we were... getting to know each other – if you know what I mean. "

Hannah had put her drink down on a small table and covered her ears with her hands.

"I don't want to know," she said, but smiled and laughed when Abby stretched out a leg and prodded her thigh.

They sat there while it got dark, trying to work out how much the gold might buy and what they should do with it, knowing that it had been hidden for a long time and that the Island had done pretty well without it.

"I'm for leaving it down there," Abby said. "Unless we've got something really special that we need."

"I wonder how much a boat would cost," Hannah said.

"I would have thought we'd got enough boats for now. I know Sophia would disagree, but some decent timber for repairs wouldn't go amiss."

"I meant something bigger. Something large enough that we could trade with the mainland direct and not be dictated to by the Recorder."

"A steamboat?"

"I suppose so."

"Wow. That would have to cost quite a bit and we haven't got anyone to crew it. We wouldn't even know how it works."

"We could learn. But I wasn't thinking of something as big as the Pride. Just big enough to go to Freetown and back and do our own selling and buying."

"Becky might know what's available, she's pretty knowledgeable about boats."

"Simon is too, if he comes over again."

"He'll come," Abby said.

Martha snored and woke herself up. She looked at both the girls. "What are you two smiling about?"

"Just thinking it was time for bed," Abby said. "And I've got to traipse back over to Hope Barton."

"Me to," Hannah added, yawning. "I'd offer you a bed for the night, but I guess you want to get back to Becky."

Abby said she liked the idea of falling straight into bed, but she'd only regret it in the morning – and the fresh air wouldn't do her any harm. They said their goodnights to Martha who, almost half asleep again, declared that she might just stay where she was as it was so comfy.

"You'll regret it," Abby said.

"Maybe one more glass," she mumbled. "A little nightcap."

Martha picked up the bottle and drained the dregs into her glass, it only half filled it. Abby and Hannah parted ways outside the store, Hannah saying she was going to stroll down to the quay to clear her head.

The wind had dropped and as she approached the harbour the water looked like a sheet of black glass. A full moon was behind her and each boat in the harbour had become two – one the right way up and one upside down. She turned towards footsteps coming along the quay.

"Hi Hannah, what are you doing here at this time of night?"

"Thinking. What about you?"

"I was wondering whether to go out fishing, but there's really not enough wind."

"I thought you liked to row anyway?"

"I do, but I'd be the only one out there."

Sophia leaned on the rail next to Hannah and they both

looked out over the harbour, enjoying the peace and the gentle slapping sound the swell made against the quay wall.

"I wanted to ask you about that boat," Sophia said.

"Becky's boat?"

"I thought her name was Bethany, the Recorder's daughter?"

"Sorry, yes, I forgot." Hannah winced at such a stupid mistake.

"If you see the Recorder, could you ask him about it. Whether he plans to take it back or leave it here? I mean it sort of should be ours as it was abandoned and we found it. And I've repaired the gooseneck."

"I'll ask Isaac. He knows the Recorder better than I do. It might be more tactful coming from him."

"Okay. I'll leave you to it then."

Sophia pushed herself off the rail and strolled lazily along the quay, towards her little cottage overlooking the harbour and Hannah made her way back up the lane to Canary Cottage, now habitable once again.

Once inside she leaned against the door, sighed, turned, and slid the bolt across. Metal ground against metal. Hannah had locked her front door for the first time in her life. She could see the garden through the glazed panel in her back door. The moon cast such sharp shadows that it was like an imitation of daylight. She bolted the back door too and made her way upstairs.

Nobody had returned her curtains yet, nor much of her furniture other than her bed. Hannah lay on it, the walls of her freshly painted room glowing a beautiful soft white as she fell asleep.

Hannah woke early and with a headache, which she was aware of as soon as she moved to get out of bed. She had never been drunk before and solemnly promised herself that it would never happen again.

She wandered downstairs and unbolted both the front and back doors, opening the door to the garden and breathing in the fresh, moist air. Mildred and Penelope clucked eagerly, strutting around their small fenced-off domain. Hannah had feed for her chickens, but no breakfast for herself. The grass was dew-damp as she walked over to their coop, delighted to find two eggs, which she gathered for breakfast.

The small fridge in her kitchen was working but the rubber seals, now rather perished, still smelled of smoke. New lengths of gasket would be available from the Pride when it called, but they were very expensive because they were imported from some far away place. But they had money now, and they could afford to keep spare supplies on the Island. That was how dipping into those gold coins might make a difference without changing everything, but it would have to be done carefully and probably not until she had replaced Isaac as bailiff.

Over the next few days Hannah restored some sense of normality to her cottage. Her prized collection was displayed again, rugs brought from the Manor made the place more like home and Joanna and her husband brought her sofa back. It was covered in a bright striped material and no longer sagged in the middle. She thought she might ban Isaac from sitting on it if she had the nerve.

She sat gingerly on the sofa, amazed at how luxurious it felt. Hannah wondered how life on the mainland might differ and remembered the Pride was due the next day. Martha had mentioned a dress when they had bumped into Isaac and Hannah decided to walk down to the stores to ask her about it.

Martha teased her, but brought out a white dress with embroidery around the neck and at the ends of three-quarter length sleeves.

"I can't wear that," Hannah said. "It will look like I'm ready to get to married as soon as he steps onto the quay."

"Nothing wrong with dropping a hint," Martha suggested.

"That's not a hint. I might as well add a wreath of flowers on my head and have string tied to my finger."

"You would look pretty like that," Martha teased. "Maybe I should keep it for you for sometime in the future."

"I think I'll stick to shorts and a pullover for now. Mornings are already cooler and I don't even know if Simon will be on the Pride."

The next morning Hannah heard the whistle of the steamship cutting through the still morning air while she was making breakfast. She cursed and hurried, a slice of toast gripped between her teeth while she struggled into her shoes. Hannah stopped outside the door, told herself to slow down and finish her breakfast, swallowing hard to make the bread disappear. She had marmalade all over her fingertips, swore again and went back inside to wash them. There was no way she was going to greet Simon with sticky fingers, assuming he was on the ship.

When she got to the quay one of the rowing boats was almost there already. The Pride had moored closer this time because the tide was already high. In the front of the boat Simon was standing up, a rope in his hands, scanning the quay. As soon as he saw her he waved.

"Hi Hannah," he called. "I'm back."

She had no idea what to say as everyone was listening. "I can see," she said and kicked herself for coming out with such an inane greeting.

He fastened the rope round a cleat and leapt onto the quay next to her.

"I've been counting the days," he said.

Hannah realised that she had been too, somewhere in the back of her head, but also trying not to admit it in order to avoid disappointment.

"Where's Gideon? Is he coming ashore later?"

"Ah, he's not well. I offered to take his place on this trip. I've been on the Pride for over a week now and the experience wears a bit thin after the first few days – not to mention the monotony of the catering."

Isaac joined them. "What's wrong with Gideon did you say?"

"I didn't say, but just the flu we hope. I haven't seen him for over a week now."

"Not the virus?"

"No, we haven't had an outbreak for ages. I'm sure he'll be better by the time I get back. But he asked me to do the usual honours with you Isaac. He said you'd know everything that needs arranging."

"Quite so, indeed I'm sure it won't be a problem. Maybe we could tidy up the formalities over dinner tonight as usual?"

"I was rather hoping to spend some time with Hannah," Simon said, turning to her. "Just us two, if that all right with you?"

"That would be nice," Hannah said.

"I suppose we can conclude most of the business down here," Isaac said and Hannah could almost see him thinking before he spoke again. "Yes, perfectly fine by me. You young things enjoy yourselves."

"I have that map for Ethan too."

Simon opened his satchel to give something to Hannah, but she kept her hands behind her back.

"Why don't you take it over to him? You know the way don't you?"

"Maybe you could come with me? Just to make sure I don't get lost."

Hannah laughed, but agreed. She told him that Ethan and her were no longer 'an item'. He looked surprise, but smiled.

"I'm sorry. I mean I am sorry but I'm not actually that sorry," his brow furrowed, "I'm not putting this very well am I?"

"You're doing perfectly okay," Hannah laughed.

"Will Ethan be all right with me and you going over there?"

"If you've got a map for him he'll be delighted to see you, even if you were dressed as a pirate with an eye patch and a parrot on your shoulder."

"Not sure I can manage that, but I think we have some chickens on board."

"We've got chickens here. But we can always use more."

They both laughed, and Hannah realised that she would either have to warn Becky or let Simon in on their secret.

Chapter 38

Isaac suggested they check the trading lists first, before they went gallivanting all over the Island. "It will only take a minute or two and then it's all done."

Simon reluctantly agreed, reminding Hannah that he was there in place of Gideon and it was his responsibility to sort these things out. She said to call for her at Canary Cottage once he was done. Martha had turned up with a posse of helpers and carts loaded with produce from the harvest – it looked to Hannah like it might take a while.

She went back home, but left the front door open, hoping Simon wouldn't be too long. After making herself tea, which she'd missed at breakfast time, she sat on her new sofa cradling a mug in her hands. She couldn't believe it had only been a little over four weeks since she had first met Simon – so much had happened in that time. She was sure she had been waiting for him for years and known him forever. Once her tea was drained Hannah picked a book on herbal remedies from her shelf and started reading. When Simon turned up at the door she was lost in the text.

"Come in," she said. "Do you want a drink or something?"

"No I'm fine," he said, patting his belly. "They feed you almost too well on the Pride. I'll have to be careful I don't end up the size of Isaac."

Hannah giggled. She couldn't imagine him ever ending up as rotund as Isaac. Simon had an almost flat stomach, his tight t-shirt showing no bulges and he was tall and rangy. Hannah grabbed a hat. The sky had cleared of early mist and the sun could be strong even that late in the year. She had to explain a lot to Simon on the way to Hope Barton and she thought it best to take a route past Abby's hut. Ethan might be on the heath with the sheep, or checking the goats or just keeping out of Daniel's way.

"I've got some things I need to tell you before we get to Hope Barton," she said. "I hope you'll be okay with it, but you need to know."

"That sounds ominous." Simon laughed. "Is it about you and your family?"

"Not my family as such."

They had left the village and a breeze blew across the fields stirring up small eddies of dust, which settled almost as soon as they had risen.

"We need some rain soon," Hannah said.

"Was that it?"

"No, sorry, it's actually about Bethany."

"Has her body been found?"

"In a manner of speaking. That is... it was never really lost."

"I don't understand."

"She never drowned."

"Now you've lost me completely."

Hannah stopped, took both of Simon's hands in hers and told him that if he wanted to change his mind about anything, about the Island, about what he thought of her, she wouldn't blame him, but what she was about to tell him had to stay a secret.

Simon said he couldn't imagine what she was talking about, but that she was worrying him.

"Do you promise?"

"Yes. I trust you. If you say it's a secret my lips are sealed."

"I mean it, I'm deadly serious."

"Okay. I can see that. I promise your secret will be safe with me whatever it is."

Hannah bit her lip, still not sure she should be telling him, but couldn't see any alternative if they were to be together.

"It's about Bethany, Beth, she's here, on the Island. We hid her."

"You hid her? You mean you kidnapped her?"

Simon pulled his hands from Hannah's. He was frowning, trying to make sense out of what Hannah was telling him. She grabbed his hands again.

"It's not like that. She asked us to hide her."

"Why?"

"She didn't want to get married, not just to you, but to anyone."

"She could have said, I wasn't about to force her."

"But her father was. She ran away from him. Sailed here. She almost died, she might have if I hadn't been there when she ran aground."

"So where is she?"

"At Hope Barton."

"With Ethan?"

"No, she doesn't want to be with a man, any man. She's with Abby."

Simon sat down on a grassy bank by the side of the lane. He patted the space next to him.

"Do you want to explain this before we get to Hope Barton?"

Hannah sat and went through everything that had happened from meeting Beth to the fire in her cottage. The only thing she left out of her story was finding the gold. She trusted Simon, but had promised Abby and Martha that they wouldn't tell a soul about it unless they all agreed.

"Wow, that explains a few things."

"What do you mean?"

"I always thought there was something different about Bethany."

"You have to call her Becky now. Nobody else must know that Becky was Beth."

"Okay, Becky it is, I'll remember that. You see I liked her, I think she quite liked me, but there was nothing there, no spark, no magic, no connection. And my mother had said things too, I think she might have guessed."

"Becky's mother knew. She told me."

"And my mother and her were friends from way back."

"Are you okay with all this?"

"Of course. Anyway, I wouldn't have met you if it hadn't been for Becky running away. I should be thanking her really."

Hannah nudged him and he pretended to fall off the bank onto the path.

"Come on," he said. "We better be getting on with this, unless you've more secrets to tell me?"

"She's going to be angry I told you. Maybe I shouldn't have."

"I love that you're honest with me and I won't let you down – or Becky."

Hannah hated that she had to keep the gold and the weapons from him. If they did end up together he would need to know, but if they didn't it would be a terrible mistake to let him in on the secret.

They walked on, but Hannah soon led him off the lane and onto a grassy track meandering up onto the heath. After fifteen minutes she pointed out Abby's hut in the distance, looking far too small for someone to be living in, even in the summer months.

Hannah knocked on the door and opened it when there was no answer. She swung it back against the wall, but there was nowhere to hide inside and Ethan wasn't to be seen. Simon looked in over her shoulder.

"Has Abby really lived here since she was eleven?"

"Only in the summer months."

"Even then... I mean there's no toilet?"

"No, no water either. It wouldn't suit me, but I have stayed here sometimes. Come on, we'd better find Ethan, he must be at the farm."

As they were walking down the lane to Hope Barton, Charlie bounded up to meet them. Simon wasn't wary of him in the way Becky had been and Hannah asked him why. He said they had dogs on a lot of their plantations.

"You're just as likely to catch the virus from another person as you are from a dog or a cat. There's no point living every day in fear. Anyway, most people think it might have run its course now."

Daniel was outside the house on his usual bench and was working on a new piece of driftwood. When they arrived he was staring at it in his hands, slowly turning it around, looking at it from every angle. Hannah found it impossible to see what Daniel saw, but once he'd started forming a creature it would become obvious to everyone and impossible to imagine how they hadn't seen it themselves. Ethan came out of the barn when he heard voices.

"Back again I see," he said.

"And I brought something for you."

Simon had a leather satchel over his shoulder from which he took a roll of thick paper, tied with a thin blue ribbon. He offered it to Ethan.

"Dirty hands," Ethan said, holding them up to show Simon. "Do you mind putting it in the kitchen?"

The three of them went inside, leaving Daniel on his bench. Simon unrolled four maps. He spread them out on the table, weighing the corners down with a salt pot and mugs, which Hannah supplied. Ethan leaned on the edge of the table not wanting to touch and spoil the paper.

"Are these all for me?" he asked.

"Yes, sure. They are a year or two out of date, but that's mainly the harbour soundings. The coastlines aren't changing any more, or not a lot."

"I don't have any money to pay for them. I could give you one of my Dad's carvings."

"They were sitting around in our office. I don't need paying. We have to make new maps every couple of years and the old ones just gather dust. Every ship has a set, so they tend to clutter the place up after a while."

"How many ships do you have?"

"Seven clippers, but they are expensive to man, four steam cruisers and three larger ships that run on bunker fuel."

"What's bunker fuel?" Hannah asked.

"It's a kind of a left-over fuel – after petrol's been refined."

"We don't have any oil or petrol on the Island," Ethan mumbled, still looking at the maps. "I didn't even know there was any."

"It's always been around, but fearsomely expensive. The price is coming down now, it drops every year. Isaac must know, Gideon would have told him."

Hannah had leaned back against the kitchen work surface, not interested in the maps. "My grandfather said oil was one of the things that caused all the problems. Anyway, it's no use to us."

"But what do you run your tractors on?"

"We have got a couple of old tractors, but they've never worked that I know of. We keep them because we don't like to throw anything away – and the kids like to play on them and pretend."

"It hadn't occurred to me," Simon said. "I haven't seen a

tractor here. I mean you wouldn't really need cars, but a tractor or two would make the land so much easier to work." He shook his head in disbelief. "You work the whole island with no machinery?"

"We've got a water mill and a steam engine."

"It would probably take a bit of work to get those tractors going again," Simon said. "But we have engineers in our company that service our ships. I could arrange for someone to come over and look at them if you want?"

"Then we'd have to buy fuel from you," Ethan said warily.

"I'm not trying to set you up as a customer, our business is sugar – although admittedly we do make ethanol from some of our crop."

"Could you send someone the next time the Pride comes over?" Hannah asked.

"I'm sure that would be possible. Or we could arrange a special visit. It's only about twenty miles here from our yards. I'm sure I could persuade my father. That way our engineers could be back at work in a couple of days, rather than stuck on the Pride for weeks."

"I can't believe Isaac doesn't know all this, about the oil and tractors and everything," Abby said from the bottom of the stairs. Nobody had noticed her there. "Surely Gideon must have told him."

"Abby," Hannah said quietly. "I told Simon about Becky. It's okay."

"Are you sure?"

Hannah nodded and Abby turned and called out upstairs. Becky came cautiously down and stayed shielded behind Abby.

"Hello Simon. I'm sorry about everything."

"Beth?"

"No, not Beth. I'm Becky."

Simon smiled at her. "Have you found what you want here?"

"I think I have."

"I understand. And it's okay with me. I never wanted to force you into something you didn't want to do. I just thought you were shy."

Ethan had washed his hands and asked if he could take the maps into the other room. "They're yours," Simon said. "Take them anywhere you want, anywhere in the whole world.

Becky and Simon went outside to talk and Abby asked Hannah if she thought it wise to tell Simon.

"I like him Abby. I think he might be the one. He has to know about Becky because he'll been bound to recognise her. I'm sure he'll keep our secret."

"Let's hope so," Abby said.

Abby hugged her. "Simon's nice. I hope it works out for you."

"It's a matter of whether he feels the same way."

"Oh, he does, take my word for it."

On their way back to the village Simon asked when she would be taking over as bailiff.

"After my birthday I suppose. We haven't really talked about it. It's not like there's going to be some ceremony where I'm sworn in and Isaac has to place a crown on my head."

"Is he okay with letting go of the reins, losing control of the Island?"

She told him that Isaac might have got the impression that they, her and Simon, were possibly going to get married and she would then move to the mainland. "I'm sorry, I didn't intend to drag you into all this," Hannah sighed. "It just happened and it got him off my back."

She explained that they thought the fire in her cottage was started on purpose and that Martha suspected Isaac, but there was no proof. Simon nodded thoughtfully, but said nothing for a while.

"So, when is your birthday? This coming of age and assumption of responsibilities."

"A week after the equinox, the thirtieth of September. We have a party on the Island for Mabon and for Yule and Ostara and Litha too."

"Can anyone come to these pagan festivals?"

"We're not pagans. My great grandmother was against all religion. She thought the old names would unite us rather than divide us. And I suppose anyone can come, but it's only ever been us, nobody really visits Hope Island."

"Except for Bethany."

"You mean Becky. And now you've come back of course."

Chapter 39

When they reached the village Simon said he needed to go back aboard the Pride and check that everything was okay. He was supposed to have been overseeing the trade transfers, but even though the crew knew what they were doing, he said he ought to check and sign the manifests on behalf of Gideon.

"You'll be back for supper? Martha is going to cook like last time, but at her place, rather than traipse all the way up to the Manor. She lives at the back of the storage barns, you know where they are?"

"I do, and yes of course I'm coming. They should have transferred a hamper ashore already. We don't want to eat you out of house and home."

"No chance of that, it's been a good harvest this year."

"I think we should ask Isaac too," Simon added. "From what you said we don't want him to feel excluded. He needs to consider his position safe."

"I'll do that," Hannah said. "You're right, we need to keep him happy."

After Simon had been rowed back out to the Pride, Hannah wandered along the quay towards Isaac's house. She knocked on his door and waited. When he answered she asked him if he would like to join them for supper at Martha's.

"I thought you and Simon wanted some time alone?"

"We've been together most of the day and, after all, you're the bailiff so you should be there really." Hannah purposefully left out the term 'guardian' so as not to offend Isaac.

"I'd be delighted to come. Usual sort of time?"

"Yes, we'll see you at Martha's."

Hannah backed away a couple of paces and smiled at Isaac. She wondered if she was overdoing it, but Isaac didn't appear suspicious and she breathed a huge sigh of relief after saying goodbye. The muscles in her neck and shoulders relaxed with every step that put distance between her and her uncle.

When Hannah dropped in to the stores Martha said she didn't need any help, she already had Sarah there, peeling potatoes. Hannah said hello to her and Sarah turned and smiled but didn't reply.

"She can talk," Martha whispered. "Just not when anyone else is around."

"I didn't know."

"I haven't told anyone because then she would feel under pressure and it might make her condition worse."

"So was it caused by the virus?"

"Not directly. I think it was shock, but I'm no psychiatrist."

"You're not a what?"

"Never mind for now, I'll explain another time."

That evening Simon arrived at the same time as Isaac. He whispered to Hannah that Isaac had been waiting for him on the quay. Sarah, usually shy and always quiet, had nothing but smiles for Simon and almost broke into giggles when she was serving him. Martha ushered her around and apologised to Simon, but he showed no sign of being offended and Sarah even managed a small thank you when he handed her an empty plate. It was very quietly spoken but everyone heard it. Martha raised an eyebrow and winked at Hannah.

Simon brought up the subject of the tractors and mentioned to Isaac that he was going to try to get a couple of engineers to come over and look at theirs – as long as his father could spare them. Isaac looked concerned.

"There's no need for that. We don't have fuel for them and we get along okay in our own way. Don't we Hannah?"

"I can't see the harm Uncle. Although I expect they will prove beyond rescue as they can't have been used for decades."

"Worth trying though," Simon added.

Isaac sighed and reluctantly agreed that they might as well look at them, but asked how much such an exercise would cost. "We don't really have any reserves for paying for that sort of help."

"No charge Isaac. I'll come over with them. I'd like to spend a little more time with Hannah than the Pride's visit allows. It will give me a good excuse."

"So so, my boy. What must be must be. But I doubt the tractors are worth rescuing so don't go to too much trouble. And you're welcome here any time you want to visit, any time."

Once again Isaac was talking as though he owned the Island, as though he was the only one who could give permission for who comes and goes.

"I've already arranged it with Simon."

"Jolly good Hannah. Although I suspect it will all be a waste of time and energy, not to mention the cost." He held both hands up, palms facing them as though in surrender. "Even if it costs us nothing in the short term, there will be the costs of fuel and I have no idea how we'd pay for that."

Hannah suggested that they could worry about that only if the tractors could be brought back to life.

"And who would operate them?" Isaac continued. "We have nobody on the Island who has ever driven anything other than our steam engine."

Hannah asked if the engineers would be able to teach them how to drive a tractor and Simon reassured them that tractors were quite simple, probably easier to handle than a steam engine. He said that even he had driven one. Isaac showed surprise that he had been involved in farming, but Simon explained that they used them on their sugar plantations and at the refineries.

"But you'll be going back to the mainland once the work is done I presume – can't leave your family business too long?"

Simon glanced at Hannah who shook her head slightly to suggest Simon didn't say too much.

"I'll ask my parents how long they can spare me. I don't think a few days will be any sort of problem."

Simon took his leave when three short blasts on the ship's whistle indicated that his boat had set out for the quay. Isaac fawned over Simon, assuring him that it had been a pleasure meeting him again and that he'd love to make the acquaintance of his family, but sadly his stomach wasn't built for pitching around on the open seas.

Martha rustled up another bottle of damson brandy to mellow Isaac, and Hannah and Simon left him at the store while they walked down to the quay where his boat was waiting. Before they got there, still hidden from the boatmen by the row of cottages, he took her elbow, encouraging her to stop.

"I've really enjoyed today, and being with you."

"Me too," Hannah replied quietly. "But we didn't do anything special."

"Simply being here with you makes it special."

Hannah dropped her head, not quite knowing how to respond. When she lifted it again he kissed her lightly on the lips. The kiss lingered for a while, neither wanting to end it.

"I ought to go," he said. "We don't want them sending out

a search party for me."

"You promise to return as soon as you can?"

"I will, and I'll teach you how to drive a tractor."

"When will you be back with those engineers? Isaac obviously felt backed into a corner, but once he thinks there might be a profit in it I'm sure he'll be more enthusiastic."

"Does his opinion matter that much?"

"It does for the time being. We don't need any more fires."

"Good point. Tell him that we'll bring enough fuel to get the tractors working. The amount you'd use here would be nothing compared with our ships, that's why I said it's expensive."

"I'm going to ask Martha and Abby whether I should arrange an island meeting to discuss it, although I can't see anyone objecting."

"My father just tells everyone what's going to happen, nobody gets to voice an opinion. Your way is much better."

I think it's the way it used to work here, Isaac's changed so much since he's been in charge."

Simon leaned forward and kissed her again. Hannah's hands were resting on his chest, about to slide up around his neck when Sophia's voice interrupted them.

"Sorry, but your boat's here. They asked me if I could come and find you."

"Do you live on the quay?" Hannah asked.

Sophia frowned, missing the sarcasm in Hannah's comment.

"You know I do, in Seaview. I'm sorry if I interrupted something important."

Hannah and Simon answered simultaneously – Hannah saying no and Simon yes.

"It's okay Sophia," Hannah softened her tone, realising that it wasn't her fault that they had been lingering in such a public place. "We were just coming."

"I could tell them I couldn't find you," she said, looking down at her feet.

Simon assured her it didn't matter and that he wasn't going to ask a search party to lie on his behalf. Sophia looked puzzled. They walked out onto the quay from the shadow of the buildings leaving Sophia trailing behind them. Simon kissed Hannah on her cheek and stepped down into the boat.

Hannah stayed on the quay when the boat pulled away. She had borrowed a cardigan from Martha, much too large for her, which she now gratefully wrapped round her body.

The boat and its crew blended into the dark water, save for flashes of reflected moonlight whenever the blades dug into the sea. When the boat reached the Pride a couple of lights hanging over the side showed people clambering aboard, but Hannah couldn't tell which of the figures was Simon. She waved anyway, hoping he could see her.

"Did you ask about the dinghy?"

Sophia had materialised next to her. It took a moment for the question to resolve in Hannah's head.

"Oh no, I forgot. I'm sorry, but so much was happening that it completely escaped my memory."

"Okay," Sophia said, but Hannah could tell by her tone that she was disappointed.

"I'll row out first thing in the morning and ask Simon."

"I can row you out. I'll come and call for you if you want. They'll be casting off early, as soon as the tide has cleared the bar."

"Okay. I'll be ready."

The next morning a persistent banging in Hannah's head woke her when it was barely light. Thinking she had another hangover Hannah swore quietly, but then remembered that she had refused all alcohol the previous night.

Simon had joked, saying that he'd give her lessons in wine tasting as well as driving tractors. The banging started again. It was her front door.

Hannah stumbled down the stairs calling out to whoever was in such a hurry that she was on her way. Sliding the bolt back and swinging the door open revealed Sophia. Her promise surfaced through the haze of sleep.

"Oh damn, I forgot, give me a minute."

Hannah ran back upstairs to dress while Sophia called after her.

"Why was your door bolted?"

"Because... it doesn't matter. What time is it?"

"I don't know, but the tides going to cover the bar soon."

Hannah slammed the door closed as they left – Sophia jogging to keep up with her. They clambered into a small rowing boat and Sophia took the oars. Hannah didn't argue, she was much stronger than her and much more practised.

The boat cut smoothly through the calm morning water. Cool air tightened the skin on Hannah's face. Gulls swooped close, recognising and calling out to Sophia, who always cleaned her catch before she landed them.

They pulled alongside the Pride. It looked huge against their small boat. Hannah had never been that close to it before. Simon appeared at the railing, leaning over the side. He must have been told of their approach.

"Is there a problem?" he called down.

"No, nothing's wrong, I just forgot to ask you about the dinghy, about Bethany's dinghy."

"What about it?"

"Do you think Gideon will want to take it back to Freetown. I mean it should belong to us as it was abandoned, but I don't want to pick a fight with him."

"I don't think he's interested in it. I would just assume it's yours. I'll tell him that I said you can keep it."

Sophia threw her arms round Hannah and blew a kiss to Simon. Then she got embarrassed and covered her mouth with her hand, realising what she had done. Simon laughed and blew her a kiss back, which made her bury her head in her hands.

Hannah took one of the oars and pushed them away from the Pride as its engines started to throb and the whistle blew. The two girls sat in their small boat. Sophia, now recovered from her embarrassment, was pulling them away from the churning water behind the Pride's huge paddle wheels.

The steamer slowly turned and drew away from them. Sulphurous smoke from her stack hung in the air and stung their throats. Simon stood at the stern waving to Hannah as the whistle blew one long blast and the Pride was over the bar and out of the harbour.

"Are you two going to get married?" Sophia asked, still staring at the departing steamer.

"Where did you get that idea from?"

"From Martha. She showed me your wedding dress."

Chapter 40

It was ten days later, and only a few days before the equinox, that a steam launch cruised over the sand bar into Newport bay. The shallow draught of the boat meant it didn't have to wait for high tide and it pulled alongside the quay with only a few villagers alert to its arrival. Sophia was, as always, loitering on the quay when she wasn't out fishing and was one of the first to spot it. She dropped the net she was mending and walked over to help.

"Wow, nice boat," she said, leaning her hand against the polished mahogany of the wheelhouse cabin. "Is it yours?"

"Belongs to the company," Simon replied, throwing her a mooring line.

Smoke was still trickling out of the fluted stack and she could see movement inside the main cabin. A small crowd was slowly gathering on the quay. This was an unusual event and word had got around quickly. Few had ever seen a boat like it. A man and woman emerged from below deck, standing behind Simon, looking cautiously at the row of houses along the quay and the growing audience.

"This is Emily and this is Harry," Simon said, half turning towards the couple behind him. "And this is Sophia," he said to them. "And the rest of the people here you'll probably get to know, I don't know them all. But I'm assured none of them bite."

Emily and Harry both smiled nervously and each held a hand up to acknowledge the Islanders.

"Do you want to give us a hand with our stuff?" Simon asked and one or two people moved forward to help.

Emily went back into the cabin and handed bags and tool-boxes to Harry who in turn passed them to eager hands on the quay. Simon had stepped off the launch and asked if Hannah was around. Sophia volunteered to fetch her and set off, running up the lane before Simon could say anything else.

"Tell her we have the engineers I promised to bring over," he shouted after her.

"You've come to mend the tractors?" someone asked.

"If we can," Emily said, having got off the boat and stood beside Simon. "We've no idea whether we'll be able to help though, not till we've had a good look at them."

"Can you take the fuel please," Harry said and Emily turned to help unload four large, green jerry cans onto the quay.

Sophia returned with Hannah not far behind her.

"Hi," said Simon. "I'm back, as promised."

He hugged Hannah who was conscious of mumbled comments from the assembled crowd and broke the embrace quickly.

"I also have a letter for Isaac," he said.

"I'll take it to him," Sophia offered eagerly.

She looked at the envelope and said it looked important. Hannah glanced at it too and saw the mark of the Recorder's Office on the front of it. The engraving was familiar from the contract sheets she had witnessed at the Manor.

"Better take it straight to him," Hannah said and Sophia set off at a run again.

"Does she ever do anything at a normal speed?" Simon asked.

"Not that I've noticed. At least not when you're around. I think she might have a crush on you."

Simon picked up a bag, the first one that came to hand.

311

"We need to shift this stuff. Where can we stay while Emily and Harry look at the tractors?"

"Martha's got spare rooms. I'm sure she won't mind."

Simon and Emily dropped their bags into Martha, who asked how many rooms they needed. Simon said just two, as Emily and Harry were married. Sophia had returned and was already leading Harry towards the barn where the tractors had been stored for decades. She was carrying a jerry can in each hand, he following with two of the boxes of tools. Hannah, Simon and Emily returned to the quay and picked up the rest of their assorted kit. They caught up with Harry at the barn, where he was already on his back under one of the tractors. Sophia was watching from the barn door, biting a fingernail.

"They're brilliant Em," Harry said when he recognised her feet close beside him.

"John Deeres," she whistled. "The old 990s aren't they?"

"Yep and in perfect condition. Whoever laid these up for storage certainly knew what they were doing."

The tractors were stood on huge, pine railway sleepers, which were black with age and tar. The wheels had been left suspended just above the ground, with no pressure on them.

"The tyres look pretty good too," Emily said. "Probably need to soften the rubber again before they take some weight."

"What's so special about these tractors?" Hannah asked.

Emily answered, listing a huge number of advantages. Hannah understood that a lack of electronics was useful but many of the other terms about synchro and hydros were a mystery to her.

"They were greased before they were stored," Harry said, lying between the rear wheels. "I think we'll have to clean some of it off. Can we get some empty cans, shame to waste it?"

Hannah said she would see what she could find and Sophia piped up from the door that she knew where she could get some and was gone.

"Looks like there's a good chance we can get them both going with any luck," Emily said, her head buried in the engine compartment of the other tractor. "They're almost like new, nothing's worn, nothing missing or broken."

Sophia had already returned with an empty can in each hand. "Are two enough? Can I help?"

"Sure," Harry said, pulling himself out from under the tractor and brushing straw from his sweater. "Extra hands are always welcome – if that's okay with you?" he asked, looking and Hannah and Simon for approval. Both agreed that it was fine by them.

"Leave us to it then. See you later."

Harry asked Sophia to bring one of the toolboxes over, pulled up an empty crate and sat her down with a bunch of rags. Simon took Hannah's hand and led her outside.

"We might as well let them get on with it. I'm not much help with that stuff."

"What do you want to do?"

"How about showing me your favourite spot on the whole island."

Hannah thought for a moment. "Okay, that would be Camp Bay. You've been past it, but we didn't stop."

"That's over the other side of the Island isn't it?"

"Yes, not put off by a walk are you?"

He laughed and they set off on the same route as when they had first met and she had taken him to see where Becky's boat had been found. The land looked different now, everything turned to the colours of autumn. The fields were bare and Ethan's two plough horses were pulling a harrow across the land, followed by women gleaning any remaining crop.

"We try not to waste anything. What we can't eat the pigs can."

The heath had turned the colour of mustard with scars of brown bracken straggling across it. Although the sun was warm, the land looked set for winter, save for a few late-blooming wild flowers.

"Your work looks largely done for the year," Simon said.

"Don't you believe it, the apples have yet to be picked and there's winter kale, onions, cauliflower, broad beans, spinach and winter salads to plant, not to mention the green-houses and pickling and..."

"Okay, okay, you've convinced me," Simon laughed.

They crested a rise on the heath and the coastline opened up in front of them. Breakers were rolling in throwing up spray, which carried the scent of salt and seaweed. Previously there had only been hints in the air. The path, now wider, took them down to Camp Bay and Hannah linked her arm through his as the wind whipped her hair across her face.

"We came here a lot as kids," she said. "My mother and Rebekah would bring us here to swim in the summer. Abby always hated swimming. She never learned, but she liked the beach and sat with my mother while Rebekah and I swam for hours. It was Rebekah who taught me to dive and how to hold my breath."

"There's a special way to hold your breath?"

"Of course. You have to breathe out as far as you can two or three times before filling your lungs for a dive."

"What difference does that make?"

"A lot. I don't know exactly why, but it works."

They had reached the top of the beach. Much of it was covered in seaweed thrown up by the wind and the tide. They sat on a grassy bank surrounded by wild flowers.

"I suppose you know what all these flowers are too?"

Simon picked one and held it front of him.

"You shouldn't pick them unless you are going to use them," Hannah scolded.

"Sorry, I didn't think."

She pointed them out in turn, naming them for him. "That's heath lobelia and red goosefoot and that pretty one you've murdered was a marsh gentian."

She laughed at Simon's hurt expression and hugged his arm.

"I'm only teasing you, but we do try to leave everything as it is unless we have a use for it or if it's a weed."

"I'll learn," Simon said and kissed her cheek.

"So what do you want from life," Hannah asked him, looking out to the horizon.

"A better life, not about money and profit and what you own."

"Are you sure about the money thing? I think it might be quite useful in an emergency." She was thinking about the gold they had stashed under Martha's store.

"It's good to have some money, but life can't be just about making more." He turned to look directly at her. "What do you want?"

"Oh, I don't know." Hannah leaned her head against his shoulder. "I'd like the life my parents planned for me, here, on Hope Island. I don't really want to change anything – except maybe Isaac. I'm not even sure the tractors will be an improvement. You saw the horses working today. A tractor can't replace that connection with the land."

"Others might not agree. Like the people walking behind the horses all day."

"I know, but you can't change one part of a jigsaw puzzle and hope the others pieces will still fit. The picture will alter and you'll have to start changing all the other pieces too."

"A pebble gets thrown in a lake and the ripples keep

getting ever bigger? My father thinks that's a good thing."

"But it's not that simple. How much of life here can change and it still be Hope Island, still belong to us all?"

They fell into a comfortable silence. The wind gradually dried the beach as the waves retreated and sand, caught in a sudden gust, flew into their faces.

"Time to be heading back I think," Simon said as Hannah buried her face into his sweater to protect her eyes.

Hannah chased Simon across the heath. He pretended to fall and then twisted out of her grasp at the last minute. They slowed to a walk when they reached the lane and, when they entered the village, Hannah freed her arm from his and they walked side-by-side back to the barn and the tractors.

"They're brilliant," Sophia said as soon as she saw them.

"What are?" Hannah asked.

"The tractors. The engines are amazing when you hear them. It's like they're alive."

Simon walked over to Harry and Emily.

"You've got them going already?"

"One of them," Harry said. "We recharged the batteries and one of them started easily. The other is a bit more of a problem. We may need to strip it down and maybe switch the batteries across. One isn't taking a charge so well as the other."

"It might take us two or three days," Emily added. "And we ought to strip the first one down too, just to get it as good as possible."

"Well, I cleared both of you with the workshops for up to a week if you're happy to stay."

"Emily would probably sleep in the barn with them," Harry laughed. "I think she's in her own version of heaven."

Martha had slid in without anyone noticing her.

"You'll be more comfortable in a proper bed."

316

"That means you'll be here for Mabon," Hannah said. "Our equinox celebration."

"Harry will stay for three months if there's a party promised," Emily joked.

"It was you who said you could live here."

"Well I could, from what I've seen so far. Do you need a full time engineer on the Island?"

"Make that two," Harry laughed. "I'm not letting you get away from me."

"When we got married you said I could choose where we lived."

"I wasn't expecting you to choose Hope Island, but I'm game if you are and there's a place for us here."

"My parents are going to kill me if they lose two of their best engineers."

"Couldn't we set up a maintenance base here?" Harry suggested. "The harbour is so well protected and we've got limited space where we are."

"Is that possible?" Hannah asked.

"I suppose anything is possible," Simon replied.

Chapter 41

For the next couple of days Emily and Harry worked on the tractors with the constant help of Sophia. Hannah dropped in on them every day and reminded Sophia that Bethany's dinghy was available if she wanted to take it out, but she was reluctant to leave the company of her new friends.

"I want to learn to drive. Anyone can fish."

Her hands and fingernails were smudged with grease and even one cheek bore a mark that looked like she was attempting to camouflage herself. Sophia had also taken to wearing cotton dungarees and heavy boots. The boots were far too large for her, but she was trying to match her appearance to Emily and Harry, who both wore Delancey overalls.

Simon and Hannah had spent their time walking the Island. He said that he wanted to see everything and joked that he wasn't going to be satisfied until he had explored every path.

On the second morning, a bright and crisp day, they climbed from the main reservoir to the top of the ridge. Hannah hadn't been up there since she was a child. From the top they could see Abby making another check of the gutters in anticipation of autumn rains. It was late for them to start, they would normally have had a few showers already, which would settle the fields and begin to fill the reservoirs. This year they were lower than usual, but that was why she had been able to dive and find the gold so easily.

"Look, over there," Simon said. "You can see the foundry opening its furnace."

Even in the sun there was an orange glow close to the sea.

Hannah and Abby had seen it as children and imagined it to be a baby dragon who lived on the mainland and wouldn't be able to fly to their island until it had grown. Simon pointed out other features, landmarks for him, but just blurs for Hannah.

"My eyesight isn't good at distances Simon."

"I didn't realise. Have you tried wearing glasses?"

"I've never needed to see beyond the Island before."

"I grew up in a house on that tall hill, just to right of the town."

"You'll have to show me when we go over there."

"I will. I think you'll like my parents."

Hannah had wondered what his family were like. They were rich, she knew that, but he hadn't spoken about them much.

"Do you have brothers or sisters?"

"One sister, she's younger than me, twelve last birthday."

"You haven't really told me anything about your family."

"There's not a lot to tell."

"But you own Delancey Sugar?"

"That doesn't mean we're weird or unusual or anything."

"But you are rich?"

"Yes. I suppose we are. Does that make a difference?"

Hannah sighed. She wanted to tell him that it didn't and why it didn't. She owned an island and thousands of gold coins, but none of it felt like hers.

"If we cut round the top of the reservoir we could intercept Abby on her way back to Hope Barton," she said.

"Sounds good. I want to be friends with Becky, she'll be there won't she?"

"Yes she keeps Daniel company, but he's so much better now with her there, not quite back to normal, but he even looks more his age now."

"She must be good for him."

319

"Either that or Ethan not being there has helped. I don't think they talked much when there was only the two of them. It's quite isolated compared to living near the village."

"It's not that far away."

"No but it feels it in the winter. You haven't been here in the winter, it's different."

Heading onto the moor they saw Abby a distance away and called to her. She had made better progress than they – probably the gutters were all clear and she hadn't had to stop anywhere. She waited until they caught up and the three of them walked to Hope Barton together.

"I hear that one of the tractors is working." Abby said.

"I think the second one will be soon," Hannah added. "Emily seems very confident she'll get it going."

"They are going to change things here. The tractors I mean."

"For the better I hope?" Simon chipped in, but neither of the girls answered directly.

"We'll keep the horses," Abby said after a while. "I like working with them."

When they got back to the farm Daniel was washing the windows. He had a bucket of soapy water and a collection of rags slung over his shoulder. The water had dribbled down his back making his shirt and trousers wet on one side. It was the first time in years that Hannah and Abby had seen him do anything but fashion pieces driftwood into creatures. Becky came out of the kitchen door with another bucket.

"Where did you find those two lovebirds Abby? I hope you didn't interrupt anything."

"They latched on to me if you have to know."

"Nice to see you both. We're just trying to get a bit more daylight into the farmhouse. The summer dust has covered the windows."

"It blows in on the southerly winds," Hannah explained.

"We get the same problem on the mainland. It's fine desert sand though, not dust. That's why it's got that slightly red tinge."

"I never knew that," Becky said.

"You need to travel more."

"Actually no, I don't. I've travelled quite far enough now."

Samson and Delilah suddenly appeared, racing round the bend in the farm lane and barking their arrival.

"What are you two doing here?" Abby asked them, fondling Samson's neck.

"They're with me," Ethan called out.

"So what are you doing here, not that you aren't welcome, " Becky said. "After all it is your farm."

"I wanted a word with Dad. Sort of on my own if that's okay?"

"No problem," Becky said. "I was going to suggest a picnic lunch, before the weather turns. We could take it over to Camp Bay."

Hannah said it sounded like a brilliant idea and within a few minutes they had filled two baskets with bread, cheese, pickles, bottles of water and biscuits that Becky had made that morning.

"Leave me a couple," Ethan said.

"He does nothing but eat does that boy," Daniel complained. "But leave me a couple too."

Hannah was pleasantly surprised that Daniel was quite so vocal and so lucid.

"Dad and I can have a chat while you're gone. I'll check on the cows too. Save you rushing back."

At Camp Bay everyone but Abby decided to have a last swim of the season. The sea was calm and even Abby paddled in the shallows while the other three swam out and Hannah showed them where the submerged house was – and the coalbunkers. She did a tuck dive and brought up a lump of coal.

"Is that's what you were doing the day you saved my life?"

Hannah laughed and splashed water at Becky. "And now look at you, you've saved my sister."

Hannah noticed that Abby had retreated to the top of the beach and said she was going to keep her company for a bit. Simon dived down and also returned with a lump of coal. Becky couldn't hold her breath long enough, but she kept trying. Hannah heard Simon explaining about the three breaths method, but she hadn't mentioned to him that it takes practice too.

Flopping down next to Abby, Hannah grabbed one of the two towels they had brought with them and wrapped it round her shoulders.

"The sea's warm but the breeze is cold when you come out."

"My feet were freezing and I was just paddling."

"You and Becky seem pretty settled on the farm."

"We are. How about you and Simon."

"We haven't really discussed the future as such. I don't know, I think this is it though. And I think he wants to be here too, with me."

"Have you told him about the gold?"

"No, not without discussing it with you first, but I do feel like I'm keeping secrets from him and I don't want to."

"If you and Simon are going to be together then you will have to tell him something."

"We don't even know what we're going to do with it. Maybe we should just forget it."

"What about that idea of buying a boat, trading with the

mainland directly? If we do that, then everyone will have to know where the money came from to buy it. We can't claim we traded some carrots for it."

Hannah laughed and agreed. She said she would tell him if she had to, because of the boat idea.

"Or maybe if he asks you to marry him? That would be a good time to point out how much money you have stashed away."

"But it's not my money. It belongs to the Island."

"Is that what Isaac would have said if he'd found it?"

Hannah was saved from answering by Simon and Becky running up the beach together. Hannah threw her towel at Simon and told him not to get her wet again. Becky hugged Abby, despite her protests.

"I am going to teach you to swim next year," she insisted.

"Many have tried, but even my mother failed on that account."

"She wasn't as determined as me," Becky said, shaking her head so that the water spiralled off her short hair, splattering not just Abby, but Hannah too.

"Get off me you pest, you're worse than Charlie."

Becky barked and pretended to bite Abby.

"I think we ought to take the children home after lunch," Simon said. "They're getting overexcited."

They spread the wet towels out to dry and Becky took a tablecloth off the top of one basket to put the food on, she'd even packed a knife to cut the bread.

"You've done this before haven't you?" Abby said.

"My mother used to take me on picnics whenever my father was away on a trip. She made them fun and looked for new places, but we both liked the beach or sitting next to a river and listening to it talk to us." Becky's voice went quieter as she remembered those times. "She made up conversations with the water about where my father was and how long we had to wait until he returned."

Simon broke the silence that Becky left hanging. "I think my mother was secretly pleased when my father went away. She would have all her friends round and they would talk forever. It was all a bit more serious when dad came back."

After they had eaten Abby suggested that they ought to be getting back. She said she didn't know how long Ethan wanted with his father, but thought he'd probably be champing at the bit to get away. They packed up the remains of the picnic and shook out the towels as best they could.

At Hope Barton Ethan was nowhere to be seen, nor Samson and Delilah, but Charlie walked across the yard to greet them and Daniel was once again on his bench with a piece of driftwood in his hands.

"I finished the windows," he said as they drew close. "Much better now."

"Sorry I left you in the middle of it Daniel."

"That's no problem girl. I didn't mind and it gave me something to do while Ethan was talking at me."

"What did he want?" Abby asked.

"Wanted to know if I was happy. Strange question, can't ever remember him asking me that before."

"And what did you say?"

"Told him I was happy as I could be without my Mary being here. I used to pretend she was still around somewhere, but I knew she wasn't really here. And I've got you two girls to look after me now. Can't complain. Although I might if you don't make some more of those biscuits, proper tasty they were."

"There's some more inside, in a tin," Becky said.

"Not any more there's not," he mumbled.

Daniel kept his head down, pretending to concentrate on his carving, but they could hear him chuckling quietly to himself.

Hannah and Simon walked back to the village late that afternoon. The sun was already setting earlier and Simon said he'd drop in on Emily and Harry before going back to Martha's.

"You don't have to sleep at Martha's you know."

"Are you suggesting?"

"Why not?" Hannah said, smiling and taking his hand in hers.

Chapter 42

Hannah woke the next morning and rolled over in bed to see Simon sleeping peacefully beside her. Voices in the lane outside the window had broken her sleep and she slid out of bed to investigate. She poked her head between the newly hung curtains, holding them tight to her neck – she wasn't wearing any clothes.

"What...?" she mumbled and then remembered it was the equinox. People were busy preparing for the festival. She made sure the curtains were firmly closed against prying eyes and shook Simon until he roused.

"What time is it?" he mumbled, but smiled when he saw Hannah through sleepy eyes. "Mmm, what a nice way to wake up."

"It's the equinox. I completely forgot. We have to go and help."

"What have we got to do? Come back to bed, I'll get you breakfast."

"We haven't got time for breakfast," she said, struggling into a pair of cotton jeans. "Come on, get up, quick."

Hannah picked his clothes up from where they were scattered on the floor and threw them at him. His trousers landed across his face, but Simon remained in bed, laughing at her.

Eventually she got him up and dressed and peeked out through the curtains to try to judge how late they were. She dragged him through the front door while he was still clutching a chunk of bread, rescued as he passed the kitchen.

"What are you doing Simon, I told you we don't have time

for breakfast."

"But I'm hungry," he moaned.

Hannah was annoyed that she was late and that anyone who saw them would know they had spent the night together. She also knew that news like that would spread across the entire island within the hour. On their way to the quay they bumped into Martha coming out of the stores.

"Did you sleep well?" Martha asked, winking cheekily.

Hannah tried to ignore her, but felt the colour rise in her cheeks and burn across her forehead.

On the quay four large, half-barrel barbecues were being set up, supported on forged iron stands and wired to the railings on the quayside for safety. Peter was supervising the procedure, making sure they were well spaced from each other.

"Hannah, Simon, I wondered where you'd got to."

Hannah let go of Simon's hand, unaware until then how hard she had been gripping his fingers.

"We got..."

"Involved in something," Simon finished her sentence, sliding his arm round her waist.

"I've got a job if the two of you are looking for something to do?"

"We're free," Simon said. "What is it you want?"

"I need someone to fetch the charcoal, it's out the back of the mill. There are a couple of dozen bags there. I meant to get it down here yesterday but had trouble with the mill gearing and had to sort that out first. Then it slipped my mind"

"Is it fixed now?" Simon asked. "The gearing, not your mind. Because Emily could help?"

"Would she? I think it's one of the bearings, they haven't been changed in living memory so I'm at a bit of a loss as to what to do."

"I'll ask her," Simon said.

"But not today. Maybe she could pop up there tomorrow?"

"Okay," Hannah said. "Come on Simon we need some extra hands and a couple of handcarts at the very least."

"We could pick up Sophia on the way. I suspect I know just where to find her. Maybe Emily could spare Harry too?"

They set off for the barns where the tractors were being restored, hearing the voice of Sophia even before they opened the door. Harry, Emily and Sophia were all there, standing together, looking at the tractors. The machines were no longer on blocks, but looked ready to run. Hannah explain about the charcoal and asked Sophia to help, and maybe Harry or Emily too if they could spare an hour.

"I can do it," Sophia said. "You two hop in the box."

Harry and Emily were both smiling as Sophia swung herself up into the cab of one of the tractors and turned the key.

"What do you mean?" Hannah asked.

"I know you weren't around yesterday, but didn't anyone tell you?"

"Tell us what?"

Sophia leaned forward in the cab and the tractor's engine coughed once and roared into life. Hannah stepped back, half hiding behind Simon and covering her ears. Sophia shouted for them to open the barn doors and then jump in the link box.

Harry and Emily watch their protégé with smiles on their faces as the tractor lurched forward and then crept towards the doors. Simon swung both wide open while Hannah watched in amazement.

When Sophia drew level with Hannah she told her that she had taken it out yesterday. "Driving is pretty easy when you know how. Hop in the link box and I'll give you a lift up to the mill."

Simon clambered into the metal box attached to the back of the tractor and held out an arm to Hannah. She cautiously took his hand. He gripped her wrist firmly and hauled her into the box. It swayed alarmingly, causing Hannah to shriek and grab the metal bar nearest the tractor so that she wouldn't fall out. The engine roared again and Simon put an arm round Hannah to reassure her.

The tractor trundled out of the barn with people stopping to watch. They headed up the lane out of the village. Sophia turned back to say something to them, but the tractor veered towards a hedge and Hannah panicked.

"Watch where you're going," she yelled.

"It's okay, it's really pretty easy," Sophia replied, without turning round again.

Although they were moving only slightly faster than a walk and nowhere near as fast as she had ridden Pepper on occasions, Hannah was terrified and never loosened her grip on the metal box or on Simon's arm until they stopped outside the mill.

When they had loaded all the bags of charcoal into the box, Hannah declared that she would walk back to the village and Simon laughed but said he'd walk with her. They watched Sophia back the tractor into the yard next to the mill, turn and head off towards the village.

It was still only a short distance ahead of them when they got back to the barns, Sophia having stopped and explained how it worked to anyone who would listen. When it appeared on the quay there were loud cheers from some while others backed off to a respectful distance, leaving space between them and the roaring monster. Hannah heard one woman complaining about the smell of the exhaust fumes.

Sophia brought the tractor to a halt beside the first of the barbecue stands and her and Peter unloaded four bags of charcoal. She had left the engine running and pulled it forward to each stand in turn, leaving the remaining bags as a stockpile a little further on. With the link box empty the more adventurous children scrambled in and clamoured for Sophia to take them for a ride.

"Go on, we've got plenty of fuel," Emily said, she and Harry having followed them down to the quay.

She drove a few children along the quay and back with the excited voices echoing off the cottages and everyone smiling and waving to them. Most people quickly mellowed to the noise and smell and even some of the adults wanted a ride, encouraging the shyer children to join them.

Sophia was delighted with her new status, smiling constantly and occasionally letting someone ride beside her while she pointed out how the controls worked. She drew the line at anyone else actually steering it, claiming that it was a skilled job and required practice.

Once the initial enthusiasm had died down, Emily suggested parking it so that she could check the brakes. A few children loitered in the link box for a while but were soon drawn away by other events being organised on the quay.

"So what happens now?" Simon asked.

"Sack races, a three legged race, maypole dancing, and there's always a rowing race round the far buoy and back. Sophia has won that for the last couple of years, but this year I suspect someone else might get a chance. There are games happening all day, no order, they just start when everyone's ready."

The barbecues were well alight by then and Simon reminded Hannah that he hadn't had any breakfast.

"Come on then, let's see what's ready."

While they were eating bacon rolls with raw onion, Isaac

joined them. He looked longingly at the barbecue, but said he had a bit of a queasy tummy and thought he might wait a while before indulging.

"What was that letter about Uncle, I meant to ask you before?"

"Ah, nothing really, simply a note from the Recorder's Office. Technical stuff, nothing to worry about today."

"So not a problem I hope?"

"No, not at all." Isaac couldn't conceal a smile playing about his mouth and made an excuse that he had to attend to the prizes for the races.

Simon and Hannah wandered along the quay, stopping at one cottage with flags draped outside.

"You've got to try this, Sarah makes it for every festival for the kids, it's such a treat."

She stopped at the door, which had a small table positioned just inside so that you couldn't walk into the kitchen beyond.

"What are you tempting me with?" Simon asked.

"Just wait a minute. Can we have one please Sarah?"

The silent girl nodded and smiled at Hannah, stole a glance at Simon and giggled. She came back a couple of minutes later with a thin, straight willow stick, stripped of bark and with spun sugar glistening in a fluffy ball.

"It's your sugar," Hannah said, offering it to Simon.

"But what is it?"

"Sarah caramelises the sugar and then spins it out before gathering it on a stick. Try it."

Simon tried to bite and then lick some off the sticky stuff, but it attached itself to his nose and chin.

"I've never had this before," Simon said, managing to eat some but getting more stuck to his face. "It's amazing."

Hannah stole a bite and when they finished it he kissed her, sticking his face to hers. They cleaned themselves with a damp cloth that Sarah offered them and moved on.

As the morning's games continued, the barbecues carried the smell of grilled fish, toasted bread and garlic to the assembled villagers.

Hannah and Simon walked to the end of the harbour, where it was quieter. There was a strip of sand showing and a bonfire had been constructed just above the high water mark.

"Isn't that a waste of timber?" Simon asked, now understanding how frugal the Island was with its resources.

"It's mostly driftwood. Some will have tar in it so no use for burning on fires because it will clog the chimneys. We only have a bonfire at Mabon.

Later they ate a supper of grilled mackerel on toasted bread, Simon tried ginger beer for the first time but Hannah stuck to diluted fruit juices, claiming she couldn't stand that hot taste. The children were the last to tire and nearly everyone drifted towards the far end of the quay. Before the sun went down, the bonfire was lit.

Most gathered round it, but a few loitered near the barbecues, finishing off the last burnt offerings.

Cider was passed round and Hannah explained the last custom of the day to Simon, one that was peculiar to that season.

"Last year's cider has to be drunk tonight before they start pressing any more. It's a tradition, the devil gets to it after today."

"We keep cider for years, it doesn't go off."

"We believe that last year's cider will turn sour if it's not drunk tonight and that it will ruin this year's pressing.

"Ah, so you do have superstitions here after all?"

"No, we know it's not true, but we all choose to believe it. What other excuse could we find to be so indulgent?"

The sat by the bonfire while stories were told, songs sung

and younger children settled into their parents' arms.

"It's beautiful here," Simon said. It's a real community. Everyone helps everyone else."

"Almost everyone," Hannah said quietly. "You're forgetting Isaac."

"He's not a problem that can't be solved."

"Stay and help me solve it then," Hannah mumbled, feeling sleepy with Simon's arm round her shoulders and the fire warming her face.

"I will if you marry me," he said quietly.

Hannah heard him, but for a second she wondered if she had drifted into sleep and imagined it.

"Have you drunk too much?" she said, snuggling in closer.

"Marry me. I love you."

Hannah didn't know what to say. She wanted to say yes but was worried about keeping secrets from him.

"I decided to ask you while I was still sober," he said, reaching into a pocket. "Even before I returned here."

He produced a ring and slid it onto her finger.

"It was my grandmother's, she told me to give it to the girl I loved."

"So why didn't you give it to the girl you were going to marry?"

"I didn't love her."

Hannah held her hand up to look at the ring.

"Yes," she said. "Of course I will."

She stretched up and kissed him.

"And now I have to tell Abby and Martha and everyone."

She dragged him to his feet.

"And once we tell them you can never change your mind."

"I never will," he said.

Hannah dragged Simon around the perimeter of the fire,

stopping and showing her ring to everyone. Abby was sat with Martha, towards the edge of the crowd and away from the few remaining overexcited children who were scampering around. Hannah dropped to her knees on the sand in front of Martha. She held her hand out, the ring on her finger sparkled in the light of flickering flames from the fire.

"Congratulations," Martha said, smiling broadly, and spread her arms out for a hug.

Hannah flung her arms round Martha's neck and kissed her cheek. "You've been like a mother to me these past years and I love you so much, and I want you by my side when Simon and I get married."

"Whoa, slow down," Martha said.

"What about me?" Abby joked. "Doesn't a sister get any role in this event?"

"You will be my maid of honour. I've read all about them and what they do."

"And there I was hoping to be best woman."

"You'll always be best woman to me," Hannah said and pulled Abby into a three-way hug.

"Wait until I tell Becky. She'll be even more excited than you are."

"Impossible," Hannah said. "I just wish she was here now to share the news."

"I wanted her to come, but she had concerns."

"I know, but I'm sure Harry and Emily wouldn't have let her secret out."

"I agree, but I can see her point. She must still be terrified her father will come to collect her."

"Ah," Simon said. "We ought to tell them too, and Sophia. If I had a megaphone it would have saved so much time."

"And been much less fun," Hannah said, grabbing his hand and dragging him back around the fire to find Sophia and share their news.

Chapter 43

The next day everyone gathered on the quay to clear up after the festivities. Harry and Emily brought their toolboxes and bags down before lunch, after they had both been to the mill to help Peter with his mechanical problem.

"We're going to send a new bearing over," Emily said. "It's a standard size and Peter knows how to fit it."

"Thanks for helping," Hannah said. "I know it wasn't what you came here for."

"Maybe we'll be back soon," Emily said. "It depends on Simon and whether he wants to lose two good engineers or start a new maintenance facility."

Yes, okay," Simon laughed. "I can take a hint, I'll talk to my father, see what he thinks."

Emily started to load their kit onto the steam cruiser and when Harry went below decks, Hannah could hear banging and scraping coming from inside the boat.

"He's getting the boiler sorted," Simon said. "The steam won't take long to get up to pressure and then we can head out."

"I'll miss you," Hannah whispered, turning the ring round on her finger.

"I could stay another week or two and go back on the Pride."

"No, better you'd better go back now. You've got to tell your parents about us and let them get used to the idea of you moving here. And I have to work out what's going on with Isaac. Something odd was in that letter I think."

"But you'll come over on the Pride when it next visits?"

"Try and stop me," Hannah giggled. "No, don't try. Meet me when it docks, I'll have no idea where to go."

Martha brought Simon's bag down to the quay. "I took the liberty of packing it for you as I wasn't sure you remembered where you were staying." She laughed uproariously at her own joke.

"Yes, very funny Martha," Hannah said. "Now leave us to say goodbye."

"I was only kidding," she said slightly affronted. "I'm just happy you two are together."

"I'll drop in for a mug of something when Simon's left." Hannah winked at Martha.

"Ah, yes, okay, I see what you mean."

Martha left them alone and Emily called from inside the cabin that they had a head of steam.

Hannah and Simon made their goodbyes discretely as a small crowd still lingered on the quay to watch the launch depart.

When it pulled away from the quay Hannah remained there, waving until it steamed over the sandbar and turned away from the morning sun. It soon disappeared behind the headland. Its whistle blew a last goodbye and Hannah saw a small column of condensed steam rising in the cool air beyond the hill.

Everyone settled back into a normal routine by the end of the day and Hannah felt at a loss as to what to do with Simon gone. Abby and Becky would be back at the farm, not requiring her company, so she helped Martha with checking over and storing some of the harvest. Soon the apples would be ready for picking and that would occupy more of her time.

A few days later, when Martha decided to have an afternoon snooze after a busy morning, Hannah walked across to Hope Barton to talk to Abby about their idea of buying a boat. Daniel told her that Becky was putting the bees to bed for the winter, checking they had enough honey to keep them alive. She had mixed up some sugar water just in case and would be up there for a while.

"Do you want me to get her lass?"

"No, it was Abby I came to see really."

"Ah, well, you're in luck then. She's in the barn mending a rake."

Hannah wandered across the lawn and through the yard. As she approached the barn she could hear Abby banging away at something.

"Hi, you in there?"

"Hannah. What brings you over here?"

"I'm going on the Pride to the mainland when it calls. I wondered if you'd thought any more about that idea of getting a boat for the Island?"

Abby leaned back against the bench, still with the head of a rake in her hands. Her thumb tested the spikes as though seeing if they were sharp enough.

"It's tricky isn't it? If we start asking around too seriously people will know we've got money. And we don't even know what they might cost yet do we?"

"We could just pretend we're interested, not say that we might be buyers."

I suppose it wouldn't do any harm."

"What about if I take Sophia. She's got a good eye for a boat and she knows a bit about engines now – probably the only person on the Island who does."

"Look, I'm happy to leave any decisions to you, just be careful."

"I will," Hannah said.

They went back to the house and Abby made tea. Daniel joined them for a while and actually engaged in their conversation. Becky and Abby's presence had made a remarkable difference to Daniel, and Hannah wondered how much of his problems had been wrapped up with Ethan. When they were alone Hannah said she would take ten of the gold coins with her and ask Simon what they were worth and how much a boat might cost.

Abby agreed, but warned her again to be careful. "I think those coins might prove more trouble than they're worth."

Martha was wary about Hannah taking ten coins with her. "That's a lot of gold," she said. "Not enough for a boat I suspect and too much for people to ignore if they found out she had them on her. Why don't you just take three, it's a lucky number and won't rouse so much suspicion."

She agreed and was going to ask Martha when would be a good time to open the vault when Isaac turned up unexpectedly.

"Ah, Hannah, Martha. I can kill two birds with one stone."

"Who do you want to kill?" Martha asked.

"Just an expression, nothing meant by it. I wanted to tell you both that I'll be travelling on the Pride when she next calls, urgent business on the mainland."

"But you don't like boats," Hannah said.

"Nonsense," Isaac replied. "It's little boats that bob about at the mercy of every ripple that I can't stand – not large ships like the Pride."

"Are you going to the Recorder's Office?" Hannah asked, remembering the letter.

"I am if you have to know, but it's a private matter, not island business."

He refused Martha's offer of tea and took his leave, avoiding further questions.

"That's odd," Martha said.

"He's up to something isn't he?"

"I imagine we'll find out in due course."

"I'll try to keep an eye on him when we're on the mainland. Simon might be able to find out what he's up to."

Hannah told Martha that she was going to recruit Sophia to go with her because of her knowledge of boats.

"I'm not sure she's that interested in them now she's got those tractors to play with."

"She might be if the boat's got an engine."

When Hannah caught up with Sophia her reaction to the suggestion was more enthusiastic than expected. She said she would be able to meet her friends again and see their workshops. Sophia also wanted to know how long they would be there and did she need to pack anything special and did she need money on the mainland.

"Harry showed me some money and explained how it works. It makes so much sense."

"Let's worry about that when we get there. I'm sure Simon will be able to sort something out for both of us if I ask."

Boarding the Pride was an emotional moment for Hannah. She was leaving Hope Island for the first time in her life. She almost panicked and asked to be rowed back to the quay. If Sophia hadn't been there with her, hyper excited, and if Isaac hadn't been talking to the captain belittling Hope Island, Hannah might even have swum back to shore.

The journey took three hours, shorter than Hannah had expected, but her home had diminished to a smudge on the horizon by the time they docked. Simon was waiting, waving to her when the Pride moored.

Freetown looked huge. Row after row of houses were scattered over the hill that rose behind the port. People, more than she had ever seen, bustled along the wharf and in the street behind it. She could see shops like the ones illustrated in old books, horses and carts, even lorries being loaded and unloaded behind Simon. And the noise was constant, people shouting, laughing, calling to each other, horns sounding, whistles blowing and there was music coming from somewhere – she couldn't tell where amidst all the din.

Isaac looked almost as uneasy as she felt when they walked down a long boarded ramp with cross struts to stop feet slipping on the smooth wood. Only Sophia was taking it all in her stride, eyes wide, pointing at something new every second and tugging on Hannah's sleeve to draw her attention to it.

Simon had a horse and trap waiting for them. They had one on the Island but it had long fallen into disrepair as there was no great use for it.

"Jump in both of you. I guess you want to see Harry and Emily?" he said to Sophia, who nodded vigorously, having lost her tongue at last.

"Isaac," he called across the wharf. "Can we give you a lift anywhere?"

"Thank you dear boy, but I have directions and transport waiting for me somewhere."

Simon set the horse off at a clip and Hannah gripped the side of the carriage. They were going faster than the tractor did. She looked round at Sophia, who was in a small seat at the back. She was smiling and enjoying every second of the ride. They stopped only a few hundred yards along the port, outside a large shed.

"This is our dry dock," Simon said. "If you wait a moment I'll take Sophia in and find Emily. You'll be quite safe."

Hannah waited, gradually getting used to the size of the place and the non-stop activity. Carts clattered by, people doffed their caps to her as they passed. She guessed that the Delanceys must command some sort of reverence in the town and it extended to her. When Simon returned a few minutes later she was breathing normally again.

"Harry and Emily will take care of Sophia, she's going to sleep at their place. She looks right at home already."

"Are we going straight to your family's house?"

"That's what I thought. Is that okay?"

The route took them closer to the shops in the main street along the front. There were fruits and vegetables Hannah didn't recognise stacked on trestles outside one shop.

"What are those yellow vegetables?" she asked Simon.

Simon laughed. "Do you mean bananas?"

"I've never seen them before. I've heard of them though."

"They're a sweet fruit. We have some at home. You must try one when we get there."

"Are your parents going to think I'm ignorant?"

"No. They'll think you're charming. Don't worry."

Her fears at meeting Simon's parents turned out to be unfounded. Although their house high on a hill above Freeport was imposing, Joseph and Danielle were both welcoming and friendly.

"Would you like some coffee?" Danielle asked. "It must have been such a tiring journey on that boat. And your first time on the mainland."

"Hannah usually drinks tea Ma."

"My wife thinks everyone prefers coffee. Being brought up in the sugar islands they drank nothing else."

"Except rum," Simon whispered to Hannah.

"Coffee would be nice," Hannah said, wondering how Simon's parents had met.

"We met when I was travelling on family business," Joseph said, apparently able to read Hannah's expression. "And here's Anya, the baby of the family."

"Do not call me a baby Pa, I'm twelve for goodness sake."

Anya walked over to Hannah and held her hand out formally. When Hannah took it she said, "It's so nice to meet you Hannah, I'm sure we are going to be best friends as well as sisters."

Hannah smiled and said she was also sure they would be.

Simon's family made her feel completely at home, although their home was nothing like Canary Cottage and she shivered mentally at what Simon had really thought of it. They said how happy they were that Simon had found someone he loved and wanted to be with.

"That Bethany was a nice girl," Danielle said. "Such a shame things ended as they did for her. But I always knew she wasn't right for Simon or Simon for her, but would anybody listen to me?"

"Thanks Ma, we all know what you mean, no need to go over it again."

"So, what are your plans Hannah? Simon tells me you are to inherit Hope Island."

"I suppose that's true," Hannah hesitated. "But it's not so much about ownership as stewardship. The island works as a community."

"All for one and one for all – or something like that?" Joseph chipped in.

"Yes, something like that," Hannah said."

She was worried that they would have wanted Simon to marry into money, and of course he was in a way, but she couldn't tell anyone about the gold yet.

"I didn't have a penny when Joseph asked me to be his wife. Love is what counts, not money. And we have plenty of that anyway."

"Hope Island has always fascinated us," Joseph said. "But the virus meant we heard so little about it. We know now of course that it was all a ruse to keep people off it.

Simon has explained it all now."

"Do you have plans to change things," Danielle asked. "Now we know that the mainland and the Island need not fear each other?"

Hannah looked to Simon and hoped he would understand. She hadn't planned to reveal her and Abby's idea yet but it felt the right time.

"We are thinking about trying to purchase a boat, one that will allow us to trade directly with the mainland and not rely on the Pride."

"That sounds admirable," Joseph said, his mouth twisting as he thought. "A boat that could carry produce to and fro, but not too large to be prohibitively expensive to run. Something efficient but spacious."

"That's exactly what we were thinking," Hannah replied.

Simon leaned back in his chair, smiling slightly as though he knew what was coming next.

"They mean the Sea Breeze," Anya piped up. "We are going to give it to you as a wedding present."

Joseph and Danielle laughed and told Anya it wasn't hers to give, but they weren't really angry with her. Hannah looked at Simon, who was grinning from ear to ear, obviously in on it.

"But that's too much, even though I have no idea what they cost."

"It's not a boat we use any longer," Danielle explained. "And if our son is to live on an island, away from his family, then we need a regular way of keeping in touch, of visiting."

"I... I don't know what to say," Hannah stuttered.

"Say nothing," Joseph said. "Consider it done."

"Can I show Hannah our gardens and the ponds?" Anya asked.

Hannah was glad for the chance to escape and breathe, everything was happening so fast.

Anya took her on a grand tour of the gardens, accompanied by Simon for the latter part. They stood on the edge of ornamental ponds while Anya pointed and listed the names of all the fish. Hannah was able to identify some plants that Anya didn't know the names of and she asked if Hannah was a botanist, struggling slightly with the word. Hannah had not heard the term, but said she was learning to be a herbalist and that they had a special garden on Hope Island with medicinal herbs.

"Like the hospital," Anya said. "A physic garden. Can I see it when we visit?"

"Of course you can. I'll give you a guided tour."

When they got back to the house, Joseph was standing on the veranda, a puzzled expression on his face, his brow furrowed.

"We've just heard from the Recorder's Office. The information may be of some interest to you Hannah."

She held Simon's arm, expecting bad news.

"There is to be a new Recorder. Apparently Gideon's illness has left him with a problem of balance."

"He's always had a problem balancing his books," Danielle joked. "I've always known the man was a crook."

"No, not that, although you may well be right. His illness is something to do with his ears, it's has left him with permanent nausea, he can barely stand up, never mind travel anywhere. No cure apparently." Joseph shook his head as though mystified. "The new Recorder is to be Isaac Davies, your uncle I believe."

Hannah's mouth dropped open. She hadn't expected anything like that.

Chapter 44

Hannah, Simon and his parents went back into the lounge and Joseph decided they should all have a drink, a strong drink.

"Only a small one for me," said Hannah. "I don't drink very much now, not since something made me rather ill."

"Can I have one too?" Anya asked.

"Not for you Anya," Joseph said. "And I think it best if you could leave us adults alone for a while. We have some important business to discuss."

"But I'm almost an adult. I should know what's happening too."

"She's right," Danielle agreed. "Anya is old enough to listen. I was not that much older when I first met you Joseph."

"Yes, all right Danielle, Anya may stay." He cleared his throat. "This news about Isaac Craig is very interesting,"

"Hasn't he always acted for the Island in trading?" Simon asked. "He'll be both buyer and seller as things stand."

"I know he's my uncle, and I don't think he's likely to return until the Pride next visits us, by which time I will have taken over as bailiff. But I don't trust him, especially if he is standing in for the Recorder."

Danielle said that they hoped Hannah could stay for a couple of weeks, so that they could get to know each other better. But that she would understand if Hannah felt she had to go back sooner.

"I would have loved to stay longer, and I will on another

occasion, but my birthday is in less than a week and I officially become bailiff on that day. I have to return for that. Especially now."

"Do you have to be there for your birthday, your ascension?" Simon asked. "I mean do you have a special ceremony?"

"No, nothing like that, but I don't know what Isaac may have already planned if he's known about this for a while. And I'd like to be with Abby on my birthday. We're going to share the role of bailiff and she's the closest I've got to family – if you don't count Isaac."

"We understand," Danielle said, letting a hand rest on Hannah's arm. "You must return for your birthday, you have to be with family. We'll have plenty of time to get to know each other in the future."

"I need to tell everyone on the Island what's happening, they won't know anything about this."

"Surely they will hear it on the radio?" Joseph said. "It's bound to be a subject of some discussion here."

"They don't have radios on the Island Pa. I did tell you."

"This will all be resolved once you have your own boat," Joseph said.

"I know, and it's amazing that you're giving us that as a wedding present, but I have to worry about now, about what damage Isaac might do in the meantime."

"The boat can be ready in a few days can't it Joseph? Then you can have it as an engagement present," Danielle said when Joseph didn't contradict her. "That way Isaac will lose whatever power he holds over you. I am assuming he is in league with Gideon and that the two of them have arranged this together."

"He had a letter from Gideon when the Pride last called," Simon said. "I took it there. I wish I'd opened it now."

"You weren't to know," Hannah held his arm.

"We can sort this out," Joseph said. "Isaac does not know how things work here, how fast news travels. He will think he has won already, he will not know he has lost."

Hannah stayed for two days and became firm friends with Anya who was glued to them while Simon showed her around Freeport. They dropped in on Sophia on the second day and she was helping service a boat, almost upside down in the engine compartment.

"This is going to be ours," were Sophia's first words on emerging and seeing Hannah.

"Who told you that?"

"Harry did. We got it in here yesterday. Isn't it brilliant?"

The boat was sturdy and sleek at the same time, much longer than the Crabber and without a mast. There was a flat cargo area taking up half the deck space and a taller wheelhouse cabin.

"There are four bunks below deck and a hold for dry goods. It's perfect for us. We can do our own trading."

Hannah could see that it would be, especially as they could make more than four runs a year.

"We have to go back tomorrow," Hannah said, and saw the disappointment in Sophia's face. "Simon is taking us back."

"Couldn't I stay and finish this. Then I can learn how to navigate at sea too. Emily is going to teach me."

Hannah looked at Simon and he shrugged and said he could see no problem if Sophia wanted to stay – as long as she wasn't getting in the way.

"She's a quick learner," Emily said, sticking her head out of the cargo hold. "It's actually a great help having her here."

It was agreed that Sophia could stay and make the inaugural trip to Hope Island in the Sea Breeze. They didn't think there was much work needed on the boat other than a regular service and Emily was going to take Sophia out to sea and familiarise her with the controls and the handling.

When they left the boat shed Hannah asked Simon if he had told his parents about Becky and he confessed that it had slipped his mind. He thought that they ought to tell them soon because they would meet her eventually and his mother was bound to recognise her, even with the change in her hairstyle.

"We can't keep her hidden forever," he said.

They decided to tell them that evening, so that there was time for questions before they left in the morning.

"My mother is going to say I told you so. She won't worry too much about it though because she has definitely fallen for you."

When they did relate the circumstances of Bethany landing on the Island, about Hannah's role in helping to hide her and change her identity and that she was now living with Hannah's half-sister, as a couple, they were surprised by the reactions they received.

"I always said she was a smart girl," Joseph said, nodding and smiling approvingly.

"Good for her," Danielle added. "I never liked her father and I was concerned about you marrying her all along, something felt wrong. It turns out I was right."

Joseph laughed at Danielle's certainty and she pushed him on the shoulder, but couldn't stop giggling herself. They wanted to know all about Abby and how Hannah and her came to be half-sisters. Hannah's story was continuously interrupted for more detail and by the time she had explained most of her family history, and that of the Island, she was exhausted.

Hannah's life was more wearing to relate than it had been to live. She left out the bit about the gold of course, and the weapons that were hidden beneath Martha's store, but did admit that she had inherited a few gold coins. Joseph was impressed when she retrieved them from her bedroom and showed them to him. Hannah let him believe that she only had a dozen or so.

"That's quite a lot of gold Hannah. It wouldn't take that many for you to have bought that boat. Be careful who knows you have them. Freeport can look very nice, but there are people here who are not to be trusted, and not just Gideon."

Hannah said she would be careful and she thought they might use them to buy fuel for the boat. Simon said her riches would last a long time if fuel was all she was going to spend her money on.

"I spoke to Emily," Joseph said. "She mentioned some idea of opening a base in the harbour on Hope Island. It does make some sense. There would be considerable benefits to our company as far as storage is concerned. Security is so difficult here. There are so many rogues."

"I'd have to talk it over with everyone, see how people feel about it," Hannah said cautiously.

"Of course we would pay a rent on land and buildings, and for the use of your harbour. And we wouldn't be paying taxes here for goods in transit so I'm not being totally selfless."

"I honestly can't answer for the Island by myself," Hannah said. "But I can't see why anyone would object."

"There's no rush," Danielle added. "Joseph is always thinking three moves ahead. He ought to enjoy being in the moment more often."

Hannah went to bed with dozens of ideas swirling round her head. She now had an idea of the significance of those coins they had found, but the value of them seemed incredible and beyond her imagination. The idea of welcoming some sort of outside business to the Island would have to be well thought out. She didn't know how everyone would feel about change on that scale.

The next day Hannah and Simon took their leave in the small cruiser, after first checking that Sophia was happy. She said that Emily and Harry were going to return with her in the Sea Breeze in a couple of days' time.

"I'll get to handle her at sea and bring her into the harbour. It's going to be brilliant."

Hannah couldn't help but smile at Sophia's enthusiasm and told her to be careful and not take any chances. "That's my engagement present you're going to be playing with."

"She'll be fine," Emily said. "Sophia I mean, but the boat will be too. We need to bring it over for a sea trial as it hasn't been used for a while. We can also see if there's enough water at high tide to get it alongside your quay. It will make loading far easier if we can."

"You'll be over quite soon then?"

"Should be," Emily said.

"Maybe you'll be there for my birthday. We haven't arranged anything special, but you're welcome to stay."

"Thanks, but it's up to Simon as to how long he can spare us."

"I'll talk to Pa," Simon said. "Come on Hannah, we need to get going while the weather's good."

The trip over to Hope Island was in calm seas and only a light breeze. The sun came out for them and Hannah spent most of her time next to Simon at the wheel. She had to take over steering for a while when Simon went to stoke the boiler. About an hour into the journey he reached forward and unclipped a small black object, like a dumpy tin, that was next to an array of dials. It was tethered to the dashboard by a curling black wire.

"Simon to Yard, checking in," he said, holding it close to

his mouth.

The box squawked a reply, that Hannah didn't quite catch, and a short conversation ensued about their progress and approximate position.

"Is that a radio?" Hannah asked.

"Yes. It's new, I was letting them know we're okay."

Hannah stared, realising that it was somehow related to the radio they had resurrected at Hope Barton.

"You can talk to people with it anywhere?"

"Yes, as long as they're in range. They've only really become reliable in the last year, with the reduction in the solar storms."

"I didn't know it worked like that. I thought you could only listen."

"I couldn't get any reception in your harbour, the hills probably block it. It's still new to all of us."

Simon called the yard a second time, as they were approaching the harbour, but Hannah still couldn't catch every word of the voice that crackled and scratched out of the speaker.

When they glided over the sand bar and into the harbour, Hannah felt her whole body relax, knowing she was home again. She looked round at the familiar houses, the crescent of sand at one end of the bay and the quay at the other. Most of the fishing boats had returned from their night's work and Becky's little dinghy bobbed cheerfully as the wake from their cruiser caught it. But there was one significant gap where the Crabber was usually moored.

They cruised smoothly alongside the quay and Hannah leapt off with the rope. By the time she had put a couple of loops round a cleat, Simon had thrown the stern rope ashore and that was being secured too. Martha had magically showed up right on time, someone must have alerted her as soon as they were seen.

"Nice to see you back safely my dear, and you Simon. What was the mainland like? Not that I really need to know." Martha leaned forward to look in the cabin. "What have you done with Sophia? Not sold her into slavery I hope."

"She's coming over in another boat."

Hannah looked at Simon, hoping he wouldn't reveal that it was to belong to the Island, or the two of them to be accurate. The concept of personal property, other than clothes or small possessions was quite alien to her.

"Where's the Crabber?" she asked Martha.

"Ethan took it. You'd best ask Abby about that. He left her a note, and one for you apparently."

"Has he gone? I mean gone for good?"

"Took some of Daniel's old carvings with him. I don't expect we'll be seeing him none too soon."

"You go on over to Hope Barton if you want," Simon said. "I'll get the boat sorted and follow you as soon as I can."

Hannah set off up the lane through the village, walking as quickly as she could, breaking into a run by the time she was on the hill. After standing on the boat for hours it felt good to stretch her legs, feel solid ground beneath her feet and push back against it. She ran faster and faster until her hair was streaming out behind her and her breath was coming hard and fast. She arrived at Hope Barton gasping for air and doubled up. A stitch caught at her side and she winced.

"What's happened?" Becky said, emerging from the house.

Hannah waved her hand in front of her, unable to speak.

"Is someone injured? Has something happened to Simon?"

"No, everything's fine," Hannah managed. "Is Abby here?"

"She's out on the fields, checking the sheep. She's due back soon though. Do you want a drink of water?"

Hannah nodded and followed Becky into the kitchen.

"I came about the letters Ethan left. Abby has them?"

"They're right here on the sideboard."

Becky picked up three letters and put them in front of Hannah. "They're not very long. Ethan isn't much of a one for writing."

Hannah sat at the kitchen table and spread the three scant letters out in front of her. She picked up the first one, not much more than a note in a spidery scrawl.

Dad, Like I said, I'm going off to seek my fortune. Just like we talked about. I hope you will be okay and I will see you soon when I'm rich. Ethan

Hannah picked up the second and third letters, one in each hand, glancing over them and then reading each one twice. They were equally concise.

Abby, I hope you and Becky can take care of dad. I know he likes you, probably more than he likes me. Thanks, Ethan.

Hannah, I'm sorry I said some of the things I did, but I didn't love you like Simon does. I've taken the Crabber because Isaac told me I could. Ethan

"He's gone then," Hannah said, breathing a huge sigh and wondering what would happen next.

Chapter 45

The island was peaceful without Isaac's lurking presence and Ethan's perennial moody attitude. But Sophia was missed. The quay seemed empty without its cheerful, bubbly ubiquitous resident.

Hannah's birthday started much like any other day in her life, except that she woke up with Simon next to her. She looked out of the window at a pale blue sky tinged with pastel shades of yellow and pink. There was a mist hanging over the lower half of the village bringing the smell of wood smoke down to street level.

The events of the past few months were already a distant memory. The mood of everyone on the Island was relaxed, even Martha was fussing less over her books and records, throwing caution to the wind now she knew they had the security of all that gold in the vault.

Martha had invited them both to breakfast, but rousing Simon was never easy, so she dressed, put a note on her pillow and hugged a thick cardigan around her body when she left her cottage to walk down to the stores. Hannah craned her neck back, looking up into the pale swirls of mist and patches of blue sky breaking through. It was good to be in the village, good to be with Simon, good to be eighteen at last, and free of Isaac.

Simon caught up with her when she was on her second mug of tea, an empty plate in front of her showing traces of egg and bacon. The aroma still filled the air and Martha made another plate for Simon. Hannah stole a piece of his bacon, but he forgave her after initially making a fuss about her being greedy.

Martha had a present for her, but apologised that it wasn't wrapped – too big she said and it would crease. She disappeared behind some shelving units and came out a minute later with a white dress, the same one she had offered Hannah before.

"I thought this might come in handy some day when you want to look a bit special."

Hannah hugged her and Martha had to hold the dress at arm's length in case she burst into tears and stained it.

"Should I be seeing that?" Simon asked.

"We don't hold with all those old superstitions here Simon. We don't usually have enough clothes to hide some away for special occasions."

"I'm going to walk over to Hope Barton this morning," Hannah said, holding the dress against her and looking down at it. "I don't suppose you want to come Martha?"

"Bit too far for my old legs my dear. But you ought to be with Abby. The two of you should be celebrating together, like you always have."

They helped Martha clear up and, by the time they left, the mist had dispersed and the sun was warming what had been a cool start to the day.

Only a few people were working on the fields, most were still in the orchards. Simon and Hannah walked hand in hand, in no hurry. The breeze was sharp, the warm caressing winds of summer gone. Hannah clutched the large thick cardigan to her. Simon put his arm round her shoulders and they walked in silence, enjoying occasional birdsong and a hare standing stock still in the middle of a field, before it saw them and sped off on a zig-zag course.

Becky was the first to notice them coming down the lane, she had obviously been in the cowshed because she was carrying a milk bucket.

"You were late milking today?" Hannah called.

"No excuse, we all decided to be lazy. I thought Abby deserved a lie-in. And happy birthday."

They all gathered round the kitchen table while Becky made breakfast for Abby and Daniel. Hannah accepted the offer of a mug of tea and Simon said he might be able to squeeze in another slice of toast, just to keep them company.

"I'm still annoyed that I missed Mabon," Becky said.

"We couldn't risk it could we?" Hannah reminded her. "Harry or Emily would have been sure to recognised you, even with your hair cut so short."

"But you're having a celebration tonight aren't you?"

Abby nudged Becky and mouthed a 'shush' at her.

"Nothing special planned," Hannah said, having missed Abby's signal to Becky. "I might have organised something if Isaac had still been here, just to make a point, but I don't need to do that now."

"Ah, okay," Becky said. "But parties are fun aren't they?"

"They are. You're right," Hannah agreed.

Becky and Daniel were going up to the bees, to check the hive weights and remove the empty feeders. They asked Simon if he wanted to join them.

"Love to," Simon said. "I've never had much to do with bees, but they are our competitors in the sugar business so I ought to learn."

Abby and Hannah were left together at the kitchen table.

"How is it going with Simon?"

"Perfect," Hannah said. "How about you and Becky?"

"Better than I could ever have hoped."

"We both got lucky didn't we?"

"And you say we have this boat coming too, the Sea Breeze?"

"Simon said we should rename it. His suggestion was

Hope Eternal, but I think he was joking. At least I hope he was joking."

"When is it going to be here?"

"I don't know exactly. I understood that it didn't need much work doing on it."

Later in the morning they all walked back to the village. Daniel had kept asking why they were going there, saying he didn't have any reason to go traipsing around the Island.

"You all go, I'll take care of the evening milking," he said.

The change in Daniel was difficult to believe. He was working on the farm independently, talking almost too much now, but he had slowed down on his carvings. He still worked pieces of driftwood, but not with the obsessive concentration that he had before.

Just before they got to Martha's, where they were going to make lunch, they were surprised when they bumped into Sophia and Anya.

What are you doing here Shrimp?" Simon asked, as Anya rushed at him and jumped into his arms.

He swung her round so fast that her legs flew out and she couldn't stop giggling.

"We came over with Ma and Pa, on our launch."

"You too Sophia?" Hannah asked.

"We didn't want to miss your birthday. We would have brought the Sea Breeze over, but we're waiting for a new part for the engine that Emily thought should be replaced."

Joseph and Danielle caught up with the two girls and Danielle hugged Hannah and wished her a very happy birthday.

"And now you're in charge of Hope Island of course," she said.

"Not really in charge. Being bailiff is more an honorary post rather than anything official."

"That was never how Isaac saw it," Abby said.

"Well, that was then and this is now. We were just going to Martha's to organise some lunch. You must join us."

"I'm taking Anya over to Camp Bay," Sophia said. "And she wants to see Spit Head too."

"Is that all right Ma?"

Joseph said it was fine, but for the two of them not to spend all day over there. "We don't want to get worried and have to send out a search party," she said.

"Sophia's going to take me out sailing later."

"Or I could take you out in it." Becky had been half hiding behind Simon and Hannah, nervous of what sort of reception she would receive.

"Oh my goodness," Danielle said, not having spotted her before. "That haircut really suits you. Come here child and tell me everything that's been going on."

Danielle took Becky's hand and drew her off back towards the quay a little way. Becky, turned and pulled a face at Abby, but she was laughing at the same time.

"Good to see you Pa. How is everything?"

"Oh, never mind about that, take me to see this Martha, she sounds like a formidable woman and I need to win her over if we're going to transfer some of our business here. I brought a little gift for her too." Joseph held up a bottle of dark liquid with a very fancy black and yellow label. "I understand Martha is partial to a small tipple now and then. I wondered whether she had encountered any of our rum before."

Abby and Hannah said they would get lunch ready when Joseph politely requested a tour of the stores. Martha was immediately won over by his charm and his interest in her organisational skills. He praised the way she had everything arranged so sensibly and expressed admiration for her breadth of knowledge on everything from food to electrical fittings.

"We could do with someone with your knowledge in our business Martha, but I doubt I could persuade you to leave Hope Island?"

"Only in a box," Martha replied. "And I wouldn't be too happy about leaving even then."

Their voices faded when Martha took him down to the cellar to show him her prized collection of pickles and bottled fruit.

"I don't think you're in danger of losing her," Simon said. "My father simply has his methods for getting on the good side of people."

Danielle and Becky returned, arms linked and obviously friends.

"I adore this place," Danielle announced. "So peaceful. No cars, no noisy lorries, no machinery filling the air with its clattering all day. It reminds me of our sugar islands, but without the dangers of course."

"Are they that dangerous?" Hannah asked. Simon had told her about the business and the faraway islands they owned, but never mentioned danger.

"The islands are lawless places where we have to keep guards and constantly be on the watch for raiders. Not a place you would choose to live, and that's from someone who grew up there."

"Ma exaggerates a little, but there are pirates of a sort in those seas. We don't get much trouble from them, but they do take smaller boats and their cargo sometimes."

"We've been lucky so far Simon," Joseph said as he and Martha returned. "But it's only a matter of time before we suffer the same way."

"When will the Sea Breeze be ready?" Hannah asked, having had enough talk of pirates and distant lands. "I'm going to have Isaac to contend with when the Pride next calls."

"Not long," Joseph said. "It is just that one part we're waiting for."

"It's not our busiest time of year for trading, but there are things we always need around now. Your sugar for one thing."

Danielle nudged her husband. "Tell them Joseph."

"Yes, well, we wondered as there has been a delay with the Sea Breeze, we might offer a solution ourselves. We could bring one of our ships over and help you out in the short term. And we have ample supplies of sugar of course."

Not just that," Danielle interrupted. "He can be so slow at explaining things. We thought you could set up a shop on the mainland, all your island produce, there's always a demand and you would get a much better price by selling direct."

We would have to tell the Recorder, or Isaac I suppose. We have a sort of agreement with the Pride, a trust."

"Isaac's cheated us for a long time," Abby butted in. "If anyone has broken our trust it's him."

"But Isaac is family. I still don't understand why he has acted like he has. Maybe we need to give him a chance to explain."

"Greed," Danielle said. "It goes hand in hand with power for some people."

"I would still like to resolve it amicably. He is my uncle."

It was left that Hannah would talk to Isaac when the Pride next called and give him notice that they would be dealing direct with the mainland in the future. Joseph had brought over a spare radio transmitter, because Anya had demanded the ability to talk to her brother when she needed to. Simon promised to let them know the outcome of Hannah's meeting with Isaac.

"So, where is this party being held then?" Danielle asked. "Our contribution is still on the launch, we should get someone to fetch it."

There was a collective groan that Danielle had revealed the secret event they had planned for Hannah.

"Oh sorry," Danielle said, putting her fingertips to her lips. "Have I spoiled a surprise?"

Chapter 46

Even though Danielle had revealed that there was to be a party, there were still secrets to be kept and Hannah was banned from asking any questions. After lunch she was told to go back to Canary Cottage and wait there until late afternoon. Simon was delegated to keep her company and bring her down when the time was right.

Danielle followed them out of Martha's and asked if she could see the quaint little cottage that Hannah had grown up in.

"I lived in the Manor for the first nine years of my life," Hannah said. "But not since my parents died. I was hoping we might make it a family home again, when Simon and I marry."

"Have you decided on a date yet?"

Hannah looked at Simon.

"We thought spring would be a good time," he said. "That way the weather won't prevent anyone from coming over from the mainland."

"And we always have a celebration for Ostera," Hannah added. "We thought we might combine the two."

"I've heard of that being celebrated elsewhere, but didn't know you followed those religious festivals here?"

"We don't see them as religious. Each equinox and solstice is a good way for us to mark the changing of the year. And I suppose we do live by the seasons here rather than by a calendar."

"It was similar when I was growing up," Danielle said. "Except we marked the seasons by rain and wind."

"This is my cottage," Hannah said. "Come in."

Danielle said it was charming, but was also fascinated by Hannah's collected oddities. She picked one of them up and turned to Hannah.

"You know you are not the only one who collects trinkets like these. Anya will be so jealous when she sees them."

"Can Anya swim?"

"Like a fish," Simon said.

"If she comes over next summer I could teach her to dive and she could find some herself."

"We must tell her," Danielle said. "She will be overjoyed. But now I need to go back and help get things ready."

Danielle kissed Hannah on the cheek, smiled and let herself out the door. "You are so charming Hannah. I'll see you later."

As soon as she had gone Hannah turned to Simon. "Are you going to tell me what's going on?"

"No," Simon said, smiling.

"Am I going to enjoy it?"

"Yes."

"Am I going to be embarrassed?"

"Hmm," Simon pretended to be thinking. "Very possibly."

She playfully beat her hands on his chest. "I do hate not knowing what's going on."

"It's not that long to wait. Do you want to go for a walk to pass the time?"

"Well I can't just sit in here all afternoon, I'll go mad."

They headed out of the village. The wind caught them at the top of the hill and whipped Hannah's hair across her face . She gathered it and tied it in a bunch on the back of her head. Once they were on the heath all thoughts of the party had been blown out of her mind and she relaxed. In the distance two figures were coming towards them.

"It's Sophia and Anya," Simon said.

"You really are going to have to find me some better glasses."

"Hello," he cried, waving to them.

The two girls sped up, running with carefree abandon, zigzagging through the heather and the gorse.

"I love it here," Anya shouted before they reached them. "I want to marry someone and live here too."

"And what about school?" Simon said.

"I could learn lots here. They have a school."

"Not really a school," Hannah said. "More of a house."

"Can I? Will you talk to Pa about it? He listens to you."

"Enough for now," Simon said. "We have a party tonight. There'll be plenty of time to talk about your future tomorrow."

The party is supposed to be a secret," Sophia said.

Hannah hugged her round the shoulders. "Not any more. And why didn't you let me know? I thought we were supposed to be on the same team."

"I think we could head back now," Simon said. "Once you've changed it should be time to present you to the assembled multitude."

"Oh God, that sounds hideous. What are you doing to me on my birthday?"

"You will just have to wait and trust in your friends."

Simon left her at Canary Cottage, saying he'd be back in half an hour, and Hannah resigned herself to putting up with whatever was coming. She riffled through the few clothes she had and ended up with the same outfit she had worn to that dinner at the Manor with Isaac, Gideon and Simon. It seemed like so long ago. When Simon returned he recognised her clothes.

"That's what you were wearing the night we first had supper together. You looked beautiful then, more beautiful

364

now."

"I don't have that many choices of what to wear, unless you think shorts and a shirt might be more appropriate?"

"You look perfect, come on, let's go."

He led her down the lane towards the quay.

"It's a bit cool to be outdoors tonight," she said, wishing she'd put that old thick cardigan round her shoulders.

"We're not going to be outdoors."

"You can be so infuriating. You do know that don't you?"

"We're here," Simon said, stopping outside the barn that housed the tractors.

"This isn't a working party is it? I'd have worn old clothes if I'd known we were going to be cleaning the tractors."

Simon rapped sharply on the door three times. There was no sound from inside, but Hannah heard and saw the bolt sliding back between the doors. They swung open, Becky on one door, Abby on the other. Hannah gasped when she saw what they had done to the barn.

The tractors had been shuffled back into two corners, their link boxes raised and a banner slung between them reading 'HAPPY BIRTHDAY BAILIFF'. Tables and chairs of various shapes and sizes formed a horseshoe and in the centre carrying was two-tiered cake.

"Ma made the cake herself," Simon whispered to her. "One tier for you, one for Abby."

Hannah didn't know how to respond, the whole island had crammed into the barn. Hay had been raked to the sides and was littered with children. Everyone was cheering her and Simon's immediate family were there along with some faces she didn't recognise.

"My aunts, uncles, some of my cousins all wanted to be here to celebrate with you," he said. "They were all crammed on my parents' launch – God knows how."

Hannah was introduced to Simon's extended family, and

365

congratulated by almost everyone on the Island. One or two sounded less enthusiastic, but Hannah wasn't worried about old alliances. She was sure those divisions would heal soon and she treated everyone with the same grateful thanks.

Food magically appeared on the tables and the village band, probably far inferior to anything Simon's family would be used to, struck up a cheerful tune after everyone had eaten their fill. Hannah had to teach Simon how to dance. It was something he admitted had been missing in his education. Joseph and Danielle were much more liberated than Hannah expected and even Martha lifted her skirt and danced, after a fashion, for one number. She then had to sit down and be revived with a small glass of rum.

The evening was joyous and chaotic at the same time. Hannah drunk more than she ever had before, the new cider being fresher and unthreatened by Isaac's hand.

When energy flagged and people began to take their leave, Hannah found herself sharing a table and a glass of Martha's rum with Danielle.

"We are so looking forward to your wedding Hannah. I think Simon has made a splendid choice."

Hannah closed her eyes and a lump came to her throat.

"He hasn't spent a winter here," Hannah said quietly. "We may yet be back on the mainland and getting in your hair. "

"Your winters can be no different to ours, we are only a handful of miles away."

"I think it's that in winter you become more aware of the isolation of Hope Island. Even some of us find it difficult when the frosts are still biting in March. And the nights are long too. We have no street lighting like you do on the mainland, no entertainment other than what we make ourselves - and you heard our band tonight."

"I think you'll survive. Simon has never been one for staying out late and gallivanting with the other boys in town. At times I almost wished he had a more boisterous side to his life, but he wouldn't be Simon if he had."

Simon joined them just at that moment.

"Did I hear my name mentioned Ma. You're not giving away all my secrets are you."

"Piffle, you don't have any secrets, that's what I was telling Hannah."

"I was saying that the Island can be a lonely place in winter, short days and nothing much to do except stoke fires, check the animals and cook."

"But we won't be bored will we?" Simon grinned. "I'll be watching you doing all that work."

Hannah dug him in the ribs. "You'll be helping me or out in the cold."

"Well said, that's the kind of attitude I should have taken years ago."

The next morning everyone gathered on the quay to say farewell. Joseph and Danielle had stayed the night with Martha and become firm friends. Anya had stayed in Sophia's cottage on the quay and was complaining that she didn't need to go home yet, that she could stay a while longer and come back on the Pride. Danielle told her that she could stay another time, in the summer perhaps, but she had school to attend for now. Simon hugged his father and thanked him for everything.

"Don't forget young man, you are going to survey the quay and take depth soundings in the harbour to see what we can arrange in the way of workshops and storage facilities here. That sandbank may prove a problem, but I suspect the Pride's reluctance to come closer to the quay may have had more to do with Gideon and Isaac than a fear of grounding."

Simon assured him that he would take soundings before the weather turned and send a chart back on the Pride when it next visited.

Half of the village had turned out to see Simon's family off. They had made a great impression on everyone, and not just because the cake had been a rare and sugary treat shared with all.

Chapter 47

Simon and Hannah were having breakfast when the Pride's whistle cut through the still morning air. Instead of the normal three, short, cheerful hoots, it gave one long persistent scream.

"Isaac's idea I expect," Hannah said.

"How do you know?"

"Trust me, that's Isaac announcing his new position."

Hannah didn't hurry her toast and jam, she was quite happy to let Isaac wait. When they walked down to the quay some twenty minutes later the Pride was moored well away from the shore and a boat had only just been lowered into the water. The tide wasn't yet full, but Hannah was sure from Simon's soundings in the harbour that it could have moored a lot closer.

Her eyes gradually made out the familiar figure of Isaac, standing in the bow of a rowing boat, one foot on the gunwales. His intended authoritarian stance was diminished as the boat approached them. The water was low enough that only his head appeared above the quayside, level with the feet of those gathered there.

"Pompous idiot," Martha mumbled from behind Hannah.

Nobody offered Isaac a hand as he hauled himself up the iron ladder and onto the quay.

"You were expecting me?" he asked, looking past Hannah to the lack of any carts or boxes on the quay.

"Of course we were," Hannah replied.

"You don't appear to have brought anything to trade?

You do want to trade I assume? You must have a list of requirements?"

"We do, but we have to discuss terms first."

Isaac frowned. He obviously hadn't been expecting any challenge to the existing system.

"But nothing substantial has changed," he said. "A fair price and a fair trade will be offered as always."

"But it hasn't really been that fair has it Isaac?"

"How do you mean my dear?"

"I've been over to the mainland now. I know the prices our produce fetch and how much many of the goods cost that we have bought from the Recorder in the past."

Isaac puffed out his cheeks and let the air escape in an exasperated blast from between his pink lips.

"Well there are expenses involved, you must appreciate that. Nothing can be transported for free, there are workers to load and unload everything, fuel costs, crew to pay, and tradesmen have to make a penny here and there. There has always been a substantial gap between producer and retailer my dear. You will come to understand that when you have more experience."

"Have you ever heard of farm shops Uncle?"

"I have come across them. But how are they pertinent to our situation?"

"Producers selling direct to customers with a fairer price for both. Simon has told me how they work on the mainland."

"But that's not really possible with Hope Island is it. You can't expect people to sail all the way over here to buy a few carrots and onions can you? I think you may have been misled by an idea that can't possibly work here."

"I don't think it's the idea that's been misleading us all these years."

"But this is unheard of." Isaac's face was turning an unattractive shade of red. "We have always traded with the Pride - even in your parents' day."

His voice had risen in volume. The crew who had rowed him ashore and had been standing behind him, gradually moved to either side. Hannah thought at first they were forming a front, showing their solidarity with Isaac, but they were facing him, rather than confronting the crowd of islanders who were growing in numbers.

"The virus was a major problem back then, I know that Uncle, but we also had better trading terms. Martha has gone over the records."

"Well I can't transport your produce for free. So who is going to offer that service so that you can sell it on the mainland in your new shop?"

"We are."

"You simply don't have a large enough vessel here to transport your goods."

Simon had been standing quietly behind Hannah until that moment.

"We have a new boat Isaac, the Sea Breeze. I doubt you know her but she's easily large enough to fulfil our needs."

"And what has all this to do with you young man. I don't see this mythical new vessel here. Are you hiding it some-where?"

Simon smiled and Hannah put an arm round his waist.

"Simon and I are getting married Uncle, don't you want to congratulate us? I thought it was something you were in favour of?"

Isaac took a moment. He looked at them in turn and a smile crept onto his lips. "So can I assume you are planning to move to the mainland to run this little shop of yours?"

"No Uncle, we're staying here. We will pay someone to run it for us. And the Delanceys will sell some of their goods direct to the public too."

Martha coughed behind them. "As long as you're not going to ask me to run it. I'm too old to be taking up any new fangled ideas."

"This is all nonsense, day dreams, it will never work and then you will have to trade with me again - and I warn you the prices will no longer be quite so favourable."

"We'll take our chances Isaac," Simon said.

"So you have nothing you want to trade today?"

"We do if the terms are favourable Uncle."

"And where is the money coming from for this new boat, this new enterprise. You can't run things on the mainland like you do here, on trust and promises."

He looked hard at Simon. "It's the Delanceys isn't it? They've put all these harebrained schemes into your head. Well I warn you, they are not as pure as you think they are. How would they have made such a fortune if they were so generous?"

"You would do well to remember I'm marrying one of them," Hannah said quietly. "Be careful what you say."

"You'll need their money young lady when this all goes wrong, as I assure you it will."

Isaac looked round at the crew who had moved even further away from him. The Delanceys were not only wealthy, they were one of the largest ship owners in the region. Nobody who earned their living at sea would want to cross them.

"Back in the boat," Isaac shouted. "We're leaving."

"As for money Isaac," Hannah said, pulling her hand out of a pocket and opening it to reveal three gold coins.

She hadn't planned to show Isaac the coins, but he was being so foul and insulting that she wanted to tease him.

"Charity from your new family I suppose?" Isaac only glanced at the coins.

"They're not from Simon," Hannah said. "Maybe you

should look closer."

"What do you mean?"

Isaac was intrigued. His eyes couldn't leave the gold and something began to click in brain. "How many more do you have?"

"Enough," Hannah said. "Take one, take a closer look."

Isaac picked one up from Hannah's outstretched palm. He turned it over slowly. His lips moved slightly as he read the date.

"You couldn't find them could you?" Hannah whispered.

Isaac looked at the other coins. Turning each one. His jaw set tighter, the muscles in his neck stretched the layers of fat covering them. His fingers reluctantly released the coins back into Hannah's palm.

"You found it," he hissed. "Where was it?"

Hannah smiled. She closed her fingers over the coins.

"It doesn't matter Isaac. It's safe now."

"Part of that is rightly mine. My inheritance from my sister."

"Did she leave it to you in her will Isaac?"

"You know there are no wills," he spat the words out. "The safe was empty."

Martha laughed, a loud snorting kind of laugh. "It was when you got there."

Isaac had turned completely red, beads of sweat breaking out on his forehead and spittle caught on his lower lip.

"Let's see what your story is when your boat doesn't materialise," he spat as he spoke. "Or your little shop fails or your marriage goes sour or the Delanceys start to cheat you and Hope Island has to trade with me again. You will be begging by the time spring comes round."

Simon managed to slip a roll of papers to one of the sailors, along with a coin, while Isaac ranted and raved. The sailor nodded and concealed the roll inside his jacket.

When Isaac turned to get back in the boat a loud, deep, throaty siren sounded from the mouth of the bay. All eyes looked to see what new vessel had arrived and Simon grabbed Isaac's sleeve before he could board the rowing boat.

"It's here Isaac, the Sea Breeze. You'll be able to see it for yourself now before you leave."

Isaac shrugged himself free from Simon's grip and climbed down the ladder to a mixture of jeers from the onlookers who were no longer afraid of him. The Sea Breeze cruised past the Pride, sounding its siren again in three short hoots and a cheer rose from the quay.

Trying to look dignified, Isaac remained standing in the rowing boat, but when the Sea Breeze passed close to it, the bow wave rocked his boat and one of the sailors had to grab Isaac to prevent him from toppling into the sea. Hannah put her hands to her mouth and called out to him.

"Maybe there are other communities that Gideon has been cheating Uncle. Maybe your luck and his have finally run out."

"I hope you're not going to ask me to run that shop," Martha mumbled again. "I can't be learning new things at my age, it wouldn't be fair."

Chapter 48

When the Sea Breeze got closer to the quay they could see Sophia through the wheelhouse window, steering the boat with a broad grin on her face. It was her who must have recognised Isaac from his size and created the bow wave that almost threw him into the sea.

Emily stood behind her, Harry was nowhere to be seen. Sophia had gone back to the mainland with Anya and her family the day after the celebrations and had now returned in style and at exactly the right moment.

On the cargo deck there was a large rectangular tank and a variety of what looked like complex farming equipment. Harry appeared from below deck before Sophia expertly brought the Sea Breeze alongside the quay. He jumped off with a bow rope and, once he had put a few turns around a bollard, Sophia revved the engine and brought the boat to a stop. Willing hands were securing the aft rope and Harry shook hands with Simon.

"Good trip?" Simon asked.

"She handles beautifully and Sophia's an absolute natural."

"A fuel tank I presume?"

"That's right," Harry said. "One of the supply ships will call in a few days and fill it up for the Sea Breeze and the tractors."

"Is that a plough?" Hannah asked, looking at something far larger and heavier than they would ask their horses to pull.

"Yes, we've also got a harrow and a seed drill to bring

over on the next couple of trips."

"Everything's going to change so much here," Hannah said, a hint of regret in her voice.

Over the next couple of days Harry and Emily, with help from others, positioned the tank at the end of the quay where the water was deepest for boats to moor. Sophia did two more trips to the mainland bringing back more farming equipment and taking some of their surplus produce over to sell. Even Martha joined her on one trip, saying she hadn't changed her mind about running a shop, but it wouldn't hurt to take a look.

The next couple of months were a hive of activity and change. Now they had a guaranteed outlet for their produce, more preserves and pickles were made and someone even suggested they should have a Hope Island label.

Sarah, known for her sketching, drew a picture of an island, rising from an impossibly blue sea, and the words Hope Island Produce in an arc over the top of it. Someone thought of adding a bee, which she did quite happily.

Weekly journeys by the Sea Breeze, back and forth to the mainland, brought occasional curious visitors. Some simply wanted to see the Island that had always been a forbidden place, others were genuinely interested in moving to what was reputed to be an island idyll.

Hannah and Abby wanted to welcome new residents, but were wary about the clash of cultures. Money was already circulating on the Island and changing the way people helped each other. Work of any sort already had a nominal value to it and the sense of everybody owning everything was quickly fading.

Abby and Hannah discussed the practicalities of new residents with Simon. Hannah thought that the only thing they could do was to formalise the occupancy of cottages and farms by lifetime allocation, but with no rents as such.

"It wouldn't be much different to what we have now," she said.

"I bet some people won't like it," Abby speculated. "They'll see it as some being given more than others. And if one family grows and another shrinks, like Daniel and Ethan, what would you do then?"

"How about a cooperative," Simon said. "You could make everyone an equal shareholder in the Island produce. Equal shares, equal profit for everyone."

"So everyone starts out with one share?" Abby asked.

"And if someone leaves the Island permanently they lose their share."

"What about if someone moves here," Hannah was struggling to understand how it would work in the long term. "Do they get a share too?"

"You could limit the number of shares," Simon suggested. "So the Island doesn't get swamped with too many people."

"Who decides who gets to stay?" Abby asked.

"I don't know, it's just an idea."

"We could do with a doctor," Abby said. "And an engineer, now we've got the tractors working."

"And our base is going to need people," Simon said. "But maybe they could be found on the Island already."

"Why is it suddenly so complicated?" Hannah asked.

"No fever to keep people away any longer," Simon said.

"And no Isaac," Abby added.

They agreed on the cooperative idea and decided to put it to an island meeting. By the time they had it organised a doctor and his wife had visited the Island and asked Hannah if they could move there. She had said yes, knowing that everyone would welcome a medical service that wasn't solely based on ancient herbal remedies.

At the meeting everyone had an idea of how property should be allocated. An idea was voiced that some worked harder than others and therefore deserved more shares – but nobody was ready to point a finger. The meeting became noisier and more aggressive until Peter stood up and banged his fist on a table – everyone quietened.

"Hannah and her family have run Hope Island with the lightest of touch for the last hundred years." There was a murmur of agreement around the gathering. "I think we're all forgetting that she owns the land and the buildings here. She is Hope Island. Anyone who wants to is now able to leave. If you think you can find a better life, then go. But I will stay. We have a good life here and nobody starves. Everyone works as best they can. Hope Island may not be perfect, but it's close enough to perfect for me that I don't want to change anything."

One person started to clap, then another joined in and a third. Soon the whole room was clapping, cheering, fists banging on tables, feet stamping on the floor. Peter held both arms up, palms facing out, trying to quieten everyone.

"I like the idea of holding a share in the Island, being part of a cooperative. People are going to want to come here and join us. And they will have to adhere to our island ethos. Isaac won't be getting a share now…" Peter had to wait for a round of cheering to die down. "But I propose Simon gets the first share we offer to an off-islander."

The universal cheers showed the general consent of the meeting and only one small voice rose above them. It was Sophia.

"And Harry and Emily," she shouted.

Applause sealed their acceptance and if there were dissenters, and there probably were, Hannah didn't hear their voices raised against the new cooperative.

Remarkably, nothing much changed on Hope Island, even though everything had changed. Simon's soundings in Newport Bay confirmed that the water was deep enough at the end of the quay for all but the largest of ships to dock, even the Pride could have moored by the quay wall had it wanted to.

Emily and Harry had taken over a small shed on the front and were fitting it out with tools and spares to service any boats the Delanceys sent there. An old warehouse, long unused, was patched up and broken windows reglazed. It would be perfect storage of valuable goods, difficult to protect on the mainland.

By the beginning of December the seas were getting high and Sophia happily put the Sea Breeze to bed for a couple of months. Simon enjoyed his first Yule, being introduced to the twelve-day celebration and Martha's Yule log.

"Do we drink and eat like this for the whole twelve days," he asked, when they were finally in bed after the first night. "I'll never last."

"It slows down, don't worry. The first night is the most important, the shortest day of the year. Now the sun is on its way back to us."

The feasting did continue, although not on the scale of that first night an,d by the beginning of January, Simon declared that if he were not careful he would end up the size of Isaac.

"I will love you whatever happens to you," Hannah told him, snuggling close under the thick bed covers. "But I'd prefer it if you didn't get quite that big, you'd squash me."

"Exercise, that's what I need," Simon declared. "Something to burn off the fat."

In the morning Hannah looked out of the bedroom window and there was a new dusting of snow over the village, making it look clean and bright and magical.

"Wake up, wake up," she shouted. "It's snowing again."

"So?" Simon mumbled, pulling the covers over his head.

"It's always cold, but we don't always get snow in the winter."

"Good."

"Don't be so miserable Simon. It looks wonderful."

He reluctantly dragged himself out of bed taking the cover with him and draping it round the two of them.

"I wonder if the reservoir has frozen," Hannah said. "It should have by now."

"Oh god, we're not going skating are we?"

"My parents used to take me up there whenever the water froze. It wasn't every year. Their blades must still be at the Manor. Have you every skated?"

Simon admitted that his mother was equally infatuated, never having seen ice until she was sixteen. He said he had been cajoled in the dubious pleasures of freezing to death while trying to balance on ice skates.

"I did get to enjoy it eventually," he said.

That afternoon the snow stopped and the sun bled through an ice blue sky. Hannah dragged Simon up to the Manor and she found a pair of skates for each of them. Wrapped up in so many layers that they could hardly walk properly, she led him up to the main reservoir. They weren't alone, other families had the same idea and there were several children, and a few parents, wobbling around the perimeter. Peter was there even though he didn't have a family and told them he'd tested the ice right into the centre, but was advising everyone to stay close to the edge to be on the safe side.

After strapping the blades to their boots, Hannah pulled a reluctant Simon onto the ice. He proved to be a better skater than she was and he guided her round the edge of the reservoir until she had found her feet. They stopped after two laps and Simon began to spin her in a circle. Hannah's balance deserted her and she fell, bringing Simon when he tried to rescue her. She landed half on top of him.

The ice was crystal clear in places and she only realised while they lay there laughing that she was directly above the cave from which they had retrieved all that gold. It was still hidden in Martha's vault, as were the stash of weapons. Abby and her had not talked about those secrets for months. The idea of diving down in the cold water that lay beneath the ice was impossible to contemplate in that weather. But she wanted to retrieve the chest next summer, certain that it held some other clue to her family's history.

She also knew that she had to tell Simon about the gold, if nothing else, before they married in spring.

"Maybe not today," she inadvertently said out loud.

"Maybe what not today?"

"It doesn't matter. It will wait. Let's skate until we fall over again."

"I doubt that will take long," Peter said from the bank, and they both laughed again.

Printed in Poland
by Amazon Fulfillment
Poland Sp. z o.o., Wrocław